I0699654

THE HOLLIS TIMEWIRE SERIES
BOOK 4

THE EMPOWERED ONES

DANIELLE HARRINGTON

FROM THE TINY ACORN…
GROWS THE MIGHTY OAK

www.AcornPublishingLLC.com

For information, address:
Acorn Publishing, LLC
3943 Irvine Blvd. Ste. 218
Irvine, CA 92602

The Empowered Ones
Copyright © 2024 Danielle Harrington

Cover design by Damonza
Interior design and formatting by Debra Cranfield Kennedy

All rights reserved. No part of this book may be used or reproduced in any manner whatsoever, including Internet usage, without written permission from the author.

Anti-Piracy Warning: The unauthorized reproduction or distribution of a copyrighted work is illegal. Criminal copyright infringement, including infringement without monetary gain, is investigated by the FBI and is punishable by up to five years in federal prison and a fine of $250,000.

Printed in the United States of America

ISBN-13: 979-8-88528-083-9 (hardcover)
ISBN-13: 979-8-88528-088-4 (paperback)
Library of Congress Control Number: 2023923100

'We all have our own unique type of light.

Many aren't gold like yours, Maddy,

but the light is still there in all of us.

Remember that."

—Hollis Timewire

$$\text{I}$$

BLOOD SEEPS FROM THE OPEN CLAW MARK ON MY CALF muscle as quiet descends on the glittering glass city of Area 19. Arthur Evandrum's broadcast to the world announcing the New World Order and the end of the institution of the Test is over, all of the street transit stops are blank now, and my head is spinning.

The morning sun is old enough to be christened early afternoon, and it beats down on us all—*puppets* and their master alike. Hundreds of citizens are still standing on the street in front of the Testing Center, bound under my control. All mine.

I flick my hand, leaving them frozen in place, and I stoop low, kneeling on the asphalt. The ground is hot to the touch, and sweat trickles down my back in the growing heat. Arthur Evandrum tricked me. The syringe meant to sedate the President was filled with poison instead. I killed President Alvaro Camille.

I'm fighting with the churning sensation in my stomach as stars shimmer in my peripheral vision. The pain in my calf muscle sharpens—as does the tingling of my ability.

Stand up, Hollis, my ability whispers. *You are not alone.*

Adrenaline skewers me, and I rise from the ground with lightning speed. The creature within hones my senses, and I shudder, feeling the heartbeat of every person under my fingertips. Their breath. The scent of their skin. Their very cells. But through the crowd of puppets, I sense a new presence. At the end of the block, twenty yards from me, a woman dressed in all black approaches. She walks quickly and without fear, her gaze directed at me. And in her hand, a black handgun glints against the beating rays of the scorching sun.

I move instinctually, slashing my palms through the air and taking hold of her, and although she stills under my command, she appears unfazed. She's looking at me with calm, collected purpose. She's different from the others. I can tell she's not a society member by the way she carries herself. I flick my wrist to open her mouth, my pulse pumping into my ears.

"Hollis Timewire," she says.

I walk up to her, stopping a few feet away. "Who are you?"

"Wren Zayla, undercover informant from the Area 19 Testing Center. And your pilot."

She eyes me like a hawk, her mouth pressing thin. Her black hair is done up in a tight bun, and her brown skin glistens in the heat. She stands quite a bit taller than me, and her body is toned with muscle. Her dark brown eyes cascade down to her stiffened body.

"Release me," she says. "We have work to do. Arthur's expecting you back at the mountain soon."

Anger boils over in my gut at the mention of Arthur, but I

don't let any of it slip onto my face. Instead, I take a calming breath to fight the pain that riddles my body.

"What work?" I ask.

"You are to take control of the Military Base and disarm the population of Area 19. Then, I will fly you back to the mountain outside Area 7 where you will receive further instruction."

I stare at her, searching her face, and my gaze lingers on the weapon in her hand. "Disarm the population?"

"Release me," she says again. She's not angry, but her words carry a commanding presence.

My ability hums through my veins, heightening my hold over everyone present. I don't know this woman, but if she works for Arthur, then I need to play my cards right. I have to get back to the mountain. I need to see if Olivia Turrick and Ashton Teel are alright. Camille shot Ashton and hurled Olivia into a wall, gashing her head open. They barely got out of the skirmish with the President alive. I don't even know if they *are* alive . . .

"You're going to take me back to the mountain?" I ask, gritting my teeth. My head is swimming, and I'm finding it hard to concentrate.

"*After* you've finished securing Area 19," Wren says. "A team will be here shortly to set up headquarters in the Capitol Building, but we must move quickly. The rest of Area 19's military elite are organizing as we speak. You're wasting time, Miss Timewire. This was all contingent upon your help, remember?"

Arthur's words slither through my head: "Miss Timewire, are you sure you're ready to do this? Because if you go to Camille, this happens tonight. You understand, yes? My people are prepared. All the Testing Centers must fall *together*. We can't give society time to regroup."

I shake myself, and the tingling in my fingertips slackens. "Yes, I remember."

The reservations within me are still thrumming to the beat of my heart, but I pull my power back, releasing Wren from my clutches.

"Good. To the Capitol Building." She holds her gun at the ready, marching through the sea of frozen citizens. "I trust you'll have my back if anyone hinders us along the way?"

"I . . . um . . . yes." I follow her, and my body spasms anew with pain. My cheek is still searing where Camille dug his knife in, and the pain in my leg is becoming unbearable, but I push forward in a trance, even though every muscle is begging me to stop.

"Can your power handle keeping these citizens in place *and* taking more?" she asks, moving at a rapid pace down the block and away from the Testing Center. "Our top priority right now is neutralizing Area 19's Military Base. But until we're sure no lingering weapons are around, you need to keep people under control."

I don't answer. My head is pounding, and my jaw is set.

"Miss Timewire?" Wren says sharply.

"Yes," I say. "I can handle it."

We move through the city streets, slinking down the deserted sidewalks. On occasion, we spot a citizen, but before they can so much as call out, they are under my control. I leave them bound in place, their terrified eyes trailing us as we move. In their mind,

I'm the worst terrorist the world has ever seen. And for now, there's nothing I can do about it. All I want is to get back to the mountain. Back to Jonah and Maddy, back to Keith, and back to Arthur Evandrum. Because I swear on my ability, he will pay for tricking me into killing Camille.

But right now, I have a job to do, and people are depending on me to do it. Area 19 has the strongest military presence, and I am the only one with a power potent enough to neutralize that threat.

As Wren Zayla and I approach the Capitol Building, I gaze up at the white flag unfurled over the side of the massive platform. A golden woman is printed on it. Her hands are in front of her stomach, palms open to the sky, and her eyes are closed. The symbol of the New World Order towers over the street, ominous and foreboding. People with powers have taken over now. The Testing Centers of the world have fallen. And the President is dead.

How long before society knows about Camille? Arthur didn't say anything about him in his speech, but once word gets out about his assassination, I'll be even more hated than I am now.

"To the platform," Wren says, pointing up above the flag. A helicopter resides atop the massive Capitol Building. "We'll take my chopper to the Military Base, and once you've taken control and our people arrive to secure the rest of the city, I'll fly you back to Area 7."

Walking up the steps of the Capitol fills me with dread. The last time I was here was when the government had Jonah. The last time I was here, I found out I wasn't the only puppet master. But now I am . . .

Camille is dead.

There can only be one puppet master.

As we enter the foyer, unpleasant memories crash over me. I can see it in my mind's eye: me and my friends charging up the steps, unaware of the danger waiting for us within. I scan over the ruby nylon carpets, the crystal chandelier hanging above the balcony, and the rose marble artistry. The rich decadence is overpowering—and the statues of the five creatures lining the spiraling redwood staircase are haunting. A bear, a lion, a wolf, a crocodile, and a viper.

But the most chilling aspect is the statue of the conglomeration of the five creatures as one. It's as if Camille were standing over me once more, leering at me and thirsty for my blood.

I pause at the start of the redwood stairs, my breathing turning shallow. Stars crowd my vision, and my face prickles with discomfort. But it's my leg that's agonizing. The adrenaline I had fighting for my life against Camille is quickly diminishing, and the longer I walk, the worse it becomes.

"Quickly!" Wren snaps.

"My leg," I say through clenched teeth. I part the ripped folds of my teal party dress to unveil the deep wound. "I . . . I've lost a lot of . . . blood."

Wren curses under her breath and jogs back down the staircase. "Why didn't you say something? I can't have you bleeding to death."

She removes her black vest and takes off her long sleeve overshirt. She's wearing a white tank top underneath.

"Sit."

I obey her, and she wraps the long sleeve around my wound tightly. I wince, fighting a bout of nausea.

"Camille did this, I assume?"

"Yes."

"Good thing he's dead."

Her statement sends ice through my veins. How many of Arthur's people knew this was going to happen? I wanted to keep Camille alive and put him on trial for the world to see. I wanted society to know the truth about him. I wanted to stop his assassination. But little did I know, I was simply a pawn in Arthur Evandrum's game.

Wren finishes tying up my wound. "I have some morphine in my med bag, but it's in the chopper. Can you walk?"

I grimace but stand up, putting my weight back onto my injured leg. "Yes."

"Then let's go."

We trek through the long, carpeted hallway past the balcony. I try to avoid looking at the paintings of the five creatures mounted along the way, but I can't help myself. It's all a nightmare, but the rage brewing within me is keeping me calm. I will do what's required of me because that's my ticket back to the mountain.

Wren leads me to the open platform—formerly President Alvaro Camille's office—and straight to the chopper. And after a five-minute overview of basic safety procedures, I'm strapped in with headphones over my ears and a shot of morphine in my leg.

Pain relief sweeps in like a soothing wave, and clarity comes back to my foggy brain. I don't feel like I'm going to pass out anymore. Wren fires up the engines, does a sound check on our mics, and then lifts off, taking us high above the city.

Shimmering glass buildings sparkle in the afternoon sun, and anxiety twists my stomach into a knot. I know I'm powerful, and I don't have anything to worry about now that I understand the voice of my ability, but I'm going to take on the rest of the military.

"We're almost there," Wren says into her mic. "I'm going to put us down on one of the helipads just inside the Military Base. Then I'll leave it to you. You take control of every person in there. We have reinforcements flying in as we speak."

My anxiety runs deeper as a thought occurs to me. "What if they shoot us down? This is a bad idea."

"This is an Area 19 military chopper," she says. "They're not expecting it to be you. We still have the element of surprise. And remember, I've worked in Area 19 for a while now. They know me. They'll let us land." Wren pushes one of the many buttons on the flight panel, and my mic cuts out. Her tone turns as sharp as a knife. "Don't say a word, puppet master."

She clicks several more buttons and starts speaking rapidly.

"Providence Tower Viper 4396 over the rock quarry inbound requesting full stop with information Echo."

A few seconds pass, and the radio crackles to life.

"Viper 4396 Providence Tower Helipad Seven cleared to land." A man's voice cuts through the audio in my headphones and my whole body goes numb. I know that voice . . .

"Cleared to land Helipad Seven 4396," Wren says.

"What's the status of the city, Zayla?" the man asks.

"Not good, sir. The city is compromised. The Diseased Ones have infiltrated the Testing Center, but they've not gained the Capitol. If we counter quickly, we may be able to hold them off."

"And the President?"

"Dead, sir."

There's silence for a beat.

"Copy that," the man says.

Wren flips a switch, and my mic turns back on. "We land in three minutes. Are you ready?"

My tongue is drier than sandpaper. "Was that . . . ?"

"General Timewire, Commander in Chief of the military elite," she says. "Your father."

I can feel all of the blood drain from my face. Only Jonah, Keith, and Olivia know what my mother told me on that dreadful day at the pond. The President of the world was my blood, and I am his secret progeny. Two puppet masters. A cruel twist of fate. And the man I grew up calling "father" doesn't know about my mother's illicit affair. All he knows is that his daughter is a terrorist who killed his wife—at least that's what Camille made it seem like when he threw her from the towering heights of the Testing Center and blamed it on me.

"This is about to be one hell of a family reunion," Wren states. "We're descending now."

The chopper lowers to the ground, blowing dust up in the afternoon's harsh light. The instant the bird lands, the monster within me comes alive. Power courses through every pore of my being, and as I turn toward Wren, she gasps, clutching her chest and swearing at me.

"Your eyes! They're black," she gulps.

I breathe in power until it hurts. As much as I don't want to do this, I don't have a choice. The military can't regroup. I must put every person in the Base under my ability. Moving with uncanny speed, I unfasten my seatbelt, pull the headphones off, and toss them onto the seat as I leap from the chopper. The darkness of my ability hovers by my side, visible only to me, and a group of military men flood the airstrip. As if in a dream, their eyes find me, and the realization behind their faces strikes deep. The leader of the second Terror War is here. It's too late for them to fight back . . .

My hands slice through the air, and I take them easily. Forty men. Mine.

The creature beside me purrs with pleasure, filling me to capacity and heightening my senses tenfold. I twitch my fingertips, and every weapon falls to the ground.

Take more, the voice says. *Feel them, Hollis. Control them.*

I march across the dirt of the airstrip, toward the building just beyond the group of men bound under my ability. And something new arises in my soul. I don't know whether it's foolishness, a sense of sentimentality, or a combination, but I'm alive with the urge to see my father. Even though he believes me to be a terrorist and a murderer, and even though he will not understand, I want him to hear this from me: that people with powers are not the threat he's been led to believe, and in time, he will come to understand.

I force the man nearest me to my side, compelling his obedi-ence. "Where is General Timewire?" I ask.

The man's eyes are bulging, and his face is flush. "The co-command tower," he stammers, pointing to the highest turret of the concrete Base behind him.

My ability spurs me onward, and I extend my hands in front of me. The invisible tendrils of my power snake out from me in spirals, and I feel more and more men. One by one, though I'm not even in the building, I put them under my power. Five hundred men. A thousand men. Three thousand men . . .

My hands shake, my lungs feel like they're going to burst, and my skin burns, but the creature pushes me further, expanding my grasp until every soul is bound to my will—six thousand three hundred and twenty in all.

Well done, Hollis, the creature rattles in my ear. *The General awaits. Call him to your side.*

My hands move as a unit, dancing into an arc, and the ties of my power fly into the building. I can feel him as clearly as if he were standing in front of me. And with a twitch of my fingertips, I force him to walk out of the command tower and onto the airstrip.

I wait with Wren at my side as the minutes tick by . . .

Finally, a metal door a hundred yards from us crashes open, and my heart leaps into my throat. Metal shrieks against concrete, echoing over the heavy silence of the Base. There, walking toward me with forced steps and a closed mouth, is General Timewire. My father. The man who turned me in the day I failed the Test.

The sun shines off of his peppered gray and blond hair. He's clean shaven, with a muscular build and clear blue eyes that never waver from me. I can feel him fighting my hold, but it's in vain. The monster of my power will not relinquish him until I allow it.

My hands move in sync, and I bring him to his knees a few feet from me. We're staring at each other, and the look he bears is one of societal restraint mixed with more loathing than he's permitted to show. My eyes bead with tears, but they don't spill onto my cheeks. I'm finding it difficult to breathe. I can't believe I'm looking into his face, after all this time. He's right in front of me.

"Father," I whisper.

I release his mouth, and he shudders. He speaks through gritted teeth, and his words pierce me like a dagger.

"I should have shot you myself when you failed the Test."

My belly burns hot, my chest heaves, and sweat beads onto my brow as the afternoon sun swelters over us. I want to cry. I feel the well of every truth I've ever learned building up in me. It's like a dam ready to burst at any second, but I don't know where to start. I don't know what to say to him. His words are a conditioned response. I understand this. But they still hurt more than I thought they would. I know what's running through his mind. I'm Hollis Timewire, *his* daughter, the leader of the second Terror War, and he wants me dead because of Camille's deranged lies.

I approach and kneel down in front of him, fighting with all I have to keep my face as emotionless as possible. But my eyes blur with tears.

"This isn't what you think it is," I say to him, my tone thick with sadness. "And I know you don't understand right now. But we're not here to kill anyone. *I'm* not here to kill anyone. People with powers are not who you think they are."

He gazes at me with fractured societal control. I can tell that he's not okay. We're a foot from each other, and I search his deep blue eyes for anything I can grasp on to—*any* humanity or compassion for the little girl he once knew. The one he raised and cared for. But I'm met with nothing but stone cold hatred.

"It's me." I peer at him with all the tenderness I can muster. "*Me.* I'm still your little girl. I'm still . . . just me." My voice breaks. "And all of this mess. I never did what Camille said I did. And I know you don't believe me, but it's the truth. I didn't kill Mother."

Silence extends between us. It stretches on and on. There's something in his eyes. I can see it . . .

Without warning, he spits into my face, and I gasp, falling backward. I catch my balance on my hands and sit in the dust, stunned. My heart is beating so loudly that it's affecting my hearing.

"Mark my words," he growls, staring at me with icy, flawless control once more. "I will *kill* you if I ever get the chance." His gaze turns upward toward Wren. "Wren Zayla, you're a traitor, and you will *die* for this." He spits on the ground at her feet. "Filthy Diseased One."

Wren stoops down to his level, a smile playing her lips. "Under the New World Order, the term 'Diseased One' is now forbidden. We are the Pure Ones, and you will address us as such. And if you refuse, the punishment will fit the crime."

He gives her a defiant look and says, "Diseased One."

She pulls a knife from her belt and grabs my father's chin, bringing the weapon up to his mouth. She forces the blade between his teeth, and he gasps. "Maybe I cut out your tongue instead of giving you a warning, General."

"What are you doing?" I shout, launching to my feet.

My hands move in a flash, and Wren seizes under the ferocity of my ability as I force her away from him. The knife thuds in the dust at her feet. Anger roars in my chest, and I have to rein back the tingling so I don't hurt her.

"Are you insane?" I snarl. "We're *not* doing this. This is *not* why we're here."

Wren's face, initially startled, slithers back into an eerie calm. "Release me, Timewire. We're both on the same side here."

"Are we?" I ask, glaring at her. My hold over her cements, power filling me to the brim. "We're not cutting anyone's tongue out because they said 'Diseased One.' To them, that's what we *are*! We can't just expect society to change because we're ordering them to do so. That's not how this works. This is going to take *time*."

Wren's tight lips split into another smile. "Whatever you say, puppet master. Now let me go. Backup will be here any minute to clear out the weapons on this Base. And you need to stay focused on keeping everyone under your power."

My hands slacken, and my grip on her vanishes, but my fierce look remains.

I turn back toward my father. He's sweating, still fighting my power with everything he has, but to the darkness hovering by my side, he's nothing but a mouse to the lion of my absolute control.

"You've killed us all, Zayla!" he says, seething. "You bitc—"

Wren turns toward him with inhuman speed and backhands him across the face. Hard. The sound of the smack seizes my stomach into knots. I grab Wren's upper arm and yank her away from him.

"Don't hurt him!" I yell.

She shrugs me off easily, her well-built frame beast-like to my small five-foot-three stature. Her dark eyes narrow, and she addresses me in a cold tone.

"The General is getting mouthy. Shall *I* gag him or will you?" She gestures to the rest of the military men on the airstrip. Everyone is silent with their mouths pressed shut under my command.

The tingling in my hands sharpens, almost to the point of hurting, but I take a deep breath and push Wren aside. I stare at my father, hating the position I'm in. But I raise my hand and close my fist, quieting him along with everyone else.

The look he's giving me makes me want to vanish . . .

"Good choice," she says. A roar sounds in the distance, and we both turn on our heels, peering up into the sky. "Ah. Right on time."

A group of a dozen military planes approaches. They soar overhead, and I watch them as they descend like a pack of vultures onto the Military Base. One by one, they land, and from their depths, men and women alike emerge, moving quickly toward the place where Wren and I stand. My head is spinning at the scope of this. I knew Arthur's reach in society was extensive, but I never imagined there would be an entire group of militarized people with powers ready to take action against society.

Wren turns to me, placing a hand on my shoulder. "Are you absolutely sure you have everyone on this Base under your power? No one's going to get shot if I send our people into that building?" She points across the airstrip to the concrete, bunker-like structure.

"I'm sure," I say. "I can feel everyone. I've got them all."

"Alright then."

Wren's hand leaves me, and she jogs over to the ever-growing group of people that have just arrived from the planes. From what I can tell, there's about eighty of them. She barks out orders in a high, clear voice.

"Bardo, you take your team into the Base and start clearing out the weapons. Take inventory of what we've got, and haul it out to the airstrip. Kirk, your team will load the weapons onto the planes. Cromwell, take your men and start bringing out all personnel in this facility. Line them up here." She gestures to the place where the forty military men are currently sitting in the dust. "Cuff them. Count them. Get their names and the names of their family members. Huxley, your team is to go to the command tower and scope out anything useful on the remaining active Military Bases in other Areas. Area 19's Base is the largest, but it's not the last one society has. Alright, let's move! We're burning daylight."

The group disperses toward their assigned tasks with quick feet, and I'm left staring at them like it's all a dream. But it's not. The Pure Ones have taken over, and I'm helping them do it.

My eyes drift in and out of focus as I gaze out across the airstrip. I'm disheveled and exhausted, still adorned in the dark teal dress that's soaked in my own blood. I'm beyond spent, and everything in me longs for the mountain. For my friends. My *family*.

Power purrs down my arms, vibrating to the rhythm of the madness in my head.

So. Much. Control.

Every breath.

Every heartbeat.

Every puppet.

From behind me, the darkness hovers like a steadfast guardian, fueling my stamina to hold every person to my will. It creeps close, snarling in my ear.

Hollis . . .

Something about the way it says my name prickles fear deep to my bones and compels a response from my lips.

"What?" I whisper.

Stay on your guard.

"Miss Timewire!"

Wren's harsh tone pulls me out of the moment, and the voice of my ability evaporates. She's standing in front of me, hands on her hips.

"Got it?"

I shake my head. "Sorry . . . what?"

"Once Cromwell detains the military men and Bardo clears out the weapons, your services are no longer required, and I'll fly you back to the mountain."

"Back to the mountain," I repeat.

"Shouldn't take more than a few hours."

"What about them?" I ask, nodding to the military men. "What's going to happen to them?"

"You don't need to worry about that," she says in a disparaging manner.

My voice turns sharp. "*Don't* dismiss me, Wren. What's going to happen to them?"

She sighs, rubbing her forehead between her pointer finger and thumb. "They're prisoners of the New World Order, Miss Timewire. And they're to be sent to a prison facility in Area 7."

My eyes widen, and my lips part, but before I can say anything, Wren continues.

"Oh, don't look at me like that. We're not imprisoning innocent citizens. This is the *military* we're talking about. They're trained to kill us. We can't have them running amok and inciting rebellion. We're snuffing that out at its source, and perhaps in time, we can come to a peaceable resolution that restores them to the new society we hope to create. Like you said: this *will* take time. But for now, they're a threat we can't afford to worry about."

"And my father?" I ask. "What about him?"

"He's going to Area 7 as well."

My pulse thunders through my veins with uncomfortable pressure. I close my eyes, trying to push past the discomfort creeping under my skin. My head is killing me . . .

"How's your leg holding up?" Wren inquires, studying me with concern.

"The morphine helped."

"That's a nasty gash. You'll need to see Beezee when we return."

"Right," I say, not really listening to her.

My mind is humming with anticipation. In a few hours' time, I'll be on my way back to the mountain. This day has shaken me to my core. It's far beyond anything I bargained for. Disarming the people? A prison camp in Area 7? Wren's threat to cut out my father's tongue for uttering the phrase "Diseased One?" And my father's hateful, poisonous, resigned stare . . .

I'm so overwhelmed, my body hurts, and all I want to do is clean the blood off of me and sleep, but the day is far from over. When I get back, I'm demanding answers, and Arthur Evandrum will have no choice but to bend to the will of the puppet master who commands him.

2

THREE HOURS LATER, WREN AND I ARE FLYING OVER A VAST expanse of open plain in a private twelve-passenger Beechcraft. Area 19 has slipped past my view, hidden under a peppering of clouds and too much distance. It's a great relief that I'm no longer holding masses of prisoners under my power. Once Wren's people had all personnel detained and accounted for, I was free to leave.

The morphine Wren gave me is wearing off, and pain is slowly creeping back into my calf muscle.

Thankfully, the journey isn't going to be a long one. Wren said it would be a two-and-a-half-hour flight from the Military Base to the mountain and that she's radioed ahead about my injuries. I'll receive medical attention upon our arrival.

I sit with clenched fists and a set jaw, staring out the window and watching the blue sky fade with bursts of orange and pink. Late afternoon is dipping into early evening. It's not even been a full twenty-four hours since Camille killed my mother.

Last night, I was at the Ability Festival with Keith, dancing and eating and pretending like I was just a kid. But my childhood was ripped away from me the day I turned sixteen. Nine months ago, this whole nightmare started, and it's far from over.

Angry tears burn my eyes, and as I close them, I shove back a sob. I don't want Wren to hear me cry. I must keep it together.

My ability tingles at the ends of my fingertips; a low buzz. Something about it comforts me. I don't feel alone. The creature I was so terrified of when I first got my power is now the essence that's keeping me sane. The more I allow it in, the more tangibly present it becomes. And the most comforting part is that no one can see her. No one but me.

It's a her. At least, I think it is. The snake-like, black body and coal-red eyes I saw when I was fighting Camille are imprinted in my mind's eye. The creature showed herself to me in that moment. Fully and without restraint. And when the voice spoke to me on the airstrip, I could see her again. But she stayed behind me, right next to me, right in my ear. Her darkness flickered in and out of my peripheral vision, like fully facing me is something only *she* can decide to allow . . .

The Beechcraft shudders as we hit some turbulence, and I clutch onto the armrests of my seat, white-knuckled and spent.

"We're almost there," Wren says, looking over at me. "Fifteen miles out. How's your pain?"

"Fine," I lie.

My brain is reeling with a hundred tangled thoughts, and my hands are humming with revenge. The wrath in my palms is palpable. It's building in my chest. More and more power. Every second, my anger turns more potent because Arthur Evandrum took away the opportunity for society to see the truth behind their leader. And the worst part: in the world's eyes, *I'm* the one responsible for the assassination. But I know the truth. Arthur Evandrum gave me poison.

"Welcome home, Miss Timewire." Wren flips a switch on the control panel and speaks into her mic. "Mountain Tower Beechcraft 237 approaching from the northwest requesting full stop with information Echo."

A woman's voice issues from the radio after a couple seconds of delay. "Beechcraft 237 Mountain Tower follow traffic at your ten o'clock."

"Traffic in sight 237."

Wren eases the plane into a slight left turn, and my stomach whirls. We sit in silence for several minutes, and with each heartbeat, the pain in my body heightens. I can't wait to get off this plane.

The radio comes back to life once more. "Beechcraft 237 Runway Alpha Ten clear to land."

"Clear to land Runway Alpha Ten 237," Wren replies.

She dips the nose of the plane down toward the earth, and before I know it, the wheels vibrate against the asphalt below us. The plane slows as flaps pop up along the wings, catching friction against the air. And when we finally come to a complete stop, I take a deep breath.

The woman from the control Tower continues speaking to Wren in a high voice. "Beechcraft 237 left at junction six then contact Ground Control."

"Copy that. Turning left at junction six Beechcraft 237."

Wren pushes a button and then says, "Mountain Ground Beechcraft 237 Alpha Ten requesting taxi to the North Hangar."

My brain spaces out as the jumble of instructions over the radio continues. I can't believe what I'm seeing. There's a whole airport carved out of the backside of the mountain. Rocky, cavernous arches gape ahead. How did I never know about this place? My stomach churns. This operation is way more involved than Arthur ever let on.

Ten minutes later, we're parked in a large, concrete hangar I've never seen before, and Wren opens the door, allowing me to exit from the belly of the Beechcraft. I tread down the extendable stairs, holding the torn folds of my dress to keep from tripping.

"Thank Heavens you're okay, child!" a honeyed voice calls out.

My body stiffens, and I have to grip the fabric of my dress tighter to stop myself from using my ability. Beezee-Day Jones is jogging toward me. In her haste, her gray braid flicks over her shoulder, and her black skin beads with perspiration. She looks like she's seen a ghost, and her brow creases together with worry.

She reaches me in a few more strides, medical bag in hand. "Wren said you have a pretty nasty cut on your calf? Heavens, look at you." She takes in my disheveled appearance and brushes the ends of her fingertips over the knife wound on my cheek.

It takes everything in me to not shrink away from her touch, but I keep still and bite my tongue. I don't want to say anything I'll regret. Even though I'm sure Arthur's the one who gave Beezee the order, Beezee was the one who fetched the syringe I stabbed Camille with. This is her fault too.

"Let me see your leg, child," she says, prompting me to sit on the concrete.

I obey, taking a seat on the cold stone and pulling my dress up above my knee. Gingerly, I untie the now soaked-through black long sleeve to reveal the deep and slightly crusted-over wound.

"Goodness!" Beezee chirps.

She rummages in her bag and sets to work. The first thing she does is pour a saline solution over the wound, which feels like a hundred needles stabbing me all at once. I inhale sharply, gritting my teeth.

"That's to help clean it," Beezee explains. "Now hold still." She places her palms over the gash, and at her touch, intense heat sweeps through my skin. I grimace, but the longer Beezee's power works, the better I feel.

She pulls her hands away, peering over the gash, which now appears to be a few weeks healed. It's still tender and clearly visible, but my skin is no longer sliced open, and instead of dark, crusted-over blood, a deep red mark is in its place.

Next, Beezee cleans the wound on my cheek with gentle strokes of a dampened cloth. She moves her palm to my face and holds it there. Heat travels into my skin, and the pain diminishes.

"Better?" she asks.

"Yes," I say. "Loads."

"Unfortunately, you're going to have scars. My ability only speeds up the natural healing process. I can't make these go away."

My stomach does several uncomfortable twirls, and I push back against the urge to vomit. Again, I hold my tongue even though I want to scream at her. I'm going to wear the reminder of the fight with Camille for the rest of my life, and there's nothing I can do about it. My leg I can live with. But my face? My eyes blur with unwanted tears as my anger burrows deeper.

I choke back a whimper. My heartbeat thuds into my limbs, my vision tunnels, and a flashback of the holographic puppets tying me to the metal throne overwhelms me. It's as if I'm reliving the moment over again in real time: I'm pushed back against the throne, the syringe is torn from my fingertips, the cuffs clamp over my wrists, and a gag is shoved between my teeth. And then Camille's wicked face is inches from my own, and his knife digs deep enough to slice open my flesh . . .

"Hollis?" Beezee's worried tone pulls me from the waking nightmare. "You're shaking. Are you alright?"

I twist my hands together. "I . . . I'm fine."

I'm not. I'm nowhere near fine. I'm trying to take control of my rampant breath, my chest feels like a hollow cavity, and adrenaline is keeping my fight-or-flight response on high alert.

"Where is Arthur?" I ask, looking around the unfamiliar hangar. I'm not sure where I am. This isn't the same place Olivia teleported me and my friends to when she rescued us from the President three months ago. "I need to speak with him."

Beezee's concern deepens. "You need to rest, child."

"I don't need to rest!" I snap. The tingling of my ability awakens, and I stick my hand directly over her heart. Pulling just enough power into the command, I say, "Tell me where Arthur is."

Beezee, compelled to obey me, points toward the double doors at the back of the aircraft hangar. "Those lead right into the mountain. He's in his office in Sector 15."

I rise from the floor, reining back my ability and releasing Beezee. She gasps as my power leaves her body and gapes at me like I've struck her across the face.

"Thank you," I say, deadpan.

And without another word, I march into the depths of the mountain.

Being back here feels impossible. When Camille locked me into the Testing Center, I thought I was going to die. I thought I'd never see my friends again. But I've returned with the dawn of a new world at my heels—one *I* helped create—and the man responsible is going to regret double crossing me.

I move through the halls with purpose, the tatters of my dress whipping around my ankles with every step. Deeper and deeper I go, until I reach the double doors leading to Sector 15.

My hands fly into the push bar, and doors to the stark white hall burst open. The darkness of my ability materializes behind me. Power is all I feel.

So. Much. Power.

My senses rise as the creature rattles in my chest, and as I approach the office, I sense three people just beyond the door. My palm slams into the scanner, it lights up, and the door folds into the wall.

Arthur Evandrum is seated in a black leather chair at the end of the oval table. He wears a crisp white suit pressed to perfection, and his white hair is gelled back, resting at the nape of his neck.

By his side, Terrace DuPont and Hugo stand at attention. Terrace's amber eyes snap to me, and he angles his head, his stringy ginger hair trailing across his forehead. Hugo's bald head dips low, and his muscled arm reaches for the gun at his hip.

Without hesitation—and before anyone can utter a word—my hands launch from me, and all three of them fall to my clutches. I can feel every cell in their bodies. Every tick of their heartbeats. Every breath drawn into their lungs.

I'm so overcome by the control that washes over me that I take a second to catch my labored breath before marching directly up to Arthur Evandrum.

"What have you done?" I demand.

I open my fist, and with it, his mouth.

He gazes at me with a look I've never encountered. Calm to the point of eerie. Piercing to the point of frightening. And so commanding that I couldn't look away even if I wanted to.

"Hollis Timewire." My name slips from his lips as if it were the most fascinating of phrases. "My, my. Look at you."

His eyes travel the length of my blood-soaked dress, lingering over my hips, and then he lifts his attention back to my face.

"What a vision of inspiration."

"You gave me poison!" I spit my words at him.

"I did."

My hand rockets up over his heart, and tingling pours from my palm into his chest. "Did you plan that from the beginning? Were you going to kill Camille anyway? Despite *everything*?"

His upper lip curls, but he's no match for my ability. He must answer me.

"Yes. I intended to kill Camille all along."

The vibrations in my hands fall to a low rumble in the wake of his statement, and I stand there, panting.

"You lied to me!"

"I never lied to you, Miss Timewire. I was *very* clear about my intentions. I told you outright: what we've planned can't happen with Camille in the picture."

I'm shaking—seething—and the creature within fuels my hold over him.

"But I must say,"—his mouth splits into a cruel smile—"watching *you* kill the President was quite a thing to behold."

I'm doused in a numbing sensation that travels from the tips of my toes to the ends of my fingertips, and I clutch the folds of my dress.

Arthur continues. "What a fight. I honestly didn't know who'd come out of that alive. But either way . . ." His eyes narrow. "I knew my puppet master problem would be half as great when it was done." He cocks his head to the side, his brown eyes burrowing into me. "You surprised me, Miss Timewire. Hats off to the winner."

"You . . . ?" Nausea is clawing its way up my esophagus. "You watched?"

His cold smile deepens. "Yes, I did."

Rage turns my vision red, and my ability surges into him. He seizes under the intensity of my grip, and I speak with inflections I've never used before, my voice running deep with wrath. "Did you know we were walking into a trap? Did you know about the steel doors?"

"Yes," he says, unable to resist me. But even though my power is pulsing through him enough to burn my fingertips, he still appears unfazed. Like he has all the power in the world.

Splotches of blue and purple streak my vision. I'm sick to my stomach. He *knew*. And he sent us to Camille anyway. All three of us could have died.

"Is Olivia alive? Is Ashton? Are they okay?"

"Yes, they are alive," Arthur responds. "What a clever trick—using your ability to command Olivia to teleport back to the mountain. And *directly* to Beezee. Truly inspired."

His eyes move from me to the clock on the back wall.

"You'll pay for this!" I growl.

Arthur's amusement only grows. "Miss Timewire, would you read me the time?"

I peer back over my shoulder. The digital display reads 1759, but I don't do as he asks. "You've ruined the only chance we had to show society the truth!"

"Miss Timewire, the time. Would you read it to me?" Arthur asks again.

My brain is slipping into a fog, and my hands begin to tremble. "I . . . it's . . ." I gaze at the clock and the red numbers glare back. "1759."

Arthur's next words chill me to the bone and steal all the breath from my body. "Let me teach you something about control, puppet master."

The clock flicks over to the next minute. 1800. And the moment it does, several things happen at once: the door to Arthur's office flies open, the nine wall screens behind Arthur's head flicker on, and my ability *dies* in my fingertips.

A huge, smothering force attacks my body, and I whirl around. Erwin, the guard Arthur had assigned to watch over Keith, is standing directly behind me with his machine gun at the ready—but he's not pointing it at me. He's pointing it at Ashton Teel.

Ashton's sickly complexion is frightening. He looks like a corpse. Bandages wrap around his ribcage, visible under his thin white shirt, and his dirty blond hair is caked in sweat. But it's not his gaunt face or death-like appearance that scares me most, it's the fact that his hand is out in front of his chest, and his power is snuffing out my own . . .

I don't even have time to react before Hugo lunges at me. One beefy arm wraps around my torso, pinning my arms to my sides, while the other twists through my hair. He yanks me around to face Arthur, and when I do, my heart drops into my gut.

There, on every display, is a live feed of a barren white room. Two people are sitting on the floor in the center, talking, although no audio issues from the speakers. The first person is a dark-haired doctor I've never seen before, but the second is a blond, curly-haired little boy.

Tears spring to my eyes, and my voice catches. "Maddy . . ."

I struggle within Hugo's grasp, but his grip on me only tightens, and I gasp, the skin across my scalp searing with pain.

The dark-haired doctor on the feed stands up, checking the watch on his wrist, and from his lab coat pocket, he withdraws a syringe. I feel all of the blood drain from my face, and every nerve in my body screams. It's the same type of syringe Arthur gave me before I left the mountain to face Camille.

"You recognize that, don't you?" Arthur asks.

"You snake! What have you done? Let Maddy go!" I cry, thrashing against Hugo. But still, I can't shake him.

Arthur looks from Maddy to me, and then back to the clock on the wall behind my head. "Miss Timewire, can you read me the time again?"

Hugo angles me so I can see the clock, but my gaze falls on Ashton instead. He's shaking, and he's so pale that he doesn't look alive. His watery gray eyes are fixed on Maddy in horror. But he doesn't release me from his power at the penalty of Erwin's gun.

Anger rips through every pore of my being. A wildness I've never felt before enters my chest and limbs, and a slew of curses escape my lips, but this doesn't seem to bother Arthur.

"Where's Maddy?" I demand.

"The time, Miss Timewire?"

I grit my teeth, panting in my efforts to fight off Hugo. "1802."

"Good. Now listen very closely to my words. When the clock hits 1805, that man has instructions to inject Maddy with the contents of that syringe. And I know you have firsthand experience with what that means." He speaks quickly, his words calculated. "Unless he hears from me in the next three minutes, Maddy will be dead. Do I have your attention?"

The rage in me, so tangible moments ago, dissolves into a storm of emotions I can't begin to name, and the suffocation of Ashton's power makes my vision swim.

"Answer me, Miss Timewire," Arthur sneers.

"Yes, you have my attention."

His cold look turns more sinister. He swivels in his chair, and his hands press together, fingertip to fingertip.

"From now on, Miss Timewire, you work for me. You will do what I say when I say it. Your ability is at my disposal. And if you do not comply with my requests promptly and without hesitation, I will dispose of Maddy before you can even beg for my forgiveness. I will not tolerate any misbehavior. I've indulged you for months now—from the moment you stepped foot in this mountain. But that's over. *I* am in charge, and what I say goes. I've let you have your little temper tantrum, but now, it's to business. Do you understand?"

The inside of my mouth turns to ash, and I stare at him. Maddy's little head bobs in the feed behind Arthur's eyes, and something in me snaps.

I writhe against Hugo's body.

With all that I am, I strain to feel my power. I reach for it with my fingertips, I try to summon the demon voice, I attempt to pull tingling into my chest . . . but nothing I do has any effect at all. And even though Ashton looks like he's going to keel over from the effort of holding my power at bay, I can't break his suppression.

My outburst seems to feed Arthur's amusement. "Tick tock, Miss Timewire. You have one minute. What will it be?"

I gaze at him with a rage so violent that I'm having a hard time breathing, but my resolve crashes. And now, panic replaces my escape attempts. If I don't say something, Maddy's going to die . . .

I claw the words out, still pinned against Hugo. "I understand."

"You work for me."

"I understand!"

His upper lip curls to expose his teeth. "Let me hear you say it."

The doctor on the feed behind Arthur flicks the end of the syringe, staring at his watch, and my heart hammers wildly in my chest.

I strain to keep pleading from entering my tone. "I work for you."

Arthur's smile turns wicked, but he doesn't move. And he doesn't speak.

Seconds tick by . . .

"Arthur!" I cry, and this time, I can't help how panicked I sound.

"It's Mr. Evandrum to you," he snarls.

His cruel expression twists his face into something deranged. He stands and walks over to me until he's inches from me. He peers down into my face and speaks slowly, his words snake-like.

"*You* belong to *me*."

There's a moment of pin-drop silence. Then, Arthur clicks a small, black, pea-sized bead on the collar of his white suit jacket.

"Jenkins, you may stand down. Do not inject the boy."

The man on the live feed nods and slips the syringe back into his lab coat pocket. I gaze at Maddy's tiny head, and my heart aches. His blond curls fall askew across his forehead. He's talking to the man with an innocent smile on his face, but I don't know what he's saying.

Without warning, all of the wall screens turn off.

Arthur's lips press into a triumphant smirk. "That will be all, Miss Timewire. You are dismissed. Get some rest. We have much to discuss in the morning." He pauses, his eyes raking over me in satisfaction. "And change out of that dress."

3

HUGO THROWS ME INTO THE HALLWAY, AND I TRIP OVER the folds of my dress, landing with a smack against the white tile. Pain riddles my body, and I lie on my stomach, stunned. It takes my brain a moment to register what's happened, and in that time, the door to Arthur's office slides shut.

With unsteady legs, I rise from the floor, and panic swallows me whole.

Maddy. Arthur kidnapped Maddy . . .

I begin to hyperventilate.

My trembling fingertips grasp the V-neck of my dress, and my vision tunnels. I swallow stomach acid that's pushed its way up my throat, and I lean against the wall for support. I'm doing my best to stay conscious. But my hands are shaking so badly that the muscles along my arms tense. So I clench my teeth and stuff my fists under my armpits to stop the violent spasming.

Minutes tick by, and the only thing I can hear is the thud of my heartbeat and the racing of my frantic breath. Once my body emerges from the panic attack, my mind clears, and I'm able to take control of myself again.

I peer down the deserted hall, and like a switch, my ability returns to me. Tingling erupts through my veins, and I train my eyes on the panel next to the door. It blinks, tempting my hand-print. But the creature rattles down my arms, prodding me away from the scanner, and I listen.

I'm completely out of my element when it comes to Ashton. And Arthur knows it. It would be foolish of me to charge back in.

Instead, I turn my untamed energy into something more useful. My hands extend from me, and the creature humming beneath my skin guides me. I close my eyes, and with the tendrils of my ability, my power snakes through the halls of the mountain. I don't take anyone under my control, but I can feel each presence. One by one, my power prowls through the souls. None of them are Maddy. He's not here. Wherever Arthur's keeping him, it's not in this facility.

Fury slithers through my blood, and my thoughts turn to the one person who could help me end this: Olivia Turrick. Her power allows her to teleport to anyone just by thinking of them—and that's something Arthur doesn't know. This ends tonight. I will not allow him to hurt Maddy. Wherever he is, I'm getting him back. Right now.

With a burst of purpose, I march toward the double doors of Sector 15, exiting through them quickly. I whip through the halls of the mountain, taking one turn after another. The people I pass gawk at me, their eyes tracing the disarray of my bloodstained appearance, but I ignore them. The only thing that matters is rescuing Maddy.

When I arrive at the medical ward in Sector 10, I allow my ability to lead me. Olivia is in the third room on the right. I can feel her, so I charge forward, and as I clamber in, I'm met with several loud gasps.

My eyes rove around the large, white, hospital-like space. There are two medical attendants present, dressed in white scrubs, and ten beds—five on each side of the infirmary. Olivia lies in the last bed on the left, and perched next to her in a plastic fold-out chair is a shell-shocked Vianne Evolet.

"Hollis?" Vianne says, looking up at me with wild eyes. Her tone is stricken, but before I can say anything, the two ladies in scrubs approach me, blocking my path. The first, and shorter of the two, waves a thick forearm at me.

"You can't be in here!" she huffs.

My palm slashes over both of them, and they succumb to my power.

"Get out!" I snarl.

They obey, scurrying through the door and leaving us alone.

Vianne stands from the chair, and as I stare into her porcelain face, I note her silver eyes. They're puffy and red. Bags hang under them, and she looks like she hasn't slept. When she speaks, the hysteria in her voice throws my anxiety to new heights.

"They took Maddy! They took him right out of my arms. Four men. During the Ability Festival. Right after the President's broadcast!" Vianne's hair changes in a rapid-fire collage of muddy browns and charcoal blacks. "Hollis, they took him!"

I run to her, and we both grip each other in a fierce hug. She sobs into my shoulder, and I do my best to fight my own cascade of tears.

"I know," I say bitterly, gritting my teeth.

"I tried to s-stop them," she gulps. "But two of them held me down. And then they ripped Maddy away from me."

She's shaking violently, and I hold her steady.

"I'm going to get him back," I say.

My throat closes as a wave of grief claims me. How could I have been so blind? I had a bad feeling about Arthur's intentions for Maddy the second Maddy arrived from the forest with the rest of my people. I should have protected him more. But the moment I left the mountain to fight Camille, Arthur made his move, and now Maddy's locked up somewhere.

"And ten minutes ago, Erwin came in here and forced Ashton out of bed," she continues. "Then he shoved his gun in my face and said he'd shoot me if I followed him. Hollis, Ashton's recovering from a bullet. He can barely stand!"

I hug her tighter. "He's . . . he's okay. I saw him."

"Where?"

"Arthur's office."

"What? Hollis, what is going on?"

I don't know what to say to her. There's too much raging through my mind, and I don't have time to delve into any of it. Not right now.

I disentangle myself from Vianne, and approach Olivia's bedside. I didn't notice until now, but Olivia's sitting bolt upright. Awake. And she's staring at me.

Her gaze turns my skin to ice.

"Olivia?" I say cautiously.

Her curly black hair is disheveled, and her dark skin is sickly. Her face appears hollow. Broken. And the skin around her cheeks is slightly sunken in, as if she hadn't eaten in days. But that's not possible. It's barely been a day since her head injury. And judging by the fact that she's awake, Beezee must have lended a healing hand.

"Olivia?" I repeat, sitting on the edge of her bed and grabbing her hand. "Are you okay?"

Her lips part, but she says nothing. I look to Vianne, hoping that she will offer information as to what's wrong.

"Did Beezee heal her head wound?" I ask.

Vianne nods. "As far as I know, yes."

I look back into Olivia's face. She seems present. Lucid. But still, she says nothing, and her arms are limp at her sides.

"Olivia, Arthur took Maddy." I grip her hand tightly. "You have to help me get him back. You can teleport me to him. I *need* you."

Her dark brown eyes begin to sparkle with tears. Finally, she speaks, but it's barely above a whisper. "I can't . . ."

"Yes, you can." I squeeze her hand harder. "Just concentrate on Maddy, and take me to him. I'll do the rest."

She shakes her head, and a pit forms in my stomach.

"Olivia, please!" My voice cracks. I'm finding it increasingly difficult to not dissolve into tears. "I need your power. You *must* help me. Arthur just threatened to kill Maddy. I have to save him."

"I can't," she repeats, hoarse.

"I don't understand," I say. "Has Arthur threatened you? Whatever it is, I can help you. Please, Olivia. We have to get Maddy back!"

I peer into her face, pleading, and a lump builds in my throat, but I stifle it. I can't fall apart right now.

Olivia's hand suddenly gains strength, and she squeezes me back. Her fingernails dig into my palm, and I wince.

"Hollis," she breathes. Her eyes pierce mine. "I don't have my ability."

A sledgehammer of shock slams into my chest, and horror streaks across my body like a physical blow. "What?"

Olivia is trembling. Her brow turns upward. She looks like she's trying not to scream.

"When I woke up, it was gone. And this was on the foot of my bed." She pulls a neatly folded letter from under her pillow and hands it to me. I open up the paper, and Arthur's familiar loopy handwriting fills the page.

Miss Olivia Turrick,

You are relieved of your position. I no longer require your services. I know your secret, and you are a liability I can no longer afford to keep. Fortunately for you, young Maddy made this decision simple for me. Instead of taking your life, which I would have regretted, I've taken your ability instead. You may stay in the mountain if you wish. Or you may go back to society. That decision, I leave to you.

It's a pity you chose to hide an aspect of your ability that would have made you even more valuable to me. But once trust is broken, it can never be rebuilt.

I meant what I said to you the day you failed the Test: Every drop of power that ran in your blood was precious to me. But you've served your purpose, and now I'm done with you. Miss Timewire is a much more useful ability, and I can't have you teleporting her away. She is mine. And where she goes and what she does is none of your business.

I won't pretend like this is the way I hoped things would go. You served me well, and your ability was critical to what we've accomplished so far. If you had any other power, I may have spared it. But teleportation is a flight risk to my new pet puppet master. I'm only glad I didn't have to kill you.

Sincerely,

Mr. Arthur Evandrum

I finish reading and look up at Olivia. All of the light behind her eyes has shattered into a thousand pieces. There's nothing left there. No fight, and no spirit. She's a broken shell of a person, feeble and empty.

I clutch the note tightly as my heartbeat pumps through my ears. In the span of a day, I've gone from the most powerful person in the world to a servant. If I can't get to Maddy, then I must do everything Arthur Evandrum says.

I'm a fully-realized puppet master, powerless to do anything but obey.

4

I WALK TO SECTOR 7 IN A TRANCE. I DON'T EVEN KNOW how I manage to put one foot in front of the other. I just move, numb to everything. Before I know it, I arrive at the training room, and I pull on the handle. The door scrapes against the stone, sliding into the pocket of the wall, and an odd sight greets me.

In the center of the training mat, four mint green dividers are set up in a rectangle, sectioning off the middle of the platform. Steam rises up from within.

I approach the dividers cautiously and peek around the edge of the opening. A tub of hot, sudsy water sits in the middle of the private space. There's also a small redwood table with an ocean-blue towel, a fluffy cream-colored robe, a cotton nightgown, and a hand mirror with a note on top. I scoop up the note and read it over.

Clean off the blood. I'll see you in the morning in my office at 0600. Don't be late.

I ball the paper up and stare at the steaming water. As much as I don't want to take a bath that Arthur Evandrum's prepared for me, I'm caked in my own blood, and my muscles ache down to the tendons and sinews.

My fingertips fumble with the zipper at the back of my dress. After wrestling with it, I unzip the garment and slip out of it, letting the fabric fall around my ankles. Hand-shaped bruises cover my arms and legs . . .

Gingerly, I step over the edge of the tub and sink into the hot water. The bath's heat prickles across my skin—hot enough to be uncomfortable—but it's working its way through me to provide relief to my aching muscles. And it feels wonderful.

But as the heat seeps in, the injuries I've sustained throb. Everything hurts. The physical pain, however, pales in comparison to the tormented thoughts running through my mind. I swore to protect Maddy. I vowed that no one would ever hurt him again. He's the innocence that made me believe I could keep fighting for a better world. The boy with the golden light. The sweetest soul I've ever encountered. And now he's under Arthur's thumb—insurance to keep me in line . . .

And my mother.

I haven't even had a minute to process the grief I feel for how violently she was ripped away from me. How Camille killed her in front of the world. How he blamed me for her death. I'll never get to see her again. Or hug her. Or hold her. And I'll never get the chance to help her believe in something new. Something better.

She's gone. And what haunts me the most is how close she

was to running away with me and leaving society behind.

I can see her so clearly in my mind. Her eyes glaze over like she's right in front of me. Her terrified face is so tangible that I can scarcely breathe.

The dam of emotion I'd been holding back since escaping Camille bursts, and I sob aloud. Cries wrack my chest, and tears fall hot against my cheeks.

My gaze lands on my blood-covered skin. It's monstrous. Gruesome. I can almost feel the phantom touch of foreign hands grabbing me all over again.

With frantic fingertips, I scrub the blood from my legs. I claw at my own flesh, and the tub water turns from clear to scarlet. I'm crying so hard my eyes blur to the point of blindness. Only colors and foggy shapes move in my vision. And my head pounds as my ragged breathing shreds my lungs.

I feel smothered. Trapped. Completely overwhelmed and alone. I'm shifting into levels of panic that are dangerous for being in water. My knees are vibrating. My eye sockets are tingling. My ankles are buzzing. I grip the edges of the tub to hold myself steady so I don't slip under the surface.

I have to calm down . . .

Though sobs still force their will over me, I begin to take intentional breaths. In and out. In and out. Until I've pulled back the reins of my racing heart. Slower and slower. Until I feel a sense of control.

When my vision clears, my attention meanders to the hand mirror that's lying faceup on the redwood table. I know I shouldn't, but I can't stop myself. I lean over the edge of the tub and grab it, holding it up to examine my face, and what I see drives my misery deeper.

There's a gash an inch long on my left cheekbone, and even though Beezee used her ability on me, it still looks ghastly. It's dark red and jagged, and something that will always draw people's prying eyes.

My fingertips trace the wound, and once again, I fall into tears. But they're softer this time. Lamentful. I shouldn't have looked . . .

I set the mirror facedown, but as I do, an inscription catches my attention. Four words are etched into the metal plating:

YOU BELONG TO ME.

Snatching the mirror up, I hurl it to the ground. It shatters, and a handful of broken fragments skid across the floor. The metal plating, however, stays intact, and Arthur Evandrum's engraved words shimmer up at me in the harsh lighting of the training room.

I curl forward, burying my face in my hands, and bathwater slops over the edge of the tub. I try to slow my breathing, but my lungs refuse to comply. Black invades my peripheral vision, and I lean over the side of the tub and dry heave.

Nothing comes up my esophagus. Nothing at all. Not even bile.

Minutes pass by, and finally, my breathing levels out, and my mind turns blank. I sit in the water, spacing in and out of reality. No plans form in my mind, and no thoughts come to me. I'm in limbo between sleep and consciousness. Exhausted, but still very much awake. Stunned, but still very much aware.

It's a wonderful mercy to sit here and do nothing. To think of nothing. To *be* nothing. Just for a little while.

A little while . . .

The bath water is tepid.

My hands are wrinkled.

My feet are pruned.

Eventually, I find the will to get out of the grimy sludge of suds and dry myself off with the towel. Slipping into the cotton nightgown and cream-colored robe, I make my way out from behind the mint green dividers. The training room is just as I had left it: couches against the far wall, tables and chairs arranged into a dining area, and cabinets, dressers, and lamps laid out into a cozy living space.

I approach the couch, and a plush rug squishes under my toes. All of the energy in me is gone. The fight. The willpower to search for an answer to this impossible situation. The spirit in me. Every piece I own—shattered like the shards of the mirror I threw to the floor.

I collapse onto the upholstery, my puffy eyes close, and I fall into the inviting arms of sweet sleep.

■ ■ ■

Abrasive hands shake me awake, and I startle, coming out of my coma-like slumber in a haze of confusion. It feels like seconds have passed since I laid down on the couch. I push the tangle of air-dried hair out of my face to see an all-too-familiar scowl. Erwin is standing over me. His beige uniform is crisp and pressed, and over his shoulder, he wears a machine gun.

"Time to get up," he growls. A smirk passes over his gruff features. "And if you don't hurry, you'll be late."

I gaze at the clock on the far wall through a blur of fatigue. 0556. I swear under my breath, jumping up as if I'd been poked with the end of a cattle prod. Arthur's expecting me in his office in four minutes. And with Maddy's life on the line, I dare not be late.

I shove my feet into my boots. I'm still dressed in the nightgown and cream-colored robe, but I don't have time to change. I don't even wait for Erwin to usher me through the door.

Pelting down the hallways of the mountain, I make my way to Sector 15 as fast as my body allows. A stitch burns in my chest, stars dance around my vision, and my stomach rumbles. I haven't eaten since the Ability Festival.

The instant I get to the panel outside Arthur's office, I place my hand to it, and it opens to admit me.

The moment I see Arthur Evandrum, all of the anger from the previous day resurfaces, and tangible rage builds in my fingertips. But upon crossing the threshold, the suffocating coils of Ashton's ability smother the energy of my power.

Immediately, I lock eyes with Ashton. He's sitting on Arthur's right-hand side, and he still looks white as a ghost. Even on the brink of passing out, Ashton's hold over me is strong. I can't do a thing.

And in this moment, even though I have no idea what's about to happen, I resolve to keep my head. I will not fall apart right now, and I will not grovel. Arthur may have Ashton to shield him, but I'm still a puppet master.

I scan the room quickly, noting who's present. Hugo and Terrace are seated to Arthur's left, and Wren Zayla is present too. She sits straight-backed and business-like, and the aggressive look she gives me sends chills down my spine.

"Miss Timewire, you're late," Arthur says.

I turn over my shoulder to look at the clock. 0602. I manage a labored reply, panting furiously. "I apologize."

Arthur tips his head to the side, studying me. "Did I not make myself clear in the note I left you?"

The stitch in my chest sharpens, and I clutch the back of the nearest chair. I grit out my words, layering contempt into my tone. "Your note was clear, Mr. Evandrum."

His brown eyes narrow, and he places his hands on the table, folding them together. "You're not used to this yet, I can see that. Miss Timewire, why are you late?"

It takes all of my self-control not to snap. "I was sleeping. Erwin woke me up *four* minutes before I was supposed to be here. How is that—"

"Let me make something crystal clear to you." The savagery of Arthur's tone silences me, and a smile creeps across his lips. He speaks in a slow and deliberately-cadenced manner. "When I ask you to do something, it is your responsibility to do it. I don't care if you're tired, or hungry, or sleep-deprived, or sick. If I ask you to jump, you say, 'how high?' If I ask you to run, you say, 'how fast?' And if I ask you to be in my office at 0600, then that's the moment I should see your pretty face." His cold smile deepens, and his tongue runs along the top row of his teeth. He looks like a wolf ready to tear me to pieces. "But since you're new to this, and so *very* valuable to me, I will forgive you this little blunder and chock it up to a moment of naivety instead of *defiance*."

I clamp my lower lip between my teeth to keep my mouth shut. I'm quivering with fury, but a wave of lightheadedness smashes through the feeling. That sprint really took it out of me.

Arthur gestures to the open chair next to Terrace. "Take a seat, puppet master."

I obey him, shuffling around the oval table and dropping into the chair he's indicated.

He turns toward the wall screens directly behind him and taps on a button panel. All nine screens come to life. Detailed blueprints, terrain maps of different Areas, and Testing Center security footage light up the space.

Arthur faces me, and he drums his fingers on the oval table.

"The Testing Center takeover was successful. Every facility we infiltrated fell as it was supposed to. And for the most part, the military presence in the smaller, less fortified Areas was dealt with swiftly and without incident." He pauses and clears his throat. "However, several pockets of resistance have cropped up. Forty-four of the two hundred and sixty-three Testing Centers are still in society's grasp. And there are six more Military Bases that remain out of our control. This is where *you* come in, Miss Timewire."

Arthur's steely gaze pierces me.

"Wren Zayla will fly you to the remaining Military Bases, and you will use your power to neutralize them."

A shiver trickles down my back. Arthur's going to use me to finish taking over society . . .

Wren slides me a derisive glance from across the table. She looks like she's ready for a fight. Her muscular brown arms bulge, and her sleek black hair is done up in a tight bun. Nothing about her appearance is out of place. She's as perfect as a society member.

"Speaking of Military Bases," Wren says, eyeing me. "I'd like to discuss your behavior at Area 19, Miss Timewire." She glances between me and Arthur, and my stomach turns over like I've missed a step. "I expected to be put under your power while making initial contact with you. I do not fault you for that. You didn't know who I was, and you had a quick brush with death, fighting that monster of a man." Her face hardens. "However, once we arrived at the Base, I did not appreciate your interference." She turns to Arthur. "Miss Timewire used her ability to prevent me from dealing with the General."

At this, my pulse spikes, and anger curls in my gut. "You were going to cut out his tongue!"

"What I choose to do with the prisoners of the New World Order is none of your concern," she says. "Your job is to use your power to help us take the remaining Bases."

"None of my concern?" I gape at her. "He's my father!"

"Yes, I could see his *gushing* affection for you." Sarcasm drips from her lips like honey from a comb. "Spitting in your face and vowing to kill you really cemented that tight-knit family bond."

"He thinks I killed my mother!" I retort. "He thinks that—"

"Miss Timewire," Arthur says, cutting across me. "You will

not interfere like this again. Your ability is for the military men, not for Wren."

Frustration enters my tone. "So, you want me to control the Military into submission while your people cut out their tongues if they dare utter the phrase 'Diseased One?' We're supposed to be showing society that we're not the monsters they think we are!"

"Do not raise your voice to me!" Arthur growls. I shrink back in my seat. "Have you forgotten your place so quickly? Or shall I remind you? Fortunately for me, Miss Timewire, you have no shortage of people you care about. Maybe instead of Wren cutting out your father's tongue, I cut out Jonah's."

Ice douses my blood, and my chest tightens. I push back my anger with strained words, and force an apology. "No! I know my place. I'm . . . I'm sorry."

There's a beat of silence so thick that fear steals all the breath from my body. I don't know what to do. Everything in me is humming with adrenaline, and I feel faint. My stomach is a pit void of any substance.

Arthur's calculated look skewers me, and he places his hands on the table.

"The days of speaking your mind are over. I don't need your input. I only require your power. You will do what you're told, and you will not interfere with Wren Zayla again. Do you understand?"

My lower jaw stiffens, and I nod, stuffing my fists under the table. If I had my ability right now, I'd let my power wrap its invisible hands around Arthur Evandrum's throat.

"Good. To the next item of business." He grabs one of the file folders from the stack to his right and slides it over to me. "You and Wren will be leaving for Area 62 at 1500 hours. You are to report to the North aircraft hangar at 1430. Area 62 is riddled with citizen unrest and has fallen into chaos since my broadcast. Its Military Base is well fortified, and it's the largest stronghold left. I hope to crush it swiftly. A large team is flying out behind you to collect Area 62's weapons and prisoners to transfer them to Area 7."

I nod again, but I'm finding it increasingly difficult to stay focused. I'm starving and exhausted, and all I want to do is leave this office and find Jonah so I can tell him what's happened.

"In the meantime," Arthur continues. "Pack your things and eat. I'll have a meal sent to your training room. You'll need your strength for this. And brief yourself on the layout of the Military Base. You have all the information you need in that folder."

I eye the folder with disdain and swallow a thick knot. I look up at Arthur, speaking barely above a murmur. "May I go now?"

Arthur leans back in his seat and puts a hand to his chin. His invasive stare rakes over me, and the hairs on the back of my neck stand on end.

"One last thing." He gestures to Terrace, who's seated directly next to me. "I want you to face Mr. DuPont, and I want you to look at him."

My eyes widen, and adrenaline douses my body all over again. Terrace DuPont's ability allows him to learn secrets just by being around someone, but eye contact helps him steal information . . .

My breath quickens.

"Miss Timewire, do as I say," Arthur states.

I swivel in my chair to face the ginger-haired man, and he, in turn, faces me. His amber eyes drill into me, and the moment we connect, I feel a strange sensation swish across my skin. He's inches away, boring into my soul, and energy seeps from me like a faucet set to drip. Several seconds pass. Then, he looks away.

Terrace turns to Arthur, an eerie grin playing his rat-like mouth. "Hollis went to see Olivia Turrick so that she could rescue Maddy."

A mix of helplessness and horror tears across my resolve like a branding iron. I try to think of something to say, but nothing comes. Even though I'm putting up a brave outward façade, I feel like I'm going to throw up.

Arthur tilts his head to the side and speaks with venom. "I don't blame you for trying to get to Maddy. I expected no less. This time, I will not punish you for your insubordination, but if I find out you've attempted again, I will not be so kind."

The silence that follows this statement is suffocating. Arthur raises his head ever so slightly, his attention never wavering from me.

"Is that clear?"

I don't answer him. Arthur's aggravation deepens.

"I said, is that clear?"

"Yes, sir."

"Good." He leans back in his seat, straightening the collar of his suit. "Every time you arrive back at the mountain, you will do a check-in with Mr. DuPont. Whatever you do out in society is *my* business, and whatever you do in the mountain will also come to light. You can't hide anything from me, Miss Timewire. Report to Wren in the North aircraft hangar at 1430. If you're late, I will know. You are dismissed."

I stand as if his words had electrocuted me. Disentangling myself from the chair, I skirt around the oval table and exit the room.

My brain is shorting out in its attempts to process the meeting. In nine hours, I'll be flying to Area 62 to help take the next Military Base. The future I wanted to create in the wake of taking down the Testing Centers is fading fast. Since learning the truth about the Diseased Ones and the massacre, I never would have imagined that they could be the monsters I learned to fear from childhood, but the political pendulum of power is swinging from one extreme to the other right before my eyes—and *I* am the unwilling force behind that pendulum's inevitable, crushing blow.

$$5$$

THE MOUNTAIN IS STILL CLOTHED IN LIGHTS THAT CAST A SOFT glow down every hallway, but the warmth they brought to the Ability Festival is gone. The walls are cold, and they swallow me whole.

A storm of rage is brewing in my soul, and the feral part of me wants to march back into Arthur's office, take him under control, and force him to tell me where he's keeping Maddy. If I were quick enough, I could take Ashton too. I could take the whole mountain under my power. I'm strong enough to do so. But I can't risk it. I have no doubt that Arthur's already accounted for the possibility of me trying to compel Maddy's location from him. If anything were to go wrong, it would be a death sentence to that sweet little boy—and on top of that, my friends are still in the mountain, and so is my teacher.

Arthur's words ring in my head: "Maybe instead of Wren cutting out your father's tongue, I cut out Jonah's."

I dare not defy him . . .

As I stride through the halls, fear slinks into my heart. What else has Arthur done in my absence? I don't have much time, but I need to see my friends. I have to make sure they're safe. And then I have to brief myself on Area 62 and eat. My stomach is so empty it hurts.

Ten minutes later, I'm outside the double doors leading to Sector 9, which houses the East Rooms. Power tingles in my fingertips as I enter into the concrete corridor, and I charge forward, hoping against hope that no one else has fallen to Arthur's clutches.

When I reach the door to Candice's room, I open it without knocking, and I'm met with four familiar faces: Candice and Keith Keaton, Ben Bryson, and Rosalie Simmons. They all run to me the moment I enter.

"Hollis, you're alive!" Keith exclaims. He wraps me in the biggest hug, and I bury my face in his chest. His strong arms hold me, and the scent of his skin calms my racing heart.

He's okay. He's alive. Arthur didn't touch him . . .

Candice, Ben, and Rosalie join in, hugging me from behind, and we all stand together, squashed into a huddle. Once the embrace ends, Candice and Rosalie both start speaking over each other in distressed tones.

"Maddy's gone!" Rosalie cries, trembling. Her red hair splays over her shoulders.

"Some men took him!" Candice spits. She pushes her dark brown hair from her face, and her blue eyes flash like she's ready to punch someone.

"What are we going to do?" Ben asks. He presses a hand

against his lanky, boyish face and begins to pace. "Did you hear Arthur's broadcast? This is crazy. 'You don't have to fear us if you don't plan to fight us?' And now we're the 'Pure Ones?' Sounds like a dictator to me. I didn't sign up for this."

"Hollis." Keith's voice pulls my attention to him, and I look up into his bright blue eyes. "What happened after the President's broadcast?" His gaze moves to my face, and his fingers gently brush the wound on my cheek. "Is Camille . . . here? Is he a prisoner?"

I shake my head and speak in a strangled voice. "He's dead. I killed him . . ."

The shocked silence that follows this makes my stomach seize. My friends are looking at me with wide eyes and open mouths.

"You what?" Keith murmurs. His brow knits together.

"Arthur gave me a syringe with poison," I say. "It was supposed to be a sedative, but . . . when I injected him . . ."

I swallow a painful lump.

"Do you know where Maddy is?" Ben asks. "Do you know why Arthur's men took him?"

I look between Ben and Keith and say words that make me want to throw up. "I don't know where Maddy is . . . and Arthur took him to keep me in line."

"To keep you in line?" Keith repeats. He grabs my hand. "Hollis, what are you talking about?"

Power lights in my chest, buzzing through my arms and into my palms. I want to scream. There's so much I want to say, but I'm scared to say any of it. Anything I do, *anything* I let slip, can make it back to Arthur, and I don't want him to target my friends. I must behave, or the people I love will pay the consequences. So I choose my words carefully.

"I work for Arthur now. He wants me to use my power to take over the rest of the Military Bases. There are still parts of society not under the Pure Ones' control."

Ben gives me a quizzical look. "The Pure Ones? So, you're going along with this?"

"Who the hell does Arthur think he is?" Candice demands. "He doesn't own you! You don't have to help him take over *anything*, Hollis." Both of her hands ignite, and flames dance on her bare skin. "I should give him a taste of my fire. He doesn't get to use you like this. And he doesn't get to take Maddy. He's a kid—not some pawn to play with!"

"Candice, NO!" I shout. I break away from Keith and march up to her. "No! Put your fire out *right now*. You're not doing this!"

She appears stunned, as if I'd hit her. "You . . . you don't want to get Maddy back?"

"Of course I want to get—" I stop mid-sentence, fighting with myself. "It's not that simple."

"Hollis, what are you saying?" Rosalie approaches me cautiously, giving me a curious look.

"I have to keep you safe. All of you!" I say, frustrated. "And I have to do what Arthur says. I don't have a choice. If I don't obey him, he's going to hurt Maddy. He's going to hurt *you*."

I peer into their faces, and I'm overcome by the position I'm in. Knowing that Arthur could choose to hurt them if I disobey him is beyond frightening. But at least if they know what's happening, then they might be able to protect themselves and put up a fight if any of Arthur's guards were to try and kidnap them.

"You can't do anything stupid," I continue. "And you can't . . . *say* anything to me."

"We can't *say* anything to you?" Candice reiterates. "What does that even mean?"

I grab Keith's hand, squeezing it tightly, and we make eye contact. I'm begging him silently to understand me. Of all my friends, he knows about Terrace's power. When Olivia teleported me back to the mountain after seeing my mother, she brought Keith to me without his guard, and I was finally able to tell him everything.

After a beat, he squeezes my hand back and then turns to his sister. "Candice." He says her name like a warning, and by the inflection in his tone, I know he understands. Relief washes over me, and some of the tightness in my chest diminishes.

This conversation is over, and I'm dreading the task ahead of me. I'm famished, and I have a pounding headache, but I need to ask my friends one more thing before I leave.

"Is Jonah safe?"

Saying this aloud steals the breath from my body. My heartbeat ticks like a bomb waiting for their response . . .

"Yes, he's safe," Keith replies.

I let out a whimper, exhaling through cracked lips. "I have to go."

I hook my arms around Keith's neck, hugging him tight to my body. He hugs me back. And then my lips meet his, and I kiss him like I'll never see him again. I kiss him until I can't breathe. With every ounce of passion I possess, I kiss him over and over again, and my eyes stream with tears I can't hold back.

When we break apart, Candice, Rosalie, and Ben are staring at us with a mixture of sadness and confusion. A heavy weight presses down on us all. I can see it in their faces—they don't understand. But once I go, Keith will tell them.

Anything I do is Arthur Evandrum's business, and with Maddy's life on the line, I must tread carefully—and they must as well.

I let out a shaky breath and then turn on my heels, exiting the room.

In a blind haze, I walk back to my training room in Sector 7. Arthur said he'd send a meal there, and I don't want to be absent when it arrives.

I clutch the folder he's given me between stiffened fingertips. I'm still dressed in this ridiculous nightgown and bathrobe. I've barely been able to rest since returning to the mountain, and the adrenaline I've experienced since coming back here hasn't helped. I feel like I've been fighting for my life from the moment Camille locked me into the Testing Center. If only I had time to fall asleep again and continue to recharge my body.

But rest must wait. I have work to do. Part of me understands that the only way out of this is to play the part required of me— and play it convincingly. I must bide my time and obey Arthur to the letter. For now, there's nothing that can be done about Maddy. And though that cuts me to pieces, I swear, I will figure this out and rescue him.

I yank on the handle of the door to the training room, and when it slides into the wall, the best, most comforting sight greets me.

"Jonah!"

I run to him, tackling him in an embrace. He drops his cane and hugs me back.

"Hollis," he breathes, gripping me fiercely.

I'm overwhelmed. All I can do is bury my face into his chest and fight to control my tears. For over a minute, neither of us says a word. We just stand with our arms around each other.

When the embrace ends, my heart begins to race. I don't know what to say to him, and I don't know how much he knows.

Jonah speaks as if he could read my mind.

"I know about Maddy, and I know about Camille," he says in a hushed tone. "After Mr. Evandrum's broadcast, he had the entire Council brought into his office with an armed guard escort, and he asked us one by one to swear allegiance to him."

Power thunders through my body, but I hold it back, attempting to breathe through the rattling sensations. "And did you?"

There's a beat of silence.

"Yes."

Jonah's response burns a hole right through my chest. Of course he did. How could he not? What else was he supposed to do to protect himself and those he loves?

"Did everyone?" I ask.

"Eli Stone didn't."

My eyes widen. "What did Arthur do to him?"

"Mr. Evandrum's guards cuffed him and dragged him out of the office. I assume he's been imprisoned in Sector 2, but I'm not sure. Hollis, listen to me, we need to—"

"Jonah!" I grab his hands, and the urgency in my voice silences him. I speak like Terrace can gather my every word. I speak like Arthur is standing over my shoulder. "I work for Arthur now. He's assigned me a pilot to fly me out to the remaining Military Bases. I'm going to use my power to take control of the rest of society."

Jonah's face pales, but I push forward before he can respond. "You have to go. You can't be here."

I check over my shoulder. The door to the training room is ajar. At any moment, someone could step through it and see us. Although Arthur didn't forbid me to talk to Jonah, he knows how close we are, and I can't risk Jonah's safety.

I'm struggling with my thoughts, trying to find a way to tell him to go talk to Keith without saying it outright. I lock eyes with him, and his tired face lines with sadness. His stubble beard has grown out a bit, and stray gray hairs mix with the brown. He looks older, like time is finally catching up to slow him down.

Jonah's hands gently squeeze mine, and he takes in my appearance. His gaze lands on my cheek. "Are you okay?"

My teeth begin to chatter between closed lips, and my chest constricts. The well of power in me is burning at the end of my fingertips like an all-consuming storm, but I've never felt so powerless . . .

"No," I whisper. "I'm not okay."

I can see it in Jonah's face: he knows my hands are tied.

"Jonah, you have to leave."

He nods and then gathers me into another hug. I wrap my arms around him and stifle a sob. I don't want to let go. I wish I could leave this place and take everyone I love with me. I wish I knew where Maddy was. I wish I never had to bury my mother or imprison my father. I wish for so many things that feel impossible right now.

Jonah's arms slacken, but then he grabs both of my shoulders gently and stares at me with fierceness in his countenance. He places his right palm above my heart, just below my collar bone, and warmth prickles across my skin. Somehow, although I don't understand it, he's using his ability on me. I've seen Jonah take on so many different powers as if they were his own, but I've never seen him do anything like this . . .

The storm of emotions I've endured through this whole nightmare cascades through my mind as if on display, and I gasp. Jonah's power pulls at each one like they were loose threads on a tapestry. The sensation is overwhelming and invigorating.

"Listen to my words, Hollis." His brown eyes, so often kind, are untamed and power-filled, boring directly into me. "You are strong. Unbreakably so."

But it's not what he says that strengthens me. Because the warmth of power leaving his palm to travel directly into my chest is saying the words he can't: that we'll figure this out, that I'm not alone, that we'll get Maddy back, and that, somehow, everything will be okay.

Jonah retracts his hand, and the warmth in my chest ceases.

As he turns to walk away, I catch his hand and say, "Keith and

I had a lovely time at the Ability Festival."

He pauses, searching my face for a few seconds, and then says, "I'm glad."

I hope my hint is enough. With everything in my soul, I hope that Jonah will go talk to Keith. Maybe *they* can come up with a plan to find Maddy and rescue him. But I can't know about it, and I can't help. All I can do is hope . . .

Jonah picks up his cane, walks to the door, and exits without looking back. I'm left alone, standing in a crushing defeat, but I don't stand there for long.

Gathering what's left of my composure, I stride over to the couch, sit down, and open the folder. There's a detailed floor plan of the Area 62 Military Base, along with a personnel count—1,478 people. I thumb through the documents, scanning over them quickly. A map of the city surrounding the Area 62 Testing Center is stapled to a blueprint containing the interior layout. This document also has a personnel count—455 people.

Tap. Tap. Tap.

I jump, clutching the documents to my chest. A girl with raven hair and an impish smile enters the room holding a tray of food.

Ice slithers through my veins. I recognize her. She's the girl I met at the Ability Festival during the talent show. She gave me a tortilla chip—and when I ate it, it made me cry. I can recall her words as clearly as if she had just spoken them: "I'm a mood eater. I impart emotion on food. Whatever emotion I want. It's thrilling and kind of boring all at the same time."

"Siena Rose," I say, eyeing her with caution.

"You're good with names, Hollis Timewire." She strides over to me and places the tray of food on the coffee table.

There's a bowl of steaming vegetable soup, a plate of small roasted potatoes, and a side of buttered bread rolls.

My stomach growls loudly, and I clear my throat to try and cover the noise. But I can't hide the fact that I'm starving. My entire mouth fills with saliva as I gaze at the meal. The smell is incredible, but the fact that Siena Rose brought this to me holds me at bay.

What has Arthur instructed her to do?

I look up at her. "What emotion did you put into this food?"

Siena doesn't respond. I try to get a read on her face, but nothing comes of it. I can't tell if she's willingly doing this or being forced to.

She hands me a scrap of paper, and I unfold it. Two curly, hand-written words stare back at me: *Eat up.*

"Siena, what emotion did you put into my food?" I repeat, this time more forcefully.

Still, she doesn't answer. Instead, she turns away from me and slips out of the room like a wisp of smoke.

I stare at the soup, potatoes, and bread with ravenous eyes, going back and forth in my mind about whether I should eat it or not. But my head pounds, and my stomach screams at me, so with delicate fingertips, I grip the spoon, dip it into the steaming broth, and bring it to my lips.

The soup slides down my esophagus, warming my insides. I wait a few seconds, and nothing happens. I dip the spoon into the bowl again, bringing the savory liquid to my mouth once more, but as I do so, an avalanche of emotion attacks my body.

Hopelessness. Melancholy. Despair.

I burst into tears. They roll down my face without mercy, and my stomach cries for sustenance. I lift spoonful after spoonful to my lips, weeping openly. I'm so despondent it hurts down to the sinews of my flesh.

I stuff the bread rolls into my mouth. They taste like sweet poison—delicious and devastating. I'm so overcome by the hopelessness in my food that I'm trying not to choke. What fresh torture is this? I fight my way through the meal, finishing every last bite, even though sobs wrack my chest and snot runs down my face.

When I'm done, the horrible sensation ends, and after a few minutes of panting, I'm able to take control of my breathing. Relief sweeps in, and my stomach settles. I'm full.

I gaze at the empty plate and bowl with disdain. Scooping them from the tray, I hurl them at the stone wall, and as they shatter, I scream. I wipe the residue tears from my face and breathe in as deeply as I can.

The creature rattles in my body, filling my hands to capacity.

Arthur Evandrum may own me, but I swear on my ability, he will never break me.

6

WHEN THE CLOCK IN MY TRAINING ROOM HITS 1415, I gather the scattered documents, tuck them back into the folder, grab my bag, and head straight to the aircraft hangar. It takes me twelve minutes to get there, but once I arrive, I'm met with bustling activity.

There's at least a hundred people here, all scurrying about, and there are several large planes. I scour the hangar, jogging down the length of it in search of Wren Zayla. I spot her standing next to the Beechcraft I arrived in, and I nearly trip in my hasty approach.

Wren checks the watch on her wrist. "Right on time." She gestures to the belly of the aircraft. Its fold-out steps are open, and I can see the interior leather upholstery. "Put your bag in there and take a seat in the cockpit. I'll brief you once I board."

I obey immediately and walk past her, grabbing the handrails of the stairs. When I reach the top, I linger and look back over my shoulder to take note of my surroundings. Even though I'm powerless to stop what's about to happen to Area 62, I can gather information on the Pure Ones' tactics and resources—as well as their approach to snuffing out society's resistance.

There are five massive commercial aircrafts, and the first one has all of its doors open. From what I can tell, the seats have been ripped out. Probably to make room for transporting weapons and cargo.

"Boeing 747," I murmur.

"Miss Timewire," Wren snaps. "I told you to sit in the cockpit."

I jump like I've been zapped with electricity, and I dip my head into the Beechcraft. The interior is lined with four windows on each side. It also has three sections of four large cream-colored seats that face each other as if it were a cozy booth.

I drop my bag onto the closest seat and shimmy my way into the cramped cockpit, taking the seat to the right. From here, I can still see a good portion of the aircraft hangar.

There are a dozen workers loading large black containers into the second Boeing 747. The word "*FRAGILE*" is printed in big bold letters on every container. My eyes wander to the yellow markings that line the lids. It's a triangular symbol. Inside of it, there's a picture of a cracked round flask next to a test tube. Dread seeps deep into my abdomen. Although I'm not a hundred percent sure what's inside these containers, I bet it's some kind of glassware. But for what? What on earth are these people planning to do?

My hands grow clammy. I hate this. I hate the position I'm in. I hate how helpless I feel. But I must do as I'm told and take every person at the Area 62 Military Base under my control. I only hope that once backup flies in to disarm the Base, the military men are treated humanely.

I continue my surveillance, noting the last three Boeing 747's. Along the side of each aircraft, there's the symbol of the New World Order: the golden woman whose hands are in front of her stomach, palms open to the sky, with eyes closed. And under her, a phrase shimmers in fresh black paint. "To be our friend is to be a soul cleansed through repentance."

My skin crawls as the words register in my mind. That's one of the things Arthur said in his broadcast. I'd bet anything that these three planes will be used to transport prisoners back to Area 7.

Fifteen minutes later, Wren is in the cockpit, and the Beechcraft's engines roar to life. I keep quiet as she hits a myriad of buttons along the control panel. Then, the Beechcraft moves toward the mouth of the hangar, and Wren speaks into her headset.

"Mountain Ground Beechcraft 237 North Hangar requesting taxi for a northwest departure with Echo."

There's about thirty seconds of silence before a chipper-sounding woman on the other end gives instructions.

"Beechcraft 237 Mountain Ground taxi to Runway Beta Six via Zulu."

"Taxiing via Zulu to Runway Beta Six Beechcraft 237," Wren says.

The plane moves along the ground at a crawl, and I gaze out of the window at the miles of open pavement marked with yellow and white lines. If only I could stop this . . .

Wren clicks something and then addresses me. "We're flying out first. Then, the other planes will follow. It's a three-hour flight. We'll land about twenty miles out from the Military Base and take a van from there. This time, we need to be more careful. Word of what happened at the Area 19 Base traveled fast. There's no doubt that they're expecting us, but that shouldn't be a problem for your power. The outer limits of the city have been abandoned, and citizens are crowding into the Military Base and the Testing Center for protection. You'll have more people to deal with than what's in the folder Evandrum gave you."

"Why are you doing this?" I ask.

Wren's jaw stiffens, and she gives me a sideways glance. "You may not agree with Evandrum's methods, Miss Timewire, but we need to get society under control before we implement the kind of change the world needs. The Military Bases must fall."

"That's not what I asked."

Silence descends between us for several minutes as our taxi continues. Wren steers the plane to the left, then halts at a set of thick, dashed white lines.

She speaks into her headset again. "Mountain Tower Beechcraft 237 holding short at Runway Beta Six ready for departure."

A few seconds later, a man comes over the intercom. "Beechcraft 237 Mountain Tower fly straight out Runway Beta Six cleared for takeoff."

"Flying straight out Runway Beta Six cleared for takeoff 237," Wren repeats.

The engines hum louder, and the Beechcraft picks up speed, zooming down the length of the pavement. My stomach does a summersault as the wheels leave the earth. And as I stare back at the shrinking ground below, I think of Keith and Jonah and silently hope that they've connected and are trying to figure out a way to locate Maddy . . .

Power plays along my arms and down to my palms, settling there at a low buzz, and even though the voice doesn't speak, I know I'm not alone. The darkness is rattling in my chest—with me every step of the way.

"You didn't answer my question," I say.

Wren exhales sharply, pursing her lips. "You really want to know why I'm doing this?"

"Yes."

"I'm tired of hiding in the crevices of this world. It's time that people with powers take back what is rightfully ours."

"And what *is* rightfully ours?"

"A chance to live."

I sober at Wren's response. I don't disagree with her. People with powers *do* deserve a chance to live, and live happily—free from the fear of being hunted down and killed for our blood. But Arthur Evandrum's forceful hand is driving the lie about the Diseased Ones further. All society sees is the monsters they've been taught to hate. And I'm the scariest monster of them all.

I stare at Wren Zayla, but I can't get anything from her battle-hardened face. Her brown skin is worn, but the way she holds herself is commanding. She looks like a soldier who's seen too many fights to count.

"Can you take control of thousands of people . . . easily?" she asks me in a gruff voice.

The tingling in my hands intensifies, and the creature of my ability comes alive inside my head, whispering into my ear.

Yes.

I repeat after it. "Yes."

Wren eases the plane into a slight right turn, and the position of the sun shifts into my eyes. I hold up a hand to block the beating rays.

"You're powerful," Wren states. "I admire that."

I don't say anything to this. Right now, I don't feel powerful at all. I'm bound to Arthur Evandrum's every request at the penalty of those I love.

"Back at Area 19," Wren continues, taking the plane out of its turn to fly level once more. "Your eyes turned black. What was that about?"

I clear my throat, pondering how I should respond. Five people know about the voice of my ability: Jonah, Keith, Olivia, Ashton . . . and Terrace DuPont.

When I was trying to figure out what I did to Ashton's power, I talked openly about the voice in front of Terrace. And that means that Arthur Evandrum is likely aware of it. I'm not sure what he could do with that information, but the less he knows about the creature, the better. Only *I* understand what she's given me: super-enhanced senses like that of an apex predator. The way that I can smell those under my power so potently. Every molecule. The way I can feel them. Hear them. Down to the vibrations of their pulse and the cells of their biology. It's incredible. Invigorating. Intimate. And it's the reason I can maintain the kind of ferocious control that can't be broken.

Unlocking the voice of my ability gave me the tools I needed to beat Camille. But I've not shared my enhanced senses with anyone—not even Jonah.

I choose my words carefully, putting just enough truth into my statement to satisfy Wren's question. "My black eyes mean I'm at my most powerful."

"You're an incredible type two, Miss Timewire. Your power is more potent than anything I've ever seen."

"I know." I can't help my stiffened retort. My power is the reason I'm in this mess.

Wren clears her throat. "Can I ask you something?"

I speak with a guarded tone. "Do I have the option of saying 'no'?"

Tingling zips down to my toes, and I stuff my hands under my thighs. I shouldn't have asked that. Of course I don't have the option of saying "no." I must do everything I'm told . . .

Wren clears her throat. "Evandrum may have a tight rein on you, Miss Timewire, but my leash isn't so short. We're not sitting around the oval table. You may speak freely. You don't have to talk to me if you don't want to, but it's going to be a long flight otherwise."

I chew on the inside of my cheek, surprised by her statement. Does she really mean that? I can't imagine that her invitation means I can *truly* speak my mind, but I'm curious. "Okay. What do you want to ask me?"

"Why do you care about society viewing us as the good guys? Society took so much from you, and it has tried to kill you over and over again. If anything, I would've thought that *you*, of all people, would be leading the charge. To be frank, I'm not sure why you're so resistant to Evandrum's ideals. He only wants to create a world where people with powers never have to die at the hands of a corrupt system ever again."

"Why do I care?" I repeat, slightly taken aback. "Because, Wren, how we treat people matters. How we do things matter."

I want to ask her if she's so sure that Evandrum has society's best interest at heart—he's imprisoning people—but I decide against it. I don't know Wren, and she's in Arthur's inner circle. So I proceed with caution.

"Isn't it enough that the Testing Centers have fallen and that we're disarming the people? We have the leverage we need to start making real structural and political change. With grace. With understanding. Citizens are not going to change their entire worldview overnight. *I* certainly didn't. I'm not sure how much you know about me, but I can assume you know enough. I believed the lie about the Diseased Ones to the point of betraying them to the government after spending *five months* with them."

My chest tightens, and I swallow the knot that's forming in the back of my throat.

"Our actions matter, Wren. That's what society will understand."

"The only thing society understands, Miss Timewire, is power—and obedience to those who wield it. You may not like it, but Evandrum is the visionary that made this happen. Society fell because of *him*. The Test is over because of *him*." She scoffs. "People will learn the truth in time."

I take a deep breath to calm the storm brewing in my soul. I'm frustrated. On the surface, it seems like Wren and I want the same thing: a future where people with powers can be free. But underneath it all, I'm scared that Arthur's method for change may be more sinister in its intentions than I'm even aware of.

Wren flips a switch on the control panel, and several buttons light up. "I'm sorry Evandrum took that little boy to keep you in check, but I can't say I disagree with him. Your power, left unguided, is too great a force. And you're the only way we can snuff out society's resistance without loss of power-filled blood."

My ability roars in my hands at the mention of Maddy, but I shove it down.

"It's a shame that it has to be this way. Truly," Wren adds. "But you were wild and opinionated from the start. Evandrum knows what he's doing. I only hope that you will come to your senses and realize that what we're leading is a *revolution*, not another Terror War."

For the rest of the flight, I keep my mouth shut, afraid I might say something that could be deemed as treasonous. And as the clouds roll by down below and the sun beams high up above, I mull over what I've learned. The people working directly for Arthur believe with all their heart that what they're doing is right. And I'm torn in my soul about it. Freeing people with powers *is* right. But imprisoning people without powers isn't.

I may not know all of Arthur's intentions for society, but I *do* know that he's willing to use people to get what he wants. Surely Wren can see this? It makes me think that something deeper is going on—something I'm not aware of yet.

As I mull this over, a memory flashes across my mind of the man I talked to in the hallway outside the aircraft hangar when I was helping my friends decorate for the Ability Festival. George. The chemist. His words ring in my head: "I can't say too much, little lady. It's top secret right now. Although . . . Everyone will know about it soon. Personally, I don't see why it has to be so secretive."

"We're descending." Wren's voice snaps me out of my thoughts. "We'll be on the ground in ten minutes. Then, we'll take the van to Area 62. Are you ready?"

My hands come alive with the force of the creature inside me, and I take in a deep breath. "Yes, I'm ready."

Once more, here comes the monster, Hollis Timewire, to terrorize the citizens of the world . . .

$$\frac{7}{}$$

7

WE MAKE IT TO THE OUTSKIRTS OF THE CITY HALF AN HOUR later and leave the van parked in front of an abandoned row of boxy housing units.

Wren pulls out a handgun and motions me to follow her down the block. I've never been to another city outside of Area 19, but everything here is eerily similar. The same street transit stops. The same glass buildings. The same perfect grid of roadways. Conformity. Perfect obedience. It's woven into the fabric of the architecture as well as every citizen's mind.

My ability snakes from me, stretching out its invisible arms to feel for the puppets that will soon be under my control, but I can't sense anyone yet. Everything is deserted. Hauntingly deserted.

"You don't need that," I say to Wren, pointing to her gun. "There's no one here."

"You don't know that," she responds.

"Actually, I do." I flourish my dominant hand. "I can feel when people are around."

She eyes me with skepticism, but then lowers her weapon. "How far out can you grab someone?"

"I don't know."

"That's not an answer. I'd like to avoid getting shot, Timewire."

"You're not going to get shot."

"How far out can you sense people?" she demands.

"This is new to me, Wren!" I bite back. "I'll know when we're closer."

If her look could kill, I'd be dead.

I hold both of my palms out in front of me, fingers splayed, and will myself to push my ability further. But still, the creature doesn't latch onto anyone. It's like she's waiting. For what? I don't know.

"Let's move quickly," Wren says. "We have a five-mile trek before we reach the perimeter of the Base. You let me know the instant you have someone under your power. Do you understand me?"

"Yes."

We slink down block after block, moving toward the heart of the city. I can see the map Arthur gave me in my mind's eye: we entered from the south side, which means the Testing Center is thirty miles to our west and the Military Base is due north.

The closer we get, the deeper my unease grows. Something within the well of power bubbling under my skin is tugging at me to pay attention. Every set of housing units, every transit stop, every street corner. Pay attention. Closer and closer—and the only sound present is our footsteps and our slightly elevated breath.

My eyes linger on the upcoming street sign as I follow closely behind Wren. Fleet Road. I recognize the name from the folder, which means we're almost there. Once we get past this block of buildings, the Base will be in sight.

Wait, the creature hisses in my ear, and fear jumps down my throat.

In the span of a microsecond, my sense of hearing sharpens a hundredfold, and I hear a myriad of sounds: Wren's pulse, the vibrations of air molecules, a metal flap hitting a plastic control panel, the adjustment of the focal length of binoculars, a sniper cocking a gun, someone's finger hovering over a button . . . and a man's gruff voice.

"The second they step foot onto Fleet Road, gas those bastards and spray the street with bullets. They're *not* getting into this Base."

"Wren!"

I lunge, grabbing Wren's arm and yanking her backward before she can step past the edge of the building onto Fleet Road. To keep her from fighting me, I grasp her with my ability and pin her against the wall. Then, I put a finger to my lips.

She looks like she wants to shoot me, so I speak quickly and barely above a whisper. "They're going to gas the street. I sense people now. Let me control them."

I lock eyes with her, a few tense seconds pass, then I release her from my grip. Wren backs away from the corner of the building.

I take a deep breath and allow my power to fill me to capacity. My hands vibrate and my chest rattles. I'm ready to split open at the seams with control, but the darkness tells me to wait. Just a few more seconds. I close my eyes as the tingling collects in my fingers, stronger and stronger. And then, at the creature's command, my ability explodes from me, and I grab the men along the perimeter of the Base.

I can feel every soul. Fifty men. My puppets.

Then, my power moves further, rolling like a tidal wave across the Base. It sweeps through the concrete buildings and over the airstrip. Four hundred people. A thousand people. Seventeen hundred people.

My arms shudder, my breath hitches, and the monster in me growls with pleasure at the scope of my capture. I'm alive with control. The sensation is all-consuming and never-ending. It's sweeter than anything I've tasted, fulfilling to the core of my being, and dangerously addictive.

No one can stop me.

When my power stills, I sense the number of my prey as if I knew them all by name. Five thousand six hundred and thirty puppets. Just like that, the Area 62 Military Base has fallen, and I haven't even stepped foot on its premises.

"It's done," I snarl, turning to face Wren.

She startles, taking a step backward and reaching for her gun out of instinct. For such a hardened soldier, her face tells me everything I need to know. I must look absolutely feral for her to be gazing at me with such poignant unease.

"I don't think I'll ever get used to those eyes," she says shakily. "Let's go."

I stride out from behind the building and onto Fleet Road.

A hundred yards from us, the heavy metal gates barring the entrance to the Area 62 Military Base gleam in the falling sun. There's also a heavily barricaded tower to the left of the entrance. As Wren and I approach, I feel the men along the border writhe under my fingertips. I'm not hurting them, but they're trying with everything they have to fight me.

I twitch my hand to command them to let us through, and without hesitation, they do so. The gates screech back against the metal fence that extends to either side of the entrance, and we walk in unharmed.

Concrete buildings lie in the distance, surrounded by pavement that stretches on and on.

"Bring me the General," Wren instructs me with a smirk. "And get all the men on their knees. Here." She points to a patch of dirt under the heavily barricaded tower.

Begrudgingly, I obey her. My hands move like I'm directing a symphony, and the group of fifty men along the chain-link fence shuffles to the patch of dirt, kneeling down in the dust. Then, my power radiates out from me like a bloodhound honing in on someone's scent. Within seconds, the creature finds the man in charge, and I compel him to us.

It takes a few minutes, but in the distance, an older Asian man emerges from one of the concrete, bunker-like structures and approaches us with forced steps.

Wren eyes him like she's going to devour him whole. The instant he's close enough, she withdraws a pair of cuffs from her belt and pulls the General's wrists behind his back, restraining him. She pushes him down to his knees, then nods to me.

"Timewire, take your power off of him."

"What are you going to do?" I ask. Nerves are edging away at my resolve as I recall how she treated my father at Area 19.

"Do as I say," she growls.

I grit my teeth but relent. My ability leaves his body, and the moment it does, he gasps as if surfacing from a deep dive. Wren pulls out her handgun and places it to the General's forehead faster than is humanly possible.

"Wren!" I roar.

"If you put me under your power, Timewire, Evandrum *will* hear about it. *Don't* interfere."

She peers around at the fifty men and speaks in a loud, clear voice. "The Area 62 Base is now under the control of the Pure Ones. You are all prisoners of the New World Order. I warn you, any resistance will be met with severe consequences."

She turns her attention back to the General and crouches down so that they're face to face. She lowers the barrel of the gun, and it dips lazily in her grip.

"General Yi, it's a pleasure to meet you." She cocks her head to the side. "My name is Wren Zayla. I have a question for you."

General Yi's jaw stiffens, and he stares straight ahead. His gray hair is trimmed to perfection, and his uniform is flawless, but his dark brown eyes hold resilience—like he'd rather be shot than open his mouth.

"You gave the order to gas Fleet Road?" Wren asks. "What gas were you going to use?"

He says nothing. He doesn't even look her in the eye.

"What gas, General?" Wren repeats. A twisted smile forms

on her lips, and then she addresses me. "Make him answer me, Timewire."

Anxiety zips down to my toes. I don't like this . . .

"Why do you care what gas they were going to use?" I ask.

"You're testing my patience," she warns. "Don't make me ask you again."

I swallow the knot of tension in my throat and direct my palm toward General Yi. I channel just enough power to force him to speak. He looks like he's going to choke, but after a few seconds, the words slip from him.

"Hydrogen cyanide," he grunts.

Wren's dangerous smile deepens, and she stands up, placing the gun back in her belt. She holds her right hand aloft and gazes at her fingers as they stroke the air. "Do you know what breathing hydrogen cyanide feels like, General?"

Her fingers continue to dance in a mesmerizing pattern.

"It's agonizing," she says. "An effective way to kill, that's for certain."

Without warning, Wren casts her hand toward the General, and he begins to thrash. Unable to catch himself because of the cuffs securing his wrists, he falls sideways and gags on the air.

"Painful, isn't it?" she says.

I gasp, running up to Wren and pulling on her arm. "What are you doing to him?" I demand. I almost freeze her in place, but her stern warning to not interfere prevents me from doing so.

The General's face and lips turn blue as he continues to choke, and Wren shoves me off of her. She thrusts her hand forward again, and this time, General Yi writhes, twisting in his restraints and contorting his body. A horrid gurgling noise issues from his throat.

"You're going to kill him!" I screech. "Stop!"

My heart is pounding into my ears, and the creature within me snarls. I could stop this. It would be so easy, but I can't disobey her orders. Arthur would hear about it. I stumble back, running both of my hands through my unkempt hair.

"Wren, please!"

At this, she pulls her hand back, and General Yi stops convulsing. He gulps for air, sucking in rattling breaths and panting like a wounded animal.

Wren kneels and grabs a fistful of his hair, yanking him into a sitting position. He groans at the sudden movement, and she speaks to him like a hungry beast. "What you just experienced is what it feels like to die from hydrogen cyanide gas." She twirls her hand in front of his face. "Consider yourself lucky I didn't kill you."

She turns back over her shoulder to glare daggers at me, and I shrink away at the intensity of her gaze. I'm horrified. Wren seemed more human to me during our conversation on the flight to Area 62. She didn't come across as kind, but she seemed less scary than Arthur. Now, I'm not so sure . . .

"Put him back under your power, Timewire," she instructs. "I need to radio the incoming planes to let them know the Base has fallen and it's safe to land."

I approach General Yi, and the look he gives me makes me sick to my stomach. He doesn't realize it, but I'm just as helpless as he is.

"I'm sorry," I whisper, keeping my face impassive.

I raise my hand, bind him under my power, and close his mouth along with the others.

As the sun sets, the planes arrive, and the next few hours are spent cataloging weapons and people. Thousands of silently resigned faces stare up at me in the harsh floodlights of the Base's airstrip. Wren tells me who to release from my power in groups as the men are cuffed and carted off to one of the three prisoner transport aircrafts.

I'm exhausted. Maintaining power over such a large group of people for hours on end is sucking the life from me. But I keep hold over them, not daring to let myself slip. I need to return from this mission with clean marks and a shining report. I must prove to Arthur that I can follow instructions. Maybe if he sees I'm following his orders like an obedient drone, he may relinquish some of his control over me. Then, I may have a chance to figure out what to do. But I must tread lightly and keep my head on straight.

The anger I've experienced since learning of Maddy's kidnapping is lapping at the edges of my resolve, threatening to pull me into a tirade of devastating power. And I'm afraid of what could happen if I unleash it too soon. Somehow, the right moment will come. I'm sure of it. Maddy will be safe, and I'll make my move. Evandrum will pay. But for now, I must wait patiently and be a good little soldier.

When the last of the prisoners are accounted for and the Base's weapons are loaded up, Wren directs me back to the Beechcraft that another pilot had collected and flown into the

Base from its spot on the outskirts of the city. It's well past midnight, and my body is spent with the extent of power I've used. I'm starving and shaking, and as we take off, all I can think about is lying in my bed back at the mountain and falling into a few hours of nothingness.

The Beechcraft's engines hum in the background, lulling me into a state of numb mindlessness. I'm struggling to stay awake, and my eyelids keep drooping over and over again.

"Eat," Wren says, thrusting a small oat cake into my hands. "You must be famished from that level of power."

I eye the treat with skepticism, thinking of Siena Rose. There's no way I could handle another bout of sobbing my eyes out right now. "No, thank you."

Wren's gaze turns sharp. "Eat it, Timewire. I can't have you falling ill." When I still don't comply, she sighs and says, "It's not poison. Please, eat."

I gnaw on the inside of my cheek and then bring the oat cake to my lips. I take a bite and swallow, and when nothing happens, I devour the cake in under a minute. It only partially satisfies the aching in my belly.

"Good," Wren says. She eases the plane to the right. "We'll be back at the mountain in an hour. Then, you can get some rest. You need it."

My stomach squirms. She's speaking to me with softness. Kindness—like she actually cares about me. And it's confusing. Back at the Base, she was vicious and commanding, and now she's nurturing. I don't trust it. What she did to General Yi makes me sick.

"Wren?"

"Yes?"

"What's your ability?"

She pauses, and levels the plane out to fly straight ahead. "I can replicate any physical sensation I want in someone's body. Any illness. Any wound."

At this, sympathy pain jumps down my throat and radiates through my arms. I grimace. "Why did you do that to General Yi?"

"Simple. He was going to do that to us. We would've died an excruciating death. But because of you, we didn't. I thank you for that. Your power really is . . . something else."

My tongue turns ashen. I want to tell her she shouldn't have done that. I want to yell at her for hurting someone who was already defeated. This isn't the way we should be treating society. She's stripping down everything I hoped would come with stepping back into the world. But I can't. Instead, I ask a more useful question.

"How did I do? What will you tell Arthur?"

There's a beat of silence, and her dark eyes look me up and down. "You did well, puppet master. Arthur will be pleased."

I lean back against my seat in the cockpit, relieved. That's all I need to know. For now, I'm a good employee, and the longer I can pull this off, the less scrutiny I'll be under. If I can make Evandrum feel like he's broken me down into compliance so quickly, then maybe I'll have a chance at getting away with things. Because I will not stop until I get Maddy back. That little boy's safety is my ticket to freedom, and then I can use my powers for good instead of evil.

8

I'm gazing into the vivid blue eyes of Keith Keaton. We're in the forest, sitting on a large rock that overlooks the river, and we're laughing. My hand intertwines with his, and my head rests on his shoulder. Being here with him is enchanting, and the view is breathtaking.

The drops of dew that litter the pine needles of the evergreens glisten in the glow of the rising sun. It's like a thousand tiny orbs of magic. And the crisp air, enriched with the scent of earth after a light rain, swirls around us.

Happiness fills me to the brim, and I cling to him. Something about this moment feels fragile . . .

Keith's soothing voice mixes with the babbling of the water below, and nature's symphony of birds and bugs blend in as well.

This feels so simple, sitting here alone with him. I miss him. I want to spend every minute of the day with him. I don't ever want to let him go. As the sun continues to rise through the thick trees, he kisses me. It's a tender kiss at first, but the longer it lasts, the better it becomes.

I wrap my arms around him, and he runs his fingers through my hair. Desire trickles through me as strong as my power. I want more of him.

Our lips move in a rhythm of passion that kindles my longing to new heights. I feel safe and wanted. He's my home. My best friend. The person I would trust with anything, and the feel of him holding me close lights my spirit.

Something deep within me is searching for a word to describe what I'm feeling for him. It's more than craving his closeness. It's an emotion stronger than fondness. And it goes beyond wanting intimacy.

When we finally break apart, all I can do is stare at him breathlessly. He smiles. Then, he leans close to me until our foreheads are touching.

"Hollis," he whispers. The way he says my name is so sweet. My breath hitches, and my stomach flutters. He's going to tell me something important. I can feel it. "Hollis, I . . ."

■ ■ ■

The dream ends abruptly as I'm pulled awake. It's Erwin again, with his rotten face and sour attitude.

"Get up," he snarls.

All of the happiness I felt from the dream vanishes like a puff of smoke. I'm lying in my bed in the training room. I only kissed Keith in the imaginings of my tormented mind. Reality is far more cruel . . .

"I said get up," he repeats. He grips his machine gun threateningly but doesn't point it at me.

I glare at him. "Are you going to pull me out of bed every morning?"

"I am to escort you to Evandrum's office."

"What does he want now?"

Erwin doesn't reply.

Frustration stirs in me. I rise from the pile of blankets, irked. I need more sleep. I've barely had a chance to rest. When Wren and I returned from Area 62, I immediately went to bed, but judging from the ball of exhaustion squeezing my gut, I'm nowhere near recovered from the mission.

I grasp the folds of my pajamas and pass air between clenched teeth. I'm dressed in a thin gray shirt and silk pants. I don't want to go to Arthur wearing this . . .

"Go wait in the hall," I tell Erwin. "I need to change."

He makes an incoherent noise with his throat then mumbles, "Make it quick."

Once the door closes, I change into a more suitable outfit and stuff my feet into my burgundy laced boots. I walk into the hallway, grimacing at what's to come. I hope I'm not being flown off to the next Base yet. I'm so drained from Area 62 that I don't know if I could handle another day of pushing my power to that kind of limit. But Arthur doesn't care about that. Unfortunately for me, I'm on his timetable now.

The trek through the mountain ends way quicker than I want it to, and before I'm able to mentally prepare myself, Erwin and I are standing in front of the door to Evandrum's office.

I place my hand to the panel, and it flashes to let me through.

When Ashton's power envelops me, I'm not ready for the

suffocation, and I stop in my tracks like I've been walloped in the stomach. The tingling in me is being strangled to death. It's so invasive that it makes me want to scream. I glare daggers at the pale teenager seated at Arthur Evandrum's right-hand side, but as I take in his gaunt appearance and silently resigned face, my anger softens. I feel sorry for him. I feel sorry for both of us.

Whether Ashton's going along with this willingly or not, Arthur's using him. Plain and simple. Ashton Teel is a prop, and Arthur Evandrum is wearing him like a cloak.

"Thank you, Erwin, for your promptness," Arthur says from his chair at the end of the oval table. "Miss Timewire, let's start our little routine, shall we?" He motions me to Terrace's side. "It's time for your check-in with Mr. DuPont."

He pulled me out of bed for this? My jaw tenses in frustration, and I ball my hands into fists, stuffing them behind my back.

"I need sleep," I state pointedly. "I did everything Wren told me to do at Area 62. You don't need to drag me out of bed to check. I understand my place, Mr. Evandrum. You've made it perfectly clear."

I say this as respectfully as I can, but there's still an edge to my tone.

Arthur's mouth curls in displeasure. "That's not why you're here. *Sit.*"

I glance between Ashton, Terrace, and Arthur, bewildered. "Okay. Then why am I here?"

"Sit down and look at Mr. DuPont first," Arthur instructs.

A storm of resentment rumbles in my chest as I obey. I can almost feel the creature stir, even though I'm shrouded in a haze of suppressed energy. I take a seat and face Terrace, looking into his bright amber eyes.

His ability sweeps over me, stealing every ounce of information from the events at Area 62. It's invasive, but I can't do a thing about it, and every second we're connected, I fight the urge to look away.

Finally, after what feels like a full minute, Terrace breaks eye contact with me and leans back in his seat, putting a hand to his chin.

"Hollis did everything she was told," he says. "Wren's report was accurate."

Arthur smirks.

Wren's report? Does he think she would lie for me? My skin crawls at the thought. It seems that Arthur's keeping tabs on everyone in this operation—even those who are fighting whole-heartedly for the cause.

Arthur taps his fingers on the oval table. "I'm glad to see you've learned how to follow orders so quickly, Miss Timewire."

I don't respond. He looks me up and down.

"Nothing to say? That's a first."

It takes all of my self-control not to snap at him. Instead, I focus on my breathing, imagining what it would be like to let the creature of my ability tear Arthur apart.

"Very well then. Tish, you may take your sample," Arthur says, motioning to the back corner of the room.

I turn over my shoulder. I didn't notice them at first, but there are three people dressed in white scrubs standing by the back wall under the clock. A woman and two men—and they're wearing gloves and masks. They approach me with hasty steps, causing adrenaline to spike through my system.

I rocket up from my seat, and it skids back a foot.

"What is this? What sample?" I demand.

The vein on Arthur's neck ticks, but he doesn't reply.

The two men reach me first, and once they do, they wrestle me back into my seat. I twist in their grasp, splaying my hands to summon my ability, but no power comes to my fingertips.

"Let me go!" I cry.

They struggle to keep me seated, and Arthur speaks in a dangerous tone, layering warning into each word. "Stop fighting them, Miss Timewire."

"Get off of me!" I yank my arms, but this doesn't break their hold.

"*Stop* fighting them," he growls. "You have three seconds to comply."

My instincts are howling at me to keep struggling, to vie for my power, to do *something* to get out of this . . . but Maddy pervades my mind, and I cease my efforts. The two men grip me more forcefully now, and the woman named Tish approaches.

The man on my right squeezes my wrist and extends my arm out toward her. She withdraws a large stretchy band from her medical bag and wraps it tightly above my elbow. Then, she wipes the flat of my arm with a sterile cloth and pulls out an empty syringe.

My eyes widen, and panic swallows me whole. My gaze flickers between Tish and Arthur.

"It has come to my attention," Arthur states, "that you never did your physical during the ability census I conducted. I've collected blood samples from everyone who arrived from the forest, but not from you. That's why you're here."

"Why do you need my blood?" My voice comes out with a roar, but it's forced. Inside, I'm terrified.

Arthur cracks a sinister smile. "That, Miss Timewire, is none of your concern."

Without warning, Tish sticks me with the syringe, and I grimace. My blood begins to fill the vial, and its dark color nauseates me.

"What are you doing with my people's blood?" I ask.

"*Your* people?" Arthur says slowly. "No, no, young lady. They are *my* people."

I swallow against a dry throat, a shiver running through me at his possessive tone.

Part of me wants to state what I know: that something is happening at the lab in Area 7, that I've talked with George, the chemist, and that he's let slip that there's some kind of serum. But the wisdom I've gained from the brutality of my life's experience tells me to keep my mouth shut. I can't let Arthur know what I've discovered . . .

Tish collects a total of ten large vials, and by the end, I feel as though I've been drained of all substance. Not only have I not recovered from the extent of power I used at Area 62, but now I've lost a significant portion of my blood.

My vision slops from side to side like the bathwater from the tub, and my stomach churns. I don't know if I'll be able to stand without losing consciousness . . .

The two men release me, and Tish packs up the vials of my blood. And without a word, the three of them exit the office.

"I'll see you this evening in the dining hall at 1800 for a celebration banquet," Arthur says. "The people of the mountain must know of our success at Area 62. That is all, Miss Timewire. You are dismissed. You may go back to sleep if you wish."

I sit there, stunned. He's expecting me to walk? After that? Any second now, I'm going to vomit. I can feel it. Shakily, I stand, and this makes my head pound. I grip the edge of the table as splotches of black and blue crowd my sight . . .

Unexpectedly, the sickening sensation dulls, and tingling returns to my limbs. The darkness of my ability manifests next to me, coiling in the air. Her presence is so real and so tangible that I momentarily forget that I'm the only one who can see her.

A small gasp escapes my lips.

Walk, she whispers.

I catch sight of Ashton, who locks eyes with me and gives me the tiniest fraction of a nod.

The creature compels me forward, and strength courses through my body—a strength that's not my own. The darkness is directing my path, and as I make it into the hallway beyond Arthur's office, I breathe in a new wave of power.

Unnatural calm descends upon me. I don't know how I'm able to put one foot in front of the other with how much blood I just lost, but every step of the way back to my training room, the creature hovers by my side. Protecting me. Shielding me. Providing me the stamina I need not to collapse.

The instant I return, she vanishes, and I sink into my bed, falling into oblivion once more.

$$9$$

HUNGER PULLS ME OUT OF MY SLEEP. RAVENOUS, INSATIABLE hunger.

I rise from my bed and down the glass of water that's on the side table. It does nothing to ease the ache in my stomach or the dizziness in my head. I need real sustenance. I feel physically ill from how much blood Arthur took, and I have nothing in my body to help replenish it.

I gaze up at the clock in my training room. 1728. I'm supposed to be in the dining hall in just over half an hour, but I don't think I can wait that long. So I put on a blue knit sweater, stuff my feet into my boots, and make the trek to Sector 12.

The whole time, my brain sloshes in my skull, pounding in splitting beats.

When I arrive, a few dozen people are bustling about the vast room, finishing the setup for what looks like a great feast. The decorations from the Ability Festival are still up, all of the tables are covered in red velvet, and fancy plates and utensils are set before every chair.

At the far end, there's a sectioned-off portion with a raised platform where several long oak tables have been pushed together to span the width of the room. A few dozen plush armchairs line the head table, but only on one side so that every seat faces the banquet hall. It looks like a giant panel. But it's the food that catches my attention. An entire roast pig, head and all, sits in the center with an apple in its mouth. And to either side, there are platters of fruit, steamed vegetables, potatoes, bread rolls, cheeses, cakes, and brightly colored sauces.

My stomach roars at the abundance, and I slink along the left wall, walking the length of it to reach the V.I.P. area. Velvet ropes hang at intervals between metal stands to bar access, but I duck under this, approaching the feast.

My entire mouth fills with saliva. I glance around. No one has noticed me, so I grab a fistful of dried figs from the nearest fruit platter and pop one into my mouth. I also grab a bread roll and a few cubes of cheese. Then, I sit on the floor in the corner so that the chair at the end of the table shields me from view.

It tastes wonderful, and once I've scarfed down the meager snack, I'm able to take control of my trembling hands. I lean back against the cold stone and take a few deep breaths, closing my eyes and cherishing this small moment of quiet. It's restorative. No one is demanding anything of me, and no one is forcing me to do something I don't want to do. It's a precious few minutes of break.

I keep my eyes shut and focus on the feel of the stone around me and the vibrations of my power along my arms. I soak it all in.

"Hollis?"

My eyes fly open, and adrenaline slams through me, but when I look up, my teacher is standing over me.

"Jonah," I breathe, relieved.

"What are you doing back here?"

He eyes me cautiously as I brush bread crumbs from my sweater. His face is creased with concern. He checks to make sure no one else is around before speaking to me. "Hollis, is Arthur starving you? Are you okay? You look like you haven't eaten in days."

I shake my head, but that makes the pounding worse. I grimace. "No, he's not starving me."

It's worse than that . . .

I say the last part to myself. I wish I could tell Jonah about Siena Rose and about how Arthur took my blood, but I'm scared to bring him into any of this. I don't want Arthur to use Jonah like he's using me.

"Are you here for the banquet?" I ask, hoping with all my heart that his answer will be yes. Maybe I could sit with him. I'd trade anything to not spend tonight by Evandrum's side. But something tells me that's wishful thinking.

"Yes, I am," he says.

Jonah offers me his hand, and I take it. As he pulls me up, my vision swims, and I grip him to keep from falling over.

"Hollis, you're not well. What's happened to you?"

All I can do is squeeze his hands and look him in the eye. We stare at each other in silence, and Jonah's brow furrows. Sadness replaces his concern.

"Keep fighting," he whispers.

The intensity of his words gives me hope. Maybe he spoke with Keith? Maybe they've come up with a way to find out where Maddy is being kept? Who knows what's happened behind the scenes during my time at Area 62. It's only been a few short days since Camille's death, but everything in my world has turned on its head. And I have to believe Jonah is fighting alongside me.

"Ah, Miss Timewire, I see you've arrived early."

Arthur Evandrum's slippery voice sends a razor sharp chill down my spine, and I spin around, inadvertently clinging to Jonah's arm. I take in Arthur's pristine appearance, and as I do so, I notice that Ashton is *not* with him.

He catches my eye with a smirk and elevates his posture ever so slightly, like he's daring me to try something. His piercing look holds brazen arrogance. Though I could take him with a twitch of my palm, I dare not. He truly does own the room—and he's slowly lacing a poisonous fear into my will to fight him. Just as before, the thought of Maddy overcomes me. Even if I were to compel Maddy's location from him *right now*, what could I do with that information? And how could I get to him before whatever other safeguards Arthur's put in place to control me go into effect? For all I know, Maddy could be hundreds of miles away from this place. And it would only take a minute for Arthur to communicate with his captors through some means that I'm unaware of. What if Arthur has given Maddy's captors instructions to move Maddy to a place Arthur doesn't know about if anything were to happen? Then what would I do?

The fact that Arthur's come to me without Ashton tells me

all I need to know: he has all the power in the world.

"Mr. Evandrum," Jonah says stiffly, with a slight bow.

"Mr. Luxent," Arthur replies, but he does not return the gesture. "Miss Timewire, please take a seat." He points to one of the plush armchairs just off center of the large head table.

I grip Jonah's arm more fiercely. "Can Jonah sit with me? Please? It just . . . would be nice to have a familiar face."

Arthur gives me a patronizing smile, like he's relishing the possibility of denying me this. He angles his head to the side, studying me with narrowed eyes. I try to appear as demure as I can, but underneath my feigned meekness, I'm fighting back a tide of anger.

He allows the moment to extend on and on, toying with me . . .

"No."

I dig my fingernails into my palms to keep venom out of my retort. "I've done everything you've asked me to do, Mr. Evandrum. Please?"

Before Arthur can say anything more, Jonah speaks up.

"Mr. Evandrum, wouldn't it be prudent to reward Hollis for her display of power at Area 62? Sitting with me is such a small request. After all, she's the guest of honor at this banquet, is she not?"

I glance at Jonah. What is he doing?

"The Area 62 Base is now under the Pure Ones' control. I can't imagine her performance was anything less than awe-inspiring." He raises an eyebrow at Arthur. "I also can't imagine that you would deny one of your most valuable assets something so trivial. I would think that rewards come to those who follow the rules?"

My heartbeat picks up, and understanding lights my spirit. I know *exactly* what Jonah's doing . . .

"What you're accomplishing in society is noble work," Jonah continues. "And Hollis's power is propelling your vision forward. Has she done something to upset you?"

He says this with so much poise and confidence that I'm momentarily dumbfounded. He's speaking like a diplomat— every word perfect and poignant.

Arthur's upper lip curls, and the vein on his neck thuds, but he gives Jonah the smallest fraction of a nod. "No, she's not done anything to upset me. Her performance has been to my satisfaction."

"Then consider granting me a seat by her side? One meal. One evening of celebration to showcase how much you've accomplished since the President's death."

Arthur fiddles with the cuff of his jacket and clears his throat. "Very well then, Mr. Luxent. You may take a seat next to Miss Timewire."

Jonah dips his head to acknowledge Arthur. "Thank you."

And with that, he ushers me around the table. I slide him a hasty sideways glance. He just used Arthur's own silver tongue ability against him. Happiness pushes its way past my disbelief, and some of my nerves settle. Jonah is going to be with me through this evening—whatever it might hold. Tonight, I'm not alone, and right now, I'm clinging to that for dear life.

Over the next fifteen minutes, the massive dining hall fills to capacity, and the head table does as well. I'm sitting to Arthur's right, and Terrace DuPont is sitting to his left. Next to Terrace are Wren Zayla and Hugo. And past them, there are the two more familiar faces: the mousy-looking Libbie Lizette and the stern-faced Caleb Stuart. They were on the Council before Arthur brought them onto his Board. I wonder what they think of all this?

Chatter fills the stone walls, and my stomach growls. I wish the dinner would start already. My stolen snack wasn't enough to tide me over, and I'm dying to eat more. But Arthur seems to be waiting for someone. There's one more seat at the head table that hasn't been filled—and it's the seat next to Jonah.

I pick at my fingernails, eyeing the bounty. Maybe I could sneak one of the grape-sized potatoes from the platter that's in front of me. I fold my hands and place them on the table next to my plate. Then, I creep them closer to the golden treats.

Just as I'm about to make my move, a scuffle comes from the end of the table as people move their chairs forward to accommodate a newcomer. Beezee-Day Jones is escorting Ashton Teel toward the open chair.

His dirty blond hair is combed over and slicked down, and he moves gingerly—like he's going to break. He's dressed in a gray suit, done up to look proper and poised. I look him in the eyes, and he looks back. His face holds some of the spite and spark I've come to know well. But I feel sick to my stomach over the fact that he's been forced out of bed over and over again after having been shot. Camille almost killed him, and if I hadn't used my ability to make Olivia teleport him to Beezee, Ashton would have bled out on the white tile floor of the Testing Center.

Ashton takes his seat, and Beezee retreats. She moves back down the length of the head table and vanishes into the crowd.

"Ashton?" I speak barely above a whisper, leaning into Jonah and away from Arthur. "Are you ..." I swallow a painful knot. "Are you okay?"

His lips press into a thin line, and he looks out over the vast dining hall. "Never better."

The way he says this chills me. I want to talk to him. I want to ask him what happened after Erwin shoved him into Arthur's office at gunpoint. I want to thank him for releasing me from his power after Arthur took my blood. But I can't.

Arthur taps on my shoulder, and I jump, stifling a gasp. He hands me a folded piece of paper and places a small fruit tart the size of a coin onto my plate. He addresses me in a low, menacing tone. "When I'm done speaking, you will stand up and read what's on that paper to the room. You will speak loudly, clearly, and *convincingly*." Arthur's eyes move to the fruit tart. "And you will eat that before you start."

It feels as though an invisible hand has taken hold of my stomach and yanked it inside out. I fumble with the paper, unfolding it with jittery hands, and I read over the text.

> I have wonderful news to share with you. Tonight, we
> celebrate a victory that mere weeks ago did not seem
> possible. Tonight, we celebrate the start of a new
> world. The dictator, President Alvaro Camille, is dead.
> (*wait for applause*)

What we've accomplished is far beyond anything our ancestors deemed possible. We are finally coming out of hiding to take our rightful place in society.

And Arthur Evandrum is the visionary that's made this possible. He has tasked me with using my power to help crush the remaining pockets of resistance, and it is my great honor to serve the New World Order in this way.

We are the Pure Ones, and soon, the future we all dream of will become a reality: a world in which no one with an ability has to live in fear of dying simply because of their blood.

You may ask how I'm certain of this, but for now, all I can share is that plans are in place to ensure the safety of all with the biomarker—and those plans will come to light soon. Tonight, we celebrate that the Testing Centers have fallen and that the remaining Military Bases are not far behind.

With all of my heart and all of my power, I will fight for you—my brothers and sisters. The Pure Ones. And I pledge allegiance to Arthur Evandrum and his cause.

I crumple the note in my fist as revulsion kindles in my stomach. I can't read this. I *won't* read this. I refuse to publicly pledge allegiance to Arthur.

Panic is thundering through me as my mind searches through

every angle of how I could get out of this. I could run, or faint, or become violently ill, or use my power to . . . to what?

I look to Jonah, but he can't help me. All he does is take my hand under the table and give it a gentle squeeze to let me know I'm not alone.

Horror settles in my abdomen like a toxin.

Arthur stands from his seat and clinks his fork against a glass full of red wine. The room falls into a hush, and every eye turns toward him.

"Ladies and gentlemen of the mountain, what a victorious past few days! You have known for many years that our goal has been to step back into society, but now, thanks to the courage of our brothers and sisters scattered in Testing Centers across the globe, we have made our move, and the beginning stages of this operation have been wildly successful!"

Spirited applause follows this, and everyone, both young and old, cheers.

"But the real linchpin to our success sits here with us tonight. We could have stepped back into society a year ago. We were ready. We had infiltrated enough Testing Centers to take down the Test. But it would have come at a great cost." Arthur's tone sobers. "And something gave me pause. Because I thought, 'with so few of us left compared to the powerless citizens of society, every drop of power-filled blood matters.' I couldn't justify moving forward knowing that the might of the military could have easily overwhelmed us in the larger Areas."

He pauses, taking a deep breath.

"For a few months, I admit, I was torn on what to do: move

forward with our operation and risk loss of precious life, or bide our time in hiding, as we've always done, and wait for a miracle. One that may never come."

The room is pin-drop silent, and Arthur gazes around at the faces staring up at us.

"But nine months ago, that miracle happened. A society girl failed the Test with a control-based, type two power more devastating than anything I've ever encountered, and it was this girl that would become our key to victory."

My entire body goes numb, and my hands tremor against my will under the table as I clutch the piece of paper.

"And I made it my mission to find her, recruit her to our cause, and finish the work we've been striving so diligently for. The reason we sit victorious tonight with no loss of life is because of Miss Hollis Timewire. Her power took the Area 19 Testing Center and Military Base. Her power conquered the Area 62 Military Base. And it is her power that will help us transition into stage two of taking back society far faster than our best-case-scenario timeline."

Cheering erupts across the room, bouncing off the high stone walls and making my ears ring.

Arthur turns to me with a face of feigned benevolence, and his gaze moves to the coin-sized fruit tart. He makes a grand gesture and says, "I would like you all to hear directly from her, the guest of honor."

His beast-like eyes stare me down. Every cell of my body, every portion of my self-preservation, every instinct I possess is screaming at me to not eat the tart, but I bring it to my lips and stuff it into my mouth.

I choke down the morsel and stand to address the room, feeling smaller than a mouse. I'm paralyzed with nerves. I'm not even sure if I'm capable of making a sound, let alone speaking loud enough for all to hear.

I hold the paper out in front of me. I want to melt into the floor . . .

But then, something huge seizes my chest, and vigor fills my lungs.

Loyalty. Pride. Admiration.

They churn together in a storm of aggressive patriotism, and I boldly call out to the room as if public speaking were second nature to me. My voice comes out loud and clear, and passion drips from every word.

I stand tall and proud, and when I read the statement about Camille's death, the room's energy explodes. The ecstasy is invigorating, and it spurs my speech to new heights. I'm practically shouting for joy, and by the end, everyone is jumping and hollering at the top of their lungs.

The instant I finish reading, the sensation dies in my chest, and disgust replaces my enthusiasm. I sink into the armchair, startled back into submission. It's like coming out of a haze. The onlookers are crazy with fervor for the cause, and Arthur stands once more. He places his hands in front of his stomach with his palms open to the ceiling and closes his eyes. The room's cheering grows even louder.

Then, Arthur raises his hand to quiet some of the wildness. "Let the feast begin!"

When I finally chance a glance at Jonah, I'm doused in

shame. He's wearing a look of stifled shock, and it almost destroys me. I had no choice but to read—he knows that—but still . . . I just displayed a disgustingly convincing show of loyalty to Arthur in front of the entire mountain. My stomach churns. What will my friends think of me? What will Keith think of me?

For the rest of the meal, I force myself to pick at the bountiful feast. I know I need to eat, but that speech made my stomach feel like a pit, crushing my ravenous appetite. I'm growing weaker, I can feel it. Keeping up my strength for the next task on Arthur's agenda—whatever that may be—is becoming increasingly difficult. Jonah encourages me to take more food than I would have on my own, and I'm grateful, but only meager mouthfuls make it into my stomach.

All night, people come up to the head table to talk to me and Arthur. They thank me for the wonderful work I'm doing. They congratulate me on the victory at Area 62. They spill their longings to be back in society and their excitement for the new future to come. And all the while, I force myself to act like the perfect representative for the cause. I grit out fake smiles and shake hands between adulations—even though revulsion seeps through me. If I could wish for anything, it would be to turn invisible and stay that way. Then, I wouldn't be the girl whose power is the key to the Pure Ones' victory.

In the span of one evening, Arthur's turned me into an icon. A legend. Everyone wants a moment of my time. The spotlight of fame is shining on me brighter than ever before, and I feel like an ant under a magnifying glass slowly being burned to death with no means to fight my way out.

When the dinner finally concludes and the hall begins to clear, I stand up to excuse myself, and Jonah stands with me. Before I can leave, Arthur grabs my wrist, and my whole body stiffens as if I were under my own power.

"I'm giving you the day off tomorrow to rest and recuperate. I thank you for your enthusiastic show of patriotism." He cracks a wolf-like smile. "You did well tonight, puppet master. You are dismissed."

He releases my wrist, and I stumble backward. Jonah catches me, and we both take the dismissal to leave as quickly as we can. I don't look back, but as I retreat around the length of the head table, I hear Arthur's charismatic voice call out.

"Mr. Ashton Teel, I'm so glad you could be here this evening. Let's talk."

Jonah and I exit the Sector with hurried steps, and once we're clear of the double doors, Jonah wraps me into a hug, and I lean against him, drained of all energy.

"I'm so sorry, Hollis," he says, and from his inflection, I can tell he's talking about the speech I was forced to make.

I breathe through pursed lips and put on the bravest face I can. "I had to."

"I know."

I look up, clinging to him for support, and my voice catches in my throat. "Jonah, please tell me that you're . . ."

But my words evaporate into nothingness. I can't say it out loud. I can't ask him for reassurance that he's working on a plan to find Maddy. I can't even think of a way to communicate with him without Terrace figuring it out. Tears of frustration spring to my eyes and I bury my face in my hands.

"We are," Jonah whispers. He squeezes me tight and then releases me from the embrace. "You keep doing what you have to. Do you understand?"

Hope ignites in my chest, and I nod. Jonah must have talked with Keith, and they're working on something. That has to be what his words mean.

The urge to ask him overwhelms me, but I bite my tongue. Right now, I feel worse than useless, but I grab Jonah's hand and whisper, "I trust you."

He nods, almost imperceptibly, and then, without another word, we part ways. I watch him retreat until he turns the corner at the end of the hall and vanishes from my sight.

This is awful. I hate that I can't talk to Jonah. I hate what Arthur's made me do. I let out a frustrated yell and kick the wall. An unpleasant twang travels up through my ankle, and I inhale sharply, cursing under my breath.

My ability stirs in my arms, and the sensation sparks energy into my body. The voice whispers in my ear.

You have more power than you think.

A jolt runs through my skin at her hiss, and I nearly topple over. I can't see her, but I can feel her presence. Right behind me. Clinging to my back.

"What power?" I ask. "What do you mean?"

She doesn't hiss again.

"What do you mean?" I repeat. "Teach me."

Silence.

I scuff the sole of my boot against the floor and let out a growl, running my hands through my hair. But as I stand there, a thought occurs to me.

Perhaps I'm not as useless as my situation seems to indicate. I may be Arthur's pawn, but I have access to him like no other person in this mountain. Maybe I can glean information about Maddy that others can't. Maybe I can work on this problem too. As limiting as Terrace's ability is, he can't read my thoughts or guess my intentions. I still own my mind. And even though Siena Rose's food can control my emotions, I still own the way I truly feel.

"I don't know what you mean," I snap at the creature. "But I hope you're right."

Her power rattles down my limbs, and she snarls.

I sigh. Tomorrow is a new day, and I'm going to spend it resting and thinking. Something is gnawing at me. The inklings of an idea are forming in my mind. I just have to ruminate on it long enough for it to come to light.

____

IO

____

It's a wonderful relief to sleep without anyone pulling me out of bed to make demands. I snooze for most of the morning, and when my body feels okay enough, I get up and change.

Immediately, my mind sets to work. How could I collect intel on Maddy? I have close, personal access to Arthur. There must be something I could do. But the longer I think about it, the more impossible the idea becomes. Arthur wouldn't dare let anything about Maddy slip when Maddy's the main reason I haven't torn him to shreds with my ability.

I sigh, shuffling my feet against the soft area rug.

As my musings wander, I recall the speech I was forced to make. The line about plans being in place "to ensure the safety of all with the biomarker" drifts to my attention, as well as Arthur's statement about me helping them transition into "stage two of taking back society."

Any witness to the event would think that I'm in the "in

crowd," but I'm just as much in the dark as they are. What is Arthur planning to do? Maybe that's where I can focus my efforts. I can investigate why Arthur needs everyone's blood. For now, I have to leave Maddy to my friends and hope that they're working on a solution.

Feeling slightly satisfied with my brain-storming session, I make my way to the East rooms in Sector 9 to go find my friends. I may not be able to talk openly, but simply being around them will lift my spirits—and that's something I desperately need right now.

But as I walk through the halls of the mountain, dread festers in me. I have no doubt they heard the speech I made last night. What if they don't see me the same way? Part of me breaks at the thought. I know what it's like to lose friends because of the choices I've made. But this time, it wasn't my choice. Surely they understand this? They must. When I saw them before flying off to Area 62, Keith seemed to understand my silent plea concerning what I can and can't say around them.

I try to shake off the nasty feeling, but it lingers in the pit of my abdomen. I sigh, rubbing my temples. This spiral of thought is exhausting . . .

It doesn't take me long to reach Candice's room, but before I can even knock, a loud voice comes from the other side of the door, and it stops me in my tracks.

"Did you hear what she said?" Ben demands. "'I pledge allegiance to Arthur Evandrum' and 'It is my great honor to serve the New World Order.' *That's* what she said."

My gut plummets all the way to my toes. Ben sounds beside

himself, but he also sounds more scared than anything else. I almost take hold of the handle and barge in, but a second voice stalls me. It's Olivia Turrick, and she speaks with exasperated notes.

"If you think for one second that Hollis had *any* choice in the matter, then you're not paying attention. Arthur controls everything she does. *Everything.* Speaking from experience, her hands are tied. Those weren't her words, and that speech wasn't her decision."

Warmth fills my chest at her response. If anyone understands the position I'm in, it's Olivia. And I'm grateful for her defense of my character.

Ben scoffs. "Well, she sure put on a show."

"Of course she did!" Olivia bites back. "This isn't a game, Ben. Maddy's life is at stake."

"We know it's not a game," a third person says.

My heart leaps into my throat at the sound of Keith's voice. I don't want him to say something I'm not supposed to hear, so I reach for the handle, but the instant I do, a monstrous force grips my body, keeping me from entering the room. Wild sensations zip down my limbs and into my face—and it's paralyzing.

What is happening to me?

"Look, if we're going to have a *chance* of pulling this off, you guys have to realize who we're dealing with," Olivia hisses. "This is a man who's been planning this takeover for over a decade, and his silver tongue ability is incredibly potent. Do you remember what you felt as he was speaking last night?"

A fourth voice pipes up with a squeak. It's Rosalie Simmons.

"I felt invigorated—like I believed him. Like I supported him."

Again, I try to reach for the door, but I'm rooted to the spot, unable to move—and my voice has been stolen from me. I'm completely captive to the buzzing that's pulsating through my body. Is this . . . my power?

"Exactly," Olivia says. "Because in that moment, you *did* support him."

Vianne Evolet joins the conversation now. "What was Arthur talking about when he said stage two? You worked for him for a while before he took away your . . ."

She falls silent.

I try to call out. But no matter what I do, my mouth won't open. I'm suffocated by the presence holding me in place, and my panic increases with every heartbeat. Then, the chilling voice of the creature comes to me and snarls in my ear.

Listen.

What is she doing to me? No. I can't listen to this. Doesn't she understand? Every second I stand here is another piece of information for Terrace. I fight her with everything I have, but to no avail. She holds me as still as a statue.

Listen, she hisses, this time more forcefully. She materializes and coils around my torso.

"Stage one was always taking down the Test and disarming society," Olivia continues. "But I was never briefed on stage two."

Ben huffs. "You don't know anything?"

Even though I can't see Olivia, I can imagine her staring daggers at Ben. Her brusque tone is interfused with caution. "The only thing I know is that something's happening at the lab in Area 7—something to do with the biomarker in our blood."

"Our blood?" Keith repeats.

Yet another voice joins in. It's Candice Keaton, and she sounds horrified. "We gave Arthur our blood!" Hysteria soaks her words. "During the physical. All of us gave him our blood! What if . . . what if something terrible happens to us? What if—"

"Shut up, Candice!" Olivia warns. "You're being too loud."

"It's okay, Candy," Ben murmurs. "Nothing's going to happen to us."

"You don't know that!" she retorts. "Arthur kidnapped Maddy! Who's to say he won't do something awful to the rest of us!"

There's a scuffle of feet against tile.

"Candice, *lower* your voice," Olivia growls. "Look, our best chance of stopping Arthur is getting Hollis out from under his control, which means finding Maddy. *That* is our priority."

"Stop him from doing *what* though?" Ben asks, frustrated. "What the hell is even happening? Ending the Test was a good thing, but all this 'New World Order' crap? And singing our own praises as the 'Pure Ones?' This is some dictator-level rhetoric. You worked for Arthur, Olivia. You've got to know more than you're letting on. I don't buy your proclaimed ignorance about 'stage two.'"

"Think what you want, Bryson!" she snaps. "But I'm telling the truth! I don't know much about it. No one does. Only Arthur's inner circle." She sounds angry enough to strike him. "Look, I get that you're a bit freaked out right now, but you don't have to take it out on me. I'm not the bad guy here."

Ben clears his throat, his tone tempering a bit. "I . . . I'm sorry. I shouldn't have snapped at you. I just—I *am* freaked out. Whatever 'stage two' is . . . clearly, there's bigger plans at play."

Keith speaks up in a calming tone. "Ben, right now, this 'stage two' thing doesn't matter. Getting Maddy back matters."

Again, I try with all of my might to break out of the creature's hold, but it's no use. I'm struggling in vain, and the vibrations that travel down my limbs only grow stronger. It's like a nightmare. All of my friends are in danger right now by plotting right in front of me, and they don't even know it.

Olivia clears her throat. "Keith's right. Arthur's thought of every conceivable way of controlling Hollis because he needs her. Hollis is the most powerful person in this mountain. Honestly? She's the most powerful person in the world. If we can take her away from Arthur, that will make things much harder for him. Let's focus on Keith's idea: stealing Arthur's memories is going to be one hell of an operation, but that's how we find Maddy. *That's* how we help her. And Hollis *can't* know. That's *critical.* Terrace can leach any information he wants from her."

"I just need to get close enough to touch Arthur," Rosalie adds. "That's the fastest way for me to absorb memories. The problem is . . . how do I pull that off without him knowing? He's seen my ability before. He knows what I can do."

All of the blood drains from my face, and my entire body goes numb. No . . . I can't know this. I can't be here. I've doomed them all. Tears spring to my eyes as I fight with the force keeping me still. What will Arthur do to them? What will Arthur do to Maddy? My friends have to get out of the mountain. It's the only way for them to avoid retribution for this …

I'm falling into a full-blown panic attack, bound in the helplessness of silence. Tears flow freely down my face now. The monstrous feeling around me sears my skin, and the smoky, black, serpent-like creature of my ability detaches herself from me. She curls in mid-air right in front of me. Her coal-red eyes bore into mine as she coils and uncoils, inches away. Then, she dips her sleek head, bowing low.

With a rapid jerk of motion, she dives back into my chest, and I'm compelled away from Candice's room. I practically sprint out of Sector 9, and when I'm past the double doors, the force vanishes from my limbs.

I begin to hyperventilate.

"What have you done?" I cry, screeching at the creature. But it feels as though I'm yelling in vain. I can't take back what I know, and I can't unhear it.

I rush back toward the double doors of Sector 9, but I'm buffeted away with a violent whip of motion. My heart hammers relentlessly against my ribcage, and I try again. But the same thing happens. Every attempt I make to push through the doors fails, and the creature rattles in my limbs, as if telling me off.

"I have to warn them!" Angry tears blur my vision, and I throw my hands forward toward the push bar, but I'm blocked by darkness. "Why are you doing this? Please let me warn them! They have to get out of the mountain. Please!"

The voice snarls in my mind but says nothing.

I back away from the double doors, panting wildly and scooping strands of hair from my face. I let out a guttural noise and kick the sole of my boot against the wall. My voice runs through savage inflections. "Why did you do that? I can't know about this! Don't you understand? I have to keep Maddy safe!"

Silence.

Cold silence.

I will myself to call the creature back into existence, and power fills my palms until they burn, but she doesn't materialize.

"Talk to me!" I yell.

Nothing.

I sink to the floor, and every nerve in me feels like it's going to explode. This can't be real. I'm dreaming. I must be dreaming...

But the longer I sit here, the clearer reality becomes, and the gravity of what I've overheard hits me like an avalanche. Terrace DuPont is going to find out about my friends' plot to steal Arthur's memories the moment he looks into my eyes.

II

ARTHUR EVANDRUM'S OFFICE DOOR LOOMS OVER ME LIKE a death sentence. It's two minutes to five in the morning, and I've been summoned for another meeting. The panel blinks, ready to accept my handprint, but I make no move toward it. All I want to do is run away.

Cold sweat beads on my skin, creeping down my back. How am I going to get out of this? I spent the remainder of the evening yesterday—and nearly all night—trying to think of what I could do to escape Terrace's ability. I came up with absolutely nothing. My friends are doomed, and so is Maddy. Arthur warned me against trying to find him, and with how ruthless he's been toward me, I can only imagine how much worse things are going to get once he's discovered the plot to steal his memories. And what will he do to Keith knowing it was *his* idea?

How could the creature do this? Her chilling hiss of "listen" is still reverberating in my mind. Doesn't she understand the position I'm in? I'm at the mercy of a man who can do whatever he pleases, and now a treasonous plot I'm not supposed to know about is floating around in my brain, free for the taking. I feel betrayed. My own power did this to me, and now everyone I love is going to pay for it.

The panel blinks again, inviting my handprint. I gulp. My tongue feels like lead, and my heart is trying to jump out of my chest. If I don't scan my palm, I'm going to be late . . .

I bring my hand up to the panel, and when the door slides into the wall, I brace myself, pushing back the emotion that's threatening to spill across my face.

I take my usual spot next to Terrace, avoiding eye contact at all costs. Just as before, Ashton's power swallows me whole. This only plunges my nerves deeper into the chasm of dread.

"Did you rest yesterday like I asked?" Arthur says, rifling through a stack of folders.

"Yes." I hold my head high and keep my shoulders poised to sell the lie, but I'm exhausted. I barely slept at all.

"Good, because Wren is flying you to the Area 147 Military Base today." He slides a file folder over to me. "In here you'll find all the information you need."

"Yes, sir."

I pick up the folder and thumb through it to give my hands something to cling to. It has the same types of maps and blueprints as the Area 62 folder.

"You'll be leaving in an hour," Arthur continues. "It's a longer flight, so you'll have time to look through the information on the way. And you'll be gone for two days. I trust you've packed your things?"

"Yes, sir."

Arthur smirks. "Well, look at you falling right into line."

His patronizing tone makes me squirm. I shift uncomfortably in the black leather chair, hoping against hope that he will dismiss me. Maybe, by some miracle, I can get out of this meeting without Terrace leaching information from me.

"Your speech inspired people last night," Arthur says.

Revulsion curls in my belly. I hate myself for the show I put on. It was disgusting. "You made me eat that tart."

"Yes, and look at the effect it produced. Whether you like it or not, people look up to you. I simply gave you a *boost*." He peers at me with curious eyes. "I wonder if, given time, you'd be willing to do what I ask of you *without* coercion?"

I can't help the glare that forms across my face. Is he seriously asking me this?

"You have the potential to be one of the most influential leaders history has ever seen. With you by my side, we could accomplish great things."

Arthur studies me like a hawk. I grip the armrests of the chair, digging my fingernails into the leather. I don't say a word.

"I know what you must think of me," he continues softly. His eyes wander the room before landing back on me. "But you don't understand the delicateness of the current world situation. You're young, and for now, I'll do what I must to guide you in the right direction. I only hope you will see that what I'm doing is for the best."

The way he's speaking to me . . . it's almost . . . fatherly, and it makes me more wary of him.

When I still don't respond, Arthur sighs, bringing a hand to his forehead as if to show remorse. "It gave me no pleasure to take Maddy from you, Miss Timewire. I know how much you care for him. But you gave me no choice. I couldn't have your untamed power running amok after the President's death."

At this, something in me sparks, and the energy in my chest builds like a bomb. I feel a violent tug within my palms. As if the creature were trying to break free from Ashton's power.

I glimpse Ashton's pale face, and he shudders.

Did he just feel that too?

I snap my attention back to Arthur. I can't explain why, but it feels like the creature wants me to ask about Maddy. Even suppressed, the urge is overwhelming, so I listen. "Is Maddy okay?"

"Maddy is fine."

"Can I talk to him?"

Arthur's nostrils flare, but he doesn't let up his strangely father-like demeanor. "I'm afraid that's not possible."

"Not possible?" I repeat.

My heartbeat spikes. What could he mean? My mind immediately moves to the worst thing imaginable, but I shake the horrid thought away. I know for a fact Arthur wouldn't give up his insurance for keeping me in line. Maddy is alive. There's no question regarding that.

Frustration surfaces in my countenance. "You can't keep Maddy from me forever. I *will* see him again!"

The instant the words leave me, Arthur's body language morphs from feigned kindness into something ferociously dark. He looks like he's about to strike me, and fear physically slinks down my spine. I shrink back in my seat. I shouldn't have said that. Why did I say that? What am I doing? I need to get out of here without Terrace looking me in the eye.

Arthur's pale face flushes red. "Did you make another attempt to try and find Maddy?"

Immediately, my head slogs into a haze. "No. I . . . I didn't."

"And you rested yesterday?"

"Yes, I rested."

Arthur tilts his head to the side, scrutinizing me. "Do you want to know what I think?"

Again, I feel the tug—this time from the pit of my abdomen. The creature is writhing under Ashton's power, like she's trying to claw off a muzzle. The sensation stirs deep within me, but she's still trapped under his suppression.

"I think you're a *liar*," Arthur hisses. "I told you that anything you do in the mountain is my business. Terrace, I think it's time for a check-in."

My heart sinks right down to my toes. What have I done? Why did I have to open my mouth? I'm shaking, and I can't hide it. I almost leap up and bolt from the room, but that would only make things worse.

"Mr. Evandrum, I didn't try to get to Maddy. I rested!"

"Then you have nothing to worry about," he replies, ice cold.

My mind is firing at break-neck speeds, but I can't think of how to get out of this. My gaze flickers over to Ashton, and we lock eyes. The tug happens for a third time. It's forceful and feral. And a singular, all-consuming thought overtakes my mind: the creature *must* break free.

Please, I think in my head, begging silently. *Let me go, Ashton.*

Terrace turns to face me.

"Hollis . . ." He lingers on the 'S' in my name until the hiss of the consonant causes a visceral response to quiver across my skin. He rolls his chair closer, practically breathing down on me, and speaks in a slow sing-song. "What are you hiding?"

I'm still staring at Ashton, pleading with my eyes. So much adrenaline is pumping through my blood that my face burns.

Please, Ashton, I think again. *Let me go.*

The instant I think this, Ashton's face lights up—like he understands something that I don't. He's staring at me, wide-eyed and alarmed. But then, his hand gives the smallest flick—had I not been watching him like a hawk, I would've missed it—and my power returns to me full force.

Did the creature just . . . communicate with him?

Terrace lunges, grabbing my upper arm with one hand and my face with the other.

With a screech, my ability comes alive, and the darkness of the creature materializes directly in front of me—tangible and huge—but still visible only to me. Her coal-red eyes and snakish features hover like a mask over my face, shielding me from the rat-like man. And her smoky, black body wraps around my torso like a breastplate. She hisses, baring teeth made of a substance blacker than the mist.

I gasp.

Terrace's face is so close I can smell the stale hint of coffee on his breath. He probes me, but I can't see him clearly through the haze of black mist covering my face. The sensations trickling through me are empowering and vibrant. My whole body is energized. And in my heart, calm sweeps in like a wave.

The creature rattles, and the vibrations skitter across my skin with warmth. The moment extends on and on. Terrace's grip on my upper arm is beginning to hurt, but I don't shrug away. The mist of the creature's body is still protecting me . . .

Finally, Terrace releases me, and I slide back into my chair. The darkness detaches herself from me, hovering forward and locking her gaze onto Ashton. Her eyes glimmer crimson with a flash, and I fear the worst. But then, she bows deep, as if to thank him.

With a snarl, the creature snakes around and dives back into my chest.

Terrace scratches his scraggly ginger beard, a strange look scrunching his nose.

Arthur looks between the two of us. "Well?" he demands. "What is it?"

My pulse quickens. I don't know what just happened, but if it's what I think it is, then . . .

"Nothing," Terrace replies. "She rested. Just like she said."

"Did she see anyone? Did she search for Maddy?"

"No."

His response steals my breath away.

The vein on Arthur's neck thuds in an irregular rhythm, and the red flush on his cheeks darkens. He clears his throat and shuffles through a few of the folders that are stacked to his right.

"Very well, Miss Timewire, I'm glad to see you're taking this seriously."

Terrace is still staring me down, clearly disturbed, so I keep my eyes glued to Arthur.

Arthur adjusts the collar of his suit. "Wren is waiting for you in the aircraft hangar. I expect a glowing report upon your return. You are dismissed."

I rise from my seat, scarcely able to believe it. "Yes, sir."

I walk around the oval table, trying to move at a reasonable pace even though I'm dying to get out of this office.

When I reach the door, Arthur's voice holds me back. "Miss Timewire?"

I squeeze my eyes shut, take a deep breath, and then open them before turning around to face him once more. "Yes?"

"Think about where your loyalties lie. And think about my offer, won't you? We truly could accomplish great things if we were working *together*."

Every piece of me hates the next words I force from my lips, but I say them anyway—and I say them convincingly. "I will think about what you've said, Mr. Evandrum."

I leave the room. The office door slides shut behind me, and once I've walked down the hall and past the double doors of the Sector, the creature of my ability materializes once more, hovering in front of me. She speaks in a growl of victory that strengthens my courage.

I will protect you.

Her coal-red eyes bore into me, and a wordless understanding passes between us. I know why she made me listen to my friend's plot to steal Arthur's memories. As twisted as that was, she taught me the only way she knew how. And now, because of her, I have the freedom to plot with them.

———

12

———

I ARRIVE AT THE AIRCRAFT HANGAR BRIMMING WITH A happiness I thought I'd never feel again. My ability saved me—*protected* me. The creature taught me something new, and somehow, Ashton sensed it too. I may not be free, but now I have a way to keep secrets from Arthur Evandrum, and that makes all the difference in the world.

I practically skip down the length of the large, warehouse-like building, searching for the Beechcraft, which I spot a minute later.

"Well, you're certainly in a good mood," Wren comments with sourness.

I drop the smile and mute my countenance. I probably shouldn't appear too pleased. I don't want Wren to report anything out of the ordinary to Arthur.

"Board the plane. I'll be with you shortly," she instructs.

I scamper up the fold-out stairs and dip my head into the belly of the aircraft. The smell of the leather upholstery mixes with the scent of jet fuel, and it churns my stomach. This is going to be another exhausting trip, and I'm not looking forward to it. The level of power I used at Area 62 drained me of my stamina, and while I've recuperated some of my strength, I'm not back to normal yet—and the lack of sleep last night has taken its toll on my body as well.

If I can keep my head down and finish this mission, I can get back to the mountain and finally talk openly with my friends. That thought alone will keep me going.

"Keep it together, Hollis," I mutter to myself, taking my seat in the cockpit of the Beechcraft.

I glance through the folder Arthur gave me, noting the number of personnel—2,356 people. But like last time, I expect there will be more. Citizens may be among the military men, crowding there for protection. Or they may be in their homes, sheltering in place. The folder gives no details about the state of the city, but whatever it is, I'll be expected to handle it.

Half an hour later, Wren and I are in the sky on our way to Area 147. Up above the dark clouds, the sun shines cheerfully, as if oblivious to the turmoil below. It's a different world up in the air. Like a dream. Everything is so clear.

"Settle in, Timewire. It's going to be a long flight," Wren states.

"How long?"

"Nine hours."

I stifle a groan, passing it off as a cough instead.

"Make sure you eat at least an hour before we land," she says. "There's food in the green backpack in the cabin. You may sit there if you like."

"Are we landing outside of the city like last time?" I ask.

"Yes."

The engines hum in the background, and the warm air in the cockpit is making my eyes heavy with fatigue. Maybe I can catch some sleep before we arrive, but something is nagging at me, and I want to talk to Wren about it before I take up her offer to move to the comfort of the cabin.

I speak delicately. "Can I ask you something?"

"What is it, Timewire?"

"More prisoners are going to be delivered to the prison camps at Area 7 . . ."

Wren gives me a side eye. "That's not a question."

I purse my lips. "Are the prisoners being treated fairly? Are there even enough resources and food to house thousands of people? Not to mention the fact that after today, we'll be adding thousands more."

"The prison camps are none of your concern," Wren says.

I fold my arms across my chest and scoff. "Why? My father's there. He's most definitely my concern."

"So you're asking because of your father?" Wren's face hardens. "Is that it?"

"Well . . . yes and no. I care about more than just him. Is the plan to free the prisoners at some point? To reintegrate them into the new society Arthur hopes to build?" I'm careful with my wording, not wanting to tread into the realm of saying anything Wren would deem treasonous.

Wren doesn't answer me, and my insides squirm at her lack of response. She stares straight ahead, and as the angle of the plane shifts, the sun reflects off her brown complexion like gold.

"I find it curious," she says after another few beats of silence, "that you are so wrapped up in the affairs of our enemies."

"Our enemies?" I repeat.

"Yes, Miss Timewire, our *enemies*," she replies stiffly.

"Shouldn't we try to leave that mentality in the past?" I offer. "We're looking to build a new future, and whether we like it or not, the powerless of society outnumber us like the stars in the sky. We *have* to learn to live together."

"Do you know that right now, if given the opportunity, society would not hesitate to kill every last person with the biomarker? They see us as vermin. The scum of the earth. An evolutionary mistake to be eliminated. They want us dead." She sounds angry, but not in an uncontrolled type of way. It's a calm, centered, and poisonous anger that breeds revenge when stewed upon long enough. "You can't truly be *this* naive still, can you?"

"I know they want us dead!" I bite back.

"Then *act* like it!" she retorts. "You say things like there's some magic spell that will suddenly make the world alright again. *Nothing* about this is alright. This is hard, and dangerous, and damn near impossible, but your power is making this happen. *You* are making this happen—for all of us. I hope you realize the position you're in and the influence you carry."

She sounds like Arthur, bolstering me into the vision of an icon—a role I never wanted, but a role that was forced upon me nonetheless.

"It would be wise of you to get on board with us," Wren adds. "I know you're only doing this because you've been coerced, but if you would just consider the opportunity you have . . ."

My insides turn to ice. Did Arthur ask her to say this? Part of me understands what Arthur's doing and why. Taking control of society with an iron fist *does* avoid bloodshed—and it is the best way to enact change quickly, but I don't trust Arthur's intentions for those who don't carry the biomarker. His rhetoric has been edging dangerously close to heralding people with powers as the only good and noble race. The Pure Ones. The phrase tastes like poison to my tongue. I'm not a Pure One, and I'm not a Diseased One either. I'm just a human being caught up in the aftermath of a bloody and dark history that happened because of prejudice, hate, and fear.

"Will I ever see my father again?" I ask, trying to steer the conversation back to my original question.

Wren sighs. "What do you imagine seeing him would accomplish? Even if the answer to that question is 'Yes.' What good would it do?"

Her words sting, and I push back the sadness that's threatening to break into my voice. "I want him to know that I care. I want him to know the truth. I hate that he sees me as a monster when I'm not one."

"You and me both," she murmurs quietly. Her brow furrows and then softens, melting away some of her toughened exterior. "You've gone through more than your fair share of trauma, I'll give you that. I don't know how you hold on to hope the way you do."

"Because that's all I have left," I say. "I have to believe that we're fighting for a world I want to live in when this is all over."

The smallest hint of a grieved smile creases the corner of Wren's mouth. "Me too."

I stare at her, perplexed. Even though she feels like my enemy, and even though she's a part of Arthur's scheme, deep down, we both want the same thing. It's confusing and encouraging all at once. I don't know what to make of her.

"You seem tired," she says. "Why don't you rest and eat? We've got many hours to go, and I need you to be alert and well-nourished. By the end of our venture at Area 62, you looked like you were about to collapse. I can't have that."

I nod. She's right. I need to sleep.

Clutching the folder for Area 147 in my hands, I scoot out of the cockpit and head into the cabin. The large beige chairs are much more comfortable than the cramped pilot seats.

I toss the folder on a small rectangular table that sits between me and the next chair and lean back in the upholstery. Closing my eyes, I rest my head against the cushion. Sleep takes me quickly, and I drift off through a sweet dream.

Keith is there, and so is Maddy. We're building a tower of blocks together in the Holodeck, and Maddy's laughter warms my spirit. He jumps up and down, pointing all the way to the ceiling, insisting that we build the tower up to the lights. And I do my best to reach higher and higher, careful to keep the pattern of colors Maddy wants.

Yellow. Then blue. Then red.

Keith hugs me from behind, rocking me back and forth in a gentle embrace. Maddy's sparkling blue eyes are full of joy as he swipes the mess of blond curls from his forehead. Higher and higher the tower goes.

Yellow. Then blue. Then red.

I'm on my tippy toes, trying to put the next block on the stack, but the height of the tower causes it to become unstable, and it crashes to the floor, blocks flying in every direction. Maddy stares around at the destroyed stack, and his eyes brim with tears.

He looks up at me and then speaks in a hushed whisper. "Help me, Hollis."

I crouch down to his level, grabbing his little hand. "We can rebuild it."

But Maddy's not looking at the blocks. He's looking directly into my eyes, and a chill quivers through me. His face is void of all emotion. "Hollis, help me."

"Maddy?" I gently place my hands on his shoulders. "Are you okay?"

Without warning, Maddy starts screaming. His strangled voice rips through me like tissue paper, and my body's fight-or-flight response overdoses my system with blinding panic. I've never heard a sound like that come from him before.

"Maddy!" I'm clinging to him, holding him close to my body, but he won't stop screaming. "Keith, help me!" I cry, spinning around. But Keith is gone, and I'm alone with Maddy in the middle of the Holodeck.

Then, the lights above us cut out, and the room is cast into darkness, but the darkness only lasts a second. When the lights return, Maddy isn't in my arms anymore. He's standing a few yards away, and his face is so pale that he looks like a ghost.

"They're hurting me," he whispers. "When are you going to save me?"

I attempt to run to him, but my feet sink into the flooring like it's made of quicksand, and I gasp. The Holodeck wraps around my ankles, holding me in place.

"I'm trying, Maddy." My voice breaks. "I'm trying to save you."

"I need you, Hollis."

"I'm right here," I say, desperately trying to pull my legs from the tile, but I'm sinking deeper into the floor. It's sloshing around my knees.

"I'm scared," he breathes, and his eyes grow so wide that it's unnatural. "They're not going to stop. They need me."

Something about the way he says this makes me feel like this isn't a dream, and a shiver of fear crawls up my back to wrap its spindling hands around my neck. This is not just my imaginings.

Something is happening.

Something real.

"They're not going to stop *what*, Maddy?" I ask. The urgency in my tone makes him tremble, and I slip further into the floor. The tile laps at my waist as if I were sinking into the sea. "What are they doing to you?"

"They're taking my blood," he whimpers. "Please, Hollis, I want to leave this place."

"Maddy, where are you?"

"I don't know where I am." He begins to cry, and he holds his hands up to his face.

I fall even deeper, and now the warping tile is up to my chest. "I'll find you," I say quickly. "I promise, Maddy. I'll find you!"

The Holodeck panels pull me down, covering my neck, then

my mouth. I don't even have breath left to scream before the
floor swallows me whole.

■ ■ ■

Rugged hands and a harsh voice jar me awake, and I come out of
my sleep with a shriek.

"Timewire! Get up!" The fog of the dream evaporates in a
microsecond. I'm back in the cozy cabin of the Beechcraft, and
Wren Zayla is standing over me, staring down with razor sharp
disdain. "We're an hour out. Eat."

She throws the green backpack at me with so much force that
it wallops me in the stomach. I grunt, grasping it with shaky
hands.

"What's wrong with you?" she demands, scrutinizing me.

"Nothing. I . . . I just had a dream. That's all. We're already
an hour out?" I ask, stunned. I peer out of the window at the
golden late afternoon sun. "Wait, who's flying the plane?"

"It's called autopilot, Timewire," Wren says, rolling her eyes.
She points to the backpack. "Eat. Now."

She turns away from me and walks back into the cockpit,
leaving me alone. I begrudgingly unzip the bag and dig out some
packaged food. I grab a strip of dried beef and unseal a bag of
dried fruit and nuts. What I just dreamed about unsettles me to
my core. Was that real? Was Maddy really talking to me?

I mull it over in my mind. The way he spoke . . . it was like I
was actually face to face with him. I don't know how that would
even be possible. But if it's true—if Maddy really did just talk to
me, then . . .

My stomach drops like I've missed a step, and a horrid feeling settles in me. What is Arthur doing to that little boy? My ability tingles in my fingertips, and I almost march straight into the cockpit to demand answers from Wren, but I hold myself at bay. Now is not the time. As much as I want to tear apart the whole world to get to Maddy, I must wait.

I bite into the dried meat and stuff my anger down as far as it will go. I have to be a puppet master now. That's what I must focus on.

The remainder of the flight goes by fast, and before I know it, we've landed outside the city limits of Area 147. Walking across the expanse of desolate dirt reminds me of the rescue mission to get Maddy out of the Area 19 Testing Center. Anticipation follows our every step, and when we finally reach the city, I extend my hands out to feel for the presence of anyone who might stand in our way.

"There are people," I mutter.

Wren nods, pulling out her handgun and staying behind me. "Can you freeze them?"

"Yes."

As we step onto the sidewalk of the first block, my hands buzz with control, and I sweep over the housing units, feeling for every soul. They stiffen under my command, and we move street by street toward the heart of the metropolis. No one is outside, but I can feel hundreds of people around us.

When we're far enough away from the initial block, I release the first batch of citizens. I don't tell Wren. I need as much of my power as I can muster for the Base, and holding on to people who are too far away to hurt us won't do me any good.

Deeper and deeper we trek, and the vibrations of my ability roll out from me with strength and direction. I breathe in power like an unending flood, creating a protective bubble of puppets around Wren and me as we get closer to the gates of the Military Base.

"We're not going to get gassed or shot at, are we?" Wren murmurs in my ear as we hug the side of a tall glass building.

"No."

"We're almost there." She nods up at the next street sign. Mayfeld Lane.

I stop walking, and so does she.

"What is it?" she hisses.

I hold my hand up to keep her from moving ahead. I don't want to take the risk of stepping out onto the street leading up to the Base. Like last time, I must take it from beyond its gates. It's the safest way. I take a belly breath, channeling the ferocity of my power out from my hands. With all the force I can muster, I call the creature alive, and my ability explodes from me, capturing the military men in a web of control that sweeps across the fortress.

My senses sharpen, my hands burn, and darkness coils by my side, relishing in the bounty of puppets. I'm shuddering from the pulses emanating from my palms. The Area 147 Base is mine, and it fell in less than one minute.

Hollis, the creature says, an inch from my ear. *Pay attention.*

"What is it?" I ask, staring into her coal-red eyes as she snakes in front of me.

"What's what?" Wren says, giving me a strange look.

"Nothing," I say quickly. "Let's go."

I march out onto Mayfeld Lane, and Wren tails me, her weapon at the ready. We approach the gates rapidly. I feel the men wriggling under my grasp, but they have no power. With a flick of my wrists, I compel them to allow us entry, and Wren and I step onto the premises of the Area 147 Military Base without so much as a protest.

Hollis, the creature whispers again. *Pay attention.*

Gooseflesh prickles across my skin at her words. What does she want me to pay attention to? I have a terrible feeling about this . . . I don't know what I'm supposed to notice, but something isn't right.

I peer out across the airstrip, and my eyes rake over the concrete buildings. The hum of my power zips through my body like fire.

Wren starts growling orders, telling me to gather the men at the entrance into a group. I do so, but still, my unease grows.

"And bring me General Whitlock," she sneers.

I slash my hands through the air, commanding the man in charge to emerge from the building in the distance. I can sense him as if he were standing before me. My ability hones in on him, pulling him out of his hiding place.

Do you feel it? My ability hisses.

"Feel what?" I whisper, low enough so Wren can't hear me. She's busying herself with the group of military men I've directed to our right, giving the same speech about the Pure Ones she delivered at Area 62.

I walk past the group of prisoners and further onto the airstrip. Something is itching in my fingertips. I can't quite pinpoint it . . .

"Timewire!" Wren barks. "Where are you going?"

I ignore her, moving further onto the premises. In the distance, a man stumbles out of the nearest concrete building. It's the General. And he moves with involuntary, labored steps. As he approaches, my sense of disquiet sharpens.

I walk toward him, and he walks toward me. He's a middle-aged man, gruff and heavy-set, with cruel eyes and a burly black mustache that matches his jet black hair.

"Timewire!" Wren shouts, jogging after me.

The moment he's close enough, I spot flecks of blood on his uniform—and also on his hands. The creature heightens my sense of smell down to the very molecules covering his knuckles, and understanding crashes over me like a nightmare.

I know what the darkness was telling me to pay attention to . . .

I spin around, aghast, and speak to Wren with frantic notes. "There are people with powers here!"

"What?" she says sharply. "Are you sure?"

I round on the General with a viciousness that rivals Wren Zayla's and speak with a growl, directing my palm over his heart. "Where are they?"

General Whitlock's eyes bulge and a gurgling noise comes from his throat. "Inside," he croaks, unable to resist me.

"Take me to them!" I snarl.

He practically leaps into the air as if I'd branded him and strides back toward the building he just emerged from. Our footsteps shuffle against dry pavement in the dusk of the falling sun, and the worst feeling twists my insides.

"Timewire, are you still controlling everyone on this Base?" Wren asks, following me with her gun at the ready.

"Yes."

The General grabs the door to the concrete building and throws it open. It slams against the wall, shaking on its hinges. Both of my hands are out, puppeting him with fury. And when the three of us step through the entrance, we descend a set of stone steps.

So much power is coursing through me that I'm having a hard time breathing, and the feeling in my stomach only grows worse. At the bottom of the stairs, we take a right down a long concrete hallway that dead ends in a heavy-set black door.

The General fumbles with a set of keys that he's drawn out of the depths of his uniform. They scrape against the lock, it clicks, and when the door opens, the stench of unwashed bodies and rot assaults my nostrils.

In the middle of the dimly lit room, there's an emaciated young brunette woman lying on a silver table with her ankles, wrists, and neck cuffed to its surface. She's blindfolded and covered in blood. Her shirt is torn, and burn marks litter her chest and stomach.

A table of nightmarish torture instruments gleam to her right, and against the back wall, there are three more captives chained hand and foot. Two older men and one young man who looks to be in his mid-twenties. They are blindfolded and gagged.

I pull my ability back, freeing them from the creature, and the instant I do, the woman on the table begins to sob uncontrollably. Her wild voice tears at her throat.

"I d-don't know where they are!" she cries. "Please! I'm t-telling the truth! We're not with them! It's just us. I s-swear!"

The young man chained to the back wall thrashes against his restraints, shouting what sounds like "leave her alone" through the gag.

I approach the young woman, and my breath catches in my chest. Blood drips from the side of the table near her waist, and I suck in a pained gulp of air. She's missing the pinky finger on her right hand as well as several fingernails.

My trembling hands reach for her blindfold. When I touch her, she screams, twisting in the cuffs. But the second the blindfold is off, she gapes at me with wide mousy-brown eyes.

Her mouth quivers. "H-Hollis Timewire?" she stammers. "Oh my God. Are you real?"

"Yes, I'm real." I'm fighting the bile that's pushing its way up my esophagus. The stench in the room is almost unbearable, and my eyes begin to water. "You're safe now."

I hold my palm over General Whitlock's face, channeling control through him. "Which key unlocks these cuffs?"

He grabs the smallest of the keys from his set and holds it out to me. It looks like it's made of pure gold. I snatch it up from his grimy hands and move to the woman, uncuffing her neck first, then unlocking her wrists and ankles. When she's free, she leaps off the table and runs to the young man, throwing her arms around him and sobbing. She pulls off his blindfold and unfastens the leather gag cutting into his cheekbones.

"Beck!" She holds him close.

"Hazel," he breathes, leaning his head against her neck. If it wasn't for the fact that his hands are shackled behind his back, I have no doubt he would be embracing her.

"Wren, help me," I say, approaching the first old man. Wren jumps into action, moving to the second old man. We remove their blindfolds and gags, and then I use the key to unshackle them. They fall limp. They're conscious, but just barely. Next, I move to the young man—Beck. Hazel gets out of my way, and when Beck's restraints are removed, he gathers Hazel into a hug, and she buries her head in his chest.

General Whitlock, who's still bound under my power, seethes. I can feel him fighting me, but he can't move a muscle. He's at my mercy, and I eye him with rage. Casting a hand toward him, I pull him closer and force him to his knees. Then, I open his mouth.

He lets out a deep, guttural growl, his face beet red. "SCUM!"

"What did you do to them?"

He can't refuse the question, and he gulps, spitting the words at me. "I tortured them for the location of the Pure Ones' base of operations."

My pulse spikes. "How long have you had them?"

"Two days."

"Are there any other people with powers in this facility?"

"No."

I look between the General, the four captives, and Wren, and the creature pulses with wrath. Wren advances on General Whitlock, withdraws a pair of handcuffs from her belt, and secures his wrists behind his back.

Then she unhooks the satellite radio from her waist and tosses it to me. "Timewire, get these people out of here and up to the airstrip. And radio the planes to tell them it's safe to land. General Whitlock and I are going to have a little *chat*."

She runs her tongue along the top row of her teeth like she's going to tear him apart, and my stomach flips. I know exactly what she's about to do.

Our interaction from Area 62 echoes in the back of my mind:

"Why did you do that to General Yi?"

"Simple. He was going to do that to us."

Wren's going to use her ability on General Whitlock, and this time, I don't want to stop her . . .

I lock eyes with Hazel and Beck. "Can you walk? And can you help me with them?" I point to the two older men, who are sitting in a stupor on the blood-covered floor of the torture room.

They both nod, and together, the three of us help the old men to their feet.

Wren cracks her knuckles. "Timewire, take your power off him."

As I help the captives through the doorway, I flick my palm through the air, releasing General Whitlock to Wren's mercy.

The five of us make our way down the hall, up the stone steps, and through the door to the outside. The sun is just beginning to set, but even the falling light of early evening is a lot for Hazel and Beck's eyes. They squint, holding up their hands to shield themselves from the retreating sun. They must have been blindfolded the whole two days . . .

Hazel begins to shiver violently, her teeth chattering together. The wind picks up her dirty brown hair, tossing it about her face. She's only wearing a thin undergarment beneath her torn shirt, and her hand is still dripping blood.

"Here," Beck says, removing his filthy jacket and draping it around her shoulders. I gasp. His muscled brown arms are covered in cut marks. And now that I'm getting a better look at his face, I can see the purple bruising that extends up his jawline. His dark brown hair is matted and covered in a layer of grime.

"We need to put pressure on your finger to stop the bleeding," I say to Hazel. Beck helps me move the two old men to a sitting position on the cold pavement. Beck is murmuring to one of them in soothing tones too low for me to catch. I move to Hazel, tear off a part of her shirt, and begin to wrap her hand as tightly as I can.

Her brown eyes brim with tears. "I can't believe I'm meeting you," she whispers, staring at me in awe. "Thank you for saving us."

I smile even though I feel like crying. "You're welcome." I look between her and Beck. "Are you . . . alone?"

She nods. "We've always been alone."

"How did they catch you?"

Beck hugs Hazel from behind. "We figured that we'd be able to find more people with powers after that broadcast. From . . . what's his name?"

"Arthur, I think?" Hazel says shakily.

"That's right. Arthur. We thought, 'Finally, more people with powers. People we could live with if we found them.' So we decided to scope out the city. Just to see if . . . if we could . . ." His voice tightens, and he hangs his head. "It's my fault we were caught."

"It's not, Beck," Hazel says.

"It is though. I took us too close to the Military Base."

Her eyes sparkle, and she shoves back a sob, hugging him. "I can't believe we're alive."

"Me too," Beck murmurs, kissing her forehead.

"I have to contact the planes," I say, clutching the satellite radio between stiff fingers. "We'll take you back with us."

"Are you with this Arthur person?" Hazel asks, mopping her eyes. She looks hopeful. "Is there really a society of people with powers?"

My gut plummets. "I am with Arthur. And yes, there's a mountain in Area 7, and it's filled with people like us."

"Did you hear that, Beck?" Hazel cries, relief washing over her gaunt face. "We're saved! I can't believe it. We're not alone anymore."

Beck pulls her tight to himself. "I know."

Beck and Hazel crouch down to the two old men and begin talking to them, relaying the information I've just shared. They look so happy that my heart aches. I can't imagine living out in the wild of the world with only each other to depend on. It's an honest miracle they weren't shot on sight. They're lucky to be alive. The only reason they're still breathing is because General Whitlock thought they knew the location of the mountain in Area 7.

Wren's harsh words stir in my mind: *Do you know that right now, if given the opportunity, society would not hesitate to kill every last person with the biomarker?"*

My heart skips with a distorted sense of justice at the idea of Wren alone with the General. He deserves it . . .

But the moment I think this, revulsion rises in me.

Is what we're doing right? That's the question I've been asking myself since Arthur took command. Until today, I would have said no. But seeing that torture room and hearing Hazel's screams has shifted something in me. For the first time since this nightmare began, I'm struck with a disturbing thought: maybe Arthur Evandrum's plan for stage one of taking back society isn't as evil as I thought it was. And that scares me to death . . .

13

THE REMAINING TIME AT THE AREA 147 MILITARY BASE FLIES by in a blur of cataloging people and weapons. Well into the night, I'm at Wren's command, following her every order. Beck, Hazel, and the two older men take shelter in the Beechcraft, which has once again been flown into the Base from the outskirts of the city. A volunteer attends to Hazel's severed finger from the supplies in Wren's med bag, cleaning the wound then wrapping it in fresh bandages.

Once every prisoner is accounted for and loaded onto the transport aircrafts, I finally board the Beechcraft, feeling like I'm about to pass out. I'm completely depleted of power. Even with the meal I ate before landing, it's nowhere near enough to sustain me. But I don't take any more food from the green backpack. I offer it to the four people we've rescued. They scarf down the dried meat, fruit, and nuts and then sleep for a good chunk of the return journey.

What a relief it must be to feel full and actually have a chance to rest. I can't imagine the horrors they suffered the past two days. What I saw in that torture room is going to haunt me for the rest of my life.

Even though I'm physically spent from using my power for hours, I don't want to sleep. I'd rather have company. To avoid waking Beck, Hazel, and the others, I make my way up to the cockpit. It's pitch black outside of the windows, but an orange light above Wren's head casts a warm, cozy glow around us. I take a seat and stare out into the abyss of sky speckled with stars.

"I thought you'd be asleep," Wren comments.

"Can't sleep," I murmur.

The hum of the Beechcraft's engines sounds in the background, and Wren adjusts her headset, looking at me with a mixture of exhaustion and something else I can't quite name. Wonder? Contemplation?

"You saved those people tonight. How did you know they were there?"

My ability skitters down to my fingertips like rain hitting pavement, and I swallow. I don't know why, but part of me feels like I can trust the woman sitting next to me. But even so, the wisest thing for me to do is avoid talking about the voice. I will guard her like she guards me. We protect each other.

"I sense things," I say. "I just . . . knew. People with powers feel different to me than people without."

The last part is a stretch of the truth, but it's not necessarily a lie. The creature allowed me to detect the presence of the biomarker from the blood on General Whitlock's hands. I didn't know I could do that until today, and I'm not sure I could explain the mechanism for the detection—or if there even is one. It was instinctual. Primal.

"They're lucky to be alive," Wren breathes, her brow furrowing. "And *we're* lucky that General Whitlock didn't capture someone who knew the location of the mountain. This whole thing is hanging on by a thread . . ."

She puts a hand to her face and lets out a long sigh.

"What's hanging on by a thread?" I ask.

"Whitlock would have sent bombers to Area 7 the second the information slipped. And then he would have killed those people without a hint of remorse." She shakes her head. "The only reason they didn't break is because they didn't know."

My stomach clenches in on itself. "Do you think . . . if they had known, they would've given us away?"

Wren's dark brown eyes search me. "Not everyone can hold out under torture like that, Timewire."

I sink back into the seat, feeling nauseated. She's right. In all honesty, as much as I'd like to think I could keep my mouth shut under torment, I don't know if I could. A nasty thought occurs to me, and it makes my skin crawl. Would my father have done that? Would he have tortured those people to get the location of the Pure Ones' base? But even as I consider this, I know the answer. He most certainly would have.

Earlier, Wren used the term "enemies," and I resisted the notion. But it's true. They want us dead. All of us. Am I foolish for thinking that people with and without powers can coexist one day? Am I insane for wanting to let go of the past?

"You did a good thing," Wren says, snapping me out of my

thoughts. "I don't know what's going on in your head right now. But you shouldn't look so downtrodden. You helped rescue people with powers. You're a hero, okay?"

I give her a weak smile and nod. But inside, I'm still reeling from the day's events.

The rest of the flight takes us into the dawn of the next day. And as the sun rises, so do my hopes. I'm going to talk with my friends—and with Jonah—and I can't wait. A sense of daring crashes over me. I don't feel silenced anymore, and for the first time since Arthur threatened me with killing Maddy, I can finally do something about it.

The entire time the Beechcraft taxis from the landing strip to the hangar, I'm itching to leave. I wait patiently, however, and keep quiet. Wren radioed ahead about the four extra people on board so that Beezee and her team could be available upon our arrival.

Wren eases the plane into its parking spot and kills the engines. I hop up from my seat in the cockpit with jittery hands. "Do you need help?" I ask. I nod over to our passengers.

Wren shakes her head. "No, Beezee can handle it. You're free to go."

I practically jump at her dismissal, but her voice halts me in my tracks.

"Timewire?"

"Yes?"

"Get some rest. You look like hell."

I stifle a grin. "I will."

I scoop up my bag and move toward the exit. Turning the

large red lever on the inside of the door, I open up the belly of the plane. The fold-out stairs extend automatically. I jog down them, taking care not to trip in my haste.

Beezee is standing there with a team of six assistants and two stretchers. She catches my eye, but I keep moving—past the group of medics, through the double doors, and off to the East Rooms.

With every step, my excitement builds, and the vibrations in my hands settle into a low hum. I can't wait to see Keith. The pitter-patters in my stomach are making me giddy.

Once I enter Sector 9, I whip down the hall and sprint to Candice's door. I bound through it without knocking. But rather than seeing my friends' faces, I'm met with an empty room.

Where are they? A little jolt of anticipation moves through me. I check the clock on the wall above Candice's bed. 1416. Maybe they're in the dining hall in Sector 12? But it's well past the midday meal.

I peek into the hallway.

Maybe they're in my training room in Sector 7? I suppose that could make sense—if they were trying to check in on me— but they wouldn't linger there if I wasn't present. I could check the medical ward in Sector 10, but that idea disturbs me more than anything else I've come up with.

I scuff the sole of my boot against the stone of the hall, at-tempting to stay calm. The jolty sensations in my stomach sharpen. I don't have reason to worry. Not yet. This mountain is huge. They really could be any number of places. Closing my eyes, I decide to use the heightened senses of the creature to search for them.

My hands move like I'm pushing through water, and the rattling creeps forth from me to scope out the facility. Within seconds, I'm able to sense Olivia Turrick, and it immediately calms me. She's in the place where she loves to spend her free time to escape reality. The place where she can enact privacy mode: the Holodeck. I should have guessed . . .

With rapid steps, I jog through the mountain, twisting down one passageway after another until I push past the double doors of Sector 1. The mirror-paneled corridor casts my reflection upon the walls, floor, and ceiling like a kaleidoscope, and I search the lighted keypads barring entrance to each Holo-room. All of them are green except one.

I approach the red keypad, take a deep breath, and knock as loudly as my knuckles will allow.

A minute passes by, and I knock again, but still, no one opens the door.

I cast a nervous glance around me to make sure no one is here. And then I hold my hand out, allowing my ability to sweep over the space. There are people just beyond this door. I can feel them.

I knock again, and this time, I knock until my hand hurts.

The seam of the Holo-room cracks a fraction of an inch, and a pair of dark brown eyes appears in the sliver.

"Hollis?"

"Olivia," I breathe, relieved.

"You can't be here!" she hisses. She keeps the door at a sliver.

"It's okay. Let me explain." I try to push the door open, but she blocks it with her entire body.

"Hollis!" She says my name like a warning. "Get out of here. I'm serious."

"Olivia." I say her name with equal force. "You don't understand. Please let me in. Nothing is going to get back to Terrace *or* Arthur."

She furrows her brow, and stress lines crinkle across her forehead. "What are you talking about?" she snaps. "You can't hide anything from him. You and I both know that."

"But I can!" I say, not backing down. "Let me in."

"No."

"When you took me to the river before the Ability Festival, you said you trusted me. *Trust* me."

"It's not *you* I distrust," she counters. "You need to leave."

I check over my shoulder again to ensure no one is in the hall. "I know about the plot to steal Arthur's memories. I heard you talking about it to Keith and the others."

Her dark skin takes on a deep crimson, and her lips part. She curses under her breath, but still, she doesn't open the crack in the door.

"My ability shielded me. The voice. She protected me," I explain. "And if she hadn't, Terrace and Arthur would already know about this. Let me in."

Olivia growls, letting air pass between clenched teeth, but she swings the door open, grabs me by the scruff of my shirt, and pulls me into the Holodeck.

I look around at the small crowd gathered within. So many familiar faces look back at me. All of my friends are here: Keith, Candice, Ben, Rosalie, and Vianne. But there's more than that.

Jonah, Audrey Rye, Libbie Lizette, and Caleb Stuart are here also. And there's two more people I recognize from the Ability Festival: Yang, the mimic who showcased his voice-replicating ability, and Siena Rose. My stomach drops at the sight of her, but then hope mixes with my shock. She must not be on Arthur's side after all . . .

And behind her, there's a dozen other people I've never seen before.

I gape at them all, awe-struck. "What . . . what is this?" I ask, turning back to Olivia.

Olivia holds her head high, a grin spreading across her face. "*This* is the resistance, Timewire." She holds her hands out in a grand gesture and gives a defiant bow. "Welcome to our band of rebels."

14

"HOLLIS, I DON'T UNDERSTAND." KEITH APPROACHES ME cautiously. "Why are you here?"

I peer around at the anxious faces in the room. They all know I work for Arthur, and judging from their terrified silence, they probably think my presence means their imprisonment—or possibly something worse.

"My ability protected me from Terrace," I say aloud, instilling confidence into my demeanor. "I'm not here to turn you in. I'm here to get Maddy back. I'm here to help."

I catch Jonah's eye, and his expression shifts from unease to surprise. "Your ability protected you?"

"Yes. I can hide things from Terrace." I want to explain the creature more fully to him, but that's not wise, given that I don't know everyone in the room.

"What about Ashton?" Jonah asks.

I grimace. The excitement I felt upon seeing everyone gathered here plummets at Jonah's question. I curse at myself internally. I definitely didn't think this through. Ashton is still an unknown factor, but he did release me from his power, and somehow, the voice of my ability convinced him to do it. I'm not sure how much Ashton understands about the incident—and I'm still unsure about it myself—but from what I can gather, he's under duress too. Suppressing me is not his choice.

"I believe Ashton is being coerced like I am," I say, treading carefully. "But he's helped me. Twice now. I think . . . I think he's on my side."

Olivia huffs, gritting her teeth together. "This is insane! Let me get this straight. Our secrecy hinges on Ashton *maybe* taking his power off of you so you can hide things from Terrace?"

The way she says this punches a hole right through my chest. What is wrong with me? How could I be so careless? I was so excited about being able to hide things from Terrace that I never stopped to consider Ashton.

I sigh, answering Olivia's question. "Unfortunately, yes."

Ben flashes up to Olivia with a burst of super speed that causes her to jump nearly a foot in the air. "Why did you let Hollis in here?" he demands. He's inches from her face. "Ashton hates Hollis!"

Olivia holds her ground with clenched fists. "*Because*, Ben, Hollis already knows about the plan to steal Arthur's memories!"

"She does? How?"

"She overheard us talking." She slides a sideways glance at Candice.

"Ben!" Candice runs up to him and pulls on his arm to back him off of Olivia. A tense moment of silence follows this.

Ben looks between the three of us and then pulls back his aggressive stance. "Sorry."

I take in the group of people scattered across the brightly lit space, and hope stirs in my heart. The fact that this gathering is made up of more than just my people gives me courage. Not everyone from the mountain is with Arthur.

I turn to Olivia. "You organized this?"

Her jaw tightens in defiance. "Arthur may have taken my ability, but he doesn't realize what I'm still capable of. It's going to take a lot more than that to break me."

I grab her hand and give it a gentle squeeze. "You're amazing. You know that?"

"Excuse me?" A woman from the back of the group speaks up in a soft voice. She's a thin, timid-looking thing with a striking blonde pixie haircut. But what stands out most about her appearance is a small, curved scar above her right eyebrow. It's deep, dark, and eye-catching. "What do you plan to do about Ashton? And what's the plan regarding Arthur's memories and the little boy? We can't just sit here and hope things will work out in our favor. There's a real possibility Arthur will learn about this meeting now that Hollis is here. What do we do about that?"

"We could take out that Ashton kid," a man mutters. "That would certainly make things simple."

Vianne rounds on the man, her hair jumping through violent shades of red and purple. She throws her hands up like she's about to transform him into some kind of mutant. "We're *not* taking out anyone!" she snarls. "Ashton is one of us!"

"Is he though?" Ben asks.

"Ben!" Candice looks aghast, and Ben holds up his hands in defense.

"Look, I'm not saying I agree with 'taking him out,' but what do we do? Pixie lady is right, we can't just hope things will work out."

"It's Delphi," the woman adds. She sweeps a hand through her pixie cut.

"Delphi," Ben nods to her. He shifts his attention back to Candice, placing a hand on her shoulder. "We need a plan. A foolproof plan."

"I agree," Jonah says. "Does anyone have any suggestions about how we make sure this group stays secret? Now that Hollis is here, we need to focus first on making sure we stay hidden before we attempt anything regarding Arthur's memories."

"I have an idea." Keith strides up to me and then faces the room, addressing everyone present. "We need to get Ashton alone. Away from Terrace and Arthur and away from his guard." He looks at me. "And Hollis, you have to talk to him and see where his loyalties truly lie."

"And then what?" Ben asks. "What if Ashton isn't going to help Hollis hide this? What do we do then?"

"If Ashton isn't going to help us, then we take him away from Arthur," Keith says simply.

"What does that mean?" Vianne asks, still fiery in her retort.

"We kidnap him. We get him out of the mountain. We leave him somewhere."

Vianne's hair changes from angry red to pale ash. "You want to strand him out in society? Are you crazy?"

Keith shakes his head. "Not in society. Somewhere secluded. Like the forest." The conviction in Keith's voice is poignant. "Hollis, you said Ashton helped you. Why?"

I take in Keith's brilliant blue eyes, and nerves twist in my stomach.

"Honestly, I don't know. But what I do know is that Ashton cares about Maddy. If he knows we're trying to rescue Maddy, then he'll help us. I know he will." I say the last part directly to Vianne because it looks like she's going to burst into tears.

Vianne's affection toward Ashton never made much sense to me. When my people arrived at the mountain all those months ago, she and Ashton were suddenly "together." Ashton helped her with her broken ankle, and he also helped her with watching over Maddy. The two of them spent quite a bit of time together before Ashton got locked up by Arthur's guards for trying to kill me. Ashton seems to have changed for the better with her. And even though I don't understand their relationship, I respect it. Vianne's my best friend, and seeing her this upset breaks my heart.

There's another moment of deep quiet, but then Mr. Stuart chimes up, his voice booming over the Holodeck. He pompously strokes his thick mane of a beard. "Mr. Ashton Teel has always been a self-centered, sniveling weasel. I don't think Miss Timewire talking to him will make any difference at all. She shouldn't waste her time. We should remove Ashton from the equation entirely. Stranding him somewhere sounds like the best course of action—and what's safest for all of us."

The coldness of his words stirs a tangible disgust in me. I advance on Caleb Stuart with a slash of my palm, and he seizes under my control. Everyone around us gasps.

Taking care not to hurt him, I stare directly into his snide, lion-like face. "*You* are a spineless coward and a pathetic excuse for a Council member. It takes a special kind of gutlessness to turn your back on someone like that. You have a habit of giving up on people and tossing them aside like garbage. I would know."

My chest heaves as the tingling builds in my fingertips. Mr. Stuart's eyes bulge. It feels strange, defending Ashton like this— but it's the right thing to do.

I continue speaking, staring daggers at the man under my power.

"Just because you're here with us doesn't make you brave or special. It just makes you smart. Because at least you can recognize what Arthur is doing. So let me make one thing *very* clear to you: you are *not* in charge anymore. You have no say in what I can or can't do. I am not giving up on Ashton until I know where he stands. And it would be smart of you to keep your mouth *shut* unless you have something productive to say."

I release him from my ability, and he staggers to his knees, dumbfounded. The creature inside of me purrs with pleasure, and I stifle a smirk. That felt good.

I catch Keith's eye. He looks like he's trying to hide the same grin, and this only makes me happier.

Rosalie, clearly trying to brush past the moment, jumps into the conversation. "Great. We get Ashton alone so Hollis can talk to him." She walks past Caleb Stuart as if he weren't there, swiping her vibrant red hair over her shoulder. "How? And if he won't help us, then how do we get him out of the mountain undetected?" She peers around. "Any abilities here that can help?"

There's a beat of silence. Curious faces stare back at her, and then . . .

"I think I can help you."

Arthur Evandrum's voice sounds from the back corner of the Holodeck, and fear wraps itself around my throat. I tense, my hands alive with power, but instead of the steely gaze of the man I've come to loathe, I'm met with the mischievous grin of a teenager, who walks through the midst of the group.

"Name's Yang," he says in his normal voice, chuckling. His spiky jet black hair glints in the harsh lighting, and he sweeps both of his hands through it several times, as if he were styling it. "Sorry for scaring you."

"That was not funny, Yang!" Siena Rose seethes, clutching her chest. She looks like she's about to pass out—and so do a few others.

He simpers at Siena. "Come on, Rosie. Where's your sense of humor?"

"In my food," she replies darkly.

Yang smirks and then turns back to me. "I could radio Arthur and Terrace to come to the Mountain Ground Control Tower with an 'emergency.' I can sound like anyone I want. That'll give you at least fifteen minutes alone with Ashton."

I nod, still trying to catch my breath from the near heart attack of hearing Arthur Evandrum's voice. "That could work."

"And I can take the kid out of the mountain if we need to strand him somewhere," an older-looking gentleman says. His wrinkled face is speckled with a splash of freckles that suit his copper, wiry hair. He coughs into his elbow then clears his throat. "I have access to the trucks we use to cart in our produce from the fields just off-site. Those trucks have emergency medical and food packs already in stock too. So we could leave the boy with some supplies, if it came to that. And no one would get suspicious of me taking a truck—I'd just come back with a load of food harvested from the fields like I always do."

"What about Hugo, Erwin, and Beezee?" Delphi asks timidly. She takes a tentative step forward. "When Ashton's not with Arthur, he's with one of those three in the medical ward. I haven't seen that boy unattended since he came back with that nasty gunshot wound."

I shuffle my stance, taking in Delphi's scar again. I can't help but stare. That's probably what my face elicits too: eyes drawn to the knife wound on my cheek like moths to a flame. But I push the uncomfortable thought away. Right now, I have bigger things to worry about.

"Do you work with Beezee in the medical ward, Delphi?" I ask.

"Yes, I do."

"What's your ability?"

Delphi goes pink in the face and mutters something about her ability being "embarrassing" and "unhelpful." She stares down at the floor, hugging herself, and Siena Rose speaks up in her place.

"Actually, Delphi, your ability would be the perfect distraction—at least for Hugo and Erwin. Someone else would have to deal with Beezee if she were the one attending Ashton."

My gaze shifts from Delphi to Siena Rose. "What's her ability?"

Siena snickers. "Pheromones."

Delphi looks mortified. She snaps back at Siena with a squeak. "I use my ability to calm patients and make people more comfortable!"

"But you *could* use it to seduce a man," Siena adds. She bats her heavily lidded eyes, puckers her lips, and twists a lock of her thick raven hair. "If either one of those losers were in the medical ward, you could pull their attention right off of Ashton and keep them *occupied*."

Delphi draws herself back into her timid shell. "I . . . I can't flirt. I can't."

"You don't have to flirt," Siena says, flashing a grin. "You just have to *bewitch*."

"I can deal with Beezee," Olivia offers. "She feels sorry for me because of what Arthur did. If she's the one attending Ashton, I'll have a meltdown and say I need someone to talk to." Olivia approaches Delphi, giving her a gentle nudge. "You may not have to use your ability at all. But if Erwin or Hugo are there, can we count on you?"

The eyes of everyone in the room land on her, and it's an odd feeling. For once, not everything rests on my shoulders. I look to Delphi as well, mustering up encouragement in my expression. Though I don't know her, she seems like the kind of woman who stays on the sidelines and doesn't stir up trouble. Whatever gave her that scar probably produced the urge to never be the center of attention again. But she was also the one who brought up the conversation of Ashton to begin with.

Delphi presses both of her hands to either side of her face and sighs. "Yes, I . . . I can do it if I need to."

The room takes a collective breath, and the tension breaks.

"What about getting Ashton to the truck?" I nod over to the old man who suggested it, and guilt guts me at Vianne's mortified face. "What happens if he doesn't want to help me and we have to get him out of the mountain? He's not going to come willingly."

"I know where Beezee keeps her sleeping drugs," Olivia says, purposely avoiding eye contact with Vianne. "We'll knock him out with those and cart him to the truck in a wheelchair."

I nod. "Okay."

"Good. We've got a plan that covers all of our bases," Olivia says, rubbing her hands together with a grin. "This can go a few different directions depending on where Ashton is and who's with him, but is everyone clear on what they're doing?"

There's a brief murmur that scuttles about the Holodeck as everyone nods.

"Then let's do this. Now."

"Now?" I repeat, going weak in the knees. "As in . . . right now?"

"Yes, right now," Olivia affirms, popping her hands on her hips. "We can't run the risk of Ashton suppressing your power in front of Terrace again. There's too much at stake now that you know about us. And the plan to steal Arthur's memories can't move forward until we deal with Ashton."

I groan. Olivia's right. Ashton must be dealt with one way or another. My stomach churns at the thought, and everything in me hopes for the outcome that doesn't involve kidnapping him and stranding him somewhere beyond the mountain. But for Maddy's sake—and for the sake of everyone in this room—Ashton Teel can't be my enemy anymore.

Vianne approaches me and clings to my arm. She looks like she's fighting back tears. "Hollis, do you think that . . ." She closes her eyes for a beat, and her hair changes through colors I've never seen from her before—colors that almost appear to glow because they're so saturated. "Do you think that Ashton will agree to help you hide things from Arthur?"

I wrap her up into a hug. "I hope so."

15

Delphi, Olivia, and I slink down the corridors of the mountain, heading toward Sector 10. According to Delphi, Ashton's only been one of two places: by Arthur's side or in the medical ward. So before leaving the Holodeck, I used the heightened senses of the creature to feel for him. To my dismay, he was in Arthur's office in Sector 15, so Yang immediately went to the Mountain Ground Control Tower to provide the "emergency."

"You'll hear me over the speakers," he had said. "And when Arthur and Terrace leave the office, whoever's guarding Ashton will take him back to the medical ward. After the announcement, I can only guarantee you fifteen minutes—maybe twenty."

The three of us continue our trek, and all the while, my nerves are on high alert. With all my heart, I hope Ashton has changed. Even though he tried to kill me, I don't hate him. And even though he's been cruel to me in the past, I don't wish him harm. He helped me with Camille when he didn't have to, and he's smart enough to see that what Arthur's doing to Maddy and to me is vile. I only hope that he's brave enough to do the right thing . . .

We enter through the double doors of Sector 10 in silence, but before we reach Ashton's room, Olivia stops us. "We can't be in there before Ashton." She pulls on Delphi's arm and nods to a storage closet across the hall. "Let's wait in there."

The three of us squeeze into the cramped space, and Olivia closes us in. The moment the door clicks shut, a business-like female voice sounds over the speakers of the mountain.

"Mr. Evandrum, sir. There's a problem at Mountain Ground Control. We need you and Mr. DuPont here immediately."

Olivia smirks, shaking her head. "That Yang kid has some guts."

Delphi looks like she's going to pass out. "This is crazy. What 'problem' is he going to lie about? How's he going to pull this off without getting in trouble? I don't like this."

"Relax, Delphi," Olivia says. "Yang's got this. We have to trust him."

My eyes wander around the closet. One metal shelving unit is full of boxes of gloves, masks, and face shields. Another is stocked with bed pans, bed sheets, and disposable undergarments. And in the corner there's a bucket and a mop. Everything smells sterile and plasticky, and the longer I stand in here, the more claustrophobic I feel.

Olivia nudges me. "You okay?"

I breathe out through puckered lips. "I'm fine."

But as the minutes tick by, I only feel worse. Talking to

Ashton feels like an impossible task, and I don't understand it. I've faced far worse than him. I've escaped death more times than I can count on one hand, so why do I feel like this?

My ability perks up beneath my palms with a jerk, and my heart leaps into my throat. "Ashton's coming down the hall," I whisper. "I can feel him."

"Who's with him?" Delphi asks.

I close my eyes, allowing the creature to tune my sense of hearing to the low murmur of conversation floating off the stone. "Erwin and Beezee."

Delphi holds her hand up to stifle a squeak. Olivia grabs her shoulder gently. "Looks like *both* of us are up. I'll go in first and get Beezee away from Ashton. Then you get Erwin."

Delphi's eyes begin to water. She claps both of her hands against the sides of her head and crunches up fistfuls of her striking blonde pixie hair. "I can't."

"You can!" Olivia hisses. Her eyes lock on to the crescent-shaped scar above Delphi's right eyebrow. "That asshole can't hurt you anymore. Erwin *isn't* Anthony."

This seems to stir something under Delphi's eyes, and she grits her teeth. She gives Olivia a stiff nod and then hugs herself.

"Okay," she whispers.

"Hollis, are you ready?" Olivia asks.

My pulse skyrockets, but I nod. "Yes."

Olivia puts her ear to the seam of the door, cracks it a few inches, and then, like a wisp of smoke, she slips through it. Delphi and I wait quietly. Soft voices carry through across the hall. There's a scrape and a grunt. Then, a wail sends shivers down to my toes.

"Heavens!" I hear Beezee say. "You're in quite a state."

The sobbing increases, and feet shuffle against tile. I have to hand it to Olivia—she's quite the actress. Weeping openly is not her style. Even when Arthur took her power, she didn't react like this.

"Come here, child," Beezee murmurs in a motherly tone. "Let's go somewhere more private. Erwin, you'll have to excuse me."

"Delphi, you're up," I whisper. "Go. Quickly."

She huffs, runs a shaky hand through her hair, then puffs out her chest. She walks out of the closet and straight across the hall with purpose. The voice of my ability hones in on her rapidly increasing pulse. My hearing sharpens, my sense of smell heightens, and the rattling sensations in my limbs thrum on high alert.

Even though I'm not in the room, I can sense Ashton, Erwin, and Delphi as if they stood directly in front of me.

"Hi, Erwin," Delphi says, mustering up a starkly different tone than anything I've heard from her before. It's thick, seductive, and heavy with desire. "I was wondering if I could have a moment of your time? In private?"

I can feel Delphi's hands twitch behind her back.

"I'm supposed to stay with Mr. Teel," Erwin grunts.

"You take your job too seriously," Delphi simpers. "Just a moment? No one will miss you. Besides, I have something I want to tell you. Something you're going to want to hear."

Again, another twitch of her hand.

Erwin's stance falters, and his voice changes. "I . . . suppose just for a moment."

There's a scuttle, and Delphi's breath hitches as she grabs Erwin's hand and leads him out of the room.

Vibrations of power sear my fingertips in anticipation, and I step out of the closet to enter the eerily white space. Ten beds line the walls, five on the left and five on the right, and Ashton's sitting propped against some pillows in the far right corner.

I approach him quickly, holding my finger up to my lips when I see his widening eyes. His chest is still heavily bandaged, and his face doesn't have much color, but it's his mouth that catches my attention. A budding bruise lingers in the corner.

"Ashton, we have to talk," I say.

"You can't be here!" he hisses. "I can't be seen alone with you."

I check over my shoulder, the jumpy nerves in me firing over and over again. "So, Arthur is coercing you too."

Ashton's lips purse, like he's attempting to keep what dignity he perceives he has left, but he can't hide the trembling that's overtaken his muscles. "Yes. He said if I didn't use my power to control you, then he'd have his men take Vianne to one of the cities and strand her there. He also said it would be 'wise of me to consider Maddy's wellbeing.'"

His words douse me in adrenaline, and the rage I've been harboring for Arthur festers deeper into my soul. I'm about to spill a lot of information, and if Ashton won't help me, then that's it for him. There's nothing more I can do.

There's still a level of risk even *if* Ashton agrees to help me because Terrace could potentially glean information from him, but if I can get Ashton to put on a show so that Arthur won't question his loyalty, then it might be convincing enough to keep Terrace at bay. Whatever the outcome, Ashton is now a part of this whether he wants to be or not.

I grit my teeth and dive in.

"Ashton, there's a plan in the works to rescue Maddy. And unfortunately for everyone involved, *I* know about it. Which means you have to take your power off of me every time Terrace looks into my eyes, or Arthur will find out."

Ashton's face turns a nasty shade of gray, but he doesn't speak, so I forge ahead.

"As long as I have my power, I can hide things from Terrace. Do you remember the voice I told you about? The one that allowed me to take your power away? The voice shielded me from Terrace's ability."

Quiet descends, like Ashton's mulling something over. I want to tell him to hurry up and talk, but I hold my tongue.

"Hollis, I can't disobey Arthur."

My heart plummets all the way to my toes. Ashton's always been so haughty and defiant, but now he looks like a shell of the person I've come to know. Feeble and broken. Like all the meanness and fight in him has been snuffed out.

I sit on the edge of his bed and stare into his eyes, speaking with fervor. "Yes, you can. You have to help me. Or a lot of people are going to pay for it."

Ashton inhales sharply. "Arthur will know I've helped you. I can't. He'll hurt Vianne."

"Does Arthur know you've helped me twice already?" I press. "You took your power off of me after Tish drew my blood and then again when Arthur was accusing me of looking for Maddy. Why?"

Ashton's jaw stiffens, and so does the rest of his body. He's pale and sweaty and so fragile-looking that a gust of wind could sweep him away. But then, a spark of fight lights behind his eyes, and he pulls back his shoulders, holding his head high.

"Because Arthur's a monster, and what he's doing to you is . . ." He falters and takes a hard swallow. "What he's doing to you is cruel. I couldn't keep suppressing you like that. I can feel something different in you this time. Your power's changed. Before the bombing, suppressing your power felt no different to me than suppressing anyone else's. But now, suppressing your power feels like taking a part of your soul away."

His breathing turns shallow, and he clutches the folds of the blanket draped over his lap.

"Your power is alive, Hollis. It feels like Camille's power. When Olivia teleported me into the Testing Center and I suppressed Camille, I felt this wildness in him. Like he was one with an animal. You feel the same. And I helped you because . . . I could feel what I was doing to you. I could feel how much you needed her . . ."

I gape at him, and my heartbeat pounds all the way up into my face. Ashton just used the word "her."

"You can sense the creature?"

He nods. "Yeah, I can."

"Then she *did* get you to understand," I murmur. "When Arthur was asking me about Maddy, I could feel her writhing under your power. And I kept thinking over and over again, 'Let me go, Ashton.'"

"I felt her," he says. "And I just knew I had to stop suppressing you. I can't explain why."

"Then help me!" I implore him. "Help me hide things from Arthur. Maddy *needs* you. If we can get him back, then I can get out from under Arthur's thumb—and so can you. I can stop Arthur from hurting anyone ever again. I'm completely powerless right now. Arthur's using me to imprison people! You've sat in on the meetings. You've seen what he's doing."

Ashton grips the blanket harder now, the skin along the back of his hands taut. "What if Terrace starts to suspect? What if Arthur—"

"*Play* the part," I say. "Arthur knows you hate me. Use that to your advantage. Make him believe you'd never disobey him. Make him believe you don't need to be coerced to do what he's asking. Be the Ashton Teel that wanted to throw me into the rapids—the one who's a snake and a coward. Fall into line! You and I have to be good little soldiers right now. Maddy is depending on us. A lot of people are. And I can't do this without you. Please, Ashton."

I stare into his worn face, and he holds my gaze in turn. Power rumbles in me as deep as my blood, and I hold my breath, hoping against hope that Ashton will agree. The silence between us stretches on and on . . .

"Okay," Ashton says. "I'll help you."

A tangle of happiness and relief catches in my chest. For everything that's happened between us—for all the anger, strife, and resentment—our circumstances have forged this clandestine bond. A covert and unexpected friendship. And as I take in the tired face of the boy who's been my enemy for so long, I can finally see past it all. Because we're both fighting a war we never asked for, and we're both being used by the same man for the same endgame.

"Thank you," I breathe. I get up from the edge of Ashton's bed, taking stock of the room once more. We're still alone, but I don't know how much longer that will be the case. I need to get out of here.

"Hollis?" Ashton's voice turns thick and gravelly, like he's trying to suppress expressing any emotion.

"Yes?"

"I'm sorry for everything I've done to you. I really am." There's a beat of silence between us. "I'll protect you from Terrace. I promise. And I'll do what you've said. I'll play my part convincingly." His brow furrows, and he speaks in a tone so gentle and kind that something in me breaks. "Just don't hate me for what I might do or say when Arthur's watching."

I give him a weakened smile. "I won't. Do what you have to do, okay?"

He locks eyes with me. "Protect Vianne, get Maddy back, and make Arthur pay."

"I will."

With one last shared look, I leave Ashton's side and slip out of the room. I practically sprint down the corridor to get out of Sector 10, and when I'm far enough away, I slow my pace. My ability purrs down my arms, and victory settles in my spirit. I'm so relieved I can scarcely breathe. Ashton is with me, and now we can come up with a plan to steal Arthur's memories.

The vivid dream I had of Maddy claws its way to the forefront of my mind. "We're coming, Maddy," I whisper. "We're going to find you. Just hold on."

———

16

———

Life in the mountain has settled into a cruel rhythm. I'm at Arthur's disposal. Constantly. He sends Wren and me out to the remaining Military Bases to extinguish the last of society's major strongholds. He makes me speak in front of the people of the mountain to update them on the Pure Ones' progress. He keeps me isolated from my friends and from my teacher by demanding nearly every moment of my time. And the time I do have to myself, I spend sleeping. I've only known this new routine for a few weeks, but I'm finding it increasingly difficult to maintain hope. Every morning I feel more trapped, and every evening I feel more exhausted. It's etching away at my will to fight, and this scares me.

From the precious minutes I've stolen to see Keith and Jonah, I've learned that the plan to steal Arthur's memories hasn't gained much ground. They've brainstormed a number of things that have all led to nothing because no one can think of a way for

Rosalie to touch Arthur without him knowing what she's up to.

The only thing I've been able to cling to is Ashton. He's kept his promise. Terrace hasn't learned a thing from me. As far as Arthur is concerned, I do what I'm told.

My exchanges with Ashton happen in silence. Eye contact. The vibrations of the creature in the moments I need Ashton to release me. A shared look of understanding between us during every meeting.

As Ashton begins to heal and step into his role by Arthur's side, he initiates a barrage of snide and savage comments—all aimed toward me. But I can see the truth behind his eyes. They're eyes that beg me to update him on Maddy and Vianne. They're eyes that grow to hold the secret of our newly forged friendship like a promise.

So I let all of his words roll off my back, because the more convincing Ashton becomes, the more freedom he gains, until Arthur deems Ashton fit to be unguarded—a feat I didn't think Ashton could accomplish so soon . . .

One morning, I awake to a new presence. Instead of Erwin's scowling countenance, I'm met with Ashton's pale and shifty face.

"Ashton?" I blink away the fog of sleep and sit bolt upright, staring at the clock on the wall. 0419. "What are you doing here?"

"Get up," he says. "I'm supposed to escort you to Arthur's office. He's sending you and Wren out again."

"What? Where? All of the Military Bases are under the Pure Ones' control now."

"I don't know. Come on. I have to get you there by 0430."

I gape at him. "Arthur's trusting *you* to bring me to him?"

He nods, checking over his shoulder in the semi-darkness of the training room. "Are you . . . doing okay?" he asks, his voice gentle.

"As good as I can be," I say. "You?"

"Fine. The worse I act toward you the better Arthur treats me." There's a stinging silence after this, and Ashton shifts his stance uncomfortably. He blows air out between pursed lips. "I'm sorry."

"You don't have to apologize," I say. "I understand. Honestly, the fact that you're here alone with me and Arthur knows about it is insane given how closely he monitored you after you got shot."

Ashton nods. "I was hoping to glean information about Maddy, but Arthur's not letting anything slip. I'll keep working on it though." He peers over to the door again before saying, "Is there any update on stealing Arthur's memories?"

My heart plummets. "No."

Ashton curses under his breath. "Nothing?"

"I wish I had better news."

He grits his teeth then balls his hands into fists. Then, his eyes dart to the clock. "Let's go. I can't be late. And neither can you."

I shove my feet into my boots and grab my jacket. My mind is firing through a slew of possibilities as to where Wren could be flying me next, but I can't think of anything. On top of that, the fact that Ashton is escorting me to Arthur is both comforting and unsettling. He must really be climbing the ranks to earn this much trust . . .

"You've certainly worked your way out from beneath some of Arthur's control," I murmur.

"What can I say?" Ashton slides me a sideways glance. "I'm good at hating your guts."

I give him a dry laugh, but it doesn't settle any of the nerves in my stomach.

When we enter through the double doors of Sector 15, Ashton grabs my upper arm and leans into me. He speaks in a chilling and nasty tone, cloaking his demeanor in his old nature with ease. "Let's put on a show, Timewire."

I grimace at his touch but allow it anyway. "Let's."

Ashton's ability snuffs out my own, and he grips my upper arm harder now. Upon reaching the office door, Ashton puts his hand to the panel, and it accepts his palm print. The moment the door slides into the wall, Ashton shoves me through the opening so forcefully that I crash into the nearest armchair.

"As you requested, Mr. Evandrum," Ashton says.

I round on Ashton and speak with a growl. "You didn't have to drag me in here like that! I can walk, you know."

Ashton's face curls into an all-too-familiar grin. "What are you going to do about it, Timewire?" He flourishes his hand in front of his face, and I can feel the creature twist in discomfort, but she doesn't fight Ashton's hold. He smirks. "You can't do a damn thing."

Ashton walks around the length of the oval table and drops into the seat next to Arthur, who appears amused by Ashton's aggression toward me.

"Thank you, Mr. Teel, for your promptness."

"Of course, sir."

"Miss Timewire, take a seat."

I glare at Arthur, but lower myself into my usual spot. "Where are you sending me now?"

Arthur riffles through the stack of folders and selects a rather large one, sliding it over to me. He's harboring an expression drenched in a sickening sort of pleasure. "Take a look."

I grab the folder gingerly and open it to scan the top page. There, printed in full color, is a photo of my father. The stark detail of the picture leaps off the page: peppered gray and blond hair, a clean-shaven face, sky blue eyes, and a hardened, muscular build. And under the photo, there's text that reads:

```
General Silas Timewire
Age: 48
Height: 5'11"
Weight: 170 lbs
Date of Birth: 1-21-2599
Status: Unregenerative
Known Family Members: Ella Timewire (wife,
    deceased); Hollis Timewire (daughter)
```

I look up from the folder as a cascade of adrenaline pumps its way through my limbs and face. What is Arthur going to make me do?

My voice comes out strained. "What is this? What's 'unregenerative' mean?"

Arthur adjusts his tie, staring me down like I'm a meal and he's a bird of prey. "A certain band of society rebels are wreaking havoc. They're bombing Testing Centers all over the world, and my people can't pin them down. They keep coming. Like cockroaches." Arthur's upper lip curls. "It seems that the military had protocols in place to establish an underground resistance should the Diseased Ones suddenly seize control of society again. And they're incredibly *well-equipped*. We've lost fifteen Testing Centers in one week."

My blood runs cold, and I clutch the folder in front of me with trembling hands.

"I am sending you to one of the prison camps in Area 7 to extract information from your father. He knows where the underground resistance is headquartered, and he's not relinquishing the location." Arthur's eyes narrow. "He's endured *much* this past week, but no one can get him to talk. He's stubborn and strong-willed. Not unlike yourself."

My gut churns, and bile rises in my throat. I stare at him with watering eyes and a weakened resolve. Feelings of empathy and horror overcome me, and my anger toward Arthur rages anew in my spirit. "You're torturing my father?"

At this, Arthur snaps, and he rockets up out of his seat. His entire body language transitions into something beast-like, and he prowls up to me, slamming his hands onto the armrests of my chair. "People with power-filled blood are *dying*, Miss Timewire!" he snarls. "Dying! And still, you seem to be concerned with the well-being of a *filthy*, powerless society member over your own brothers and sisters!"

I gasp, shrinking back into my seat, trapped by Arthur's arms.

"Do you truly care about your *father* more than you care about people with powers? Was that compassion in your tone for someone who would gladly kill you without a moment's hesitation?"

"Mr. Evandrum, I—"

"I'M NOT DONE SPEAKING!" he roars. "You would do well, Miss Timewire, to get on the right side of history before it catches you in its teeth and tears you to pieces! We are fighting an enemy who outnumbers us a hundred thousand to one. *Every* drop of power-filled blood matters. And you'd better start acting like it matters to you too, or I swear you will regret it. You think I've made your life difficult? You haven't seen *anything* yet!" Arthur's face creeps closer to me until he's inches away. "I asked you to think about where your loyalties lie. Because you can't have it both ways. You're either with society or with me."

My heart jackhammers through my chest, and my vision tunnels along the periphery. All I feel is the suffocation of Ashton's power and the claustrophobia of Arthur's presence, but I force out a reply to temper the crazed man standing over me.

"I'm with you."

This does nothing to back Arthur off, and I begin to shake more violently now. I can't help it. Arthur's outburst has pushed me into new realms of adrenaline, and I'm struggling to keep myself from falling into a full-blown panic attack.

Arthur maintains his offensively close stance, and his foul breath trails into my nostrils. "You will go to your father and compel that information from him, and then we will crush the head of this underground resistance before it can take any more lives. And when you return, you will *publicly* condemn the actions of your father for harboring information regarding the resistance, and then you will announce his execution. He will be put to death for his crimes against the New World Order." Everything in me dies at his next words. "Consider *this* your test of loyalty. Do you understand?"

Arthur's cruel gaze is void of all humanity and compassion, and I'm caught in a limbo of rage more intense than anything I ever felt for Camille. I want to take him in the clutches of my power and let him writhe. I want to fight him. I want to hear him scream for mercy, but instead, I force a reply through strained vocal cords.

"I understand."

Arthur removes his hands from the armrests and leers at me. "Wren is waiting for you in the aircraft hangar. You leave now, puppet master. I *eagerly* await your return."

17

My eyes sting with frustrated tears the entire walk
to the aircraft hangar. I wipe them away over and over again, but
they still come. When I reach the Beechcraft, I take a seat in the
cockpit before Wren can get a good look at me. I stay silent
through her pre-flight check, and I angle myself away from her,
trying to shield my face by pretending to be occupied with
peering out of the window. But as we begin to taxi down the
airstrip, she steals a glance at my eyes—which I'm sure are
splotchy and red.

"What's wrong?" she asks.

I don't answer. Instead, I continue to stare out of the window
and imagine myself transforming into a bird. Then I could fly far
away from this place and be free.

Wren speaks into her headset, and I tune it out.

My body feels like it's been weighed down by a bag of rocks.
My father is going to be executed. The thought plays over and
over again in my mind. I've tried so hard to stay hopeful through

this. With everything Arthur's forced me to do, I've kept my head. I've kept the vision I had for a better world in my heart and mind. And even though I'm the reason so many are imprisoned, the Pure Ones aren't killing people. We're just establishing control—at least, that's the tagline.

But this? Publicly putting someone to death? And Arthur making me announce it? Condone it? I hate him. I want to scream. I want to wrap the tendrils of my power around his throat and never let go. With everything I possess, I want to challenge him so I can stop this. But I can't because Maddy is still entirely out of my grasp.

Arthur's chipping away at every piece of me, and soon, I don't know if I'll have enough shards left to keep myself whole.

The Beechcraft's engines roar as the plane picks up speed, and within thirty seconds, we're in the air, leaving the mountain behind.

"Timewire," Wren says. "What's wrong? You know where we're going, don't you?"

"Yes," I say flatly.

Her brow knits together. "I thought you'd be happy. I thought you wanted to see your father again."

"I do."

She purses her lips, drawing herself up in a commanding manner. "Then what's wrong? You haven't said a word to me. That's very unlike you."

I turn to face her, and my eyes burn with the anger that's been bubbling underneath my skin. But I do my best to keep calm. "Wren, what's 'unregenerative' mean?"

Her face darkens, and her cheeks gain a bit more color. She grips the yoke that controls the plane with stiffened fingers. "Don't change the subject. Something's wrong. Spit it out."

At this, I break, and I yell at her. "You want to know what's wrong? Arthur's going to execute my father after I force him to tell me where the resistance is hiding! And he's going to make me publicly condemn his actions against the New World Order! That's what's wrong!"

Wren's fierce grip on the yoke slackens, and her shoulders fall, along with all the gruffness in her tone. "Oh . . ."

My throat closes, and fresh tears streak down my face. My ability gives me a nudge, and tingling showers through my arms, as if the creature was trying to encourage more words from my lips. But should I say anything more? Wren works for Arthur, and while I can hide things from Terrace, I can't control what Wren reports.

"I'm so sorry," Wren says gently.

I look at her, and another piece of me breaks apart. The creature nudges me again, and this time, I listen. "Can't you do something to stop this? You're high up in Arthur's ranks. You could speak to him."

Wren lets a shifty breath pass between barred teeth. She doesn't appear angry, but I can tell my question bristled her the wrong way. "No, I can't."

I grab fistfuls of the fringes of my jacket to stop myself from shouting "Why not?" Because I know why not. Whether she agrees with Arthur's decision or not, she would never go against him. And she would never question him to his face, especially about me.

If Wren had been cold toward me from the start of our forced partnership, I never would have opened my mouth, but she's been kind in an unexpected way. Always job-oriented, and a bit rough around the edges, but kind. She's grown to care about me in her own way. I can see restrained sorrow in her face. It almost borders on compassion, but Wren's soldier-like personality holds it back.

"I can't offer you any comfort concerning your father," she says, sobered. "But you're about to save a lot of lives by extracting this information. I can only guess that Arthur hasn't thanked you for what you're doing. It's important work. Work only you can do. So . . . thank you."

I look at her, and tears spill out all over again. "Wren?"

"Yes?"

"Help me get through this."

"I will."

The flight doesn't last long. After only twenty minutes in the air, Wren speaks into her headset with someone from the prison camp, and we land five minutes later. The airstrip here is much smaller than the one at the mountain. There's only a single paved lane covered in dust, and beyond this, there's nothing but open desert.

When I step out of the Beechcraft, the chill that sweeps my skin comes from more than just the cold air of early morning. Barbed wire chain-link fences surround rows of barracks that stretch on as far as I can see. Everything is dilapidated, colorless, and caked in dirt. And men with machine guns walk the perimeter of the encampment at intervals. From the look of it, this seems like a terrible place to be trapped.

Dread hangs in the atmosphere as if it were a thick blanket of fog, and I stay behind Wren all the way up to the front gate.

A spindly, tall, gaunt-looking man with deep-set eyes and a crooked mouth greets us. He's wearing a gray uniform that scarcely covers his ankles and wrists, and the smell of his unwashed body makes me gag.

"Hollis Timewire," he says with an off-putting leer. "Welcome to PC-7A." The chain-link gate slides to the side. "Wren Zayla, it's lovely to see you."

Wren looks like she wants to crinkle her nose at the man's stench, but she holds herself at bay. "Mr. Briggs."

"The warden is waiting for you." His toothy smile displays a mouth riddled with yellow-stained enamel. "Follow me."

He leads us across the dirt and down a row of barracks. In the distance, there's a concrete dome with a heavyset metal door, and when we reach it, Mr. Briggs types in a code on the keypad just under the handle. The metal hinges squeal, and the hairs along my arms stand on end. If it weren't for Wren, I would've already turned on my heels and marched straight out of this place.

"This way," Mr. Briggs says, extending his lanky arm out.

Wren and I step over the threshold into a well-lit concrete antechamber. To our left, there's three doors—each with an armed guard—and to our right, an open hallway curves around the dome and out of my line of sight.

Mr. Briggs takes off to the right, his long legs propelling him forward at an uncomfortably fast pace. I have to jog to keep up.

Along the curve of the hall, we pass door after door, and I start counting them to ease some of the twisting sensations in my stomach. It doesn't take me long to notice that every door carries a sprayed-on image of the golden woman. She's disturbingly serene with her hands open to the sky and eyes closed—like she's in a world all her own.

A wail echoes off the stone of the passageway, and I spin around, halting in my tracks. My hands fill with power. "What was that?"

Mr. Briggs waves it off with a crooked smile. "Never mind your pretty little head about it."

I give the man a scathing look as another wail sounds, this time from farther away. It floats in the air, giving me an eerie frisson that steals the breath out of my lungs. Wren flashes me a quick glance, and her narrowed eyes tell me to not ask any more questions, so I don't.

Mr. Briggs halts abruptly at a door to our left and knocks three times.

When it opens, I have to clamp my hand over my mouth to temper my look of horror. It's a small, dark hole of a room with a rotten stench, and at its center, under a single hanging light bulb, my father sits bound hand and foot to a metal chair. His lower lip is bleeding, his left eye is swollen shut, and bruising extends across his jawline—some of it a few weeks old. He's skinnier than when I last saw him too, his barren chest diminished of some of the muscle mass he had before.

A beefy man with a thick mustache and a balding head stands beside him, and when he sees us, his hardened face splits into a relieved grin.

"Wren Zayla," he says.

"Warden Kane," she replies.

"Thank the powers you're here." His gaze shifts to me, and he eagerly ushers me forward. "Come in, puppet master." Kane speaks with an evil enthusiasm. "Daddy dearest is so longing to see you."

My father stirs under Warden Kane's cruel stare, and the moment he sees me, his one good eye expands in recognition. He curses and tries to pull his arms from the cuffs keeping him restrained. Without warning, Warden Kane whirls around and strikes him full across the face with the back of his hand. My father grunts, barreling forward, though the chair holds him in place.

I shriek. "Stop!"

My protest does nothing to temper the Warden's look of satisfaction. He stares at me expectantly and holds his arm out in a grand gesture. "Go ahead. Make him talk."

The creature rumbles in my chest, and immediately, she tells me without words that I need to talk with my father alone. The instinct is overwhelming and urgent, and the tingling in my hands jumps, searing my palms. Her strange guiding force is becoming more potent with every decision I make, and deep in my soul I know I need to listen to her. It isn't even a question.

I glance between Warden Kane, Wren, and Mr. Briggs, who's hanging back in the hallway. "Let me speak to my father alone."

Warden Kane's piercing light gray eyes crawl over every inch of me. "Excuse me?"

"I said, let me talk to him alone."

His face darkens, and he bares his teeth, creeping closer to me. "Is this some kind of joke to you?"

I have to stuff down the tingling in my fingertips to keep my ability back. I elevate my shoulders. "Not at all. I'll make him give you the information, but you need to let me talk to him first."

"You think you can make demands?" he growls, now getting offensively close.

"I think I can," I say pointedly, holding my ground. "It's my power you need."

"Mr. Evandrum said you had a spirited defiance in you," he leers, licking his lips. His invasive stare roves over me, and my entire body shivers. "You will do what you're told, girl."

"You can't make me do anything," I snarl. My pulse is thundering through me wildly. I'm taken aback by my own gall. I haven't made a threat like this since Maddy was taken.

"Why you insolent little—"

"Warden," Wren interjects. "Give the girl five minutes." Kane's mouth drops open, but before he can say anything more, Wren continues. "It's the girl's father. Let her say goodbye. Five minutes isn't going to change General Timewire's fate,"—Her eyes snap to me—"and the girl isn't going to try anything stupid. Arthur's made sure of that."

Her words sting, but I'm grateful for them. She's right. I'm not going to try anything stupid. I can't stop this. All I can do is talk to my father one last time. Deep down, I know what I'm about to say won't change his perception of me, but I'm going to say it anyway.

Warden Kane's cheeks flush purple, and he gets in my face. "Five minutes, girl. Then you're compelling the location of the resistance from his lips in front of me, or I swear I'll make you listen to his screams."

He storms into the hall, and when the door closes, there's a muffled garble of yelling that issues through the seam.

"Dad." I speak the term barely above a whisper. I approach my father with quick steps, and my eyes burn at the sight of him. His injuries look worse up close. I suck in a sharp breath. "I'm so sorry this is happening to you."

His bruised face holds nothing but loathing. "Save your pity. I don't want it."

More yelling comes from beyond the door, and my heartbeat spikes. I don't have much time . . .

"Camille was the one who killed mother," I say quickly. "I had nothing to do with it. I swear."

Something stirs under my father's gaze, but his injuries make it hard to decipher.

"Camille was a Diseased One. He had a power. My power. He was a puppet master too. And I know how crazy that sounds, but it's true. He wanted me dead because he couldn't have another puppet master challenging his control. And when I escaped execution at the Capitol, he bombed the Area 34 Testing Center to lure me out. He told society it was me, but it wasn't. And then . . ."

Rage and grief fester together in me like a poison, and my throat constricts.

"And then Camille used his ability to force mother to step off the ledge of the Testing Center. He killed her to get to me because he knew that would make me come to him. And I did."

I pause, fighting the bloody images of my mother's broken body. This is grief I've still not fully processed. I don't know how to cope with what's happened. All of it storms through me—every jagged piece—intent on ripping me to shreds: our conversation at the pond, my mother's illicit affair out of desperation to conceive, the President's identity . . .

Of all the things my father's had to endure, I won't make him endure this truth. I won't tarnish my mother's reputation. Because I know how much he loved her. Her secret affair stays with me.

I lock eyes with my father, and heartbreak drives my anguish deeper. "I swear to you. I didn't kill her. I would never hurt her. I loved her."

The last statement seems to spark life into my father again, and he strains against the cuffs. "You're a liar!"

"I'm not!"

"You are with them!" he spits, and blood dribbles down his chin. He's like a caged animal, more emotive than I've ever seen him before. And a small piece of me dies at the thought of my father crumbling beneath the circumstances of his capture. "You're not here for me, you're here for information. So don't pretend to care by appealing to me about Ella. You don't get to speak to me about her."

His tone carries so much feeling that it temporarily paralyzes me. He's a wild shadow of the man I expected. Torn in two by the torture he's had to endure. My eyes glisten, and I walk all the way up to him, placing my hand on his.

He shrinks away from my touch, even though his restraints barely allow any movement.

"Dad, I don't want to steal information from you." I look back over my shoulder and lower my voice. "I'm being forced to do this."

My father scoffs. "Another lie! You've single-handedly imprisoned the military forces of the world, and now you're going to crush society's last chance to defend itself. You're a monster!"

"I'm not a monster!" I shout.

My father slinks back into the chair, stunned by my outburst. I run my hands through my tangle of blonde hair and suck in a huge breath, shaking with so much power. The creature rattles through my chest, but it only makes me feel helpless and small.

"There's so much you don't understand! So much I wish I could show you . . ." My voice breaks in frustration, and I look at him through a blur of tears. "After I failed the Test, I had to fight tooth and nail to undo the brainwashed ideologies of bad blood. For so long, I thought I was evil. That I was a mistake of evolution. But I'm not! I'm just a girl with a power everyone wants to use. And I'm being used over and over again."

Tingling works its way into my face, but I push past the uncomfortable sensation.

"I didn't want to imprison you. I was forced to. I never meant for this to happen. I just wanted to show citizens the truth about people with powers. That we're good. That we never went crazy a hundred years ago. That we never had bad blood. But now, everything's so messed up, and I can't do anything to fix it. I can't . . ."

The words die in my throat, and I hang my head. So much of me is bursting with the weight of truth I've come to know, but it all seems futile. Five minutes is not enough time to make my father see. And I hate Camille and Arthur for the monster they've painted me to be.

"You really expect me to believe you're good?" He says this so softly that it's chilling. He angles his head, and his jaw tightens. "They're going to kill me. Did you know? I'm unregenerative."

A chill slams its way through my body, and I look up at him. "What did you just say?"

"Don't force me to tell them the location of the resistance," he says, ignoring my question. "Let me die protecting the only thing I have left. You can't let them know."

"What does unregenerative mean?" I'm shaking. I can't help it. My entire body is going numb with panic. And the creature nudges me from within, prodding this line of questioning. Is this why she wanted me to talk with my father alone?

"Dad, what does unregenerative mean?" I ask again.

My father scrutinizes me like he's unsure of whether this is an act. Then, his cracked lips part, and something lights behind his one good eye. "You really don't know, do you?"

I shake my head. "I told you. I'm being coerced into doing this. I don't know anything about these people's plans. Please,"—my eyes dart to the door—"tell me what you know."

There's a moment of silence. My father is still staring at me like it's a trick. I hold my breath . . .

"Your people are going to kill me because I won't take the serum," he says. "That's what unregenerative means."

My entire body floods with ice, and I stagger back at his statement. So many pieces of this puzzle are crashing through my mind: the blood samples, George's chemical formula, the secretive nature of the project at Area 7, and now, confirmation of what I suspected before: the existence of a serum. But still, I have no clue what's going on. It's all one big mess with more questions and no answers.

"What is the serum for?" I ask. My nerves are firing on high alert. Any second now, I have a feeling that the Warden is going to crash back through that door.

"They told me the serum would purify me, and if I didn't take it, then I had no place in the new world that is to come. But I would rather die than take whatever's in that serum." He growls out the last sentence, falling back into his animalistic fervor. "I refuse to be a science experiment."

I look at him, horrified. The shouting outside the door continues, and I press my father for more answers. "But what does the serum *do*?"

"I don't know. But they're offering everyone here a chance to take it. And anyone who refuses is going to die." He sputters, and blood leaks from his mouth. His face, always so stern, is pleading and broken. "That's why you can't compel the location of the resistance from me. If you have any shred of loyalty left in you . . . please, Hollis. At Area 19, you said you were still you. Be who I raised you to be. Don't make me do this. Fight them."

Tears roll down my face, and another piece of me chips away. I've never seen my father like this. He's desperate. And the begging in his voice is so unlike the hardened military leader I grew up with.

I open my mouth, and my heart fills with hatred for Arthur

Evandrum. "I have to. Or Arthur's going to kill someone I love."

My father's look hardens, his whole body stiffens, and the pleading in his demeanor evaporates. All emotion saps from his face, and his tone falls back to that of a society member. "Then you are as dead to me as the day you failed the Test."

"Dad . . ." I hold my hands up to my chest, clasping them over my heart. "I don't have a choice."

Bang.

The door slams open, and Warden Kane storms back in. He marches straight up to me and grabs my upper arm with his beefy hand, practically lifting me from my feet. His thick face is an inch from my own. "Your five minutes are over! Compel the information from him!" he bellows, shaking me within his grasp as if I were a rag doll.

My ability shoots down my arm with the quickness of a viper, and I force him away from me with a slash of my palm. He skids a few feet across the cold stone with a grunt. His pudgy mouth parts in shock, revealing crooked teeth.

"How dare you use your power on me!" he seethes.

He barrels forward, arms outstretched, but I hold both my hands aloft to challenge him. "Don't touch me!" I shout.

He stops in his tracks, and then his bright gray eyes turn to slits. "I'm sure Evandrum would love to hear about this. Using your power when you're not supposed to?" He licks his lips in pleasure. "I was told Evandrum has the means to control you *and* punish you."

My heart leaps into my throat, but still, I don't lower my hands.

"ENOUGH!" Wren barks, stepping between the two of us. She addresses Warden Kane with disgust. "Miss Timewire is not the prisoner here. And if you lay your hands on her again, I will report you. Evandrum doesn't take kindly to interference."

"What interference?" Kane scoffs. He sticks a thick forefinger in my direction. "She's the one who's caused a delay by demanding to talk to this piece of scum instead of doing what she was told."

Wren steps closer to Kane, towering a whole head above him. She peers down with amused spite. "I'm sure Evandrum would be interested to know about how you assaulted Miss Timewire while she was trying to extract critical information for the cause."

Kane blinks. "Assaulted?" he repeats. "You can't be serious."

"I am." A dangerous smile plays on her lips. "Keep your hands to yourself, Warden, or you're going to have bigger problems than simply tracking down the resistance. Have I made myself clear?"

Warden Kane falters under Wren's fiery gaze, and when he doesn't challenge her further, it only confirms what I suspected: Wren ranks higher than he does, and he dares not cross into Evandrum's bad graces.

"Very well then," he murmurs through tight lips. "Make him talk, puppet master."

Wren nods me over to the bloodied and broken man bound to the metal chair. "It's time, Timewire. Let's get the information and go."

I look into my father's face, and his cold hatred falls into grief for the little girl he's lost. He's gazing at me with one last silent plea.

I raise my hand over his heart. "Please forgive me," I breathe. I channel my power into him gently, pushing just enough tingling to do the job. "Where is the resistance headquartered?"

My father grunts and sputters, but he can't resist me. He grits his teeth through his reply. "There are four underground bunkers located beneath the foundations of the Testing Centers in Areas 19, 89, 122, and 207."

My father gasps when I pull my power from his body, and Warden Kane's face splits into an evil grin.

He approaches my father, his gaze tracing over the gruesome injuries. "After all you've endured . . . it's all come to nothing. You lose." There's a deafening quiet that follows this. Then, the Warden faces me, but keeps his distance. "The New World Order thanks you for your services, puppet master. Now get out."

When I don't move, Wren pulls on my shoulder, ushering me to her side. She gives the Warden a curt nod. "Kane."

He sneers at her but dips his head back in return. "Zayla."

I steal one last look at my father. His head is bowed, and one good eye is filled with anguish. What I just did broke him . . . and I can't take it back.

Wren steers me from the room, and my father vanishes from sight. I clutch the folds of my jacket with white-knuckled fists. My lungs are burning, and my chest begins to expand and contract faster and faster. Tingling explodes down my arms and legs.

"What have I done?" I say aloud, choking on the emotion that scalds my vocal cords.

Wren grips me between firm hands. "Walk," she says. "And breathe."

All the way back to the Beechcraft, Wren never lets up her supportive hold. She walks by my side in silence. My guardian. The morning sun casts a deep orange glow over the barracks, glinting off the barbed wire. If I weren't in a prison camp, it would've been a spectacular sunrise. But the burst of light awakening the world to a new day feels hollow and empty.

My father is going to die—not because of his crimes against the New World Order—but because of his refusal to take a serum. George's serum. And now, a whole new group of citizens will be joining the prison camps because of me, and they will all likely meet the same end.

18

When we reach the plane, Wren helps me up the fold-out stairs and into the cabin. I'm numb. Drained of all substance. Empty. I didn't just break my father, I broke myself too.

I sit curled into a ball on one of the plush chairs in the cabin. My eyes well with tears, and when I rest my forehead on my knees, I let out a sob. Wren doesn't say a word. She simply lays a hand on my forearm and holds it there for a moment.

After a few seconds, she withdraws her touch and heads into the cockpit. The only sounds present are the rumblings of the engines as they start up and my heavy breathing. Within minutes, we take off into the sky. The mountain awaits me. And so does Arthur Evandrum.

I don't want to break down like this, but I can't stop myself. It's like a waking nightmare. Soon, I'll be back, forced to announce my father's execution to everyone.

My chest begins to expand and contract faster and faster,

stars circle my vision, and tingling pulses through me.

I clutch at my chest.

"I can't."

I say it quietly at first, but then the phrase grows louder in my mind, building like an anthem of doom.

"I can't!" I cry, pulling at my hair and slipping from the arm-chair onto the carpeted floor of the cabin.

"I CAN'T!"

I scream it, and the plane shudders, buffeted by some turbulence that throws me forward. I catch myself on my hands.

Abruptly, the snakish body of the creature emerges from me, coiling through the air to face me. Her eyes lock on to mine as she hovers, and with each looped pattern, she gets closer to me until her diamond head touches my forehead. Warmth sweeps my skin, and calm descends through me. It's like magic. Inexplicable and wonderful. The creature holds me steady with her gaze, and in her red eyes, I sense the fierce protectiveness she holds for me. Like she would burn down the whole world to keep me safe. And as we look at each other, my heart rate begins to slow, my breathing backs off from its high, and my sense of control returns to me.

It's not that she's made me forget what I did to my father, it's that she's made me feel like I'm not alone. That I can get through this. That I can still fight.

I am with you, she hisses.

I swallow hard, my eyes streaming, and I whisper to the creature. "Thank you."

She bows and then dives back into me, and the rushing sensation this gives me forces me to my feet.

My hands light with power, and I breathe deep, savoring the control that washes through my limbs.

"Timewire, are you alright back there?" Wren calls from the cockpit.

I try to say "yes," but it gets lodged in my throat, refusing to leave my lips.

"Timewire?"

There's a clicking sound and a myriad of tapping noises, then Wren shuffles out of the cockpit. Her fierce brown eyes find me, but as she takes in my face—which is still smeared with tears—she softens her expression.

"Sit," she instructs, gesturing to the chair behind me.

I obey her, slumping down into the leather upholstery. The energy in me falls, and I sit there without words.

Wren looks me up and down and then sighs, putting a hand to her face to squeeze the skin between her eyebrows. She looks like she's struggling with herself, but finally, she says, "I'm going to tell Evandrum you need to rest. Whatever he's having you do next can wait."

My lips part, and my eyes brim over again, but this time, relief claims me instead of more pain.

I can barely get the words out, but I manage a "Thank you."

Gratitude wells in me like a spring bubbling forth from the ground. It's strange. Wren is not the person I expected her to be when I met her on the streets of Area 19. And right now, she's more human to me than she's ever been before.

"When we get back to the mountain, I want you to go to sleep. I'll talk to Evandrum. You take care of yourself."

She gives me a stiff nod and then turns back toward the cockpit. There's several more clicking sounds as Wren takes the Beechcraft off autopilot.

For the rest of the flight, I sit in the cabin in silence, staring out of the window. The clouds reflect the golden rays of the rising sun like a canvas. The world is waking up again with all of its brokenness and beauty, and I take it in with glistening eyes and a heavy heart.

When we land, Wren assures me again, telling me to get some rest and not to worry about Arthur. I do what she says and go straight to my training room. I stop for nothing. And once I sink into the fresh sheets of my bed, I fall into a deep slumber with no dreams.

*   *   *

"Timewire."

A soft voice coaxes me awake, and the delicious scent of roast chicken fills my nostrils. I bat my eyes open, confused, and through the groggy haze, I see Siena Rose staring back at me. She's crouched by my bedside, her thick raven hair done up in a messy bun.

Behind her on the coffee table by the couch sits a tray stuffed full of the most mouth-watering foods I've ever seen. A half a chicken with crispy golden skin, a mound of fluffy mashed potatoes, a steaming pile of carrots, green beans, and peas, and a bowl of mixed berries with a glass of amber-colored liquid.

I sit up quickly, my eyes bouncing between the meal and Siena Rose.

"I'm not eating that," I say flatly. My stomach cries in protest, but I keep all indications of my hunger from my expression.

"I didn't tamper with it this time," she says, standing from her crouched position and walking over to the couch. She flops down on it, making herself a little too comfortable for my taste.

I glare at her, unsure of whether to believe her. "Why are you here?"

"It's lunchtime," she says simply, but I get the feeling there's something more to this visit.

I check the clock on the back wall. 1200—fifteen minutes into the midday meal, which means Sector 12 must be packed right now.

"Did Arthur send you?"

"Yes."

A shiver runs down my spine, and I stare at the small feast again. "Then I'm not eating that."

She sighs and holds out her hand. A small, folded note sits on top of it, and this finally pulls me out of bed. I walk to the couch, snatch the note from Siena, and unfold it to read Arthur's curly handwriting.

Miss Hollis Timewire,

Thank you for your important work at PC-7A. You helped save many lives. Rest, recuperate, and enjoy the meal. I've decided to give you the day off before your announcement. You've earned it.

Sincerely,

Mr. Arthur Evandrum

I reread the words with a furrowed brow. After Arthur's psychotic yelling episode and threats of making my life even worse, this is not what I expected upon my return to the mountain. It doesn't make any sense. If anything, the note only increases my anxiety. Could Wren have something to do with this?

My eyes snap to the tray on the coffee table and then back to Siena Rose. "You didn't tamper with it?"

"I didn't. Use your ability on me if you want."

The way she says this is so laid-back it stuns me.

With a guarded posture, I take a seat next to her on the couch. There's a mystery to this girl that's driving me crazy. One day, she's forcing emotions of despair and sadness into my food, and the next, she's in Olivia Turrick's band of rebels. I don't know what to make of her.

"Is Arthur . . . coercing you too?"

I'm almost afraid to ask the question.

Siena lets out a stiffened laugh, and her hooded eyes flash. "No, but I know when to play my cards." She picks at the cuticles of her fingernails. "Sorry about that first meal. That one was particularly nasty of me."

I grimace at the memory of the vivid sensations of Siena's power coursing through my body. My stomach growls again, and I'm tempted to start eating, but still, I make no move toward the feast.

"Seriously, use your power if you don't believe me," Siena says, folding her arms across her chest. "You need to eat."

"Fine, I will." Without hesitation, I flick my hand over Siena's chest, and she freezes under my control. "Did you use your ability on my food?"

She gulps, and then "No" tumbles from her, forced from her lips.

Relief floods me.

I release her and she gasps, leaning back against the couch cushions and clutching the collar of her shirt. Her mouth parts, but then a slippery grin slides onto her face. "I didn't think you'd do that."

"You don't know me very well."

"I suppose I don't."

There's something so familiar to this conversation. It's like I'm back in the Holodeck, having my first clandestine meeting with Olivia Turrick about going to see my mother. I don't know anything about the girl sitting next to me other than what her power is and the fact that she's one of the people helping with Maddy's rescue.

Tingling thrums down my limbs, and instinct guides my next question. "Why are you really here? If you didn't mess with my food, anyone could have brought that to me." I gesture to the feast.

Her gaze flickers to the door of my training room, like she's checking to make sure we're alone. She lowers her voice. "Because, Keith's figured out a way for Rosalie to steal Arthur's memories. And I happen to be the least suspicious person to come and talk to you right now." She nods over to Arthur's note. "And you're wrong about 'anyone' being able to bring you food. I do what Arthur tells me, same as you."

An explosive wave of happiness and urgency hits me all at once, and I sit bolt upright. "Are you serious? He did? Why didn't you start with that?" I demand, feeling slightly irked.

"Because, Timewire, you need to eat. And I need to deliver a mostly emptied tray back to Arthur."

My stomach rumbles a third time, and finally, I give in to it. I grab a leg of chicken and stuff it into my mouth. The taste is incredible, but I glare at Siena Rose nonetheless. "Are you happy now?" I murmur in between bites of everything.

Siena smirks. "Are you?"

I grab the cup with the amber-colored liquid and take a swig. It's cold and sweet and immediately gives me a boost of energy. "Yeah, I guess so."

It takes me ten minutes to eat until I'm satisfied, and Siena watches me like a hawk the entire time. It's odd, but I don't say anything, and when I'm finished, I immediately press her for more information about Keith's plans.

"Go to the Holodeck. I can't come with you. I need to go to Arthur's office right now."

Anxiety fires through me as an uncomfortable thought occurs to me. What if Siena Rose was supposed to put emotion into my food and she didn't? Why would she have to deliver my emptied tray back to Arthur? I give her a quizzical look.

She notes my demeanor, and her eyes narrow. "Look, I know you don't trust me yet. I can see it in your face, but there's a lot of people involved in trying to get Maddy back, so you're just going to have to trust that everyone is doing their part right now."

Surprisingly, her words stamp out my suspicions. Seeing Siena at Olivia's initial meeting in the Holodeck should be reason enough for me to trust her, mysterious as she is. And all I can think to say is, "You're right."

"Now go to the Holodeck." She collects my tray from the coffee table and stands, giving me an encouraging nod before slipping out of the training room.

With anticipation following my every step, I quickly make my way through the halls of the mountain fortress. I'm so elated by Siena's news that I can't help the smile that's come over me. It's foreign on my face, but I welcome it in, and hope builds with every footfall.

Once I reach Sector 1, I traipse through the double doors and into the hall of mirrors, heading straight for the red-keypadded door at the very end. This particular Holo-room is the one the group collectively decided to meet in each time to avoid any mix ups if multiple Holo-rooms were in use.

I knock on the door with even raps. Two knocks. Then four. Then another two. It's the pattern that lets everyone inside know it's a friend.

The door cracks, and Keith's handsome face greets me. "Hollis," he breathes with the biggest smile. He opens the door wider, pulls me through, then shuts it without hesitation.

He hugs me, and the warmth of his body relaxes me. It's like finally being able to take a deep breath. I hug him back fiercely, shoving down every overwhelming feeling that threatens to make me cry.

"It's so good to see you," I say, closing my eyes tight and taking in the scent of his freshly washed shirt. "Arthur's kept me so busy that I can't-"

"I know." His strong hands hold me steady. "Did you speak with Siena Rose?"

I nod, relinquishing the embrace. "She said you've come up with how Rosalie's going to steal Arthur's memories? How?"

I peer around Keith's shoulder. It's only now that I notice the others who are also present. Jonah, Vianne, Rosalie, and Olivia gaze at me with warm smiles.

My heart fills with affection. It's been so long since I've been able to steal a moment with Jonah that I run to him, tackling him in a hug. There's so much I want to tell him—to tell all of them—but first, Keith's plan. That's why I'm here. Even though this is "a day off," I can't be lackadaisical with my time.

"So what's the plan?" I ask, staring around at them all.

Keith gives a nod to Vianne and then to Jonah. "Show her."

Vianne squares her shoulders and Jonah does the same. They both hold their hands out toward Rosalie, and then with a flick, Rosalie's hair begins to lighten. Her vivid red turns to a pleasant blonde. But it doesn't stop there. Her stature shrinks, her face shape thins around her jawline, her eyes change from green to hazel, and her freckles vanish. And within seconds, I'm staring at myself. The transformation is chilling. I've seen myself in memories, but I've never seen myself like this.

I approach Rosalie, scarcely able to believe my eyes.

"What do you think?" Rosalie asks, and I nearly jump back. She doesn't sound like herself. She sounds like *me*.

I turn to Vianne, awestruck. "I thought your ability only

allowed you to partially change someone's appearance."

Vianne beams. "I've never pushed myself this far, but when Keith suggested it, I thought . . . why can't I change someone all the way? Shapeshift them." Vianne's hair shifts from auburn to a muddy blonde. "And Jonah helped me fine-tune it. I've been working on it for a week already, but when he doubles my power, it's perfect."

"Well, not quite," I say. My hand traces the deep red scar that marks my left cheekbone, and Vianne claps a hand to her mouth.

"Oh, Hollis! I . . . I forgot. I'm so sorry. I . . . I shouldn't have forgotten that. I . . ."

She looks incredibly disappointed with herself, almost angry. She begins tripping over her words more violently now, going pink in the face. Olivia raises an eyebrow at this, but I know why Vianne is reacting this way. She has scars of her own, given to her by the dogs that killed her parents. She hides them from everyone with her ability. If anyone knows what it's like to carry scars on her face, it's Vianne Evolet.

I walk up to her and grab her hand gently, pulling it all the way up to my face. I place her fingers on the jagged line. A wordless look of camaraderie passes between us, and then her hand falls from my face.

Determination replaces her shame, and she focuses back on Rosalie. Her fingers make quick work. A line of deep red spreads across Rosalie's cheekbone, and after a few references between the two of us, I'm staring at my exact double—this time, in every way.

"I genuinely can't tell who's who," Keith says.

"Don't worry, Keith, I promise I won't kiss you," Rosalie teases.

The joke breaks the tension of the room. Olivia and Jonah smirk, and Vianne bursts out in a laugh. Keith, however, looks a little embarrassed. I chuckle at the jab, but decide to throw a light punch at Rosalie's shoulder.

"Hey!" Rosalie holds her hands up, backing away from me in defense, but she's smiling nonetheless.

"This is incredible!" I breathe, excitement bubbling up in my chest.

Keith nods, matching my energy. He rubs his hands together. "The plan is that Rosalie goes to Arthur as you. And that way, when she touches him, he won't know what's happened."

"It will have to be without Terrace present, of course," Olivia adds, saying the words aloud right as I think them. "Because Terrace would immediately know that Rosalie isn't you."

"We just need an opportunity for Rosalie to talk to Arthur alone," Jonah continues, scratching his gray and brown beard. "More specifically, a believable reason for her to approach him without being summoned. I assume you only go to him when you're called?"

I nod.

Vianne's muddy brown hair darkens into charcoal black, and she speaks with conviction. "We also need a topic of conversation. Something easy for Rosalie to play off of. Ideally, something that only you would know about, Hollis."

Jonah clears his throat, and this pulls my attention back to him. His face is fierce. "The reason and topic, we leave to you.

Only you know what you've been through, and only you know what might work. Rosalie may be your twin on the outside, but she needs something more that will convince Arthur. We can't have him suspect."

My stomach clenches into horrible knots as the perfect idea comes to me. Jonah's right. I would never intentionally seek out Arthur unless summoned, but I know exactly what would make me approaching him on my own believable.

My heart jackhammers through my chest, and my breath hitches. I might as well rip the bandage off quickly because everyone will know about my father sooner or later, and I'd rather tell them what Arthur's forcing me to do before they have to watch another gruesome performance.

"Arthur is going to execute my father and he's going to make me publicly announce it *and* condone it in front of everyone."

They visibly stiffen, but before they can say anything, I forge ahead.

"It's going to be my test of loyalty to him."

Anger burns hot in my belly, and wrath courses to the ends of my fingertips. I hate Arthur with everything I possess, but the speech he's forcing me to make might just be the perfect cover for Rosalie.

I fight with myself over what I'm about to say, but really, it's what would work. I clench my hands into fists and take a deep breath.

"Rosalie, after my speech, when Arthur dismisses me, we're going to switch places. And then, you'll go to Arthur and tell him that he was right about my father, and that I was wrong for thinking he might change. You're going to tell him that you're loyal to him and that you understand that what he's doing is right. You're going to tell him that you're sorry for how resistant you've been to his ideals and that you see things more clearly since visiting PC-7A. You're going to apologize for your obstinate attitude, and then you're going to promise him you'll do better."

My eyes burn, and my voice grows thick.

"And I'll put on a show. I'll make him believe I've changed before we switch. And then, you'll seal where my loyalties lie. That's how we pull this off."

Everyone is staring at me with a haunted silence. Keith and Jonah's expressions are grave. Olivia and Vianne appear shell-shocked. And Rosalie's hazel eyes glisten with tears.

It's so surreal, seeing myself tear up. But they all know by the conviction of my tone that it will work.

For a few moments, no one speaks, but then Olivia breaks the silence. "I'll make sure Terrace isn't anywhere near Arthur. I know a few people who can help me too."

"When is this speech happening?" Keith asks, coming to my side and taking my hand.

"I don't know, but probably tomorrow. I think it was supposed to happen today, but Wren asked Arthur to let me rest."

Olivia's lips purse. "She did?"

I nod.

Keith wraps his arms around my shoulders and I wrap mine around his waist. There's still so much I want to tell them about what my father told me. About the serum, the real reason for his execution, and the impending death of all those who refuse to take it, but that's a much larger conversation for a different time. And I want everyone from the band of rebels present when I drop that bomb.

For now, I need to focus on the upcoming speech. Because after I make it, I'm really going to have to play along.

19

I SPEND THE REST OF THE DAY IN MY TRAINING ROOM WITH Keith, and it makes my heart happy. For a few hours, I'm able to shove away the nightmare of my predicament.

Part of me feels nervous about spending time with him, as if Arthur could appear at any moment, see us together, and intentionally do something awful to Keith. Through all of this, Arthur's never told me who I can and can't spend time with, he's simply made it impossible to have a personal life.

I lean against Keith's chest as he strokes my hair. We're sitting on the couch, and it's well into the evening now. We passed the day talking about anything Keith could think of to distract me.

It was actually lovely—moving from one silly topic to another. We talked about how to make ice cream from scratch and how to play Poker—a card game I've never heard of. We daydreamed about what it would be like to ride horses along the beach, or picnic by a lake, or hike up a mountain just to see the view. We debated if a cat or a dog would make a better pet—or if something like a chicken or a fish would be a more adventurous choice. We even discussed if Ben and Candice might get married one day, to which we both agreed "Yes."

Something deep in me stirred at the thought of one day getting married myself. And it gave me a feeling of profound happiness when I imagined it being with Keith.

And for a little while, I felt normal. I actually laughed. I imagined a better future away from this place and this war.

But the day is over now, and tomorrow is fast approaching. Someone will drag me out of bed, and I'll be thrust into the chaos all over again. It makes me want to cry.

"I don't want to be alone. Stay with me tonight?" I ask, peering up at Keith. His chest rises and falls in a calming rhythm, and I snuggle closer to him, wrapping my arms around his middle.

"Of course," he replies, still stroking the top of my head.

My eyelids are heavy, and they droop shut. I flutter them open, fighting sleep. I don't want tonight to end. I want more of this. More of him. More time to feel human again.

"Sleep," Keith breathes, taking in my tired eyes. "I'm right here."

And as Keith continues to gently brush my hair with his fingers, I doze off, safe and protected against his body.

■　■　■

I'm standing in a bare white room with no windows and a single door. There's a stark lack of any stimuli at all, and an eerie quiet steals my breath away. Something is off about this place.

I gaze around, unsure of why I'm here. Finally, I move toward the door and take hold of the handle. I want out of this room. But when I pull, it doesn't budge. I try twisting and jimmying it. Nothing.

"Hollis," a tiny voice whispers.

I spin around, yelping and clutching my chest. My heart rate spikes. A pair of blue orb eyes are staring directly at me through a tussle of blond curls.

"Maddy?"

He gives me a huge smile. He looks thinner than when I last saw him. Dark circles hang under his eyes, and his face is pale.

Without a second thought, I run to him and scoop him up into a hug. His little hands hook around my neck, squeezing me tight. As we embrace, the uneasy feeling in my gut grows. It's that sensation I get when my power is telling me to pay attention.

I set Maddy down, gazing at him with so much affection my heart could burst.

"I did it," Maddy murmurs, almost to himself. "You're here."

The way he says this sends chills zipping through my body. I take in his sickly complexion once more, and my mouth parts. Something about this feels almost . . . real. But is that possible?

My heart begins to hammer faster. A strange sort of cold adrenaline is pumping through me, and my voice comes out shaky. "Maddy, is that really you?"

He nods, and then he looks over his shoulder at the blank white wall for a few seconds before turning back to me.

Tears collect in my eyes. I crouch to his level, grabbing his hands in my own. They're small and cold and so real it aches.

I stare at him, aghast. "But I'm dreaming. How am I talking to you?"

"The golden light. It can find you," he says simply.

I shake my head. "I don't understand. What do you mean?"

Maddy looks like he's struggling with words that are beyond him. His face scrunches up, contemplating something. Then, his orb eyes glue onto mine with intense focus. "You're the only person I've ever given the golden light back to." His little brow furrows. "You dreamed of me. And I could feel my power. The golden light helped me talk to you."

Immediately, I recall the dream I had of Keith and Maddy building blocks with me in the Holodeck. Maddy had screamed and begged me to save him, and I slipped into the tiles of the flooring. Maddy seemed so real to me in those moments, like he was actually talking to me, but I brushed it off as a vivid nightmare.

I gape at the boy before me. "That was real? You were really talking to me?"

He nods again. His little hands tremble in mine. "It scared me. I didn't know how I was doing it, but then I thought . . . I could talk to you again if I tried."

He looks back over his shoulder a second time to check the blank white wall, as if he was listening for something.

"Maddy." Saying his name brings his gaze back to me. "Do you know where you are?"

He shakes his head, and my gut plummets.

"Can you tell me anything about where you are? What does it look like?"

Maddy considers the question, then says, "There's the number eight over all the doors. And they take me to a room that has glass everywhere. Glass walls. Glass cups. And big machines."

"What happens in the room with the glass?" Fear ripples through me, and urgency floods my veins. I don't know how long we have to talk before this dream ends . . .

"They take my blood, and then they mix it with stuff."

I inhale sharply and grip Maddy's shoulders, overwhelmed by the helplessness I feel. My mind searches for what to say next.

"How often do you go to the room with all the glass?"

"A lot. I don't know how many times." He begins to shake, and his voice turns to a whimper. "Hollis, when are you coming to get me? I don't want to be here anymore."

"Soon," I say, and my throat constricts. "I just have to find you. But I will. I swear I will. I'm close, okay?"

Maddy looks like he's going to burst into tears.

I press him further. "Is there anything else you can tell me about what's around you? What does your room look like? What do the people watching you look like?"

"My room has a bed. It's small. There's a keypad next to the door. The doctor man doesn't think I'm looking, but I'm smart. He types in 3-3-4-6-7 every time he comes to take me to the glass room. And his name is Jenkins. He has a funny eyebrow. It's cut in the middle."

Maddy checks the back wall for a third time, and this only increases my sense of urgency. Immediately, I begin to repeat the numbers Maddy's said over and over again in my head.

"Jenkins says it's working now." Maddy's face turns ashen, and his grip on my hands tightens.

"What is working now?"

"I don't know. But they take me to the glass room more and more. I . . ." Maddy sucks in an uneven breath. "My arms hurt."

He pushes me away gently and stretches out both of his arms. They are bruised at the crux of his elbows, and needle marks litter his skin.

I feel sick to my stomach at the sight, and anger for the people doing this to Maddy festers in my soul.

"I'm coming for you, Maddy," I say.

Bang. Bang. Bang.

A harsh knocking sound echoes across the room, and I jump. But it's not coming from the door. It's coming from the white wall directly behind Maddy.

Maddy gasps, spinning around to face the noise.

"What is it?" I ask, alarmed.

The banging continues.

"I can't let them see the golden light!" He tackles me in a hug, wrapping his arms around my neck. "Please find me soon."

I hug him back, and I can feel his little body shuddering. "I will. I promise."

Bang. Bang. Bang.

With a blinding flash, Maddy vanishes from my arms, as if he had been nothing more than a trick of the light. And then, a violent tug pulls me from the dream before I can even call out Maddy's name.

■　■　■

I awake on the couch in the training room with a cry, and Keith wakes up as well, startled by my outburst.

"Hollis! What's wrong?" He asks, bleary-eyed, but alert.

I'm panting, clutching Keith's forearms and staring at him in disbelief.

"I just talked to Maddy."

"You what?" Keith looks around us, alarmed, as if Maddy could be hiding behind the couch. "What do you mean you talked to Maddy?"

"In my dream," I say, still unable to believe it. As my mind searches for some kind of explanation, pieces click into place in rapid succession. "I think Maddy's using his ability to communicate with me." Energy spikes through my body, and I clutch Keith's hands. "Maddy said I was the only person he's ever given an ability back to. That day at the river, before we went to rescue Jonah, he used the golden light. And I think . . . I think somehow his power created a link with mine." I stare at him, stunned, when it finally hits me. "Oh my God . . . a connection point."

"A connection point?" Keith repeats.

A growing anticipation churns in my stomach. "Jonah taught me about them. It's when two biomarkers interact to produce a unique effect. Basically, Maddy's power and mine have connected somehow. And I think it's because Maddy absorbed my biomarker into himself when he took my power away. But when he gave it back, the golden light linked to my puppet master ability." As I say it, excitement and dread mix in me. "I remember Jonah said that since Maddy's so young, he hasn't explored what he's capable of yet. This is amazing. He used the golden light to talk to me! He said he doesn't know where he is, but he told me some details that could help."

I list them off to Keith quickly: the code to his room—3-3-4-6-7, the number eight above all the doors, the doctor named Jenkins with the cut in the center of his eyebrow, the glass room where they draw Maddy's blood, and the fact that "it's working now."

Keith listens intently, crinkling his brow at the last statement. "What's working now?"

My heartbeat pounds through my chest like a drummer is beating on my insides. During the dream, I didn't realize what Maddy was talking about, but now I do. I haven't told anyone about George's formula or the truth behind my father's impending execution, but I have no doubt in my mind that Jenkins meant the serum—the one that the Pure Ones are forcing the prisoners of the New World Order to take.

I had hoped to tell everyone in the band of rebels together, but talking to Maddy sparked my need to share this burden. At least one person should know the truth before I'm forced to broadcast my father's execution. And so, with watering eyes and a constricted voice, I tell Keith everything my father told me.

As I speak, Keith's face pales, and his body language turns stiff. When I finish, we both sit there in silence for nearly a minute.

"This serum," Keith says. "That's got to be what Arthur means by 'stage two' of taking back society."

I nod. "I think so."

Keith's grip on my hands increases in strength until it's almost uncomfortable. The way he's looking at me is fierce and encouraging and sorrowful all at the same time. "Get through the speech and focus on convincing Arthur you've changed. Because we're getting his memories. *Today.* And I have a feeling we're going to discover a lot more than Maddy's location."

Fear grabs my insides. I didn't even think about that, but Keith is right.

"Hollis, I'm so sorry Arthur's making you announce your father's execution." He gathers me into a hug, and I lean my head against his chest. "But this will be over soon. We're going to find Maddy, and when we free him, we're going to free you too. I promise."

I hold him tight, and with all my heart, I hope his words are true. Today is going to chip away another piece of me, and I pray I have enough strength to get through it.

—————

20

—————

When morning comes, I ask Keith to leave. I don't want him to be here when whoever it is comes to fetch me. There's a growing knot of tension in my gut. It's like the kind of anticipation I had in school before taking an examination, but ten times worse.

Before long, the door to my training room opens, and Ashton Teel slips in. Though nerves stab through me, I'm relieved to see him.

"Where are you taking me?" I ask.

"The aircraft hangar," he says. "Not the one with all the planes. The one Olivia teleported us to when she brought us here from the forest. Arthur's gathered everyone for some kind of announcement. Is this . . . the thing about your father?"

My stomach flips, and I nod. "Yes." I don't say anything else because there's more pressing matters to catch Ashton up on. "We're stealing Arthur's memories. Today. After I'm done speaking."

Ashton's eyes widen. "There's a plan?"

"Yes."

"What's supposed to happen? How can I help?"

I catch him up quickly and note the importance of keeping Terrace away from Arthur while Rosalie is talking to him. I also tell him that Olivia supposedly has a plan to keep Terrace occupied.

As a last resort, I add, "Maybe you could be there when Rosalie speaks to him? And if Terrace shows up, you could suppress his ability? Because Terrace would know Rosalie's not me in an instant."

Ashton's stance turns shifty, and he rubs the back of his neck. "Let's hope that doesn't happen. I don't think I could explain that away. Terrace would know I'm suppressing him. He doesn't use his ability on me, and I don't want to give him a reason to."

I twist my hands together in frustration. He's right. The last thing we need is for Terrace to get suspicious of Ashton, because what he knows would blow our cover.

"Rosalie won't need more than a few minutes, right?" Ashton offers the question like an encouragement.

"That's the idea."

Ashton checks the clock on the far wall. He clicks his tongue. "We have to go. Arthur's expecting you in nine minutes."

The tingling of my ability showers down my arms. I want to scream, but I grit my teeth together to pluck up my courage. "Let's go."

We arrive at the balcony section of the aircraft hangar just in time. When I step through the double doors to the upper section, ice fills my veins. Easily a thousand people are crowded below, and Arthur, Terrace, Hugo, Wren, and a few other Board members stand along the balcony overlooking the giant space.

"Miss Timewire," Arthur says, walking to my side. One of his spindly hands grasps my shoulder, and I shudder under his touch. He steers me away from the edge of the balcony and closer to the back wall so that my view of the people below vanishes.

From his suit jacket pocket, he pulls out a folded piece of paper and hands it to me. I take it with stiffened fingers.

"This is your speech," he says, narrowing his eyes. "Do you remember what I said about loyalty?"

I look directly at him, and though my ability rumbles in my chest, ready for my command, I hold it at bay. "Yes, I remember."

Arthur pulls a second item from his suit jacket pocket. It's small and wrapped in silver foil.

"Hold out your hand," he instructs. I do so, and Arthur places the small, foiled object on the flat of my palm. "Your boost."

I unwrap the foil to see a square of chocolate, and my insides recoil.

"You're up when I'm done speaking," he murmurs close to my ear.

He spins around, pristine in his societal composure, and steps up to the balcony railing. He motions me to his side, and I step up as well. A hush falls over the people as every eye finds us.

Arthur clicks the pea-sized microphone on his collar and begins. "Ladies and gentlemen of the mountain, I've gathered you here to share grave news." Arthur sobers, taking in a deep breath. The room below seems to hold its breath. "Society rebels have bombed fifteen Testing Centers in the past week, and we've lost some of our own."

There's a rumbling of distress that cascades through the crowd, and already, I can hear stifled cries of women and men alike.

Arthur clears his throat. "It burdens my heart to tell you this. And I am deeply sorry to the families … I …" He pauses and swallows hard. "The names I'm about to share with you were some of our brightest and best."

He pulls a sheet from his pocket. It looks like it's been crumpled and flattened back out many times.

The stifled atmosphere of the aircraft hangar presses in on us all. Then, Arthur begins.

"Katy Fallow."

There's a cry from the far back corner of the room.

"Henry Perset."

A wail issues from the center of the crowd.

"Dean Griff."

More crying. More shrieking.

As Arthur continues to read names, the commotion in the room grows. I've never heard such sounds. Grief tears through the souls, merciless in its sharp reality.

I even begin to tear up. I didn't know any of these people, but they were people who died fighting for a better world. People who had likely been undercover in society for a long time, separated from their families to help bring down the Test.

Arthur finishes reading the list. Thirty-one names. Thirty-one families without their loved ones.

The weeping below is palpable. Hair-raising. Puncturing to the sinews and marrow.

"I am truly, deeply sorry for your losses," Arthur says, and his voice grows thick with emotion. "Know that they did not die in vain." He places a hand to his forehead, gathering himself before continuing. "I know there is nothing that can be done to bring back those who have passed, but we can bring justice to their murderer, Silas Timewire."

At the mention of this name, a roar rips through the aircraft hangar, and I'm doused in a panic that I have to quickly shove down. Some people wear expressions of loathing, like they would tear me apart if they got their hands on me. Others wear looks of shock and sympathy, as if they could imagine how horrible this news must be for me too.

"General Timewire knew the location of these groups of society rebels, and yet, he did not relinquish the information. Instead, he allowed our brothers and sisters to die." Arthur raises his posture and gestures to me. "But Miss Hollis Timewire used her ability to compel their location from his lips. And in the past twenty-four hours, we've captured these society rebels, snuffing out their deadly assaults."

I shift from one foot to another. Maybe that's why Arthur gave me the day off yesterday. He certainly made quick work of the information I forced from my father's lips.

"And now, I want you to hear from Hollis herself. She has something to announce, and I hope it will bring you some comfort."

Arthur unclips the pea-sized microphone from his collar and

then clips it to the collar of my jacket. The entire time he does this, he stares me down. When he finishes, he nudges my curled hand—the one that has the chocolate in it.

I face the room, then I look down at the flat of my palm, gazing at the small treat. My eyes move from the chocolate to Arthur Evandrum, and with my heart in my throat, I hold my hand over the railing and intentionally drop the candy over the edge.

Arthur's entire body tenses, and my eyes never leave his. I cup my hand over the microphone on my jacket and lower my voice so only Arthur can hear.

"You said you wanted to see my loyalty. Well, here it is."

I uncover the microphone, unfold the paper, and speak boldly to the room, and in my heart and mind, I call the creature of my ability to life, beckoning her to my side. She materializes and coils around my chest like a guardian, spurring my resolve and strengthening my spirit.

"My brothers and sisters," I say, compassion filling my voice. "I want you to know that I condemn the actions of my father. Silas Timewire may be my blood, but he is not my family. *You* are my family."

My chest rises and falls, and the creature surrounds me, fueling me with an energy that's not my own.

"He is a traitor to the Pure Ones' vision, and he is a coward. For his crimes against the New World Order, he will be put to death."

I say the words with conviction, holding nothing back. I stand tall and proud and filled with love for the people staring up at me.

"I hope with all my heart that his death will bring you some semblance of peace," I continue. "For he represents the evil in this world that we are so desperately trying to stamp out. His death will be a symbolic death—a death that makes it clear to all who oppose us that we will not be stopped and we will not back down. The Pure Ones will continue to thrive, despite the vicious opposition of those who wish us dead."

My words boom over the large concrete space, echoing off the walls.

"Mourn tonight. Spill your tears and hug your loved ones. Come together as one people."

My hands start to tremble as my eyes find the last line written on the page. I push the deep anguish I feel down.

"Silas Timewire dies at dawn."

I turn back to Arthur, unclip the microphone, and hold it out to him. The creature hisses, exposing her fangs of peppery mist. I'm wearing a look that's muted and business-like, as if that didn't just rip my heart to shreds.

Arthur takes the microphone, peering at me with intense scrutiny, and then he clears his throat, clipping it back onto himself. He faces the room once more.

"Please retire for the rest of the day. Take a break from your work stations. Be with your families. Rest and mourn. Tomorrow, we face a brighter day. You are all dismissed."

There's a great amount of scuffling and footfalls as the crowd disperses. Some leave immediately. Others gather in pods to console one another. There are people sitting on the floor in tears or in shock. My heart breaks for them, and my heart breaks for me too.

With the slightest twitch of my hand, I let the creature know she can go. She uncoils herself from my torso and snakes back into my chest, vanishing from my sight.

The energy in me dissolves.

Arthur's fierce gaze rakes over me, but I hide my feelings well, and I simply stare back, satisfied with my performance.

"You continue to surprise me," he murmurs. The vein on his neck ticks. I can tell that dropping the chocolate was a dangerous move on my part. I blatantly defied him to his face.

"I didn't need the boost," I say. "I can be loyal without it. You want me to show you where my loyalties lie? This is the start. I'm loyal to you. Not society. Not my father. *You.* The chocolate wouldn't have been me speaking. It would've been Siena Rose's version of me."

This seems to quell some of the tension in Arthur's face, but I can see he isn't fully satisfied. His upper lip curls. He presses his hands together, fingertip to fingertip.

"Very well, Miss Timewire. Take the remainder of the day along with the others. I will see you in my office at 0500 tomorrow morning. You are dismissed."

"Yes, sir," I reply, keeping all emotion from my tone.

I scan the balcony, quickly taking stock of who's still here. Wren and Hugo have already left, but I spot Terrace immediately. Whatever Olivia's plan is, she better do it now.

As if on cue, Olivia enters through the double doors of the upper section. Arthur's eyes snap to her, but she doesn't even acknowledge him. She marches straight to Terrace, pulling on his arm to turn him around. "Terrace, Delphi needs you."

Terrace raises an eyebrow at this. "What for?"

"She's very upset over Katy Fallow's death, and she's demanding to talk to you."

Terrace sighs, putting a hand up to his face like he knows exactly how this situation is going to end. "I've told Delphi before, Katy was out of my control. Katy volunteered to work in society. This isn't my fault."

"I don't care what you've told her before," Olivia shoots back, ice cold. "Go talk to her. Now."

She folds her arms across her chest, and Terrace groans. "Fine."

The two of them exit through the double doors, and I can scarcely believe how smooth that went.

Ashton and I lock eyes, and he gives me a nod. I wait about thirty seconds before exiting the balcony myself. When I do, my heartbeat quickens.

I reach out with the tendrils of my power to find Jonah, Vianne, and Rosalie. They're down below, and I launch myself into the stairwell, descending to the lower level of the massive concrete room.

My senses are firing on high alert as I approach Jonah.

"This way." I beckon them, and they follow me out of the lower section and into the stairwell once more. When we reach the top, I steer the three of them down the hall away from the double doors and into a small storage closet.

The space is cramped and filled with plastic buckets and mops.

"Arthur, Ashton, and a few stray Board members are still up

here," I whisper rapidly. "Olivia got Terrace away from Arthur already. We have to do this. Now. Before Terrace returns."

Vianne's pale and sweaty face flushes with color. Jonah looks grim. And Rosalie looks like she's on the verge of passing out.

I grab both of Rosalie's shoulders. "Do you remember what you're going to say?"

She nods slowly.

"You can do this, okay?"

She nods again, words lost on her.

"Vianne, are you ready?" Jonah asks, positioning his hands in mid-air toward Rosalie's chest.

"Ready."

Vianne raises her hands in a beautiful arc, floating them over Rosalie's body, and her transformation begins. She shrinks, her hair turns blonde, her freckles disappear, and her eyes change to hazel. Then, the scar blossoms across her left cheekbone. She's my double in every way.

I look her full in the face and give her an encouraging nod. "Go. We'll be right here when you're done."

And without another word, Rosalie slips out of the closet and into the hall.

The second the door shuts, I call the creature alive with my hands, and I will her to sharpen my senses. I hone in on Rosalie. Her scent. Her ever-increasing heartbeat. Her shaky breath.

I track her down the hall, and the second she steps foot through the double doors, I allow the creature to expand my senses again, until I feel every person on the balcony: Arthur Evandrum, Ashton Teel, two other Board members, and Rosalie Simmons disguised as me.

My hearing turns sharp as Arthur turns on his heels at Rosalie's arrival.

"Miss Timewire, what is it?" he asks, surprised at her presence.

"I need to tell you something," she begins, and I can perceive the smallest tremor in her vocal cords.

"Yes?"

She moves closer to him, and her heartbeat picks up.

"Visiting PC-7A really put things into perspective for me. You were right about my father."

Arthur's posture raises ever so slightly. I can feel him gazing at her with intense focus, like something is out of place.

"He doesn't care about me, and it was wrong for me to let my guard down thinking he would. When I saw him at Area 19, I thought things could change. I thought *he* could change." Slowly but surely, the confidence is building in Rosalie's tone. She inches closer to Arthur. "But I was wrong. People like him can't change. Their hate runs too deep. I'm sorry for how opposed I've been to your ideals, Mr. Evandrum. I hope the speech I made tonight is the beginning of me proving myself to you. I meant it. Every word."

Rosalie's breath hitches.

"My father wants me dead. He made that clear when I visited him. His death tomorrow will serve us all. I understand that now. I can see that what you're doing to take back society is the only right way. The way we survive."

Again, Rosalie takes one more step in Arthur's direction until she's three feet from him.

"Please forgive me for my naivety and my lack of vision. I was wrong, and you were right. I hope that moving forward things will be different. Better."

The silence after Rosalie's words extends far longer than I'm comfortable with. I can feel Arthur's prying presence bearing down on her. Calculating her. My own heart rams itself against my chest, hoping against hope that he doesn't suspect . . .

"Why, Miss Timewire, this has been quite an unexpected turn of events." His tone sends razor sharp chills down my spine. It feels as though, somehow, he *knows*. But I can also sense an uncertainty in him, as if he's working out whether his gut instinct is simply a figment of his imagination.

Rosalie holds her hand out toward Arthur, and I can scarcely breathe.

"To new beginnings?" she says.

Arthur considers her for a moment, and then, as if in slow motion, he grasps her hand in his own and shakes it.

"To new beginnings."

An electric shock wave makes me gasp as I feel the intensity of the power transfer from Arthur's hand into Rosalie's. This, however, doesn't faze Rosalie at all, and I can feel the ball of tension dissipate from her abdomen.

"I will see you tomorrow, Mr. Evandrum," she says.

Arthur is still eyeing her intently, and his posture shifts. He still is trying to place what's wrong with Rosalie. Something about that handshake bothered him. Abruptly, he addresses Ashton. "Mr. Teel, please escort Miss Timewire to her training room. She needs to rest."

Ashton jumps, startled by the request, but then he moves to

Rosalie's side at once. "Of course, Mr. Evandrum. Let's go, Timewire."

He pushes Rosalie forward and she nearly trips, but she collects herself, and the two of them exit into the hallway.

The double doors to the balcony swing shut, and I let out a sigh of relief, victory in my heart. I turn to Jonah and Vianne. "She did it," I whisper. "She got the memories."

But just as I'm about to celebrate, my senses hone in on a snarky voice and a pleading one, and my blood runs colder than ice. Terrace DuPont and Olivia Turrick are marching down the hall, shouting at each other, and they're headed directly for Ashton and Rosalie.

I spin around to Jonah, stricken. I keep my voice low, but I can't keep the panic out of it. "Terrace is in the hall!"

"You barely talked to her!" Olivia shouts, pulling at Terrace's arm. This does nothing to halt his steps.

"I don't give a damn about what that whiny bitch has to say!" Terrace retorts, wrenching his arm out of Olivia's grasp. "I don't deserve to be berated for something that's not my call!"

"Terrace!" she roars.

Abruptly, Terrace stops in his tracks, eyeing Ashton and Rosalie, and my heart leaps into my throat. Before I can even think of what to do, Ashton steps in front of Rosalie and his hands cut through the air. I can feel Terrace stiffen, and then he advances on Ashton, cold and calculated.

"What the hell do you think you're doing, Teel?" he snarls. "Take your power off me!"

Ashton smirks, standing tall and fearless, even though

Terrace is nearly a whole head taller than him.

"Oh, I'm just messing around." The way he says this is saturated with mocking.

"You little piece of—"

"I think it's fascinating," Ashton says, cutting Terrace off. He moves his hand in front of his face, stroking the air with his fingertips. "Your ability, Terrace." He cocks his head to the side. "You're *so* useful. Aren't you?"

"Return my power. Now." Terrace threatens, stepping even closer to Ashton.

"You're so useful, yet, you can't do a thing against *my* power. No one can." Ashton nods over his shoulder. "Not even Timewire here. And she's a fully-realized puppet master."

Terrace stares him down. I can feel a palpable rage growing in Terrace's chest. But Ashton is calm. Eerily calm.

"So what does that make you?" Ashton grins, taunting. "Nothing special really."

"You give me my power back right now or I'll—"

"You'll what? Tell Arthur?" Ashton says this like it's nothing of consequence. He leans forward, as if inviting Terrace in for a secret. "You know, I'm thinking that in a few years, I could be Evandrum's right-hand man."

Terrace grabs the front of Ashton's shirt and shakes him. Rosalie gasps, stepping back a few paces, and Olivia joins in, once again pulling on Terrace's arm. But this only angers the ginger-haired man. He shoves Olivia violently, and she falls backward onto the floor.

Terrace turns to her, still keeping an iron grip on Ashton,

"Get out of here, Turrick. Or I swear I'll have Evandrum banish you from the mountain."

Olivia trembles. I can feel her glance between Rosalie and Ashton. But then, she scrambles up from the floor and sprints from the hall, leaving them.

Terrace places his attention back on Ashton, and Ashton's heart rate increases. My mind is firing as well. What is he going to do? Rosalie begins to retreat down the hall in the opposite direction, but Terrace stops her.

"Not so fast, Timewire!" he barks. "Something's going on here, and I'm going to find out what it is. Teel, if you don't take your power off of me right now, you'll regret it. I've been Arthur's right-hand man for *years*, and this little stunt of yours doesn't scare me."

Ashton tries to put up a brave front, but it's fading fast.

"Help me," I whisper frantically to the creature. She materializes by my side, hissing and coiling through the air. I stare into her coal-red eyes, panicked. "What do I do?"

Her gaze is fiery and intensely focused, and within seconds, she brings to my mind the image of how she shields me. She bares her teeth, looking between me and the door.

"Okay," I say, nodding to her.

"Teel, you have three seconds to stop suppressing my power, or I'm dragging you straight to Evandrum," Terrace threatens, shaking him.

But Ashton doesn't budge. He presses his lips together into a disdainful smile and says, "You can't make me do a damn thing."

"But I can," I murmur from the other side of the closet door.

With a flick, I compel Ashton with my ability to stop suppressing Terrace, and in the moments of this exchange, the misty creature dives through the door, crossing the distance between me and Ashton within microseconds. I can feel her black body expand, encircling Rosalie and Ashton and pulsing alive with protective fury.

Terrace grabs Ashton's face, staring him dead in the eye, searching for any information he could pry from him for his insolence.

For several seconds, I hold my breath. I can sense the creature's vibrations. The power of her shield. The strength of her stealth. The moment stretches on and on, and then Terrace shoves Ashton away.

Ashton appears dumbfounded. He looks at his hands, then back to Terrace, and before he can do anything else, Terrace moves to Rosalie, repeating what he had just done to Ashton. He grabs Rosalie's face, and she whimpers, caught off guard by the roughness of his touch. But the creature holds steady, providing a misted barrier.

Terrace pushes Rosalie away as well, swearing under his breath. I can tell that the frustration in him is rising to dangerous levels. He approaches Ashton and pins him to the wall by his neck. Rosalie squeaks, holding a hand up to her mouth.

"I warn you, Teel, you ever do anything like that again, and I'll kill you."

Ashton struggles under his grip, but this only cements Terrace's hold over him. He glances at Rosalie in disgust. "Let me make one thing *very* clear. You and Timewire are only here because of your abilities. You two are nothing more than a means to an end for him. But I'm here because Arthur's my uncle. He's my family. And you will *never* replace me. I mean more to him than you *ever* will."

Terrace releases Ashton, and he stumbles forward, sinking to his knees and coughing violently. Terrace glances between Rosalie and Ashton, and then says with a growl, "This never happened. Are we clear?" He stalks off, his nose in the air.

Ashton and Rosalie stare at each other, panting, and once I sense Terrace has moved out of sight, I turn to Jonah and Vianne, who are staring at me in confusion and awe. "Take your power off of Rosalie. Now."

Jonah and Vianne simultaneously pull their hands back, and Rosalie transforms back to herself.

I burst from the closet, joining Ashton and Rosalie's side.

Rosalie is shaking from head to foot, and Ashton is as white as a sheet. I stare at him, unable to believe it. Ashton Teel protected Rosalie. He protected *me*—and he did it without any hesitation.

"What just happened?" Ashton asks.

"My ability shielded you," I say. "The creature. She shielded you from Terrace like she shields me."

Ashton gapes at me, and so do Jonah and Vianne. But Rosalie is growing evermore pale and sickly. With a violent gasp, she clutches her chest with one hand and covers her mouth with the other, sinking to the floor. She's paler than I've ever seen her. Cold sweat clings to her brow, her hands are trembling, and her eyes glaze over.

"Rosalie!" Vianne cries, crouching in front of her. "What's wrong?"

Rosalie doesn't respond. Her eyes move back and forth, vibrating faster and faster, like she's in a dream state. Her pupils are so wide it's scaring me.

I crouch too. "Jonah! What's happening to her?"

Jonah checks the hall and then kneels, scooping Rosalie into his arms. His tone is urgent. "Let's move. Quickly. To another Sector. Rosalie's watching Arthur's memories. We can't let anyone see her. This can happen when she absorbs a lot all at once. I've seen it before. The memories play out within minutes in her mind. Like a burst."

Rosalie jerks within Jonah's grasp, her eyes still glazed over.

"Move!" Jonah orders, and we all jump into action, whipping down the hall and up the concrete staircase until we've arrived at a new Sector.

Luckily, the new stone corridor we walk down is deserted, and we find another storage closet.

After shuffling in, Jonah sets Rosalie gently on the floor as she continues to convulse.

"Jonah!" Vianne whimpers, grabbing his arm and looking away from Rosalie.

"She's okay. We just have to wait."

The next thirty seconds seem like an eternity, but then Rosalie's body stops shaking, and she becomes still.

"Rosalie?" I murmur.

She snaps awake with a shriek, and her limbs flail like she's fighting off someone.

"Rosalie!" Jonah says, kneeling and grabbing hold of both of her wrists. It takes a few moments to get her to come back to reality, but once she realizes Jonah is the one in front of her, she stills.

She's panting wildly, gulping the air. "I . . . I saw the memories! Jonah, I saw all of them!" She clings to Jonah's forearm, vice-like upon him.

Chills creep down my back. "What did you see?"

She shakes her head, and tears begin to stream down her face.

"Rosalie, what did you see?" I repeat.

She's shaking so much that Jonah's having a hard time steadying her. All of us look at each other, alarmed. What could Rosalie have seen that's producing this kind of reaction?

Hot tears stream down her face and onto her sweater. And what she says next chills me to the bone. "No, Hollis, you have to watch them for yourself."

$$21$$

I'M STANDING IN THE CENTER OF THE HOLODECK, SUR-
rounded by my teacher and my friends. The moment Rosalie
came out of her memory-induced haze, Jonah ushered us through
the halls of the mountain to Sector 1, shuffling everyone into the
last Holo-room and turning on Privacy mode. Ashton went to
find Olivia, Keith, Ben, and Candice—per my request.
Whatever these memories hold, I can't watch them alone. I want
all of them by my side.

There are nine of us in the Holo-room. Keith and Jonah
stand next to me like guardians. Olivia, Ashton, and Vianne are
huddled against the far wall, and Ben is standing behind
Candice with his arms hooked around her waist. Everyone looks
grave, but it's Rosalie who's the palest of us all. "Hollis, are you
ready?"

My heart leaps into my throat.

Rosalie falters, her bright red hair splaying unkempt around her shoulders. She's already sweating profusely. "Just . . . remember what we got these for, okay? We're going to get Maddy."

Her words are strange, and dread settles deep into the back of my mind. I take hold of Keith's hand to steady myself, and I look to Jonah for strength.

"I'm ready," I say.

Rosalie bites her lower lip and screws up her face in concentration. She breathes in and out with a rhythm, centering herself. Then, she throws her hands forward, and black mist spills into the Holodeck, immediately chilling the surrounding air.

Two figures seep from her fingertips: Arthur Evandrum and Olivia Turrick. They're both standing in the middle of what appears to be Olivia's bedroom. A cot appears, along with a side table and a lamp, and Arthur's harsh voice booms.

"It's almost been a month since the government bombed their compound, and still, you've been unable to find her! Why is that?"

Arthur stands tall and menacing, bearing down on Olivia. But Olivia doesn't shrink away.

"I've been looking, okay?"

"For a month?" The vein on Arthur's neck pulses, and he narrows his eyes. "You're particularly adept at finding people, Miss Turrick. They can't have vanished, so where are they? I need that girl."

"I know you need her!" she retorts. "You've made that extremely clear. But I can't magically make them appear. I've searched the site of the bombing over and over again. I don't know where they went. They've hidden themselves well."

"Not good enough!" Arthur breathes his words like fire. "You will continue searching every day until you find her."

At this, Olivia snaps, and she yells at him, throwing her arms up. "I don't want to do this anymore, okay? I'm done! You can't keep asking me to push myself like this. I'm exhausted, and I haven't slept in weeks. I've looked a dozen times over! I don't know what else I can do! I can't find Hollis Timewire." Her mouth trembles at her next statement. "So maybe . . . maybe you have to figure out what moving forward without her looks like."

Arthur stares Olivia down, his posture changing nearly imperceptibly. His voice turns sinister and quiet. "You're done?"

There's a stiff silence that hangs in the air.

"Do I need to remind you of what you owe me?" he sneers. "Perhaps I should pay your family a visit and expose you. Your parents were crushed by your death when you went in for your Test, but imagine their reaction if they found out their daughter was a Diseased One? They would *hate* you. You must know this. You're a smart girl. The shame you would bring them. The grief." Arthur's upper lip curls, and he steps toward Olivia, getting uncomfortably close. "I've kept you out of the world news. I saved your life! You aren't known in the way Hollis Timewire is, and you should be grateful. Fame of that nature is destructive beyond anything you could comprehend. Do you *want* everyone in the world to know your name?"

Olivia's head falls to her chest, but Arthur grabs her chin and tilts her head upward, forcing her to look at him.

"You're not done until I say you're done. Keep searching."

All of Olivia's resistance melts away, and she resigns herself to his request.

"Yes, sir."

The peppery mist dissolves as the scene shifts. Rosalie's hands shudder, and a new burst of mist pours into the Holodeck. Arthur's office materializes, and the memory zooms in to the nine wall screens. A live feed plays, and President Camille addresses the world.

"Citizens, I have wonderful news for every man, woman, and child. We have captured Hollis Timewire and her fellow Diseased Ones."

The feed zooms out, and I see myself, Keith, Candice, and Ben standing on the platform of the Capitol Building, held captive between Camille's puppets. Rosalie lies curled into a fetal position in a pool of her own blood, and Jonah lies near Camille's feet, bound and gagged.

The memory snaps to Arthur, who leaps up from his chair, gaping at the feed like he can't believe his eyes. "What is she doing? Why isn't she fighting?"

Camille's voice roars over the audio. "Their reign of terror is over! And they will pay for their crimes with their lives."

"You have a power, Timewire. What are you doing? Use it!" Arthur cries, unable to take his eyes off the feed. He runs his hands through his gelled-back white hair.

"It is my solemn duty, as your leader, to publicly put an end to this," Camille continues. "Their defiance and hateful destruction of all we hold dear will not stand. Hollis Timewire and her accomplices will die, and once again, the world will be at peace. True and lasting peace!"

At this, Arthur curses loudly and bounds out of his office at a sprint, knocking over several chairs in his haste. The memory follows him through the corridors of the mountain.

It takes him less than a minute before he collides with Olivia at the double doors of Sector 15.

Olivia shrieks, caught off guard, and Arthur grabs her to keep her from falling over. His pale face is flushed.

"She's at the Capitol! Camille's going to execute her!"

"I saw!" she says, gulping the air. "It's on every screen in the mountain."

"GO!" Arthur cries, turning on his heels to run back the way he had come. There's an intense flash of blue as Olivia vanishes from the hall, and the memory dissolves again, reforming back into Arthur's office.

Terrace DuPont bursts from Rosalie's fingertips. He enters the office out of breath, his ginger hair plastered to his forehead.

Arthur is pacing at the far end of the oval table, but he stops the moment Terrace appears.

"We got her. She's here. And unharmed."

Arthur breathes a sigh of relief, brushing a hand along the side of his face. Then, he laughs out loud. It's a manic and piercing laugh that echoes off the stone walls. He pulls on the bottom corners of his white suit jacket, composing himself.

"Does the girl have her ability?"

Terrace nods. "Yes, she used it on me and Olivia once Olivia teleported her to the aircraft hangar."

"Then *why* was she almost shot?" Arthur slides a chair out of his way as he approaches Terrace.

"I don't know."

Holding a hand out in front of his chest, Arthur motions Terrace to lead. "Let's go. And bring Hugo along. I want to be cautious. Something's not right here. She shouldn't have almost died."

The memory implodes in on itself, and Rosalie's arms shudder. With a snap, the scene reforms, sharp and poignant, and a new setting materializes from her fingertips.

Arthur, Terrace, and Beezee appear in one of the largest rooms in the medical ward. Beds line either side of the space, and a cabinet chock-full of various supplies sits against the far wall.

"The girl's alive, but only *just*," Beezee says, flipping her long gray braid over her shoulder. Worry creases her forehead. "That boy broke her jaw and fractured a few of her ribs. If you hadn't pulled him off of her when you did, I don't know what would've happened. It's a miracle she's not dead."

"You can fix her, right?" Arthur asks.

Beezee huffs, popping her hands onto her hips. "Oh, I can fix her alright, but it's going to take some time."

Arthur growls in frustration. "I need to speak with her. *Now*."

"You'll do no such thing!" Beezee scolds. "Her jaw is wired shut! You're not talking to that girl until she's healed. I need her *walking* before you do a thing with her. And that's that."

Arthur rounds on Terrace. His eyes narrow, and his words come out with a snarl. "How could this happen? I thought you said the girl had her power, but that boy almost killed her. Why didn't she use her ability?"

Terrace holds his hands up and backs away a few paces. "She

does have her power! Look, I'll show you. Wren sent this about an hour ago."

Terrace moves to the wall screen mounted to the left of the door. He taps on several menus until he opens up a folder labeled "Area 19 Street Cam Footage." It begins to play. There I am, standing before the Capitol, hands outstretched as a thousand military men are forced to their knees in a torrent of devastating power.

Arthur looks from the screen to Terrace and then back again several times. His lips purse. He whips around to face Beezee and glares daggers at her. "The moment that girl can walk, you bring her *straight* to me."

Flash.

The peppery mist of the memory swirls like a vortex, and we're pulled into Arthur's office. Thirty Board members pop into existence, sitting around the oval table, along with Arthur, Terrace, Hugo, Beezee, and me.

Beezee's sharp words hum. "Arthur, your time is up! I'm taking Hollis back to her room. If she doesn't rest, then there's no point to any of this, so I'm sorry, but this meeting is over."

Arthur clicks the cuff of his sleeve, and the nine wall screens behind his head turn off. "Your timing is impeccable, Beezee-Day. We were just finishing." He addresses me next. "Miss Timewire, please get some rest. We will discuss what can be done about President Camille later."

"Come with me, child," Beezee says in a soothing tone. "I'm sure you're quite exhausted from all of this."

The instant I vanish, Arthur's entire poised and professional façade evaporates, and a dark expression falls like a shadow over his features. No one in the room says a word. It's so quiet that the silence stabs at my ears, and the temperature in the Holodeck drops by a significant amount.

"President Alvaro Camille ..." Arthur murmurs, teeth clenched. "A second puppet master. The leader of the world and my shiny new *pet*... unable to control one another." His gaze flickers to Terrace. "I must admit, this is beyond anything I bargained for. And Miss Timewire is certainly her own little force, isn't she? Making demands of me already. How very brazen of her."

"At least she agreed to help us, and she told us where her people are," Terrace comments. He puts a hand to his chin and leans back in his chair. "Although, I got their location from her on the walk over here. She looked me right in the eye. Practically stared me down. We didn't need her to tell us."

"Yes, well, I'm glad she willingly offered the information," Arthur muses. "It gives her the illusion that she's in control."

Terrace chuckles. "In a way, she is. No one here is a match for her ability."

Arthur doesn't look amused. "She may have agreed to help us, but I sense a resistance in her. I need to get her on my side. It's *imperative*. So for now, I'll play by her rules." His gaze sweeps the other Board members. "*All* of us will."

A slippery grin forms on Terrace's face. "I discovered something else from the girl. Something Aleda's kept quiet about."

Arthur leans forward, eager. "Do tell. Aleda's always been a thorn in my side."

Terrace folds his hands and places them on the table. "The

day the girl betrayed her people—the day of the bombing—Maddy took her power away, and *Aleda* was the one who convinced her to give it up. I suspect she was going to broadcast that victory to the world after killing Timewire. I bet she thought Camille would reward her handsomely for removing the ability of the most powerful Diseased One *and* striking her down in one go. What an accolade for Aleda to add to her resume as Chief Overseer of Area 19."

Arthur's entire demeanor shifts, and understanding lights behind his eyes. His hands creep onto the table like two spiders, and a bold look of excitement flashes through him. "But then . . . if the boy took Timewire's ability *away* . . ."

Terrace nods. "Then that means he gave it back. That kid might just be the answer we've been searching for. All this time, and no one thought the 'secret weapon' of the Terror War could *give* power too."

A shared look passes around the room, and a murmur bristles through the Board members.

"Extraordinary . . ." Arthur breathes. He appears to lose himself in thought, and low whispers travel around the oval table. At first, it's soft, but then the noise grows as the Board members' excitement builds.

Arthur scoffs, and the conversations around the room die. "Of course Aleda would keep something like that to herself. She removes Timewire's power but can't gloat about it because Timewire escaped . . . not to mention Aleda's miserable failure when the girl managed to steal Maddy away from Area 19."

"*And* Timewire stole Maddy *without* her power," Terrace

remarks in a tone that suggests admiration. "She's certainly something, isn't she? A timid society girl turned rogue by her circumstances."

Arthur's brow furrows, and he speaks in low, menacing notes. "She's a loose cannon."

Terrace smirks. "An extraordinary one."

Arthur glowers at Terrace, perturbed, and Terrace shifts in his black leather chair, falling silent. A myriad of uncomfortable glances fire around the oval table.

Arthur adjusts his tie then says, "What do we do about Camille? Of all the things I thought she'd say, it wasn't that. We aren't prepared to deal with two puppet masters."

He looks to everyone present, but no one offers an idea.

Arthur drums his fingers on the tabletop. "We can't move forward with stage one of taking back society until we have a solution to this. Camille's tried to kill her twice now, and he's clearly stronger than her. I can't send her to Area 19 with him there. Anyone?"

Still, no reply.

He balls his hands into fists at the Board members' silence. It stretches on for an unbearable amount of time before Arthur speaks up again.

"Terrace, keep an eye on our new pet puppet master, and see what else you can glean from her."

"Of course, Uncle."

A blur effect transitions the space, and all of the Board members vanish. When the mist reshapes itself, only Arthur, Terrace, and Hugo remain.

A bold red wine stain appears on Arthur's white suit as he stands over the table with his chair pushed back, seething. The vein on his neck thunders, and his cheeks are crimson.

"She won't let me near Maddy! She challenges me in front of my own people! And then she threatens me to force my hand! Tonight was about building rapport with Eli Stone and his associates. But she made me look *weak*. I wanted the Keaton boy to stay *out* of the equation!" He rakes his hands through his gelled-back white hair then slams them onto the table, causing Terrace and Hugo to jump. "If he beats her to death, then what will we do?"

"I don't sense Camille's power anymore," Terrace offers. "I don't think we'll have another incident. As far as I can tell, Keaton is safe."

"I don't have the means to control her." Arthur's gaze skewers Terrace. "Have you discovered anything else from the girl? Something tangible I can use?"

Terrace fidgets with the sleeve of his jacket, looking down at his fingertips. "She cares about protecting her friends."

"Who are her friends?"

"The Keaton siblings, a boy named Ben Bryson, and two other girls named Rosalie Simmons and Vianne Evolet."

"See what you can discover from them."

Terrace nods.

"Anything else?" Arthur asks.

"She views people who protect others as good and noble." He says this like he hopes it will suffice. "Maybe you could show Timewire that you're on her side by removing anyone who opposes her? Like you did with Mr. Thomas tonight. Throwing him out made quite the statement. Besides, she doesn't trust you right now."

Arthur gives Terrace a dark look. "I'm well aware. But I need something more!"

He turns to Hugo, whose bald head shines in the lighting of the office. Hugo strokes his burly mustache with his thick fingers, and his beady eyes spark to life, like he knows exactly what Arthur's about to say.

"Hugo, I think it's time you take a dream walk in Timewire's subconscious. Give her a nightmare and see what you can dig up. I want to know what she cares about and what scares her. I want to know what I can *use*."

Hugo's sinister smile takes over his entire face. He cracks his sausage-like knuckles. "With pleasure."

Arthur waves a spindly hand through the air. "I also need an excuse to examine Maddy. Something that Timewire will allow."

"Let's see what Beezee can come up with," Terrace says.

Flash.

The scene evaporates, and the speckled flakes of Rosalie's power fall like soot over the Holodeck. Within seconds, the medical ward appears, and Beezee bustles about, grabbing items from the drawers of a cabinet and stuffing them into her medical bag. Arthur stands there, watching her.

"I think an ability census should do the trick," Beezee states, matter-of-fact. "And we can make a physical examination part of the requirement. That way, I can get blood samples from everyone new." Beezee's long gray braid whips around her shoulder. "Plus,

I'd like to know what new abilities we've got."

"That's perfect, Beezee-Day. Thank you. I'll suggest it to Eli Stone, and I'll have Hugo handle the scheduling. Once we test Maddy's blood, we may finally see results."

Beezee tisks. "Just because the boy is a type two doesn't mean it will work. I hope you know that."

Arthur folds his arms across his chest. "Type two blood has been the only thing that's shown promise. And now we have more of it. This boy . . . he's special, Beezee-Day. I can feel it."

She studies Arthur's ever-increasing earnestness with skepticism. "You may be right, but we won't know until we have his blood, will we?"

She turns back to the drawers of the cabinet to continue rummaging within its depths.

"How many new type two's do we have anyway?" she asks. "Because it's not a matter of *more* blood, it's a matter of the *right* blood." She shakes her head. "I suppose I'll find out when I complete the ability census."

"I'll ask Timewire's ability teacher. He should know. But I don't think they have many."

The medical ward shudders and then vanishes. More black mist pours from Rosalie's fingertips, and the memory expands, buffeting us back to the periphery of the Holo-room.

Arthur, Hugo, and Terrace sit at the end of the oval table, and Hugo wears a smug look of satisfaction.

"The girl dreamed about her mother dying in her arms," he says. "She was in her home back at Area 19. She killed all of the military men with her ability. It was brutal. Her power made their skulls implode. Like fruit dashed against stone. I've never seen such rage."

Terrace sucks in a hasty breath, almost as if he could feel sympathy pain on the military men's behalf. He grabs the glass of water to his right and takes a sip.

"I'm sure we could use her rage," Hugo comments, a speck of spit landing on his fat lip. "She cares and feels deeply. She also has an incredibly powerful sense of justice. I could do another dream walk to dig up more if you'd like."

Arthur contemplates Hugo's report for a moment. "No, for now that will suffice. Thank you, Hugo."

Hugo dips his head.

Arthur turns to Terrace. "I was thinking about what you said earlier: get the girl to believe I'm on her side by removing anyone who stands against her. I think I've come to a solution that will help all of us."

Terrace and Hugo exchange quick glances, and then Terrace raises the glass of water to his lips once more.

Arthur smirks. "Why don't we kill the President?"

Immediately, Terrace chokes on the water. He coughs violently, spewing it down his front, and his eyes begin to water. But he manages a reply. "That's a bold move."

"But that could work," Hugo adds. His ruddy complexion turns ashen, and his forehead shines with sweat.

Arthur clasps his hands together, placing them on the table. "It's the perfect solution. Camille wants Timewire dead, and Timewire can't control him. So, we eliminate the threat. That way, I protect the girl from a fight she can't win, and she can take Area 19 without resistance."

The blur effect happens again, swirling the vapors of Rosalie's power around. The memory darkens, the mist reforms, Hugo vanishes, and I appear. Arthur's office, however, remains.

Arthur addresses me with deep conviction. "Miss Timewire, should we find no alternative solution, we move forward with *my* idea. One way or another, what we've planned can't happen with Camille in the picture, I trust you know that. And our brighter future won't come without loss. It is the unfortunate nature of war."

"War?" I repeat.

"Yes, war."

"I don't think killing is necessary to achieve what you want to do, Mr. Evandrum."

Arthur's eyes narrow. "Think what you will. But you will soon learn that few things come without this kind of cost."

I glare at him. "And *you* will soon learn that I can be quite surprising."

"Then *surprise* me."

"Don't worry, I will."

I watch myself leave Arthur's office with my head held high, and when the door closes, Arthur grabs the stack of files folders from the table and throws them to the floor, letting out a growl. He stands, knocking over his chair.

"She doesn't want us to kill him!?" he roars. "What am I supposed to do? I can't force the girl to do anything! I've accommodated her, placated her, offered her a solution to this mess, and *still*, she resists. She didn't see the assassination as an offer of protection at all. She views it as irreparable damage to our reputation as the Diseased Ones . . . I need her to *want* to kill Camille. There *is* no alternative. She can't take Area 19 with another puppet master there. I don't care how hard she trains."

Arthur kicks the fallen chair out of his way as he begins to pace. Terrace waits a moment, as if sensing he should let Arthur's anger dissipate before joining in.

He sweeps ginger strands from his face then says, "Maybe we need to take what Hugo said into consideration. Play off of Timewire's sense of justice. If she feels things as deeply as Hugo's dream walk seems to suggest, then let's use that. Appeal to her emotions. We can talk all day long about how killing Camille is the logical choice, but that won't matter. At least not to her."

Arthur's heated stance relaxes, and he stops pacing. He takes a moment to compose himself and then picks the chair up off the floor, standing it upright. He eyes the mess of folders scattered around his feet.

"Perhaps you're right," he mutters. His attention wanders to the screens mounted against the back wall. "I need to do some thinking."

Terrace pops up, scooting himself around the end of the oval table. "I'll leave you to your thoughts."

The scene seems to fast-forward. Shapes and figures zoom in and out of Arthur's office. A collage of grays and blacks shimmer like a splash of stars in the void of night, and then the memory resumes its normal speed.

There are a dozen Board members present, and Terrace is back. His mischievous face holds a secret.

"I found out something interesting," he says, hand to his chin.

Arthur's focus cleaves to Terrace. "What is it?"

"When Timewire was living in the forest, a boy named Ashton Teel and another boy named Darren Mitchell tried to kill her by throwing her into the river. They had a third accomplice—Pierce Bodegard—who was caught, but the Council never caught them." He smirks. "This could be another opportunity for you to show Timewire that your goal is her protection. It may help win her over."

Arthur glances around the room, taking in the people seated before him. He checks the clock on the wall. His face slowly slips into a twisted smile. "Terrace, collect four guards from Sector 2. Brief them on what you've learned, and have them arrest the boys." His eyes flash. "Tell them to make a *scene*. I want the whole of Sector 12 to witness this. Let's see how the girl reacts."

Terrace can hardly hold in his excitement. He bounds up, heading for the door. "On my way. I'll be back shortly."

Again, the memory speeds ahead. It's moving so fast that the only concrete visual is the oval table. And when it plays in real time once more, I appear—along with Rosalie, Ashton, Darren, and the four guards.

Arthur nods to the men holding Ashton and Darren. "Remove these boys from my office."

"Right away, sir."

There's a scuffle as the men escort Ashton and Darren from the room, leaving Rosalie and me behind.

I give Arthur a stiff nod. "Sorry for the interruption. We'll show ourselves out."

"My first priority is keeping you safe, Miss Timewire. They

tried to kill you. You understand, don't you?"

"I understand."

"You're valuable to us. We need you."

"I know."

I hook Rosalie's arm and steer her from the office. A few beats of silence follow.

"That was promising," Terrace says.

"Indeed," Arthur muses. He swivels in his chair to address Hugo. "I'd like you to give the girl another nightmare. This time, let's amp it up, shall we? I wonder what you could glean from her subconscious if you killed her in the dream."

Hugo squeezes his beefy hands together. "No problem."

Arthur stands and turns toward one of the wall screens, tapping on a series of menus. "I'm going on a short trip, gentlemen," he announces. "I have some business to attend to. Hugo, I look forward to your report upon my return."

The foundations of the memory tremble, and it's at this point that the temperature of the Holodeck drops to frigid. Peppery swirls of ink-black twist in a deadly waltz as a tornado-like funnel churns at the center of the room. When the funnel dissipates, the new setting steals all the breath from my body.

Arthur Evandrum is standing in the Capitol Building, in the very room where my friends and I almost lost our lives, and President Camille sits behind his desk, pristine in his societal control, staring Arthur down. Although the two of them share the same stature and build, Camille's jet black hair starkly contrasts with Arthur's shocking white hair.

"I'm curious to know why you've traveled all the way from

Area 7 to seek an audience with me?" Camille begins. "I don't often entertain meetings of this nature. But I'm told you're rather convincing." He cocks his head to the side. "What do you want, Mr. Evandrum?"

The corners of Arthur's mouth quirk upward. "I think the better question is, what do *you* want, Mr. President?"

Camille's black eyes narrow. "Do not waste my time. Why are you here?"

"I have an interesting proposal for you." Arthur bows his head ever so slightly. "And it comes with the opportunity of killing Hollis Timewire."

At the mention of my name, Camille's whole demeanor shifts from on guard to untamed. "You better speak quickly, Evandrum, before I accuse you of knowing where the girl is . . ."

The threat doesn't ruffle Arthur, and he maintains his poised posture. "I'm simply here to point out something your advisors haven't."

"Oh? And what might that be?" Camille leans forward, calculated. His hands look like they're itching to use the power that lies underneath.

Arthur smiles, expressing himself in a manner he shouldn't. "Forgive me, Mr. President, but your attempts to find the girl have been so *feeble* I can't help but conclude that your heart isn't truly in it."

Camille rockets up from his seat. His eyes darken, his jaw stiffens, and he bares his teeth. For a fraction of a second, the beast within makes him appear feral, as if he might launch himself over the desk and strangle Arthur to death with his bare hands.

"You are *dangerously* close to speaking your last words, Evandrum!" he growls.

Arthur appears unfazed. He takes a few steps forward, stopping three feet from the President's desk. "No matter how hard you search for the girl, you won't be able to find her."

"What do you mean?" Camille snaps. Again, it appears he has to restrain himself from grabbing Arthur with his ability.

"If we've learned anything from the Diseased Ones, it's that they hide *well*. Otherwise, they'd all be dead, wouldn't they? What you need to do is *lure* Hollis Timewire out. Then, you can kill her."

Some of the viciousness in Camille's feral appearance tempers. "What's in this for you? You're already a Chief Overseer. There's nowhere higher to climb. You've reached the top."

"All I want is recognition for aiding in the girl's death. Credit, if you will. The notoriety and fame are what I'm after."

Camille considers him, studying Arthur like it might be a trick. But then his expression changes, and his tone turns pensive. "Lure her out, you say?"

"*Yes.*"

"Go on."

Arthur throws his arms wide open, as if inviting Camille in. "What if there were a bombing? Let's say, at a Testing Center. And it was due to Hollis Timewire's terrorist activities. Drag her name through the mud. Blame her for the deaths that occur. Slander her to society's face and broadcast it across the world." Arthur brings his hands back together as he delivers the final statement. "I have no doubt that will bring her out of whatever hole she's hiding in. Because she's too *noble* to let lies like that stand."

Camille's face contorts as the idea takes hold, and then his mouth splits into a cruel smile. "And all you want is credit?"

"After the girl is dead, yes. I'll be the most celebrated Chief Overseer in history."

"What an idea . . ." Camille murmurs, now struck deep in thought.

"Indeed. Just keep Area 7 out of it."

The President throws his head back and laughs. It's a gruesome noise. "Of course, Evandrum. You have my word."

The mist breaks apart like shattering glass, expanding out in every direction. With a crack, it shoots back toward the center of the Holodeck, and Arthur's office forms anew. It's the middle of the night, and Arthur's wearing a pair of black cotton pajamas. Hugo and Terrace are dressed in sleep apparel as well. Then I materialize, and I'm seething at the three men. I shove a chair out of my way. It skids across the floor with a hair-raising screech, and I place both of my hands flat on the table. "I'm going back to bed."

I watch myself turn away, but Arthur's voice stops me.

"Miss Timewire?"

I spin around. "What?"

"Use your time wisely. Camille isn't a patient man. And neither am I."

I scoff and trudge out of the room. The office door slides closed, and Arthur lets out a guttural cry of rage. He tears at his hair and slams his fists repeatedly over the top of the table. He's like a wild beast with shifty eyes and a thirst for blood.

"That infernal, headstrong *BITCH!*" He practically screams it. "I've been planning to take down the Test for over a decade, and after *everything*, I'm stalled by a sixteen-year-old girl with devastating power and a savior complex!"

He gets up from his seat and shoves Hugo out of his way when he doesn't move quick enough.

"I've done everything I can possibly think of to get her to agree to this assassination. I even convinced the President to *bomb* a Testing Center and blame it on her!"

He laughs aloud like he's unable to believe his own gall. He begins to pace, and the wildness in him increases.

"I've played by her rules. I've given her time to train. I've even entertained her foolish ideas of keeping Camille alive by giving her a month to come up with a plan. But she has none, and she has no will to kill him!"

He rounds on Hugo, yelling at him. "You said the girl has a powerful sense of justice! You said she feels things deeply!"

"She does," he murmurs.

Arthur scoffs, still trudging back and forth, restless. "Why didn't the bombing convince her to move forward with the assassination?" He puts a hand to his chin and furrows his brow. "I'm missing something . . ." Abruptly, Arthur barks up at Hugo. "Report on the second dream walk. What happened?"

The beefy man is pale and sweating. Even though he's larger than Arthur, he quells under the intensity of Arthur's fury. He coughs to clear his throat, then proceeds in a cautious manner.

"In the dream, her mother was standing on the roof of the

Testing Center. It looked like she was going to fall, and the girl fought tooth and nail against the military men to get to her—even though her power was gone." Hugo scratches his fat chin. "And then when I pushed the dream to kill her, this metal throne appeared. She was terrified of it. But even as the men tied her to the throne, she wouldn't stop trying to get to her mother. And Camille . . . well, he was the one who stabbed her to death in the end."

At this, Arthur's animalistic energy calms down a bit. There's a palpable silence. The mist of the memory grows thicker. Then, realization appears to strike Arthur. His eyes grow wide, his lips part, and he places a hand to his forehead.

"Two dream walks with mother dearest, huh?" An evil grin spreads across his face. It's so unnaturally wide that all of his teeth become visible. "Gentlemen, I've got it."

"What are you thinking?" Terrace muses with the same chilling smile as his uncle.

"Terrace, why did the girl go to the Capitol in the first place?"

"Camille had Jonah."

Arthur claps his hands. "Precisely! It was personal. It was someone she cared about. *That's* what pushed her to action. This bombing—it wasn't personal."

The three men share a look, and then, like a collective, the idea takes hold.

Arthur's toothy smile deepens. "Camille can use the girl's mother to get her to come out. If Camille kills her, Timewire will *have* to act." He pats Hugo on the back. "You mentioned Timewire's rage when her mother died in her arms during the first dream walk? Imagine if she *actually* died and Camille was responsible? The girl would burn the whole world down to kill that man."

Terrace laughs and then chimes in a playful sing-song. "You're a monster, Uncle. I love it."

Arthur leers. "No, Camille's the monster, and this time, I'm going to make sure Timewire sees it."

The swirls of mist shift like the sands of a vast desert, and Hugo and Terrace disappear from the room. Only Arthur remains. He transforms out of his black cotton pajamas and back into his crisp white suit.

He's hunched over a file folder, feverishly writing down notes, when the door to the office opens. Terrace strides in with an impish glee, rubbing his hands together. "You'll never guess what rabbit hole I've just gone down." He pulls a chair out and sits.

Arthur stops writing. "I know that look. What did you discover?"

"I was able to look directly into Ashton Teel's eyes, and I leached some *very* interesting information from him. Before he got locked up, he spent a lot of time with that metamorph girl, Vianne Evolet. And do you know who Evolet spends a lot of her time with? Miss Hollis Timewire." Terrace's enthusiasm builds. "When I looked into Teel's eyes, I saw a conversation he had with the metamorph, and she shared something that Timewire said. Apparently, Olivia knew the location of Timewire's camp all along. She was lying to you. Hiding them from you."

Arthur perks up.

"But that's not the best part," Terrace adds. "I went snooping to see what else Olivia was hiding. I slipped into her room while she was sleeping, and I discovered two things: one, Olivia Turrick can teleport to a person just by thinking of them. That's how she found Timewire and her people in the forest."

Arthur's eyes widen.

"And two," Terrace continues. "She and Timewire are planning to go to Area 19 to see Timewire's mother. They're going to leave the mountain when you leave for the Quarter review."

Arthur looks like he's won a prize. His mouth curls, his eyes grow hungry, and his posture elevates. "My, my . . . what *scintillating* news."

"Do you want me to stop them?"

Arthur considers him for a moment then shakes his head. "No, let them go. It will make her mother's death all the more tragic."

"What about Olivia? Hiding a portion of her ability from you? Lying to you?" Terrace scratches his red stubble beard. "I'll admit, I've been lazy when it comes to using my ability on her. I should have known something was off when she stopped looking me in the eye. She should be punished."

Arthur waves a hand at him. "I'll deal with Miss Turrick later. For now, let her think she can still hide things." He closes the file folder, sweeps it off the table, and stands. "I leave for the Quarter Review early tomorrow morning."

"Do you think Maddy's blood will make it work?"

"That's what I hope to find out. Beezee sent his blood to the Testing Center lab at Area 7. I have a good feeling about it." He moves toward the door, and his eyes flash. "Wish me luck, Terrace, because I'm about to convince the President to kill Ella Timewire."

The scene dissolves, and a new setting forms. Rosalie's hands shudder. Dark black tabletops appear, followed by test tubes, beakers, Erlenmeyer flasks, graduated cylinders, and hot plates. Then, cabinets materialize, filled with different hazardous chemicals and powders. And two people coalesce into existence: Arthur and George, the chemist.

George is dressed in a white lab coat, and he wears gloves and safety goggles. He's pouring a dark liquid into a ten milliliter graduated cylinder, carefully measuring it out.

When Arthur approaches, George stops his work. He steps back from the workbench and degloves, pulling the material inside out and tossing it into a waste receptacle.

"Mr. Evandrum, the serum is showing remarkable progress!" he says excitedly. "I've never been able to get the biomarker to bind to the host's red blood cells, but when I mix Maddy's blood in, the reaction appears to work. Without overcomplicating the scientific explanation, I simply take the donor blood sample, add a few drops of Maddy's blood to it, and when it's injected into the host's blood, it takes. Look at this!"

He gestures Arthur over to a microscope that's set up on a workbench to his right.

Arthur leans in, placing his eyes to the viewing port.

"This slide is a failed attempt to bind. Do you see how the red blood cells look deflated? Like all the water has gone out of them? And do you notice the gray color around the edges?"

Arthur nods. "Yes, I see."

"If you'll step back a moment," George says. He takes the slide that's clipped under the microscope and exchanges it for a new one. "Now look."

Arthur leans in again.

"That's what the red blood cells look like after I've used Maddy's blood."

Arthur grabs hold of the knob of the microscope to adjust it. He's gaping at the sample. "Are you sure this thing's working properly?"

"I'm sure."

"But the cells . . . they're glowing."

"I know. It's incredible!" he exclaims. "I've exhausted my supply of Maddy's blood. I'll need more to confirm and run additional tests, but I think that I've finally cracked it."

"Do you have a test dose ready?"

George nods. "One. Like I said, I'll need more of the kid's blood before—"

"Test it," Arthur says.

George falters, and some of the excitement in his countenance falls. "But I don't know what the effect will be. There's still so much I need to—"

"I'll get you more of the boy's blood, just test it."

George stares at him blankly and puts a finger up like he's about to challenge the request again.

Arthur's eyes narrow. "Do we not have any test subjects? I thought I made myself perfectly clear."

"We do, it's just that—"

"Then lead the way." Arthur holds out his arm, and after another moment's hesitation, George resigns himself. He grabs a small vial and a syringe, pocketing them.

"This is the only dose, Mr. Evandrum."

"I promise you, the boy will be yours. Now, let's go."

The memory moves with the two men, snaking through the halls of the Area 7 Testing Center. Within minutes, they stop at a room with a large steel door guarded by four men with machine guns. George murmurs something to the tallest man, and he turns toward the door, tapping a code into the keypad that sits at its center.

The memory sharpens, chilling the air of the Holodeck down to ice cold, and the door groans.

"We've secured two test subjects," George says. He wipes his brow with the back of his shaking hand.

"And what have you told their families?" Arthur inquires.

"For the boy, we said he panicked during his Test and tried to stab his nurse, so he was shot. And for the girl, we said she had a stroke after her blood draw and passed away."

"Good."

The large steel door creaks open to reveal two sixteen-year-olds: a boy with brown skin and black curly hair, and a girl with strawberry blonde hair and freckles. They're both sitting on the bare stone floor, chained to the back wall by their ankles, and they appear incredibly malnourished. Their clothes are dirty, and their skin is covered in grime.

The girl shrinks back at Arthur and George's approach, but the boy goes wild, jumping up and yelling at the top of his lungs.

"You can't keep us in here forever! We didn't fail the Test! We're not Diseased Ones! When my father finds out what you've done, you'll be sorry!"

He's completely abandoned his societal restraint. He charges forward as far as the chains around his ankles will let him.

Arthur smiles wickedly. "Your father thinks you're dead. You don't exist anymore, young man. Your purpose is now far greater than it ever would've been outside of this place." Arthur nods to the guards. "He'll do. Restrain him."

The men move in unison to arrest the boy's arms, causing the girl to shriek. He kicks and fights, but he's no match for them.

"Keep him still," Arthur instructs. He turns toward the pale scientist at his wake. "George, you may proceed."

George walks up to the boy and pulls out the vial and syringe. With quick fingers, he expertly withdraws the dark fluid from the bottle.

"What are you doing?" the girl squeaks, unable to keep herself composed.

George ignores her and sticks the needle into the boy's arm, emptying the contents in its entirety.

"You may release him," George says to the guards.

They obey, and the boy shoves them off. He stands, panting and glaring at Arthur. But then, he doubles over, gasping and clutching his stomach. His face contorts, he falls to his hands and knees, and he starts to writhe. His screams echo off the stone walls, sharp and terrible.

After thirty seconds, he becomes still, and George stares at him in silence.

But then, the boy sits bolt upright with bloodshot eyes. He's staring at his hands in horror. A soft red glow shines under his palms, like the embers of a dying fire. Abruptly, a flame dances to life on his bare skin. He screams, swatting at it until it dies. But the flames have already done their damage; scorched flesh remains.

The boy's face goes white. He vomits and begins to cry. He looks between Arthur and George with watering eyes. "What have you done to me?"

Arthur's look of triumph is contrasted by George's look of shock.

"Congratulations, young man," Arthur says, giving him a sweeping bow. "You're a Diseased One."

Without another word, Arthur leaves the room, and George scampers after him. The heavy door shuts, sealing the teenagers in.

The scientist stumbles over his words. "It works! I—I did it! It—well, it's not supposed to burn him. That vial was 'fire,' but using his power shouldn't have burned him. I need to do more tests. The serum isn't perfect, but . . ." He gapes at Arthur. "I gave him a power."

Arthur claps him on the back, and his voice booms. "You did, indeed."

The two of them stride down the hall with a new spring in their step.

"As promised, I'll deliver Maddy to you. He will stay here, at the Area 7 lab, safe and secure. I'll have Jenkins prepare a room for him."

George nods, still overwhelmed by what he just witnessed.

"Well done, my friend." Arthur grasps George's hand and shakes it. "You've just changed history—and you've saved us all."

Flash.

The Area 7 Testing Center vanishes, and the Capitol Building takes its place. Arthur is standing before President Camille once more, and Camille is enraged. He advances on Arthur.

"You said the bombing would work! You said the girl would come out, but she hasn't! And now I've lost a Testing Center. All for nothing!"

"I was mistaken," Arthur replies calmly, holding his hands up in a gesture of surrender. "But I think I know what will work now."

"Why should I listen to a word you have to say?" Camille demands.

"Because, this time you'll be using someone the girl *loves.* Isn't that why she came to you before? You caught that Diseased One and threatened to kill him to get her to come to the Capitol. Well? Why not do that again?"

Camille's black eyes rove over Arthur, and his aggressive stance tempers. "I'm listening."

"Why not use the girl's mother? Make it something she can't possibly ignore. It should be a public spectacle. A broadcast so devastating that the girl *must* act." Arthur appears to mull something over, then he puts on a devilish leer. "You could throw her mother off the roof of the Testing Center and let the world watch. Now *that* would be a spectacle."

Camille's interest piques, and he grins, eager and beast-like.

"You've surprised me in a way not many have, Mr. Evandrum."

Arthur dips his head at the compliment. "I have one other idea you may find helpful."

"Oh?"

"I don't know how you plan to kill the girl, but may I make a suggestion?"

"Please do."

"The girl controls people. That's her disease. So why not use Holo-tech against her? She can't fight if there are no puppets." Arthur's face cracks a sickly smirk. "And why not kill the girl in the metal throne she was meant to die in when she failed the Test? It's poetic, in a way. A full-circle moment. The throne is a symbol of the Test, an institution you've worked your whole life to uphold."

Camille lets out a dark laugh, and he eyes Arthur with pleasure. "How poetic indeed."

The memory shudders and begins to unfold on fast-forward. The peppery flakes of the Capitol room blur, and figures move in and out of focus. When the scene resumes, it feels like my heart has been ripped from my chest.

Two of the President's puppets carry my mother into the room, throwing her to the carpet at Camille's feet. She hits the floor. Hard. And when she lifts her head, blood dribbles down her chin from a busted lip. Arthur and Camille tower over her, leering down at her.

"W-why am I here?" she whimpers.

The two men glance at each other, smiling in a depraved manner.

Camille kneels down to her level. "Because, my dear, I'm going to kill you."

She turns as white as a ghost and begins to cry. Tears flow from her gaunt, corpse-like face. "I've f-followed the rules!" she wails. "I've been an obedient citizen!"

Camille grabs a fistful of her hair, yanking her to a sitting position. His hand caresses the side of her face. "Oh, Ella," he coos. "You and I both know that's not true."

"P-please."

"This isn't personal," he continues. "It's business. Your death has a purpose. All I really want is to kill your daughter."

At this, my mother's jaw trembles, and she puffs out her chest, putting on the bravest face she can muster. But tears still trace her porcelain cheeks. "You won't be able to find her."

Camille chuckles. "I know that. I'm not looking for her anymore. Did you know? I'm going to get her to come to me. That's why I need *you*."

My mother's face falls, and she shakes her head in horror.

Camille's wolf-like smile deepens. "Look at you, putting two and two together. She'll come out of hiding for you, Ella. And then, I'll kill her, because this time, thanks to Mr. Evandrum, I'll be prepared."

"Please don't kill her! Please!" she begs. "I'll do anything if you spare her! I'll give you anything! Please!"

Her words seem to fuel the President's fun. He pulls my mother up from the floor, pinning her against himself so that her back is to his chest. His lips brush her ear, and he strokes her neck with his free hand. "You have nothing left to give me, Ella. I've already had my way with you. And you kept it a secret all these years like a good society girl."

My mother strains against him, but he keeps her in place. He puts his nose to her hair and inhales deeply. "Mmm, this reminds me of that night. You smell the same. So sweet. Like a rose."

"That night wasn't what you think," she says, gritting her teeth. "You didn't take advantage of me. I took advantage of *you*."

Camille sways her back and forth in a forced waltz, still keeping her pinned to his body. "Whatever do you mean, my dear?"

A fire lights in her spirit. She inhales sharply. In her face, I can see all the determination and fight she's suppressed for so many years. It's like she's accepted her own death but won't accept mine. She puts all of herself into her next words: "She's yours, Alvaro."

Camille stops swaying. There's a deafening silence. All of the color drains from the President's face, and Arthur, who has stood quietly watching from the sidelines, gapes at her.

Camille spins Ella around, grabbing her by the throat and pushing her back until she slams into the bookcase. She gasps.

"What did you just say?" he growls.

Her eyes are streaming, and her voice comes out taut with emotion. "She's yours. Your daughter. I slept with you to get pregnant, and it worked." Her whole body trembles as she grasps Camille's forearms, looking him right in the eye. "So kill me if you must, but please don't kill Hollis. She's yours."

Camille stands back from her, releasing her neck. She coughs, clinging to the bookshelf.

It's like Camille's been punched in the face. A stricken look flickers over him, but then it's swallowed in a boiling rage that brings out the beast. With a powerful blow, he backhands my mother across the face, and she shrieks, falling to the floor. He stoops down and grabs her by the hair, dragging her back to the center of the room.

"SHE'S MINE?" he roars.

He releases my mother and screams, tearing at his hair with a howl of madness. The black in his eyes expands, and Arthur steps back a few paces.

Camille gets on his knees, pinning her head to the carpet with the flat of his palm. He seethes, getting within inches of her face.

"Listen to my words, Ella. I'm going to take *great* pleasure in killing Hollis, and you're going to listen to every excruciating detail of my plan. Because I want you to know that this is *your fault.* If you thought you could appeal to my better nature, I have none! Hollis's death is on you! And you can do *nothing* to stop me." He glances at Arthur. "I have Mr. Evandrum to thank for his inventive suggestions and sadistic ideas. He's made quite a useful new advisor."

"She won't come for me," she says, crying and struggling against him, but he keeps her head pinned to the floor.

"She will!"

My mother glares at him with the strength she has left. "You won't win, Alvaro. Change is coming. And *she's* that change."

Whoosh.

The scene slips away, and we're sucked back into Arthur's

office in the mountain in the blink of an eye.

I'm standing in front of Arthur in my teal party dress, and Arthur's writing a note. Terrace sits by his side like a shadow. When Arthur finishes, he hands the paper to me.

"Give this to Erwin."

"Thank you. Am I free to go?" I ask.

"Yes, you're free to go. Have a good evening with Mr. Keaton."

I exit the room with quick steps, and when the door closes, Arthur's attention meanders to the wall screens. He appears pensive and focused. "Terrace, I've come to a decision I never thought I would."

"Oh? And what's that?"

Arthur stands, readjusting his tie. "For a while now, I've wondered if killing Hollis Timewire is better than keeping her alive."

Terrace shakes his head, shocked. "What do you mean?"

"After meeting with the President, two things have become clear. Alvaro Camille is a threat only in that he possesses a power stronger than anyone who could oppose him. But he's a simple man driven by his animalistic side and isolated from everyone because of the ability he hides. Even if I hadn't used my silver tongue on him, I would've been able to convince him to carry out my plans." He pauses and presses his hands together. "Hollis Timewire, however, is a far more dangerous creature. She's powerful and intelligent in a way that's infuriating. She pushes back. She's driven to do things *her* way, and as she matures, she will only grow in her ability to bend circumstances to her favor.

I recognize a leader when I see one. She's a force I will have to deal with one way or another."

"But isn't the girl crucial to taking back society? I thought you wanted to do this without losing people with powers to bloodshed along the way?"

"*Not* if I can't control her," he replies coldly. "Her response to her mother's death tonight will tell me which path to take. If Timewire decides she wants to kill Camille, I'll warn her of what's waiting at the Testing Center. I'll tell her not to go, and then we'll plan Camille's assassination. She will have finally bent to my will—and that's all I really wanted from her. But if she persists, I'll let her go to Camille and allow the cards to fall where they may."

Terrace takes a hard swallow. He tugs on the collar of his shirt like he can't get enough air. "What if she survives Camille?"

Arthur's eyes flash. "That is an outcome I'm currently mulling over. I have a few ideas, but for starters, I'm going to kidnap Maddy to keep her in check. If Timewire chooses to go to Camille, the guards have instructions to take the boy. But if she decides in favor of the assassination, I'll have to figure out a different way to collect him. Either way, the lab needs his blood."

Arthur strides over to the door and his face twists with sickening pleasure. "Hollis Timewire's fate is in her own hands now. Let the games begin, and may the best puppet master win."

The memory roars like a feral beast, and then it shatters into a thousand peppery pieces. The black mist falls over the Holodeck, enchanting and devastating, and all of us are left in a heart-pounding void of death-like silence.

22

I SINK TO MY KNEES.

It's like I'm falling through time. Back and back again. Flashes of what I've just witnessed capture me and hold me hostage. It's paralyzing. Everything I've done. Every decision. Every secret. They were never mine. From the moment I stepped foot in this mountain, Arthur Evandrum was the mastermind, and I was simply his chess piece.

He killed my mother . . .

A scream lodges itself in my throat, but I can't force it out. Instead it chokes me, suffocating me with its cruel claws. Colors streak across my vision. Muffled voices echo around me. Someone's hands clamp onto my shoulders.

"Hollis! Hollis?"

Jonah's face comes into focus. Sweat clings to his forehead, and shock creases his brow.

My ability hums underneath my skin, and strength finds its way back into my body.

"

I grip Jonah's forearms with iron intensity, and anger laces my whisper. "Arthur killed my mom."

The sadness etched into my teacher's expression mirrors the grief clawing at my heart.

We stare at each other for what feels like an eternity, and I can sense that Jonah's trying his best to keep himself collected.

I remember the moment I lost my mother. I can still see it so clearly in my mind's eye: her tear-stained, gaunt, beautiful face . . . then she stepped into nothingness and fell to her death. The rage I felt for Camille, the absolute hatred, the desire to kill him . . . all of that feels dull compared to the fire of wrath that's coursing through my veins now.

The scream pushes its way up my esophagus, but still, I can't release it. It's like a branding stick, white-hot against my throat.

The creature's energy builds in my chest, vibrations skitter down my limbs, and my lungs heave. With a burst, the snakish animal of my power comes alive, and she curls around my torso, baring her fangs.

All of my senses explode. The clarity of my vision quadruples, the range of my hearing increases, and the sensitivity of my smell sharpens. I'm a beast with a thirst for vengeance, and my power prowls beyond the walls of the Holodeck, ready to strike. Within seconds, I can detect the scent of every person in the mountain. I can feel every heartbeat. I can hear every breath.

I hone in on Arthur Evandrum like a bloodhound, and my hands raise.

There's a collective gasp.

"Hollis, NO!" Jonah roars, gripping me by my upper arms and shaking me.

The creature growls, and my attention snaps to him. His brown eyes appear so sharp to me, almost as if flecks of gold were glowing deep within his irises. I can feel Jonah's deep panic. His pounding heart rattles to the pulsing of my power.

"Don't." His tone has softened, but his grip on me hasn't. "You can't confront Arthur. Not yet. We don't have Maddy."

I'm still gazing at him with a wildness beneath my chest, and the creature is fueling it. Jonah can't stop me. No one can. It would be so effortless. And I could finally make Evandrum pay . . .

"Hollis, stand down," Jonah coaxes, still firmly keeping me in place.

The smoky snake encircling my chest hisses at Jonah's words. I turn my gaze toward her. Her deep red eyes bore into mine, and I can feel her violent protectiveness over me. She would do anything for me. I can feel her rage and my own twisting together to create a storm of devastation. Like we could end the whole world together . . .

But deep in the recesses of my mind, Maddy pulls at my heart. Jonah's right. I can't face Arthur without rescuing Maddy first.

"Go," I whisper to her. "I'll be okay."

The creature inclines her head, still boring deep into my soul, and then she bows, slinking back into my chest and vanishing from my sight.

I look back to Jonah, rage still tangible in my abdomen.

He pulls me into an embrace and rests his chin on the top of my head. I hug him back, attempting to ease the erratic thumping of my heart.

"We found Maddy," Jonah breathes.

I cling to him, and the pieces of my resolve shatter around me. I've learned so much in the past hour and my brain is simply refusing to cooperate. It's shorting out and overloading all at once, flying through the revelations with unsettling speed. My mother . . . the true nature of the serum . . . Arthur's plan for society . . . the Area 34 bombing . . . Arthur's willingness to let me die by Camille's hand . . .

"Can you stand?" Jonah asks.

My fingernails dig into Jonah's skin as he helps me to my feet. All of my friends are staring at me. There's a silent horror playing across their features like a haunted symphony. I must have had black eyes when the creature emerged . . . or perhaps they're as shell-shocked as I am from what we've discovered.

Rosalie approaches me, tears speckled across her freckled face. She wipes them away with the back of her hand. "We're going to get Maddy."

"Hollis." Keith says my name like an enchantment, joining my side and grabbing my hand. "Tell them what you told me. About Maddy."

I'm shaking, but I grip Keith's hand fiercely, intertwining my fingers in his. I peer around at my friends, and then my gaze lands on Jonah. "I talked to Maddy. In my dreams. I don't understand it, but Maddy's power has formed some kind of connection to mine. The golden light helps him."

Jonah's mouth parts, and his eyebrows climb his forehead. "He talked to you? Are you sure?"

I nod. "He described some things about where he is. He told

me there's the number eight above all the doors. He's got to be on the eighth floor of the Area 7 Testing Center. A man named Jenkins watches him. He has had a cut on his eyebrow. Maddy also gave me the code to his room. 3-3-4-6-7. And then he said that . . ." I swallow hard. "It's working now. George's serum."

The memory of the teenage boy's scalding flesh rips through my subconscious. His screams. His convulsing body. How horrifying to get the first ever dose. My eyes burn, and my stomach roils. This can't be real. This can't be happening . . .

"This is crazy!" Ben pipes up. His lanky, boyish features are as pale as a sickly person. He slaps a hand to his forehead. "Turning people into Diseased Ones? What does Arthur think he can do? Force everyone to take the serum?"

"That's exactly what he thinks," I say, revulsion ripping through my insides. "That's why my father is going to die. Not because he hid the location of the rebel group, but because he won't take it. Arthur's offering all of the prisoners the chance to take it, and if they don't, they die."

There's a collective intake of breath from everyone.

"He can't do that!" Rosalie squeaks. "If people here knew what was happening, they wouldn't stand for it. They would push back."

"But people don't know!" Ben snaps. "That's the point. That's why Arthur's been so secretive." His jittery fingers twist through the hair at the base of his neck, and his skin shimmers with sweat. He looks like he's had too much caffeine. "I knew I had a bad feeling about this stage two thing."

"Okay, but Arthur's going to have to tell people eventually, right?" Ashton says, joining in. "If he's planning to turn everyone into Diseased Ones, people *will* find out. And when they do, they'll put a stop to it. No one's *actually* going to support this. There are sensible people here. Nobody is anywhere near as psycho as Evandrum is."

Olivia grinds her teeth together, laughing out loud. It's a harsh laugh that startles everyone. "You really think Arthur's going to announce that he's killing people who don't take a power? No, he'll make sure everyone sees that this serum is for the betterment of humanity. He'll probably make it optional at first. When he announces this, it's going to seem like our salvation—the Pure Ones' key to survival. A new world where everyone has a power. Where no one will have to die because of their blood, because everyone will have the *same* blood."

Olivia's statement grabs a hold of my brain and yanks it back to Arthur Evandrum's hope-filled words as he sat sipping red wine at our welcome meal: "If we accomplish what we've set out to do with this research, no one with an ability will have to suffer and die at the hands of society *ever* again."

Candice takes a timid step toward Olivia, tucking a lock of brown hair behind her ear. "Do you think—if more people knew about this *before* Arthur announces anything—that we could stop this?"

"Yeah, we need more people on our side," Vianne insists. Her hair changes through a collage of color, settling on a deep blue. "We need our band of rebels to get bigger. We have twenty-six people. That's it. That's not enough to stop anything. We should tell everyone what we know before Arthur has a chance to twist things his way."

Olivia pinches the skin between her eyebrows, letting out a frustrated noise. "It's not that simple. As much as I'd love to recruit more people to our secret meetings, we have to be careful. There are people who are fiercely loyal to Arthur's vision—people who are prejudiced against society members. They were raised their whole life in hiding, knowing that the world would love to see them dead. Society members are evil to them. This thinking runs deep, and it's generational. We can't go blabbing about things, because we don't know who will report it to Arthur. How would we explain knowing this information?"

Ben shakes his head. "But we were raised in hiding too, Olivia." He gestures around. "And we don't hate society members. Yeah, it sucks that the government lied to people about the Diseased Ones, but we recognize it for what it is."

Olivia sighs. "I don't know what it was like for your group, Ben, but you guys were small. About four hundred. Right? Your culture may have been one of acceptance and moving on. Learning to forgive because you couldn't change things. But that's not the culture of the mountain. There are thousands of us here. Not to mention thousands more who chose to go undercover in society to pull off this takeover. The idea of living out in the open again has been ingrained in the minds and hearts of everyone here. For generations. And Arthur's finally accomplished that. There are so many people who are willing to do whatever it takes to further Arthur's cause."

"Even at the cost of society members?" Vianne asks.

"*Especially* at the cost of society members," she affirms. "We need to be careful. We can't talk about this with just anyone.

We'll tell our group of twenty-six for now, but that's it. We can't risk anything more. Especially not without Maddy in our hands."

"Olivia's right," Jonah says. "No one besides those who are involved in Maddy's rescue can know about this. Not yet. For now, we let things play out on Arthur's timetable. Our priority is Maddy, and now that we know where he is, we can plan a rescue."

There's a stiff silence that falls across the Holodeck. It feels insane that we've learned the truth and can't speak about it. It's like having a hot coal on the tongue—unbearable, but spitting it out would start a fire that would make things unimaginably worse.

Ashton rubs his hands together, a look of determination coming across his face. "Getting Maddy back will help stop Arthur. The scientists need his blood, right? That's why the serum works. If they don't have his blood, they can't make more doses. I don't know how many doses exist already, but that will halt production."

I breathe a sigh of relief, staring at Ashton with a sense of wonder in my heart. He really has changed. I never imagined the boy who hated me enough to try and kill me would be on my side, but here he is, ready to fight with us.

"So, what do we do now?" Candice asks, hugging Ben's arm.

The fire at my core ignites anew. My ability, still churning with rage, zips through my limbs with electric energy. I let go of Keith's hand and take in every anxious face around me. These people are more than just my friends. They're my family. We're in this fight together, and I'll burn the world down to protect them. I grit out my words with stone cold determination. "We're going to gather the rest of the band of rebels, we're going to tell them what we know, and then we're going to do whatever it takes to get Maddy back. I may not be able to save my father, but I'll be damned if I don't save that little boy."

My hands curl into fists, and my heart screams in my chest. It feels like my blood is on fire. I wish I could run away with all of the people I love, go into hiding, and forget about this world. I wish I could live in blissful peace. But that's not possible. I can't run away from this serum, and I can't run away from this new world. I must face it head on. I must be what my mother thought of me in her dying moments: the change.

I'm the leader. I'm the one who has to end this. Deep down, a part of me knew this all along. To be a puppet master. To carry the power I hold. It's my responsibility to wield it for good no matter what.

All of the hate I've been collecting for Arthur laces deep to my bones and broils there like a dark plague. To know that I must pretend to be fully on Arthur's side is a cruel poison to choke on. But I'll be his good little puppet master. I'll be his perfect, submissive pawn, because when the time is right—when I'm no longer under his thumb—I'm going to kill Arthur Evandrum.

23

THE EARLY MORNING SUN PAINTS ORANGE HUES ACROSS A baby blue sky dotted with gray clouds. There's a crowd gathered on the airstrip outside of the mountain, and as the chill of dawn sweeps across the pavement, so does the chill of death.

A crisp breeze tosses loose strands of blonde across my forehead. I make no attempt to sweep them away. I keep as still as a statue, even though there's a storm of unnamable emotions brewing in my soul. Twenty yards from me is a metal platform with a silver square post sticking up from its center. The execution platform.

To my left, Arthur Evandrum stands tall and proud, his white suit pressed to perfection. To my right, Wren Zayla taps her finger in an eerie rhythm on her bicep. Behind us, the families of the fallen huddle together, gazing ahead at the platform and waiting with baited breath. I can practically feel their hatred at my back, but I don't look at them. I keep my attention on the silver square post, and with all that I am, I hold the shards of myself together.

My ability rages beneath my skin, boiling my blood and searing my fingertips, but I forbid the creature to come. I'm too afraid of what I could do to the man inches from me—the man I loathe with everything I possess. The man who, after today, will have taken both of my parents away from me.

There's a hushed spattering of whispers and a scuffle of footsteps. It comes from the depths of the crowd. As they part down the center, it takes every ounce of my self-control not to break the façade of no feeling that's etched across my face. Two men in beige uniforms lead my father toward the platform. He's chained hand and foot, so his movements are slow. The injuries he's sustained from torture look gruesome. Sickening. His pepper-gray and blond hair is streaked with dirt, his frame is thin and frail, and his sky blue eyes look like he's lost the will to fight.

And then those sky blue eyes find me . . .

I can't stop the physiological reaction of tears. They well up faster than I can staunch them. But my face? I keep it as stone cold as a society member's because Arthur Evandrum is staring me down.

The two guards bring my father forward. With quick steps, they pull him up a set of metal fold-out stairs and take him to the square post, chaining him there with his arms behind his back. After they finish, they retreat down the steps and join the line of guards standing a dozen feet from the edge of the platform—ten men in all, and each has a gun slung over his shoulder.

My heartbeat thuds into my ears, and sweat beads across my body. The morning air tosses my hair again, this time whipping it off of my face. It's frigid, and I suppress a shiver. I'm fighting to keep the trembling in my chest from entering my limbs. I hate this, and I hate Arthur. But most of all, I hate that I have the power to stop this and can't.

Arthur turns to address the silent crowd, and like an obedient drone, I turn with him. I gaze upon the faces of the people who have lost their loved ones. They're a mix of melancholy and madness.

"Brothers and sisters," Arthur begins, his tone deep with sorrow. "We are gathered here to witness the execution of Silas Timewire. This morning, justice prevails. This man's death will not bring back those we have lost, but I hope it will give you some peace of mind and heart. He will never be able to hurt anyone ever again."

There's a bristling of menacing murmurs that waft over the airstrip. Arthur faces my father and calls to him in a loud voice. "Silas Timewire, on this day, by firing squad, you shall meet your end. You have been condemned to die by your own actions. Do you have any last words?"

My father shifts his gaze to Arthur. There's a beat of silence. Then he lifts his chin up in defiance, pressing his cracked lips together and mustering a stone cold front.

"Very well then," Arthur says, nodding to his men.

The group of ten guards raise their guns in unison.

My father's face burns a hole right through my heart. One of his eyes is still swollen shut, but with the other, he's staring at me like he's asking for help—begging for it. I want to look away. I don't want to witness the moment his soul leaves his body. But I keep my gaze on him, the sadness I'm not supposed to show now soaking my expression. My hands shudder with power, though none of it leaves my fingertips, and I mouth the words, "I'm sorry."

The guns go off with a noise so loud it causes my heart to leap. My father slumps down the post. Just like that, the light in him is gone, and blood seeps through the holes in his prison shirt.

I clamp a hand over my mouth to stifle my cry. It feels like a huge fist has seized my chest, sucking the air from my lungs. I feel a firm hand on my shoulder, and fear jumps down my throat. I can't pretend to be okay right now. I can't look at Arthur, or I might tear him apart.

But it's not Arthur's hand that grasps me. It's Wren's. She steers me away from the crowd, away from the platform, and further onto the airstrip.

When we're a fair distance from all the commotion, Wren purposefully places herself between me and the platform so that her body blocks my view of it.

She doesn't say anything. She simply stares at me with a look that gives me permission to fall apart. I bury my face in my hands and let out a sob. The cry wracks my body. Air passes out from my lungs like I'll never get it back. Like I could suffocate and die from the pain. After a violent spasm, I suck in a new breath and sob again.

Wren stands with her arms across her chest, silent. Her

battle-hardened face is neutral. Patient. Waiting.

I allow one last bitter cry to escape my mouth, and then I shut it down. Snot runs from my nose, so I wipe it away on my sleeve as my chest heaves. Slowly, I take back control of my breathing.

In and out.

In and out.

All the while, Wren still blocks the platform from my sight. We stand there without speaking for almost ten minutes, and when my eyes are dry and my face is no longer littered with tears, Wren gives me a stiff nod.

"Let's go back," she says.

I follow her soundlessly, and in my heart, I'm grateful that she pulled me away from Arthur. It's as if she knew I needed the space to break down. But now my walls are back up. Now my face is hardened once more.

We approach the platform. My father's body is no longer there. The only thing left is a pool of blood with smeared footprints. I can't bring myself to ask Wren where they've taken him. I don't know what Arthur plans to do with his body, but I can't show that I care.

Just past the platform, the crowd has thinned to half its size. People are clumped in groups, crying and comforting one another.

When we reach the scene, Arthur strides up to me, business-like and unbothered, as if he didn't just give the order to have my father killed in front of me. "Miss Timewire," he says, fiddling with the cuff of his jacket. "We're going on a little trip. I have something I need to share with you now that you've seen reason."

My stomach does a summersault. "Where are we going?" I glance back at Wren, but her jaw is set. She's not going to say a word.

"To see an old friend of mine," Arthur replies, a sinister glimmer in his eye. "Wren, is everything ready?"

"Yes, sir."

"Then let's leave."

Wren marches off in the direction of the aircraft hangar, and Arthur takes my shoulder and pushes me forward. His touch makes my skin crawl, and my ability snarls in my head. Moving ahead, I join Wren's side so I don't have to walk next to him.

The Beechcraft is waiting for us with the stairs folded out and ready for passengers. I take a hard swallow, nerves firing up through my chest and squeezing the air from my lungs. Where are Arthur and Wren taking me? Who is his old friend? A sense of foreboding hangs in the air, and it mixes with my mourning heart.

"Keep it together," I murmur to myself.

Arthur doesn't hesitate climbing into the belly of the aircraft. Wren doesn't either. She slips in like a wisp of smoke, and I'm left standing on the concrete staring up at the Beechcraft wanting to run away.

"Miss Timewire?" Arthur says.

His voice jolts me to move. I climb the stairs and enter the interior, with its overpowering new leather smell. In a grand gesture, Arthur indicates the seat he would like me to take, and I sit with a stiffened posture. The sound of the Beechcraft's door slamming shut makes me jump. And once the belly is closed and secure, Wren starts up the engines.

Arthur strides over to the seat directly across from me. He sits, sweeping the tail of his suit jacket out as he does so.

His gelled-back white hair and pristine societal look is nauseating. I feel trapped in a storm of rage that I can't unleash. So I simply stare back at him with tight lips and a fake confidence.

His brown eyes rove over every inch of me, examining me, searching me for what lies underneath. But I won't break. Whatever this mission is, I'm going to prove myself to be his loyal soldier once again.

Arthur tilts his head to the side as the Beechcraft begins to taxi onto the airstrip. "I'll admit your change of heart surprised me." His hands creep onto the built-in table that's situated between our two plush armchairs. "It's time for a new chapter, Miss Timewire."

The atmosphere of the cabin is stifling. I can't breathe properly. My head pounds, and my heart thuds, and still, I keep my face impassive.

"Did you mean what you said to me about new beginnings?" he inquires, raising an eyebrow.

I channel focus into my answer. "Yes."

Arthur is scrutinizing me like my response is a trick. His upper lip curls. "Are you quite *sure*? I couldn't help but notice your reaction to your father's execution. Your eyes still have a lingering rim of red."

His words dig into me like a knife, and tears threaten me; my anger, however, helps me hold them at bay. I speak candidly, despite the lump building in my throat. "I needed a moment. I don't like the sight of blood. I'll say this once, and once only: I'm *glad* he's dead but … he was still my father. I just—I needed space to compose myself. Is that so wrong?"

The look Arthur gives me doesn't bode well, so I forge ahead, layering conviction into my tone.

"I meant what I said to you, Mr. Evandrum. I was naive before. I didn't understand why you were imprisoning people, but I do now. You're protecting us—establishing control with an iron fist so that no one with power-filled blood has to die. I understand. I'm ready to continue doing my part for the New World Order. *Willingly*. And I will keep proving myself to you until you believe me."

He folds his hands together, and his eyes narrow. I want to look away because the sight of him makes my insides roil, but I don't. Silence ticks by second upon second. I can see something working behind his steely gaze …

"Do you have any idea where we're going, Hollis?"

His use of my first name elicits a shiver that runs down the length of my spine. I'm so thrown off by this that my stoic look slips into one of surprise. I quickly compose my face again.

The Beechcraft's engines roar, and the plane picks up speed, zooming down the runway. I grip the armrests of the chair as Wren takes us down the pavement and off into the sky. The sudden change in momentum is enough to make my stomach drop like I've missed a step.

"No, I don't know where we're going," I say.

"We're headed to Area 19."

My heart does a pitter-patter, and I grip the armrests more fiercely. "Why?"

He doesn't answer me. Instead, he fixes his gaze out of the window to study the rays of the awakening sun. Dawn has transformed into a breathtaking sunrise, the oranges more vibrant than before.

"Do you remember the Chief Overseer of Area 19?" Arthur inquires.

A razor blade of memory slashes through my mind. Tall, terrifying, and power-hungry—with dark eyes, silver hair, and cornered spectacles. She's the woman who persuaded me into giving up my power. She showed me the video of the twins—Maddy and his sister—and it was at that point that I discovered the government's "secret weapon" was a pair of children. She's the one who shot Tiffany Chang when Tiffany teleported back to the Testing Center to save me. She's the one who placed a tracker on Tiffany's sweater, leading the government right to our doorstep. And she's the one who ordered the bombing of the underground compound that left over a hundred people dead . . .

"What about her?" There's a tremor in my voice that I can't help.

"We're going to pay her a visit."

My chest feels like it's been plunged into icy water. "What for?"

"I'm hoping I can convince her of something," he muses, hand to his chin. "Do you remember when you asked me about the term 'unregenerative'?"

The word stirs the rage I'm trying to suppress, and my father's death replays in my mind. I should have looked away. His body going limp from the bullets is something I'll never be able to unsee. Dread is filling me to the brim. Arthur thinks he's going to give me some big revelation, but I already know what "unregenerative" means, and I already know what the serum does. Unregenerative is the term for those who refuse to take the serum. It's for the powerless of society who choose to stay powerless.

I continue to play along. "Yes, Mr. Evandrum, I remember."

Arthur's fierce eyes fix onto me. "Today you're going to learn a lot of things—things I've yet to share with the majority of my people."

My heart beats faster, and the hairs on the back of my neck stand on end. I stare at him with a guarded look. Is Arthur about to tell me his plan? *Me*? The girl he's been unable to control for so long? My ability pricks at my fingertips, and power simmers in my palms, so I tell myself to keep breathing to distract myself from the ever-growing need to unleash the beast.

The secret tugs at the corners of Arthur's mouth, but all it does is drive me crazy. He's so smug. When he doesn't say anything more, I speak up.

"What are you hoping to convince her of?" I ask. "Maybe I can use my ability to help?"

"No, I'm afraid that won't work. This is something she must do willingly."

I don a bewildered expression, but I know where this is going, and bile threatens to push its way up my throat. The pieces fall into place in my mind: Arthur's going to try and convince the

Chief Overseer of Area 19 to take an ability. The idea is horrifying. I wish I could say aloud the thoughts that are whirling through my brain. That I know what he's up to. That I vehemently oppose this. That I—

Arthur's next words snap me out of my spiraling.

"When we get there, I want you to keep her under your ability while I speak with her. Just as a precaution. We don't want any *accidents*, do we? I trust that you'll keep Wren and I out of harm's way?" He eyes me like a snake does a mouse.

In all reality, I would love for there to be an accident. I imagine the Chief Overseer shooting Arthur through the breast pocket of his blemishless white suit. In my mind's eye, the crimson spreads over his torso like ink spilled from a bottle . . .

"Of course, Mr. Evandrum," I say. "I will keep the two of you safe."

"Very well then." He leans back in his plush armchair and resumes staring out the window of the Beechcraft. "We will be there in a few hours. Get some rest before we arrive."

I take the invitation to move to the cockpit, not wanting to spend another moment in Arthur's presence. I shimmy into the cramped space, taking the seat on the right. Wren's gaze is set forward, her headset in place. Her brown muscled arms hold the yoke of the plane in a grip far more delicate than seems possible for her built physique.

My tongue runs over my teeth, and I press my lips together. "Thank you, for earlier."

She doesn't look at me. "You're welcome."

And that's all we say to one another. It feels odd. On all the trips I've taken with Wren, she's been open to talk, but there's a stark difference in her this time. She's more closed off and business-like than I've seen her before. So I set my eyes upon the bright morning sky and let my gaze dance upon the speckled clouds below us. We'll be at Area 19 soon.

The blood rushing through my veins turns as cold as ice. I can't help but think of Tiffany and how she came back for me. In the moments of my betrayal, she teleported me out at the cost of her own life. She was shot in my place—a shame I must bear for the rest of my days.

I swallow hard, dread capturing me. In a matter of hours, I'll be face to face with the woman who meant that bullet for me.

24

THE GLITTERING GLASS CITY OF AREA 19 SHIMMERS IN THE distance. I peer out of the cockpit, and my stomach curls into knots. How am I here *again*? It's a cruel joke that fate keeps sucking me back to this place like some cosmic magnet.

The Beechcraft descends, but instead of landing outside the city like Wren and I did on our missions to take down the Military Bases, we fly over the buildings, aiming for the landing strip inside the Area 19 Military Base. Wren begins to talk into her headset, but I'm not listening. I'm too focused on the Testing Center. It seems so much smaller from up in the air. Even still, the sight of it squeezes the air from my lungs. It's only when we pass overhead that I'm able to draw in a deeper breath.

We circle the landing strip once, then Wren takes the plane down. When the wheels hit the pavement, I ball my hands up, fingernails pressing into my palms. The sensation grounds me. Power courses at my center, and this helps calm my nerves as well.

"Alright, Timewire," Wren says. "Let's move."

I walk into the cabin of the Beechcraft. Arthur's already up from his seat and unlatching the door of the plane. He swings it open, and the metal fold-out stairs lower to the ground.

The moment I exit the Beechcraft, hot wind hits me like a wall. It's sweltering outside, and the sun beating down on us from overhead burns my skin. The air here is more humid than the air back at the mountain.

Wren and Arthur begin to walk toward the building in the distance where a row of vehicles are parked outside. I quickly follow them, glancing over my shoulder at the Beechcraft. How I wish I could fly that thing myself—then I could escape. But I'm stuck, so I trudge on.

To my surprise, when we reach the building, we don't go inside. Instead, Wren pulls open the driver's side door of the first truck in the row and hops into the front seat. Arthur takes the front passenger side, and I, after a moment's hesitation, open the rear door and slide into the back seat. I fumble with the seat belt, but I'm able to click it into place.

"She's not at the Base?" I ask Arthur, feeling like that would've been the most logical place for the woman to be if she were a prisoner at Area 19. But maybe she's not a prisoner at all.

Arthur turns over his shoulder to look at me as Wren starts up the engine. "No, we'll be making a house call."

Wren throws the truck in reverse, backs out of the row of vehicles, then floors it toward the exit of the Base. I peer out of the window, examining the wide expanse of concrete. Up ahead, there's a gate, and the person manning it opens it wide like they were expecting us.

Once we're on the street, my stomach threatens to lose the meager meal I ate earlier this morning. Being back in the city brings the familiar feelings of dread and panic. The streets appear as though nothing has changed. It's like I've been cast into my past. I remember sitting in the white van on my way to the Test, passing street transit stops and reciting that garbage pledge to my government. It seems so long ago, but it's not even been a year. I rub my nose with the flat of my palm, trying to recall how many months it's been since I failed the Test.

I murmur the numbers quietly to myself. "Five months in the underground compound, one month in the forest, three months in the mountain before . . ." I trail off as my brain spirals. How long have I been living like a prisoner under Arthur's control? How long has Maddy been kidnapped? My mind searches for a timeframe in the blur of chaos since Camille's death. "A month and a half in the New World Order," I finish.

The words taste like poison. Maddy's been in that lab for six weeks. I've been Arthur's pet puppet master for six weeks . . .

"What did you say?" Arthur shifts in his seat to glance back at me.

"Nothing, I was just . . . counting."

His jaw stiffens, and he clears his throat. "We'll be there in a few minutes."

The truck lurches left at the next intersection of buildings, and boxy housing units appear. No one is outside, but I can feel the presence of citizens in their dwellings with the tendrils of my ability. Has everyone in Area 19 been put under house arrest? Or are they all too frightened to make leaving their home a regular occurrence? In all honesty, I'm not sure what's happened in the city since Camille's death. All I know is that the Pure Ones have full control over the Testing Center and Military Base and they've disarmed the population, imprisoning all military personnel. Beyond that, anything else about the current workings of the Capitol City is a mystery to me.

Wren slows the vehicle, taking one last turn and stopping in front of a white and gray housing unit that stands out above the rest. For one, it's on the corner of the street, and it's three times as large as any of the units surrounding it. Its rectangular, boxy framing mirrors the style of the rest of the neighborhood, but its grandeur is clear. This is the house of a Chief Overseer.

We all exit the truck, and Wren pulls out her hand gun, but Arthur waves it away.

"No weapons, please."

Wren begrudgingly holsters it, and Arthur dusts off the front of his suit jacket with his hands, though not a speck about his appearance is out of place.

"Miss Timewire? If you will. Just as we discussed."

He gestures me up the cobblestone path that leads to the front entrance of the unit. I swallow as tingling pulses through my palms. I raise a hand in front of my chest and feel for the occupants of the grand house. Only one person resides within. Taking a deep breath, I allow my ability to grab her, and she stiffens under my command.

"I have her," I say to Arthur. "It's safe."

"Good. Let's go."

He marches up to the large stainless steel door. It's etched with a pattern of squares that alternate sinking into the surface and coming out of it. Taking the handle, Arthur pushes the door, and it swings inward in a wide arc.

The three of us enter the grand foyer of the home. To our right, a white marble staircase curves up the side of the dwelling, hugging a wall that's made entirely of glass. Above our heads to the left, a wooden balcony connects to the top of the stairs. Interlocking cream-colored tile bleeds into a living room that's furnished with gray couches, a large wall screen, a rectangular rose marble coffee table, and a set of metal, tree-like lamps. An island of dark brown glossy wood separates the living room from the kitchen area, which is tucked into the furthest nook of the space. It's huge. But it's not the size that shocks me.

The floor is littered with glass bottles of various sizes. Silver plates with intricate printed etchings and metal cups sit on every available surface. There's trash everywhere. It also overflows from the receptacle installed into the kitchen wall. And the stench of rotten food and alcohol assaults my nostrils.

I gulp, and my eyes begin to water. There on the couch, sitting as stiff as a statue, dressed in a pair of gray sweatpants and an off-white shirt that clearly hasn't been washed in who knows how long, is the Chief Overseer of Area 19.

Her silver hair is greasy and unkempt. Dark bags hang under her eyes. And she's not wearing her cornered spectacles. She looks like a completely different person, like I've stepped into an alternate reality where order, cleanliness, and perfection were never ideals to begin with.

Arthur steps into the living room, and I note how his nose

fights a crinkle, as if he were trying not to gag at the smell of the place. The woman's eyes snap to him, and they grow wide, but when they land on me, fear slips into her expression. She doesn't make a sound, however, because she's rigid under my power.

"Aleda Sagespark," Arthur says in a slippery tone. His eyes rove over the dozens of bottles scattered around her. "Chief Overseer of the Capitol City's Testing Center, my professional and political rival, the *wolf* of society..." His mouth curls in disgust. "Reduced to drinking herself to death on a dilapidated couch."

My hand twitches, allowing her the freedom to speak.

"What do you want, Arthur?" she says in a strained voice. Her uncontrolled tone is miles past the collected and terrifying woman of my memory; she's a mere shadow. "Have you come to gloat? You've finally bested me in the climb to the top. I knew you were a snake, but I never imagined you would be a *filthy* Diseased One."

Arthur's mouth splits into an amused grin. "No, I've not come to gloat." He walks further into the living room, and Wren and I follow him. He glances around the mess of trash, bottles, and dishware. "I've come to talk."

Her gaze flickers to me, and she bares her teeth, her wolf-like demeanor emerging. "I see you've brought the leader of the second Terror War with you. Were you in league with her the whole time?"

Arthur chuckles. "No. I've only recently acquired her."

"I find that very hard to believe," she sneers.

Arthur ignores her comment, sighing and placing a hand to

his forehead. There's a palpable shift in his tone. It becomes softer, more poignant. He gestures around himself to the filth of the house. "You're better than this, Aleda."

"Am I?" Her unnaturally dark eyes narrow. "What's left for me now? The Diseased Ones have won. We're all dead anyway. You could kill me right now if you wanted."

"I don't want to kill you," Arthur says. He takes a moment to sweep discarded bottles of booze off the armchair that's facing the couch. He sits, his attention cleaved to Aleda. A determined glint hides in his eyes. "What if I told you that you could still serve a purpose? I know you think your life is over, Aleda, but it's not. There's so much you don't understand. What if your life could have more meaning than it ever had as the Chief Overseer of Area 19?"

Aleda laughs out loud. It's the type of laugh that would shake a person's body, but she's still bound under my power and awkwardly slouched against the cushions. "Then I would say you're as delusional as you are ambitious."

Arthur purses his lips as if the word "delusional" pricked at his ego. He folds his hands together and rests his elbow on his knees. "If there's one thing I know about you, Aleda, it's that you can't resist power. You've pursued it your whole life. Worshiped it. Tied yourself to the altar of it—like a moth to the flame. No one ever stood a chance against you when you set your sights on something. You outperformed and outperfected everyone in your climb to the top. I admire that. Truly, I do. A hunger for power as strong as yours is rare. So, I'd like to make you an offer." He tilts his head in a calculating manner. "I'm about to change the world, and I want you to be a part of it. What if I told you that you could have more *power* than you've ever had before? Power that will satisfy that itch? Power that will run as deep as your *blood*."

Aleda's expression sparks with a glint of hunger, but she presses her lips together as if to maintain her dignity. She speaks with measured control, exuding a commanding presence. "What game are you playing, Evandrum?"

"A *revolutionary* one." Arthur's mouth splits to a smirk. "And I want *you* to lead the charge."

From her face alone, I can tell that Arthur has piqued her interest. A glimmer of her Chief Overseer demeanor has returned to her countenance, and unease grips me by the throat. I know she can't hurt me, but seeing the subtle switch in her face is enough to make me feel like I can't breathe.

"I'm listening," she says.

Arthur dips his head to acknowledge her, and then he glances back at me. Our eyes meet, and my stomach drops. This is it. This is the moment Arthur is going to say it outright. My heartbeat jackhammers against my ribcage.

He turns back to Aleda, elevating his posture in the armchair.

"Out of fairness and respect to you, I will speak candidly," Arthur begins. "No tricks and no beating around the bush. I've developed a serum—a serum that, when injected into the bloodstream, gives the host a power. Simply put, I've created a serum that gives people the biomarker."

A look of horror flickers across Aleda's face, and I force it to flicker across mine as well. A small intake of breath passes my lips, and with all my heart, I press into the act. It *must* appear as though this is shocking news to me. My effort is met with a satisfied look from Arthur. He only glances at me for a fraction of a second, but it's enough. I've sold the lie.

Arthur holds out his arms as if inviting Aleda into the fold. "The biomarker that runs in my blood can run in yours too. I'm offering you the chance to have power. *Real* power."

Aleda can't help the slack jaw that's captured her mouth. It hangs there, wide and revealing. "You want me to become a Diseased One?" she whispers. Her face pales so fast that it looks like a trick of the light.

"I want you to become a Pure One," he answers. "I want you to take the serum live in front of the whole world. And I want you to convince the other Chief Overseers to take it too." Arthur cracks a dangerous smile, a triumphant gleam in his eye. "Then I want you to convince everyone in Area 19 to take it . . . and then I want you to convince *all* citizens to take it . . . until every last person has a biomarker flowing through their veins."

All the years of no emotion couldn't have helped Aleda Sagespark suppress the feeling that spills across her face. Her eyes go wide, her mouth quivers, and a lick of perspiration forms at her hairline. I can feel her shudder under the control of my power, though no movement is visible in her limbs.

"And if I don't?" she murmurs, horror-struck.

"Then you die," Arthur says simply. "There's a long list of Chief Overseers I can go to next. But you're too smart for that, my dear. I came to you first because you are driven, intelligent, charismatic. You inspire obedience—even fear. *You* are the woman for this job. With your help, the transition can happen in record time. People will listen to you, Aleda. Other than the late President Alvaro Camille and myself, you are the most recognizable face in all of society. If you take the serum, so will they."

Aleda's eyes are unnaturally wide. She breathes out her words. "You're a monster."

"No, I'm a visionary. Be one *with* me, Aleda!" Arthur urges. "Be the society member who leads the charge into the new world. Join us."

"I will not taint my blood!" she exclaims, clenching her teeth. The wildness in her is back full-force, and I can feel her fighting my power.

Arthur curls his upper lip, scrutinizing her rigid form. There's a palpable and tense moment of silence. He looks between me and Aleda, then he gives me a stiff nod. "Miss Timewire, would you please remove your ability from her?"

I hesitate, heart in my throat. What is he going to do to her? Kill her? I take a hard swallow, discomfort wriggling in the pit of my abdomen. Slowly, I raise my palm, and with a flick of my wrist, she's free.

Aleda gasps like she's coming out of water for a breath of air. She moves so quickly I barely have time to register it. She dives over the coffee table that separates the couch from the armchair, launching herself at Arthur. A flash of silver metal comes out of nowhere, and the two of them tumble to the bottle-strewn carpet, Aleda on top.

I jump backward, and Wren pulls out her handgun as the

knife in Aleda's hand comes down toward Arthur's neck.

Before Wren can intervene, Arthur grabs Aleda's wrist, twisting it. And in one fluid motion, he disarms her, throwing her onto her back and pinning her to the floor under the weight of his own body. He straddles her, trapping her left arm under his knee and pushing her right arm above her head so her wrist is next to her face.

"I'm fine, Wren! Stand down!" Arthur says, panting. I move to encase Aleda again, but Arthur waves me away with his free hand. "No! Don't!"

Wren and I back off.

Aleda strains under him, her dark eyes beast-like and her expression feral. She hisses like a snake, but this only solidifies Arthur's hold over her. He brings Aleda's own knife to her throat.

"Let's take a breath, shall we?" he says, his chest heaving from the altercation.

She spits into his face, twisting herself under him, but he doesn't budge. He presses her wrists into the floor with more force and digs the knife into her skin. She winces and ceases her escape attempts.

Part of me wants to stop Arthur, but I'm torn between letting this play out and saying something. Would Arthur actually follow through with his threat? My breath catches in my throat. The small amount of sympathy I feel for this woman is stamped out by an onslaught of memories from the bombing. This woman killed over a hundred of my people. This woman killed Tiffany Chang. She doesn't get my sympathy. This plays out how Evandrum decides it does.

Aleda huffs, glaring at Arthur. "I thought you said you didn't want to kill me?"

"I don't," Arthur counters. "Join me. Take the noble blood of the Pure Ones into your veins. Be a part of something bigger. You have a chance to be a leader, a forward thinker, a visionary like me! You have nothing left besides this. *I'm* your chance at salvation! Do you really think society has the means to fight us? You have no weapons, you have no Testing Centers, you have no military, and you have no hope. The old ways are finished. Hunting us for our blood is done. The institution you dedicated your life to is dead, and there's nothing that can resurrect it."

Arthur's words are laden with conviction. Wild and melodic all at once. A delicate dance of a monologue. My ability tugs at the back of my mind, and the creature communicates with me wordlessly. My stomach clenches at the realization . . . Arthur's using his silver tongue on her, and he's holding nothing back.

"Don't be a fool, Aleda," he continues. "Aren't you tired of being afraid? Aren't you exhausted of hiding behind the guise of the Test to ease your conscience? Citizens know the truth now. We have *powers,* not bad blood. But you knew that from the start. All Chief Overseers did! Do you remember the day they briefed you on the *real* history of the Terror War? Or should I say . . . *massacre.* Tell me, did you not think for a moment about the ramifications of killing people you knew were *people* and not animals? Did you never stop to question it? I am doing something that will end the bloodshed once and for all. *I* am providing hope for a new world where we can finally move past this stain of history and *live!* If everyone has the biomarker, then no one will have to die for the sake of their blood ever again!"

The gravity of his statement washes over all of us like a powerful wave. Though he's not directing his power at me, I can feel Arthur Evandrum's words. They rage like a storm in my heart, and hope for a new world stirs in my soul. It's powerful. Incredible.

Aleda stares at Arthur, her lips parted ever so slightly. She appears spellbound, almost enchanted. Arthur pulls the knife away from her throat and tosses it across the tile leading to the front door. It clatters and skids to a stop.

"This has been a long time coming," he says, still keeping her pinned to the floor. "This is happening with or without your help. But I hope you have the vision to see that *you,* Aleda Sagespark, can be the start of this transformation. Because you know the truth. You've known it from the moment you became a Chief Overseer. You simply let the power of your position keep you silent for fear of losing what you worked so hard to gain."

Aleda's breath comes out heavy, and something shifts behind her eyes. "I . . ."

"Don't stay silent anymore," Arthur urges. "Take the serum and tell the world what you know. Atone for the sins of what you've allowed and what you've caused."

Tears of anger form in my eyes. There's no doubt in my mind Arthur is talking about the bombing . . .

Aleda's throat bobs as she swallows. All aggression has left her face, and a pensive look replaces it. Her expression is still muted out of habit, but today she's shown more of herself on her face than she likely has in a lifetime. The wolf of society, as

Arthur put it, has fallen to the emotions she's fought so hard to suppress.

"You always did have a way with words," she whispers. "It's almost like . . ." The realization dawns on her as she trails off. "Your power?"

Arthur nods. "Yes. Not a brain mutation. A gift. A treasure. And you can have it too."

Her lips begin to tremble, her voice turns hoarse, and her eyes glaze over for a moment. "They went crazy and tried to kill us all. Bad blood. A brain mutation. A mistake of evolution. They went crazy and tried to kill us all . . ." She sounds like she's reciting it, slipping into some trance-like state.

The light comes back to her face as quickly as it had gone.

"Sometimes I tell myself that over and over again because I can't . . ." Her words grow thick in her throat. "I can't bear what I've done. I want it to be true."

Her words are eerie. Ghost-like. They fill the pin-drop silence of the house like an out of tune flute playing its final song.

"But it's not true," she murmurs. She gazes into Arthur's eyes, and something in her breaks.

"It's not true," he affirms, his voice now gentle and compassionate. "Please, Aleda. Take the serum. Help me change the world."

The moment hangs between them like a boat on the cusp of plunging down a cascading waterfall. Once over the edge, there is no going back. I hold my breath, unable to take my eyes off of the Chief Overseer of Area 19.

"Okay," she says. "I'll take the serum."

Arthur breathes a sigh of success. It's subtle but powerful. All of the hunger returns to his features, and the compassion slips away as if it were never there in the first place. He releases Aleda's wrist and unpins her arm from under his knee, getting off of her and offering her a hand.

She sits up slowly, and with trembling fingertips, she accepts the gesture.

Arthur pulls her to her feet with a wolf-like grin, triumph lacing his whole demeanor. "Welcome to the program, Aleda Sagespark. You're about to make history."

―――
25
―――

Upon getting Aleda to agree to his terms, Arthur instructed me to take her under my power again for the ride back to the Military Base. He told her that she must earn his trust, seeing as she nearly stabbed him to death. Once Aleda was secured at the Military Base to await further instruction—which was a whole ordeal in and of itself—Arthur, Wren, and I took to the skies . . .

■ ■ ■

I sit in the plush leather chair farthest from the cockpit, gazing out the window of the Beechcraft. It's well past sunset. I can't see a thing past the glass. Pitch black night is all that greets me beyond the cozy glow of the cabin.

My eyes droop with the weight of the day. This morning my father was executed, and only a few hours later, Arthur Evandrum managed to convince the Chief Overseer of Area 19 to take the serum. Now, we're off to the next thing—whatever that may be.

I feel sick, exhausted with grief, and overwhelmed. This act of full devotion to the cause is breaking me. All I want is to get back to the mountain so I can meet with the band of rebels and hash out a rescue plan. At this point, knowing Maddy's location is the only thing keeping me sane.

I glance up at a shuffling noise that comes from the nose of the Beechcraft. Arthur is making his way down the aisle toward me. I fold my sweaty palms together in my lap, catching his eye. I haven't said a word to him since Aleda's house. Fatigue coils around my insides, pushing me toward a breakdown, but it seems Arthur's here for a conversation. He's tired—I can tell from the dark shading under his eyes—but that doesn't detract from his innate ability to command attention.

He sits across from me, placing his folded hands on the bolted table between us.

I don't know what to do with myself. The muscles along my arms and shoulders tense up as if to betray that I had known Arthur's plan for the serum all along. But I must keep up the charade.

"How long have you had this serum?" I ask, adding just the right amount of guardedness to my tone.

A smile tugs at the corners of Arthur's mouth. "I've been working on it for three years, but I've only recently seen success. Two months ago today, actually."

I have to stop myself from shuddering at the memory of the boy with the burned hands. His look of sickly panic is imprinted in my mind. This "success" Arthur speaks of isn't true success;

that dose went horribly wrong. However, now that Arthur has decided to recruit Aleda Sagespark to the cause, my guess is that George has fixed the problem.

"And the serum works?" I ask, barely above a whisper.

"Yes." Arthur leans forward, his eyes never leaving me. "I can give people powers. What do you think, puppet master?" His words feel like a challenge—like he's daring me to slip up.

"I never would've imagined something like this could be possible," I admit. "It's . . . extraordinary."

This is not, strictly speaking, a lie. Never in my wildest dreams did I think there could be a world filled *only* with people who have powers. What I'm against is Arthur killing those who refuse to take it. The idea is horrifying. It's like we're on the cusp of the massacre all over again. Only this time, it's directed toward people *without* the biomarker.

"When will everyone know?" I ask.

"Once I've gathered enough Chief Overseers who will agree to take it together. Aleda won't be enough. I need a show of unity to present this to the world. It will take more than one person to convince society that this change *must* happen."

I exhale steadily. Even though the idea of convincing citizens to take a power seems like an impossible feat, a group of society's most revered and celebrated leaders all becoming Pure Ones at once would make quite a statement.

"Tell me, Hollis, as a former society member, what do you think of my plan?" Arthur inquires. "You have a unique perspective. I'd like to hear it."

There it is again. My first name. I hate that he's using it. It feels slimy coming out of his mouth. It's like he's treating me as an equal, though I'm far from it. I would like nothing better than to tell him the truth, but I bite my tongue to keep it to myself. Instead, I pretend. It's something I've become good at through this whole experience.

"I think that citizens will be resistant, but a good portion of them will likely cave upon seeing the Chief Overseers become Pure Ones," I say.

Adrenaline douses me as an idea comes to mind—an idea that will probably earn me another tick mark of trust from the man I so desperately despise. Clearing my throat, I force myself to continue.

"I think every Chief Overseer who agrees to take the serum should do so publicly. Broadcast it every time. You may not be able to get all of them to take it when Aleda does, but each person who joins the Pure Ones should be made into an event. A spectacle. The more citizens see it and the more it becomes normalized . . ."—I take a deep breath,—"the more people will take it."

I'm disgusted with myself, but my words have sparked something behind Arthur's eyes. His posture shifts, and he sits up taller, studying me. I hold his gaze, not giving in to the overwhelming feeling of wanting to look away.

He presses his lips together, a sinister look befalling him. He speaks slowly, his tone calculated. "What happened in that prison camp? You've become a whole *new* person since then. So obedient. So agreeable. So . . . *helpful*." His eyes narrow, and I have to keep my wildly beating pulse in check. It's like I've become *too* amicable for his taste now. "What's your angle, Miss Timewire? I know how much you despise me. Let's not pretend otherwise."

I let out a quick breath, drawing the creature out. I'm going to need her help to sell this. She emerges from my chest, snake-like and coiled, and with her presence comes a burst of energy and resolve. She hisses at Arthur but stays by my side, fueling me with her strength. I decide to leaven in an ounce of truth with my carefully crafted tangle of deceit.

"I'll admit that when you took Maddy, I hated you," I say, keeping my eyes firmly fixed on him. I swallow, the sensation unpleasant. "And when you made me kill Camille . . . I was angry. But I've come to understand a lot since then. When I visited my father at PC-7A, I finally saw it, like the shattered pieces of everything I've been through finally clicked into place: no matter what I do, or what I say, or how hard I fight . . . I'll always be a Diseased One. To them, I'm a mistake. My blood is something I have no control over, but my blood is who I am. And even though you forced me to help you, I . . ." I trail off, fighting with myself. The creature stares at me with her coal-red eyes, as if giving me permission to say it. "You couldn't have done it any other way. You *had* to control me so I could learn—so I could see—and now I do. I think your plan has merit. If everyone has the biomarker, then no one will have to die for their blood anymore. It's the perfect way to prevent history from repeating itself. I know I've been stubborn, but I've changed. And I think the world you're imagining, Mr. Evandrum, is the world we need to *survive*. Like I've said before: I'll keep proving myself to you until you believe my loyalty."

Arthur's expression still holds some skepticism, but it's tempered a bit. I feel like I can't breathe. I've done everything he's asked me to do and more. I can only hope he doesn't press me further.

"Very well," he mutters.

Thoughts of relief flutter through me. He's not prying more.

Arthur stifles a yawn behind the flat of his palm, and this only reminds me of how tired I am. He clears his throat to hide his exhaustion. "I'm going to require your assistance over the next few days. We have many house calls to make. When we return to the mountain, pack your things. We'll be gone for a week. This will be a quick stop. I'm on a rather tight schedule."

"Of course," I say with a small dip of my head. This makes me want to cry. The fact that I can't rest after this extremely taxing and emotionally devastating day is insane.

■ ■ ■

The rest of the flight doesn't last long, and before I know it, Wren has landed the Beechcraft back at the mountain, and the three of us deplane. Arthur catches my arm in an icy grip before I can run off. I nearly squirm out of it on instinct.

"Don't say a word about the serum," he warns. "If you do, I will know."

"Yes, sir," I reply. "When are we leaving again?"

"In a few hours. Meet me and Wren at the Beechcraft at 0500."

I suppress a groan, biting back a retort and nodding in

agreement. Then, he releases me. Even though I would like nothing more than to pass out in the training room for a bit of rest, I can't. I need to talk to the band of rebels.

I waste no time in finding Olivia. Yes, it's the middle of the night, but that doesn't stop me from asking her to gather everyone in the Holodeck.

She eagerly accommodates my request, and before long, the Holo-room is packed to the brim. All of my friends are present, as well as my teacher. The others from the initial meeting are there too: Siena Rose, Yang, Libbie Lizette, Caleb Stuart, Audrey Rye, Delphi . . . To my shock, I also see Beck and Hazel—two of the people I rescued from the Area 147 Military Base. And there are dozens more. Some I briefly recognize, and others I've never seen before. Our group has grown since last time. With a quick count, I land on fifty-seven members.

I lean into Olivia, speaking low enough so only she can hear me. "Are you absolutely sure you can trust everyone here?"

"I'm positive," she affirms. "I've been hard at work. And so has Keith. He's been an incredible help."

"What about Terrace?" I ask. "With so many people here, what if he learns something?"

"Terrace doesn't care about most of the people in this room. He only cares about checking up on the people Arthur cares about. Namely, *you*. Besides, everyone here knows to steer clear of Terrace and keep their heads down until we have Maddy."

"I suppose," I murmur.

"It's going to be okay, Hollis," Olivia says. "These people want to help."

I eye Hazel and Beck. The fact that they are here when they were literally tortured by a society member is telling. If they are able to recognize that their rescuers are not in the right, then I have hope that more people in the mountain may join us.

"Thank you, everyone, for being here," I call out to the room. "I'm sorry for waking you up, but this is important."

The low whispers of the crowd dwindle to silence. Every eye is on me. I take a deep breath, the anticipation of this moment traveling like electricity through my veins. I'm about to spill a bunch of information, and finally, after six grueling weeks, we're going to hash out a plan to extract Maddy.

"I have a lot to tell you," I announce, and without waiting, I dive in.

I start with the serum and explain everything in detail. I describe what it does, and I lay out how Arthur plans to get the Chief Overseers to take it first. I tell them about how Arthur wants to create a world where everyone has a power and how he plans to kill anyone who doesn't join the cause.

Then I move on to Maddy. I share how Arthur's kept him secured at the Area 7 Testing Center. I explain how his blood is the key to making the serum work and how rescuing him will not only free me but will also stop the production of doses. Maddy is the key. Maddy's blood is what started this, and Maddy's blood is what will end this.

Horrified and pondering looks are engraved on the faces that stare back at me. The gravity of these revelations weighs heavy, and for a moment, no one speaks. Then, the silence is broken by Delphi, the pixie-haired blonde woman with the curved scar above her right eyebrow. She clears her throat, speaking in a much more confident manner than she had at our first meeting.

"Well, let's go get the kid then," she says. "We know where he is, so why wait?"

Keith walks into the midst of the Holodeck. "How do you propose we do that? Olivia can't teleport anyone to him. How do we get to the lab? And more importantly, how do we do so *secretly*?"

A bristling murmur skitters about the room. An older-looking gentleman with wiry copper hair raises his hand. I recognize him as the man who volunteered to drive Ashton away from the mountain if Ashton had not agreed to join us.

The man's wrinkly, freckled face creases around his eyes as he offers his idea. "We could drive there. The trip would take two days to arrive at the lab. Four days round trip in the best of circumstances. The downside: it might draw attention—having a truck missing for that long—but we may be able to think up a cover story for using it." He coughs into his elbow, pausing to collect his breath. "Only five people could come. Taking multiple trucks is out of the question."

"Who would go?" Vianne asks, gazing around. Her silvery hair flickers to a soft brown. She's standing next to Ashton, who furrows his brow, contemplating the question.

"What abilities would be best for this? That's the real question," Jonah adds from behind me. I glance over my shoulder, my pulse ticking in an uneasy rhythm. Part of me already knows the answer to this . . .

"I don't mean to sound like an ass," Ashton begins, "but the best abilities here belong to me, Jonah, and Hollis. Do we need more than that? The Area 7 Testing Center is run by people with powers. I can suppress everyone we encounter, Hollis can control them, and Jonah can double us. Should anything happen, Hollis's power protects me, and mine protects her. No one will be able to do a thing about it."

Ashton and I lock eyes. He's got a point, we would make quite the team.

Siena Rose pipes up, twirling a lock of her thick raven hair between her fingertips. "I agree. Realistically, there's no other abilities here that could take on the people in that facility." She scans the room as if to double check. "Sure, we have a few powerhouses." She points to a muscular Black man standing in the back of the crowd. "Theo has super strength, but that can't stop a bullet. And Neriah,"—she nods to a tall woman with high cheekbones and dazzling purple eyes,—"she can shoot laser beams from her eyes. But unfortunately for us, our little band of rebels consists mostly of mundane powers. Lyla can make flowers bloom, Harper can communicate with animals, Quinn can see in the dark . . ." She trails off, and her heavily lidded eyes flash. "No offense to anyone here, but Hollis, Jonah, and Ashton are superior. Hands down. They're the ones who should go."

I gaze around, a twisting sensation tugging at my gut. Siena's got a point. Our three powers are plenty. The real crux of the issue is that Ashton and I are both nearly always with Arthur. And I don't see Arthur giving me *four* days off. Even if he did, he wouldn't do the same with Ashton. I sigh, twisting the ball of my foot into the flooring of the Holodeck.

"Ashton, there's no way both of us could 'go missing' for several days without Arthur knowing something's up. We wouldn't even make it to the Testing Center before our absence would be noticed."

His face falls, eagerness replaced by a troubled look.

Rosalie joins the conversation now. Her soft voice is melancholy and woven with stress. "Arthur will move Maddy if he thinks something is wrong. I've seen enough of his memories to know." She grimaces, holding my gaze with a lamentful look. "I gathered more memories than what I showed you, Hollis. Arthur has an entire team of people guarding that boy—and they have orders to whisk him away at the first sign of *anything* out of the ordinary. They check in with Arthur often—and at random times too. Arthur's taken every precaution to keep Maddy in his care."

"Two days is too long, let alone four . . ." I whisper, almost to myself.

I'm sick to my stomach. If I suddenly vanished along with Ashton, there's no doubt in my mind that Arthur would act. Maddy would be gone, likely locked away in some other facility for his safekeeping, and everything we did to steal Arthur's memories will have been for nothing.

Dread seeps deep to my bones. I know what I have to do. The idea burns in me like an unquenchable fire. It's crazy, but it's the only way to get to the Area 7 Testing Center fast enough. I look up at Jonah and swallow, clamping my hands into fists. "We'll fly. The Beechcraft can get us there in a matter of hours."

Jonah pales, and so does Ashton. Everyone in the Holodeck

freezes like I've cast my ability over them. Stealing a plane is going to be one hell of an operation, and in many ways, it's far riskier than stealing a truck. But realistically, it's the only way to get to Maddy quickly.

"Hollis, none of us know how to fly," Jonah says in a guarded tone.

By his face, I can tell he understands where I'm going with this.

"We don't have to," I say. The creature pulses alive within my veins. "Because I'm going to make Wren Zayla fly us there."

The silence that follows this statement is loud. Even as I say it, my heart thunders through my chest like a violent storm. The sensation sweeps the breath from my lungs, and I have to take a second to refocus myself.

"Great. Steal a plane. We've got our transportation," Ashton says. "Wren won't be able to refuse you, and she won't be able to warn Arthur. Sounds good to me."

I pinch the bridge of my nose between my thumb and pointer finger. I'm so exhausted I'm finding it hard to think. "I wish there was a way we could extract Maddy without storming into the lab, powers blazing."

"Why?" Ashton asks, raising an eyebrow. "Once we get to the Testing Center, who cares? No one will be able to stop you. We'll get Maddy and run away. Why does it matter if Arthur knows what we've done by that point?"

I shake my head. "No, I can't run away from this. I have to stop Arthur. I have to confront him—and truthfully, I'd rather have the element of surprise. If there's anything I've learned, it's that Arthur's always been ten steps ahead of me. I can't let that happen this time."

I take in the room of people standing all around me.

"We're in this together, and whether we like it or not, we're all going to have to face the world Arthur's creating. I don't want to live in a society where everyone has a power if that's not everyone's genuine choice. Arthur's vision may have merit, but his means for accomplishing it are wrong. I'm not going to turn my back on this. As much as I'd like to, I can't run away. I have to face him. I have to put an end to this."

Scattered nods of agreement come from the crowd. But it's Keith and Jonah who catch my attention. They're both looking at me like they're proud of me, and my heart overflows with affection.

"Excuse me?" Hazel says timidly, holding her hand up.

She steps into the middle of the Holodeck, and my focus snaps to her. Her brunette hair is tucked up in a loose ponytail that frames her thin face. It's still gaunt, although her skin has gained back some color since being rescued, and she doesn't look as emaciated. "I think I can help."

"Hazel." Beck catches her arm. "You really want to step back into society? After everything you've been through?" His fingers brush her bandaged hand where her missing pinky finger is. Images of Hazel chained to the torture table at General Whitlock's mercy fire through my mind, and sympathy pains jump through me.

"I wouldn't be stepping back into society," she counters. "The Testing Center at Area 7 is filled with people who have powers."

"People with powers who are *bad*," he says.

"Then why are we even here?" She throws a hand up. "I thought this was about doing something real. Making a difference. I can help. You know I can. Besides, I would have Hollis, wouldn't I? This time, I'll be safe."

I approach both of them, and they stop talking. Beck swallows, running a hand through his dark hair. His brown complexion looks healthier than before, like he's gained back some of his strength from being held captive. I lock eyes with Hazel.

"What can you do?" I ask her.

She glances back at Beck and then sighs when he doesn't say anything. She spreads her hands apart. Quicker than I can blink, the two of them disappear, and everyone in the Holodeck gasps. Then, with a rippling of the air around the vacant place where they once stood, they reappear. It's like watching a mirage turn into reality.

"I can make myself and others invisible," she says. "Like a shield, I shift the air to conceal."

My breath hitches in my throat. I can't believe it. But then a thought occurs to me, and I give Hazel a quizzical look. If she can turn herself and others invisible, how were they caught by General Whitlock?

It's like she can read my mind.

"Dogs," she says, hugging herself. "We got too close to the Military Base trying to find other people with powers after Arthur's broadcast to the world. They sniffed us out and cornered us. That's how we got caught."

Her face burns hot with shame, and Beck hugs her.

"Never mind that," he says. "Besides, I blame myself, not you. I'm the one who suggested we check out the Military Base. Even invisible, that was a stupid idea."

Hazel's face changes from embarrassed to determined. She looks between me, Ashton, and Jonah. "I can shield you three. We can get into the Testing Center without anyone seeing us. And we'd only have to use your powers if someone caught us. We can get Maddy out before anyone knows he's missing."

Jonah and I exchange quick glances, and I can't help the smile that tugs at my lips. Like a gift from the Universe itself, the perfect power has fallen into our midst.

"Okay," I say to her. "That's what we'll do."

"When do we leave?" Ashton asks.

I purse my lips. "Hilda, what time is it?"

The automated voice of the Holodeck chimes up. "It is 0327."

I curse, frustrated. Unfortunately, Arthur has me for the next week. There isn't time to fly to Area 7 right now. As much as I would like to, Arthur's expecting me in the aircraft hangar in less than two hours. And I haven't packed my things.

"We'll have to wait until Arthur gives me another day off," I say. "I'm supposed to meet him at 0500. He's taking me to meet with more Chief Overseers. I'll be gone for a week. But when I return, we'll go."

"Wait a minute," Ashton says, brow furrowed. "Why can't we take the plane and go now? Hollis, I know you said you wanted to rescue Maddy from the lab without storming in, powers blazing, but why not control Arthur? Just grab him with your ability, take Wren too, and let's go. We know where Maddy is. The only reason you haven't used your ability on Arthur yet is because you didn't know Maddy's location *and* you didn't have a plan to get to him. But now we have both, so puppet Arthur. He won't be able to stop us."

Rosalie shakes her head so furiously that I'm taken aback. She marches up to Ashton and grabs his shoulder to turn him around. "No! That's a bad idea!"

"Why?" he asks, surprised by her show of force.

Rosalie sighs, frustrated. She places a delicate hand to her forehead, her red hair swishing about. "Were you not listening to me before? The people guarding Maddy check in with Arthur on a random schedule. What if they try checking in with him while you're flying to the lab with Arthur as a captive? If they don't hear from him, they'll move Maddy. That's their orders. We can't risk it. Besides, the only way Hollis can safely confront Arthur is if Maddy is in *our* hands, not his. Stealing Maddy back in secret is our best option."

Ashton's expression falls.

Olivia swears aloud, raking both of her hands through her tight black curls. Her attention diverts to me. "Of course Arthur would be taking you on a weeklong trip. What timing! I was hoping we could get Maddy back *before* Arthur drops the news about the serum. Do you know when Arthur plans to announce this?"

I scrunch my nose. "Kind of? I know he's planning to announce it once he gets enough Chief Overseers to agree to take the serum together. And it's going to be a worldwide broadcast."

Olivia purses her lips. "So, probably at the end of your trip."

"Probably."

"Why were you hoping to get Maddy back before Arthur shares the news about the serum? Why does that matter?" Candice asks, speaking up for the first time since the meeting started. She's huddled together with Ben, who looks like he's sleep-deprived. His hair is pressed in a cowlick up against the left side of his head—a definite sign of being pulled out of bed.

"Because," Olivia says, hands on her hips. "Once everyone in the mountain hears whatever speech Arthur's cooked up, it will be harder to convince them that this serum is *bad* news."

"But isn't that obvious?" Hazel asks, confused. "Forcing citizens to choose between taking a power or dying is *definitely* a bad thing."

Olivia shakes her head. "You're new, Hazel. You don't know how convincing Arthur can be."

Delphi rocks herself up onto her tip toes. "Then we'll have to convince people that Arthur is in the wrong." She gazes around at everyone present, and her voice rises like an anthem. "We may not have abilities as powerful as Hollis or Ashton, but we know the people here. All of us. They're our friends. Our family." Fervor lights in her spirit as she continues. "We have a voice. And if we can't rescue Maddy before Arthur makes this announcement, we can still do our part. Besides, it's clear that not everyone is in agreement with Arthur. Look at all of us. There *has* to be more! And once Hollis confronts him, we'll have planted the seeds of standing up against this serum in the minds and hearts of a lot of people."

There's an encouraging murmur of agreement that sweeps the room.

A jumpy sensation seizes my stomach; it's excitement and anticipation grabbing hold of me. We're going to do this. I'm going to get Maddy back, and then I'm going to make Arthur Evandrum pay for everything he's done to me. He will never be able to use anyone for his own gain ever again.

Determination and the creature rattle together as one in the depths of my chest, and power ignites down my arms, showering to my fingertips and flying up through my face. Control washes over me, and it's like being able to take a deep breath after holding it for far too long.

I spend a few moments searching the faces of the people gathered in the Holodeck. They're all here for Maddy—for *me*—and my heart swells with gratitude beyond what I can express.

"Thank you, all of you." My voice catches in my throat. I'm on the verge of tears, but they aren't sad ones. They're hopeful.

"We're here with you," Keith says, approaching me and grabbing my hand. He gives it a gentle squeeze. Then he pulls me into a backward hug, and I let my head rest against his chest, closing my eyes.

"Hollis." Jonah's voice sucks my attention to him, and my eyes fly open. The way he says my name is cautious, and it skewers me with adrenaline. "When are you going to confront Arthur? The timing is important. If we're flying back to the mountain with Maddy by our side, you need to have a plan. It's not safe for Maddy here."

"I'm going to confront Arthur the moment we return from rescuing Maddy—the moment the plane touches down," I say with conviction. "I'm taking Arthur under my power along with anyone else who gets in my way. He won't be able to hurt Maddy."

Jonah puts a hand to his chin, a pensive look overshadowing his tired face. "When you finally face him, what are you going to do to him?"

The question burns a hole right through my chest. I want to kill him. But I've kept this thought to myself. I haven't even voiced it aloud. As I ponder it once more, it takes hold of me, but this time, it scares me. Abruptly, a physical sensation of pain mixed with panic claws its way through me. Could I actually take a life intentionally? Would the creature do it for me? Would killing him break me in a way I'm not prepared to deal with? Ending Arthur's life is certainly the easy answer and the one I've been stewing on. Realistically, what would I do otherwise? How else could I stop him?

My hands begin to shake, and Keith holds me closer, sensing my discomfort. His strong arms give me something to steady myself on.

"I . . ." My voice trails off, now sounding weak. Nearly hoarse.

Say it. Just say it. I want to kill him.

My mind fires through a tangle of one horrible thought after another. Am I really ready to kill him? In my anger after seeing Arthur's memories, I would have said yes. But in this moment, right now, despite everything, I can't find the will to say the words aloud. What is wrong with me? Arthur's taken everything from me. He's hurt so many people. He *deserves* to die . . .

"I don't know," I say, meeting Jonah's gaze.

My own statement unnerves me. One thing is clear: when I confront Arthur Evandrum, there's no turning back. In the aftermath of this, I'll be the one in charge of the Pure Ones. Leadership, for however brief a time, will absolutely fall on *my* shoulders. Would the people of the mountain follow me if Arthur were still alive? But then, a more sinister question suffocates me, closing its icy hands around my throat. Would the people of the mountain follow me if Arthur were dead?

26

I USE MY ABILITY TO ENSURE THAT THE HALLS OF THE MOUNTAIN are deserted before sending the band of rebels away. Keith is with me, standing by my side as if to indicate he's not going anywhere. I'm glad. I want to spend as much time with him as I can before leaving the mountain.

I grab his hand as people file out of the Holodeck in small groups. "Stay with me while I pack?" I ask. "I don't want to be alone."

Keith gathers me into a hug and rests his chin on the top of my head. "Of course."

We stand there, waiting for the majority of people to leave. No one says much. Groups of three or four slip out in two-minute intervals, slinking off in silence and shrouding the mood of the Holodeck in somberness.

Vianne approaches me, her hair dancing through shades of dark brown. "Hollis?"

I glance at her porcelain face. I can tell she's been suppressing tears because her eyes are glassy but her face hasn't gained the right amount of pink. Her lower lip trembles, and she takes a shaky breath. Before I can say a word, she opens her arms wide and pelts me with a hug. I embrace her back, closing my eyes to fight off shaky breaths of my own.

"We're going to get Maddy back, right?" she whimpers.

"We are," I say firmly.

It's like my words break her, and she lets out a quiet sob.

"Hey," I say, pushing her gently out of the hug to look her in the face. "It's going to be alright. Like Ashton said, we have the most powerful abilities in this place. We'll be okay, and so will Maddy."

I catch Ashton's eye, and he gives me a stiff nod. He walks up behind Vianne and brushes her hand with his fingertips.

"And that new girl, Hazel," Ashton adds, "she'll hide us when we go. No one is going to catch us."

Vianne's eyes shimmer with more tears. "Maddy only has us. All that time I spent watching him after we rescued him from Area 19…" She pauses, clasping her delicate hands together. "We're it. We're his family. I just want to hold him in my arms again. I want to keep him safe and let him be a kid. He doesn't deserve this! Not after everything he's already been through." Anger now flashes across her features, and her hair turns scarlet. "I can't believe Arthur is taking his blood over and over again! That *monster*! Maddy's a *child*! I'd love to transform Arthur into some mutated beast. I could make him go blind or deaf. I could make him hurt, if I wanted. There's plenty I could do if I had the chance."

Her hands curl into fists. The darkness in her tone is something I've never encountered from her, but I know what she means. Three distinct memories come to mind. The first is when she transformed Ashton into a mutated dog with fat disfigured lips, yellow bulging teeth, and orange hair. She did it because he was teasing her about liking Ben. That feels like a lifetime ago. The second is when she was on the roof of the Testing Center as we were fleeing the military men. She was the last person Keith flew up to grab. I don't know what happened on that roof, but Keith's ghastly expression of shellshock told me all I needed to know. Vianne did something terrible to those men with her metamorph ability. And the third was the story of how Vianne lost her parents to the dogs. Those dogs almost took her life, but she managed to kill them with her ability by mutating their faces. And that's why she has scars—scars that she still chooses to hide. Vianne is incredibly powerful and can inflict serious harm.

I gently grab her upper arm, pulling her attention toward me again. "This is going to be over soon. I promise."

She grits her teeth, fire in her tone. She looks at me in a way she's never looked at me before. "Whatever you decide to do, make Arthur pay for it."

The squirmy sensation of panic returns full force, and my mind draws a blank. What *am* I going to do when I confront him? With the clock on Maddy's rescue now ticking down to zero, I have to come up with a plan. The fate of society rests upon my decision. What happens to Arthur Evandrum affects us all.

The Holodeck is empty now. The only people that remain are Vianne, Keith, Ashton, and myself.

Keith nudges me. "I know you said you don't know what you're going to do to Arthur, but . . . do you have *any* ideas?"

Spots of light flicker in my vision, and I have to grab Keith's arm to steady myself. Adrenaline doses my blood. Again, I'm caught in a tongue tie of wanting to say the words out loud but being unable to do so. The tangled mess of emotion tugs at my gut, causing me to grab my stomach and grimace.

"Hollis, what's wrong?" Keith asks.

"Nothing," I lie.

Ashton and Vianne exchange quick glances, and Ashton steps forward. "Hey, I may not be as close to you as these two are,"— He gestures to Keith and Vianne—"but even *I* can tell you're lying."

I cast my gaze to the floor, struggling with myself. "I just . . . I want to . . ."

The words die in my throat. I fight to say it all over again, but still, nothing happens. I let out a frustrated sigh, scuffing the sole of my boot against the brightly lit panels of the Holodeck.

"You want to what?" Keith prods.

I look into his eyes, and part of me begs him to change the subject, but I know that's not going to happen. The three of them simply stare at me. I clench my teeth, the muscles along my jaw tightening. I might as well say it, because if I can't even say, how will I do it? Taking a deep breath, I channel tingling into my chest and limbs.

"I want to kill him."

Vianne pales, and Keith and Ashton sober, but they don't protest. As I search their faces, I can see it in their eyes: they support this decision. Some of the tension in my chest dissipates, and I let out a trembling breath between pursed lips. I feel like I have to justify myself.

"Ever since I saw Arthur's memories, I've wanted to kill him. It was Arthur's idea to kill my mom. He's the reason Camille bombed that Testing Center and blamed it on me. He took Maddy. He's kidnapping society children to test the serum. He forced me to—"

Keith's places a hand on my shoulder, and it stops me. "You don't have to explain, Hollis. We all saw the memories."

I'm frustrated and ashamed. Tears blur my vision. Why do I feel stupid for wanting to kill Arthur when I never wanted to kill Camille? In some ways, Camille was just as vile. But part of me already knows the answer. Keeping Camille alive served the purpose of showing citizens the lie they were living under. All that time I spent fighting against the assassination plot had a direction. An intention. Sparing Camille's life would have been proof that the Diseased Ones weren't murderous creatures. But that's exactly what Arthur is turning us into. Take the serum or die.

Camille and Arthur are not the same . . .

Vianne begins to shiver, her hair shifting to the color of snow after a fresh snowfall. "How are you going to do it?" she whispers.

"I don't know." I chew on my lower lip, creasing my brow. Nerves are flaying my stomach alive. It's a horrible sensation. "I'm afraid that when it comes down to it, I won't be able to kill him. Even though I want to. I'm scared. I hate what Arthur's done to me, but I also hate what he's turned me into." My voice catches in my throat, becoming thick and sorrowful. "I'm so angry all the time. I feel like I've lost myself. I feel like everything I was afraid of when I found out I had powers is going to come true. The creature . . . she's become my companion and guardian. But sometimes, she becomes all consuming. Controlling. She would burn the whole world down for me, and part of me is afraid to let her. Like, somehow, if I give in, I'll be bad. Does wanting to kill Arthur make me a bad person?"

Keith puts his arms around me, pulling me close to his chest. "Hollis, listen to me. You're *not* a bad person. You've just had bad things happen to you."

I sink into his arms, and I can't help the shaking that enters my limbs. "Sometimes, I just feel so alone. Because I'm the one who has to do it. I'm the one who has to end this."

"You're not alone," he breathes. "We're here for you."

I nod, clinging to his arms. "I know."

Ashton furrows his brow, putting a hand to his chin. He seems to be mulling over something. His eyes trace the paneled flooring while he mutters under his breath. Then, he looks up at me. "I have an idea."

"What is it?" Vianne asks, peering at him.

He locks eyes with me then puts on a guarded tone, holding his hands up in a gesture that suggests surrender. "First, I'd like to say . . . I'm not here to tell you what to do, Hollis. If you decide to kill Arthur, that's your prerogative. But if you don't, or you can't . . ." He clears his throat. "Why not turn off his biomarker like you did with me? In a way, you're like Maddy. You could take his power. Besides, more than half the things that man's been able to accomplish has been because of his silver tongue. It's almost like he puts people under a spell when he uses it. You've seen the way he makes a speech. Everyone hangs on his every word. But if he didn't have his power, I wonder how many more people would be on our side? Just something to consider."

My mouth hangs slightly ajar. I'm struck by the simplicity of the idea. How come I've never thought of that before? Ashton's right when he says it's like Arthur's put a spell over people. My mind immediately jumps back to what I witnessed when Arthur convinced Aleda to take the serum. His voice was like magic in the air—and *I* wasn't even the one he was trying to convince.

The hate I've been collecting toward Arthur wants to strike down the idea. So much of me still wants to end his life, but if I can't, then at least I have a backup plan. Something concrete. Something I know I can do—*and* something I fully understand.

"Ashton, that's brilliant," I say.

He dips his head toward me, a hint of a smile pulling at the corners of his mouth.

A little pitter-patter of nerves fires through me as I remember I have to be back at the Beechcraft soon. "Hilda, what time is it?" I ask.

The voice of the Holodeck answers promptly. "It is 0411."

I grab Keith's hand. "I have to go to my training room and pack, or I'm going to run out of time."

I approach Vianne, giving her a quick hug. She hugs me back, squeezing me like she'll never see me again. When the embrace ends, I take in her silver eyes. I can see fear there, still digging itself deep into her soul, so I reassure her once more. "When I come back from my weeklong trip, we'll steal the plane, and we'll get Maddy. Then I'll confront Arthur. It's going to be okay. You'll see."

She nods but doesn't say anything else.

"Keith, let's go," I say.

With quick steps, the two of us exit the Holodeck, leaving Vianne and Ashton behind. We walk the halls of the mountain with ease. I made sure to check no one was milling about before leaving Sector 1. When we arrive at the training room, I set about throwing clothes and toiletries into a duffle bag that I dragged out from under my bed. I also grab a small pillow and shove it into the folds of canvas-like material.

Keith offers to help me, but I decline, and within ten minutes, I've got everything I can think of. Glancing at the clock on the far wall tells me I have thirty-three minutes left until I'm supposed to be at the Beechcraft, so I plop onto the couch, exhaustion sweeping over me. I've been awake since before my father's execution, and my eyelids are heavy with fatigue and grief.

"Don't let me fall asleep," I warn Keith. "I don't want to be late. I'll just sleep on the plane."

Keith sits next to me, putting his arm around my shoulder. I snuggle up to him, wanting nothing more than to sleep in his arms.

"Hollis?"

"Yeah?"

"I've been thinking."

I stifle an exhausted giggle. The laughter feels foreign in my throat, like I've forgotten how to do it.

"What?" Keith muses.

I peer up at him. "That's just a very *you* thing to say."

He gives me a look that's half exasperated and half amused. "I suppose it is."

"You always have a spot where you go to think too. Up in the little cave in the ceiling at the old compound, by the river at night when we were in the forest..." I pause, studying his face. "Where's your spot here?"

He sighs. "When I was confined to a cell in Sector 2 after attacking you, it was there."

"That doesn't count."

"Well, lately, it's been here, in this room." He regards the training room with his free hand. "When you're gone, I come in here to think. I guess it makes me feel closer to you, in a way." The color in his cheeks intensifies, as if he were suddenly embarrassed to admit it, but my heart swells with affection for him.

"That's sweet," I breathe.

He smiles then stares at the empty training mat for a beat. I follow his gaze, and memories of me and Jonah training to improve my power come back to me. It all feels like so long ago, but it's not been long at all.

"Well?" I say. "What have you been thinking?"

He lets out a breath, holding me close. "I've been thinking... what is this all going to look like after Arthur's regime is over?"

His question sinks into me like a stone that's been thrown into the sea. I'm going to be taking leadership over an entire group of people, and by extension, over society itself. Whatever I decide to do with Arthur has nothing to do with the decisions

I'll have to make after the fact. There's so much to consider that it overwhelms me. I have no experience rebuilding a society from the ground up. All I know is that I'm vehemently against the one Arthur's working to create. Suddenly, I feel like a child again, despite the responsibility on my shoulders and the power under my fingertips.

"That's a big question that I'm not sure I have the answer to," I admit. "But I know I won't have to face that question alone. I have Jonah. And I have you."

"Me?" Keith raises an eyebrow in surprise.

"Yeah, you're a leader too, you know. You've been working hard with Olivia to organize the band of rebels. You were the one who came up with the plan to get Ashton out of the mountain if he didn't agree to help me. And you were the one who came up with the idea of stealing Arthur's memories to find Maddy. You're a part of this."

He gives me a tired smile. "I suppose I am."

"I remember the day you told me about your parents . . . and how they died on a rescue mission."

Keith sobers and doesn't say anything in response.

"You said you wished you could do something like they did," I continue. "And you did exactly that when you helped rescue Maddy from the government." I grab the front of his shirt gently. "I also remember you saying how your parents believed we might be able to rejoin society one day. Imagine how proud they would be if they could see you now. You're helping to change things. And after all this is over, we *will* be able to rejoin society."

The corners of Keith's mouth tip upward. I can't quite

pinpoint the emotion that works its way over his face. It's a mixture of pride, happiness, and something else. Determination?

"Thank you for saying that, Hollis," he breathes. "It means a lot to me."

I smile at him, affection filling my heart to the brim.

"Well," Keith says, shifting a bit to readjust his arm. "Speaking of rejoining society, if you could snap your fingers and magically make the world alright again, what would you do?"

I laugh. "I'm a puppet master, Keith. I'm powerful, but I'm not *that* powerful."

He playfully nudges me, unrelenting. "Humor me. What would you do?"

I sigh, my eyes landing on the empty training mat once more. My mind wanders down paths of possibility. There's so much good the world could accomplish if we could learn to get along . . .

"I guess I would turn the Testing Centers into Education Centers where people without powers can learn from people who have powers. The massacre stemmed from fear of the unknown, right? Well, I would make us known in an environment where people feel safe. Where people can develop a new culture together—one where it's okay to be whatever you want to be. As much as I hate the concept of this serum, it's truly incredible. Maybe one day the world could be a place where people get to choose to have a power. People wouldn't have to take one if they didn't want to—and we would have to find a way to do it without Maddy's blood—but science is always evolving. And there would be jobs for all citizens suited to what they do best, power or not. Kids wouldn't have to grow up being afraid anymore. We could teach people how to feel again and how to express emotion. Displays of affection wouldn't be condemned, but embraced. And there would be a memorial plaque installed in the foyer of every Education Center to remind people of what happened. We would teach it to everyone, the whole truth this time, and future generations would grow up to do better than us because they will know that hate and fear only lead to death and that love and acceptance is the only way forward."

I end my speech feeling slightly breathless and a little wistful. Keith is staring at me with the biggest grin on his face.

"That sounds wonderful."

"It does, doesn't it?"

"See? And you were nervous about taking charge," Keith teases.

I give him a shove in the ribs, and he gives a fake yelp.

"Ha. Ha." I say flatly. "Yeah, this will be *so easy*. I don't know what I was worrying about. Silly me!"

Keith chuckles, pulling me in to kiss the top of my head. "That's the spirit!"

We fall quiet for a minute, both of us gazing at each other. I can feel Keith's heartbeat quicken with the subtle tendrils of my power. He's suddenly nervous. I can tell from the clamminess in his palms and the slight change in his breath.

"What is it?" I ask, still holding his gaze.

He doesn't answer me right away. Instead, his piercing blue eyes take me in, and I can feel the heat creep across my face. It's a fluttery, wonderful feeling. He lets out a shaky breath, and then grabs my hands. "I love you. I don't know why it's taken me so long to say it, but I've loved you for a while now."

My breath hitches, and warmth flows through me. Without hesitation, I lean into him, and our lips meet. Showers of acceptance and happiness burst through me. As we sink further into the kiss, I forget everything, and I live in this moment alone, as if everything in the world were alright again. When we break apart, I hold his gaze, squeezing his hands within my own.

"I love you too."

Keith smiles, pushing a strand of hair from my face. "I suppose there's one good thing that came out of this crazy situation. It finally gave me the courage to say that."

I laugh. I can't help it. I lean in for another kiss, and all over again, I fall into bliss. When the kiss ends, I'm pulled back to the present, and my circumstances come crashing over me once more. The clock on the wall ticks mercilessly ahead, and I groan. I'll have to leave soon, and it makes my heart sad.

"I have one more question." Keith's voice has now turned soft and pensive.

"Yes?"

"What do *you* want, Hollis? When all of this is over, what do you want for *yourself*?"

My lips part. No one has ever asked me that before, and as I stare into Keith's vivid blue eyes, my own fill with tears.

"I want to be happy," I whisper.

Silence falls between us, and it makes my stomach flip. Right now, happiness seems so far away, but I hope with all my heart to find it soon. I've caught glimpses of it through this past year. It's in the way Keith makes me feel. It's part of Maddy's joyful laugh, and it's imprinted in the memory of my mother's warm embrace. It's woven into the fabric of Candice and Ben's humor, and it's found in the steadfastness of Jonah's undying encouragement. It's part of Vianne's scars. It's in the poignant scenes of Rosalie's storytelling. And it's in the courage of Ashton's choice to put aside his hatred for me to fight alongside us. Happiness. Hope. I want that feeling to stay with me. And maybe one day, it will.

All that's left for me to do is rescue the boy with the golden light so I can topple the silver-tongued man's apocalyptic regime.

$$27$$

THE BEECHCRAFT'S BELLY IS ALREADY OPEN WHEN I ARRIVE at the aircraft hangar. With my duffle bag in hand, I march straight toward the plane and board, taking the seat all the way in the back. I dig into the folds of the duffle to withdraw the small pillow I had squashed in there. I'm so exhausted I can feel it in my gut, and all I want to do is fall asleep for however long I'm allowed.

Wren is up in the cockpit, doing her normal pre-flight check, but Arthur is not here yet. The small digital clock embedded in the panel directly above the entrance to the cockpit reads 0506. I shake myself, squinting at the red numbers again to make sure I'm seeing it right. Six minutes past five. Arthur's late.

A shiver runs through me. Never once during this whole hellish experience has he been late. I was practically flayed alive for being two minutes late at my first meeting with Arthur post Maddy's kidnapping. And now Arthur's six minutes late?

The clock flicks over to the next minute. 0507.

I peer out of the window of the Beechcraft, scanning the large aircraft hangar. Hardly anyone is here. I only spot three people busily carting crates into the cabin of a huge Boeing 747.

I get out of my seat, treading toward the cockpit with silent steps. Wren is clicking buttons on the control panel and muttering to herself. I wait a moment, hoping she will notice me. When she doesn't, I clear my throat.

"What is it, Timewire?" she asks, her voice a bit more gruff than usual.

"Where's Arthur?" I ask.

She doesn't answer my question. Instead, she continues to tap on various buttons. This only makes me more nervous, and the fatigue threatening to pull my eyelids closed vanishes.

"Wren, where's—"

"He'll be here soon," she says sharply.

The edge to her voice shuts me up. Sighing, I decide to go back to my seat rather than pry further. I'd rather not get under her skin if I can avoid it.

I situate myself with the pillow and keep my gaze fixed beyond the window. The next thirteen minutes feel like an eternity, and my head pounds with the desire for sleep. But I'm not relenting until we're in the sky.

At 0521, Arthur emerges through the double doors at the back of the hangar, and I perk up, watching him stride quickly across the concrete. He clutches a stack of folders and a large white briefcase. When he reaches the Beechcraft, he climbs in, carefully setting the briefcase down as if it were made of the most delicate glass. Then he places the stack of folders on one of the bolted-in tables and pulls in the plane's fold-out stairs, securing the airlock.

When I catch a glimpse of his face, I suck in a hasty breath. The bags under his eyes are far worse than they were before. Gray skin sags beneath his lids, and his normally pristine gelled-back hair is a bit disheveled. He looks seasick or like he's eaten something that didn't agree with him. The crisp folds of his white suit are crinkled, and as I study him, I notice tiny capillaries of red that streak the whites of his eyes. His forehead is also pale and sweaty.

I swallow unpleasantly. "Are you okay, Mr. Evandrum?"

In all honesty, I don't care how he is, but I'd be lying if I said his untidy appearance and late arrival didn't bother me.

He sits in the chair catty-corner from me, attempting to smooth out his hair and straighten his suit. It's a gesture I've seen him do so many times—his hands running down the smooth white fabric of the jacket as if flicking off water—but it's hasty now. Like he's been caught rolling out of bed and he's trying to pull himself together. I've *never* seen him this unkempt, and it doesn't sit well with me.

"I haven't slept in three days," he croaks, his voice rough and jaded, exhaustion riddled in his tone.

Part of me doesn't buy his excuse. Why was he late? What was he doing? Why does he look *so* undone? And in front of *me* no less. I'm hardly someone he would consider to be in his inner circle of trusted people. I'm not like Terrace or Wren, and yet, here Arthur sits, in more disarray than what I witnessed from his memories. Anxiety weaves through my veins. I can't help the nagging feeling that something is wrong.

Arthur swivels his chair, calling up to Wren. "Let's go. We have a lot of work to do."

The Beechraft's engines roar up under us, and my stomach jolts.

Arthur leans back and places his folded hands across his eyes. "I'm going to get some sleep. I suggest you do the same."

Though my body feels on edge as a result of seeing Arthur in such a state, it's also screaming at me to sleep, so I listen. I tuck the pillow up under my head and adjust myself against the window. The ball of weariness at my core finally dissipates as I drift off into a blissful period of REM sleep. Dreams flicker in and out of my subconscious. It's a tangle of events with no purpose. I float from one meaningless encounter to the next, interacting with people I don't know but feel like I've seen before. It's all fuzzy and unfocused.

As the dreams continue, my body begins to recharge. Strength collects in my limbs, as if my ability were feeding off the sleep too . . .

The fuzziness ends abruptly, and I'm sucked into a bare white room with no windows and a single door. My blood runs cold as my mind clears. Everything turns sharp. I know this place. I've been here before. My bare feet pad silently toward the door, and I pull. Just like last time, it's locked.

"Maddy?" I call out tentatively.

"Hollis."

I turn toward the little voice, and my hand rises to cover my mouth. My stomach sinks all the way to my toes. He's horribly thin and sickly, even more so than in the previous dream. His face is devoid of color, and his lips are so pale they look white. His blue eyes, normally full of life, are sunken and sad. He looks like he's about to collapse.

I rush to him, wrapping my arms around him, and he sinks into me. We both sit on the floor. "Maddy," I whisper, clinging to him. His little body is trembling within my grip.

"Hollis, have you found me yet?" he whimpers. "Are you coming?"

"Yes!" I say fervently, fighting the well of tears pooling in my eyes. My throat closes up, and I have to take a second to compose myself. "I've found you. You're at the Area 7 Testing Center. And I'm coming as soon as I can. Ashton's coming with me. And Jonah too."

Maddy peers up at me. A faint smile comes across his face. "Ash?"

I nod. "Yeah, Ash is coming. We're going to get you out of there."

"And will I see Vivi again?"

"Of course you will. She's very excited to see you. She misses you."

"I miss her too."

His head falls against my chest, and he curls in on himself. It's like all the life has been sucked out of his tiny frail frame. He takes a few labored breaths, clinging to the fabric of my shirt. I feel helpless. I'm not actually with him. This is only Maddy's power helping him to communicate with me in my sleep. It makes me want to scream.

My shoulders stiffen as a thought sharper than a knife digs through me. Maddy reached out to me *on purpose*. I can't initiate whatever this connection is. He's the one doing it, which means there must be a reason. I lift his head up gently with my hand.

"Maddy, is there something you need to tell me?" I ask.

My words seem to lift him out of his stupor. His blue orb eyes shine, and a trembling overtakes his tiny mouth.

"Be careful," he says in a quiet ghostly voice that spooks me.

"Be careful of what?"

"Of Jenkins. He's the man that watches me. When you come, whatever you do, don't let him touch you."

My heartbeat quickens, and I hold Maddy closer. "What is Jenkins' power?"

Maddy presses his hands to his cheeks. His face screws up in concentration, and he remains quiet for several seconds. It seems like he's having a hard time forming the right words. "He helps me so I don't deplete."

I give him a strange look. It sounds like he's simply repeating something he's heard. "So you don't deplete? What does that mean?"

Maddy blinks a few times. "He makes sure I'm strong after they take my blood. But he can do bad things too. Really bad things." He peers over his shoulder to look at something I can't see, and then he tilts his head to listen. He stays like this for a few beats before continuing. "He's supposed to come and help me, but he hasn't yet. I don't feel good, Hollis. They took a lot of blood today."

"Maddy, I don't understand. Can you explain?" I press him. "What does Jenkins do?"

"He puts his hands on my chest, and when he does, I feel better again." Maddy's eyes grow unnaturally wide, and his little voice gains strength. "But you can't let him touch you or Ash! You have to be careful! Promise?"

He grabs my hands forcefully, and I nod. "I promise, Maddy. I'll be careful. I won't let Jenkins touch us."

I still have no idea what Maddy means, but one thing is clear: whatever Jenkins' power is, I better not be on the receiving end of the bad part.

Maddy slumps against me again, barely able to keep himself upright, and fear leaps through my chest. The way he's acting scares me. Last time I saw him, he simply looked sick, like a long weekend of rest and a handful of hearty meals could bring life back into him. Now he looks like a tiny corpse. I know Arthur needs his blood, but I reasoned that since Maddy is such a critical piece to Arthur's plan that he would be in better condition. Apparently, that's not the case.

To keep myself from falling apart, I trace my fingers through his blond curls, rocking him gently and cherishing the feel of my arms around him. I begin to hum under my breath. It's a tune I remember my mother humming to me when I was little. I don't know why the melody comes to me, but it's comforting.

Maddy closes his eyes, and his breathing steadies. His little chest rises and falls in an even rhythm as I continue to hum the string of notes. He looks so peaceful. It's like we're back in the mountain and Maddy's fallen asleep on my lap after a long day. My heart aches at the thought.

The melody stirs up words from the recesses of my mind. I

had forgotten that the tune had lyrics, but something about holding Maddy like this has sparked a deeply buried memory of my own mother holding me when I was sick. My mother's beautiful voice sings in my head as I sing aloud:

> Sleep, little one, safe in my arms
> Dream of a place where worries can't swarm
> In morning's light, you'll be strong as can be
> For healing and love surround you, you see
>
> Though you're weary tonight
> I promise tomorrow you'll be alright
> And with the sunrise, you'll fix your eye
> To gaze at an endless cerulean sky
>
> Once night dances away on silver streams
> And flows under moonlight's sparkling beams
> You'll wake anew as light greets your face
> Chasing all aches far from this place
>
> Sleep, little one, safe in my arms
> Dream of a place where worries can't swarm
> In morning's light, you'll be strong as can be
> For healing and love surround you, you see

I stop singing and lean down to kiss the top of his head. Even though this dream space isn't real, I'm clinging to every moment of it.

"Hold on, Maddy," I whisper. "I'm only a week away, and then you won't ever have to give your blood again. I promise."

Maddy's head suddenly jerks upward, and his body begins to shake again. He clutches my hands. "Jenkins is coming. I have to go. He can't see the golden light!"

I grip his hands fiercely. "One more week, Maddy," I assure him. "One more week."

A violent banging issues from all around us, and Maddy disappears in a flash of light. Next thing I know, I'm being ripped from the dream space and pulled back into reality. I awake with a gasp as the Beechcraft materializes around me. The engines' steady rumbling fills my ears, and the scent of the leather upholstery wafts into my nose.

I gulp, coming out of the dream feeling more helpless than ever. At least I have another tangible piece of helpful information to cling to before the rescue mission: don't let Jenkins touch anyone.

Arthur is still out cold, sleeping soundlessly with his head against the window. My eyes travel from his pale face to the stack of folders on the table directly in front of him—then they land on the briefcase under his feet.

Curiosity gets the best of me, and I rise from my seat. I make my way over to the table silently and ease myself into the chair across him as slowly as I can. All the while, I'm holding my breath so as not to wake him.

I reach for the folder on top of the stack, carefully pulling it toward me. I flip open the top page. A picture of a man with dark skin, a neatly trimmed beard, and clean-styled haircut is pinned next to a block of text. I read over it quickly.

```
Chief Overseer Faruk Hadi
Testing Center: Area 171
Age: 55
Height: 5'10"
Weight: 230 lbs
Date of Birth: 5-14-2592
Status: Unregenerative (pending)
Known Family Members: Salma Hadi (wife); Amira
    Hadi (daughter); Jode Hadi (son)
Notes: Faruk is ambitious and clever, securing
    the job of Chief Overseer at a mere twenty-
    six years of age—the youngest age for a
    Chief Overseer on record. While he is
    fiercely loyal to his government, he is
    more loyal to his family, consistently
    demonstrating his willingness to put their
    needs above anything else. Offering
    security to Faruk's family in the New World
    Order is the key to getting him to take the
    serum.
```

I grab the next folder as delicately as possible and open the top page. This time, I see a picture of a blonde woman who looks just as terrifying as Aleda Sagespark. Her piercing green eyes, pointed teeth, and sharp jawline give her the appearance of a wild cat ready to devour anyone who would dare cross her. My eyes dart across the text.

```
Chief Overseer Eden Nova
Testing Center: Area 34
Age: 42
Height: 6'2"
Weight: 170 lbs
Date of Birth: 8-28-2605
Status: Unregenerative (pending)
Known Family Members: None
```

    Notes: Alvaro Camille bombed the Area 34
        Testing Center, publicly blaming it on the
        terrorist Hollis Timewire. Eden survived
        the explosion with minor injuries. She has
        lost everything. If she knew the truth
        about Camille's plans for the bombing, it
        may shake her trust in the former
        government enough to convince her to take
        the serum.

As I move to select the next folder, Arthur stirs, and my blood laces with adrenaline. I freeze, my hand hovering over the stack of papers. Arthur's mouth twitches and he shifts, but to my relief, he doesn't wake. I lift the next folder up with silent hands.

The picture inside the front flap is of a much older-looking gentleman with wildly graying hair and a long beard that's been trimmed into a sharp triangle, the tip of which goes down to his mid-chest.

    Chief Overseer Sebastian Windward

    Testing Center: Area 201

    Age: 73

    Height: 5'11"

    Weight: 165 lbs

    Date of Birth: 2-19-2574

    Status: Unregenerative (pending)

    Known Family Members: Claudia Windward (wife);
        Eustace Windward (son); Kassandra Willet-
        Windward (daughter-in-law); Seeme Willet-
        Windward (granddaughter)

    Notes: Sebastian is one of those rare men that
        embraces and encourages change. His long
        and accolade-filled career as Chief
        Overseer has granted him the opportunity to
        push the frontier of science, with his lab
        at Area 201 producing the most cutting-edge
        technology and medicine the world has ever
        seen. Nothing is off limits to him when he

```
considers scientific advancement. Appealing
to his devotion to the progress of humanity
is the key to getting him to take the
serum.
```

The stack still has seven folders left, but I close the three I've already opened and return them to their place in the order I took them. This is undoubtedly the list of people Arthur is going to visit in an effort to have them join Aleda in taking the serum. My stomach does an uncomfortable dance, and then my gaze falls on the white briefcase once more. It's wedged beneath Arthur's legs under his seat, but it looks like there's enough space for me to slide it out if I were careful.

I debate going back to my seat and letting it go, but I can't. Something about this case intrigues me. I want to know what's inside. With cautious movements, I position myself in the aisle of the Beechcraft, stooping down by Arthur's side to reach for the briefcase. My fingertips brush the metal handle . . .

An ice cold hand clamps over my wrist, and adrenaline sledgehammers through my limbs. I'm met with a murderous stare. Arthur yanks me to my feet, pushing me down the aisle a few paces. I gasp as his face comes within inches of my own.

"*Don't! Touch! That!*" he grits out in a dangerous growl. "Do you understand me?" When I don't respond immediately, he shakes me. "I said, do you understand me!?"

I have to suppress the skitters of power that shower through my veins. If I were following my instincts, I would freeze him on the spot, but that kind of a response is out of the question.

"Y-yes," I stammer, staring into his wild eyes. He appears less haggard now, like the sleep restored his energy and spirit. He only holds me for a moment longer before releasing my wrist. I stagger backward, clutching the place where his hand had just been. An uncomfortable pang throbs there from how forcefully he grabbed me.

"Take a seat," he hisses.

I obey him, turning on my heels and stumbling to the chair with my pillow on it. My heartbeat is thundering in my chest, and twinkles of light sparkle along the edges of my peripheral vision.

Arthur brushes off the front of his suit jacket, a sudden spring in his step. He calls up to the cockpit. "Wren, how much longer until we reach Area 171?"

There's a slight delay before Wren's voice sounds from the cockpit. "Two hours and thirteen minutes."

"Lovely," he responds.

His gaze whips around toward me once more, and he purses his lips, a dark expression clouding his features. I avert my eyes, pretending to be interested in the spattering of clouds beneath the wing.

Area 171. That's Faruk Hadi's Testing Center. I take a slow calming breath to rid myself of the jitters from the altercation. I need to stay focused and hope I can get through this week with my head on straight.

When I'm sure Arthur's not staring at me anymore, I chance a glance back at the white briefcase, and an uneasy feeling settles in me. After successfully stealing and watching Arthur's memories, I feel like I know so much about him, but clearly I don't know everything. What could he be hiding in that case? And why doesn't he want me to see it? My curiosity is driving me insane. I ball my hands up on my lap, letting my mind wander through a whole host of uncomfortable thoughts. Arthur's late arrival to Beechcraft, his overly tired and unkempt appearance, and now this mysterious case? I don't know what to make of it. Perhaps it doesn't matter. All I know is that this game I'm playing is about to end, and I can't wait until it does.

I keep the words I spoke to Maddy in the dream space close to my heart: *One more week, Maddy. One more week.*

28

THE NEXT SIX DAYS PASS IN A FLURRY OF ACTIVITY THAT demands every moment of my attention and near constant use of my power. Wren flies us from Area to Area as we make our house calls. Same routine, different speech. I use my ability to capture the Chief Overseer—and any other people in the dwelling—and Arthur uses his silver tongue to convince them to take the serum. Each visit, magic-filled, fear-instilled words flow from Arthur's lips; a spellbinding melody of language that twists together into a symphony of compelling reason. It's an incredible thing to behold. Even with the full knowledge of how his ability functions, Arthur's silver tongue captures my thoughts and steals my attention. But I keep my wits about me. Each time we leave a Chief Overseer's house, the spell breaks, and I claim my mind once more. It's like coming out of a fog.

After each visit, Arthur sends in a separate plane to collect the Chief Overseer and send them to the Area 19 Military Base.

It seems the spectacle of taking the serum in front of the world will happen there. It's like clockwork: meet the Chief Overseer, persuade them to take the serum, fly them off to Area 19.

Of the ten Chief Overseers Arthur talked to, only one outright refused him: Gemma Gray, Chief Overseer of the Area 14 Testing Center. No matter what Arthur said, Gemma stood firm on her decision. She was a small woman—barely taller than me—but she had a fierce determination about her that was unrivaled by her peers and a deep hatred in her heart for people with powers. With no family to threaten, no prize to offer, and no angle to exploit, Arthur simply couldn't get an edge over her mind. Even with the threat of death, Gemma didn't budge. So, with calm and collected poise, Arthur walked over to Wren, grabbed her gun, and shot Gemma Gray in the forehead. No hesitation. No regret. I jerked violently in response as the creature relinquished her hold over the woman.

"I have no need for someone as stubborn as her," Arthur said, handing the gun back to Wren as though he had dismissed an assistant applying for a job and not murdered the woman in cold blood.

Gemma Gray was the last on Arthur's list.

And just like that, the week was over, and we were back in the Beechcraft on our way to the Capitol City . . .

The entire flight, I'm riddled with anxiety. I park myself in the farthest seat from the cockpit and huddle down with my pillow, trying to get some rest, but it evades me.

"Almost," I whisper.

It's the word I've been reciting to myself like a mantra. A

prayer. I'm almost out of this hell. *Almost.*

Gemma Gray's cold dead eyes keep flashing up in my brain. The blood oozes from her forehead, the spatters of crimson stain her tile flooring, and the ringing of the gun buzzes in my ears . . .

I didn't think Arthur would actually do it. I don't know why I thought such a foolish thing. But until I witnessed it, I truly didn't think he would kill her. But that bullet shattered the last inkling of delusion left in my mind. Arthur is a monster bent on one thing, and one thing alone: power. I've known his true colors for a while. I've seen them in his memories and in my father's execution—and now I've seen them in Gemma Gray.

"We're twenty minutes out," Wren calls from the cockpit, and her words bring me relief. I can't wait to get off this plane. At least at the Military Base, I might be able to snag a moment away from Arthur. Spending every second of every day with the man has been unbearable. Sleeping on the plane, maintaining my demure and obediently helpful attitude, eating meals with him, keeping up the façade of my dedication . . . it's draining the life from me.

My trips with Wren weren't as bad as this. At least she would talk to me and make me feel at ease between the directed times of working the mission. But with Arthur present, she's barely said a few passing comments to me. It's isolating. I know Wren isn't anything close to what I would consider a friend, but we worked well together, given the circumstances. And she's been kind to me. Now, it's all business all the time—a fronted wall of professionalism and dutiful focus.

To my great relief, the remainder of the flight doesn't last long, and the Beechcraft touches down on one of the runways of the Area 19 Military Base. Arthur quickly jumps to his feet, delicately handling the white briefcase—which he kept by his side constantly throughout this past week. With his free hand, he yanks on the lever to open the door of the plane, and the extendable stairs ease out to the pavement.

"Let's go," he says to me, gesturing me out first.

I grab my duffle bag, but he shakes his head.

"You won't be needing that. We're headed back to the mountain tonight. You can keep it on the plane."

"We're going back to the mountain after today?" I say with a little too much happiness in my voice. I temper it immediately, dropping my bag on the seat. "That's good to hear. It's been a long trip."

Arthur doesn't reply. He simply ushers me from the Beechcraft into the mid-afternoon sun. Wren follows suit, and in silence, the three of us traipse across the burning pavement toward one of the concrete buildings in the distance.

The sky above is the clearest of blues with not a cloud to be found, and heat seeps under my clothing, layering a sheen of sweat down my back. Thankfully, when we reach the towering concrete structure and enter through the thick metal doors, cool air washes over us.

The foyer of the Military Base looks like a grand hall. The floor is made of dark marble—the walls of a similar color and material. But it's the columns of blue pearl royal granite that impress the eye. Ten of them line each side of the space, making the room appear as though it were filled with a splash of stars. In between the columns, doors of rich olive wood sit at intervals with letters above their frames.

A stoutly-built bald man dressed in a beige uniform greets us with hurried steps, diverting my attention away from the grandeur.

"Mr. Evandrum, sir," he says, saluting him. "The Chief Overseers are waiting in conference room B."

"Thank you, General Myers," Arthur replies.

"We've accommodated them during their stay, per your request. Anything they could want, within reason of course. And they've stayed under guard," Myers says. "Although they've been less than thrilled about that part."

"Is the stage set up?"

"Yes, we've transformed Aircraft Bay 6 according to your specifications. The camera crews are waiting there already."

"Excellent. And are there guards in conference room B?" Arthur asks.

"Of course, sir."

"Dismiss them."

The man's face pales in concern. "Sir, I would highly recommend keeping the guards present for your meeting."

"There's no need for that. Miss Timewire is all the security I require. Dismiss them. These people have chosen to join the Pure Ones. They are our friends, not our enemies."

The man dips his head. "Of course, sir. I'll take care of that right away."

He turns away from us and approaches the olive wood door marked "B," disappearing for no more than a minute before emerging accompanied by six men with guns. They file past us and out the doors we came through. General Myers walks up to Arthur, sweeping his hand toward the conference room.

"They are all yours."

Arthur eyes me. "Don't use your power unless things get out of hand. I want to present myself as their equal."

"Yes, sir," I say.

"Let's go."

Wren and I follow Arthur across the dark marble floor, and my heart begins to beat faster. I'm about to enter a room full of Chief Overseers, who, until very recently, made it their life's mission to see me dead. Even though I could easily overpower them, it still doesn't do anything to calm my nerves.

When the door opens, I feel like I can't breathe. The conference room is not unlike Arthur's office back in the mountain. An oval table fills the space, and around it sits a group of ten Chief Overseers, Aleda Sagespark among them. Each one of them is terrifying in their own way. Whether it's their physicality, their presence, or simply the way in which their beady eyes hone in on me, as if they'd like nothing more than to rip my throat out. I push back the violent urge to freeze them.

Arthur takes the seat at the head of the table, tucking the white briefcase between his legs. Wren sits to his left, which leaves me the seat to his right. I slip into it gingerly, my fingertips vibrating with power at the ready. I'm not letting *anything* happen. If anyone so much as twitches the wrong way, I'm taking them under my control.

"Ladies and gentlemen, today is a very special day," Arthur

begins, folding his hands together and setting them on the table. The eager look in his eye and the bold confidence in his voice steals the attention away from me. "Today you will become Pure Ones. By your example, you will light the way for others to follow in your footsteps."

There's a palpable shift in the group of Chief Overseers, and Faruk Hadi holds his pointer finger up. "Mr. Evandrum, what powers will you give us?" he asks, his accented deep baritone voice carrying across the room. He looks around at his colleagues, all of whom appear stoic and collected, but I can pick up the subtle increase of their heartbeats. "You said nothing of this when you came to talk."

"I have carefully selected a power for each of you, Mr. Hadi," Arthur replies. His gaze lands on Aleda Sagespark, and he stares at her for an uncomfortably long time before continuing. "I have thought long and hard about what each of you could bring to the might of Pure Ones. Because you ten are the first, I have chosen a selection of abilities that will dazzle the world. I want a *show*. Something so incredible that it will leave citizens in awe."

"So what have you selected?" Aleda asks sharply. She sits opposite Arthur at the far end of the table, and she wears a dark expression. She seems to have thrown out all sense of societal restraint. It makes her presence even more terrifying, and I have to keep myself from shrinking down in my seat.

"Patience, my dear Aleda," Arthur chides.

She bares her teeth at him, not hiding the disgust in her tone. "How are you *so* confident in us, Arthur?" She leans forward. "Tell me, what's to stop us from killing you with our powers the moment you gift them to us?"

Arthur's mouth splits into a deranged smile so off-putting that Aleda falters. "You won't do that. None of you will."

She laughs at him. It's a high-pitched, cold laugh that prickles my skin and yanks at my insides. Even the others in the room seem to flinch at her flagrant display of emotion.

"Is it the girl?" Aleda points to me. "Are you banking on her protection?"

Arthur enunciates his response with a hiss. "*No.*"

His answer surprises me, and it seems to surprise Aleda as well. This whole week, Arthur's used me as a shield, and he's given me explicit instructions to keep him and Wren safe.

"Then where does the *delusion* come from?" she growls.

"Are you saying you plan to kill me when I give you the serum?" Arthur studies her with amusement. "Haven't we already had this fight? You gave it a valiant effort when I visited you in your home, but you failed. I seem to recall pinning you to the floor and holding a knife against your delicate throat."

He smirks as the rest of the Chief Overseers exchange glances of muted shock. No one else had an altercation with Arthur as he collected them. No one else besides Gemma Gray— and none of the Chief Overseers know she's dead.

Aleda glares at him, a bestial look overshadowing her. The slightest hint of color rises in her pale cheeks. Clearly, she didn't want that information to come to light. I glance at Arthur, noting the subtle way his nostrils flare out. He's relishing this moment of making her look weak in front of the others.

"Don't embarrass yourself any further," he sneers. "To answer your question: once you taste the power I'm about to give you, you'll realize that you've never truly *lived* at all. You'll never draw breath the same way again. There will be no more thoughts of bad blood or hate for us. You will *be* us, and this frivolous prejudice you may still carry in your heart will vanish, because then you will truly understand what we are. Not Diseased Ones. Not the enemy. Not a mistake of evolution. But the pinnacle of it. You won't want to kill me, Aleda. You'll want to shake my hand."

Arthur's eyes linger on her to take in every detail of her face. Then he shifts his attention to look at each person around the table. One by one.

"I promise you, today you'll finally understand this biomarker in a way you never could have imagined. We are all on the cusp of a historic day. But first, a set of ground rules and a warning." Arthur's shrewd expression deepens. "During the broadcast, you will stand on the stage, directly over your mark. It's a strip of tape with your name on it. Next, when my assistants step up to deliver the serum, you will hold out your right arm. Before they inject you, they will hand you a piece of paper. Read it carefully, for it contains the description of the power you will be receiving. And now, the warning: my head scientist, George Perry, has run a sufficient number of tests to perfect the serum, but there are still immediate side effects that may occur. These side effects are listed under the description of your power. You may or may not experience any of them. But rest assured, the serum is safe and effective. According to George's tests, within the first minute, you may feel a change in your body. A buzzing in your chest or your fingertips. All I ask is that when you're ready and you've felt the transformation occur, try it out. The paper will give you a set of initial things to keep in mind while attempting to use your power. Remember, this is about *showing off*. This is about *showing* the world."

Arthur stands abruptly, and everyone gives a little start. He carefully grabs the white briefcase and says, "Let's go, my friends. The cameras await."

My mind is reeling, and my breath hitches as the rest of us rise together. I can't believe this is really happening. We exit conference room B in silence. Arthur, Wren, and I lead the way, and the ten Chief Overseers follow suit.

As we walk, I keep looking at the white briefcase clutched between Arthur's fingertips. Are the serum doses in there? My brain spins at the thought. That must be what's inside, and that must be why Arthur's been so protective over it.

Our group marches down the black marble foyer and through a labyrinth of concrete hallways. As we go, I keep my hands poised to strike and my senses on high alert. I call the creature, and she snakes out of me, curling around my torso to bolster my strength. Her presence calms me quite a bit. She gives me a sense of courage, and though she doesn't speak, she makes me feel like things will turn out alright.

Aircraft Bay 6 is massive. Everyone's footsteps sound off the high walls as we approach the large metal stage set up at the mouth of the bay. It's open, and sunlight mixes with the artificial lighting. Camera crews are set up at intervals along the front of the stage, which faces the outside, and guards line either side of the steps leading up to the platform. There's also a black podium adorned with the image of the golden woman with her eyes closed and her palms open to the heavens in front of her stomach.

Arthur carefully climbs the steps to the left, taking his place behind the podium. I keep by his side. He carefully sets down the white briefcase then straightens himself up. Wren lurks off to the side behind the stage, out of view of the cameras. Each Chief Overseer walks to their mark—five to Arthur's left and five to his right.

People shuffle about, readying the camera angles and holding out boom mics to capture anything that may happen.

The lead cameraman looks at Arthur and gives him a thumbs up. "Mr. Evandrum, we're ready when you are."

Arthur turns to me, lowering his voice so that only I can hear him. "Are you ready to witness history, Miss Timewire?"

The creature curls tighter around my torso, and I bury every sprout of hate shooting up in me. "I'm ready."

Arthur gives a stiff nod to the lead cameraman, donning a charismatic and camera-fit smile. "Then let the show begin."

29

"WE ARE LIVE IN FIVE, FOUR, THREE, TWO . . ."

The lead cameraman gives a silent point of his finger on "one." Arthur puffs out his chest and looks directly into the lens, drawing himself up to his full height.

"Citizens of the world, greetings. It has been seven event-filled weeks since the Pure Ones took back their rightful place in society. Though many of you still fear the unknown of what the future might hold, I've come to you today to share our plans. What you're about to witness is humanity stepping into the future. It is a future where *equality* will finally be enforced. I am joined by ten of society's most esteemed Chief Overseers." He gestures to either side of the podium, and the cameras focus in on each face as Arthur lists off their names. "Faruk Hadi, Tess Bane, Eden Nova, Sebastian Windward, Ava Ply, Silver Chessens, Aleda Sagespark, Mizzen Frank, Sylee Hasten, and Victor Quill."

The camera angle moves back to Arthur.

"My fellow Pure Ones, first, I'd like to speak to you. You have known for quite some time that I've had plans in place to ensure the safety of all with the biomarker—plans that would allow us to walk freely in the world, unhindered by our blood, safe in our homes, and protected for the remainder of our lives. I am both humbled and thrilled to announce that *today* is the day those plans come to light. And now, citizens of the world, I address you. I ask only two things of you: one, that you watch what I'm about to show you with an open mind, and two, that you consider carefully what side of history you'd like to be on. Times have changed, your Testing Centers and Military Bases have fallen, and you're on the cusp of a new world. Consider what it would mean to join us instead of fight against us. And now, to the main event."

Arthur sweeps his hand in a broad motion, and ten assistants in white lab coats walk onto the stage, each carrying a small roll of paper. The cameras zoom out, taking in the entirety of the stage. My gaze lands on the white briefcase under the podium.

The assistants hand the pieces of paper to their respective Chief Overseers, and they all unfurl their instructions, reading them over. They wear muted looks of awe and apprehension, each doing their best to maintain their societal presence despite the insanity of what's about to happen.

Again, the white briefcase lingers at the front of my mind, and my brow furrows. Why isn't Arthur grabbing it? Perhaps an assistant is going to fetch it to distribute the doses once Arthur gives the signal.

There's a good amount of shuffling as the assistants all withdraw a small silver case from the depths of their lab coat pockets. With careful and delicate movements, they unlatch the clasps in sync and open the cases to reveal syringes filled with dark liquid. They hold up the doses so the cameras can see.

My stomach somersaults, and once more, my eyes land on the white briefcase beneath Arthur. Whatever's in there, it's not the serum for the Chief Overseers . . .

Arthur's voice booms, making me jump. "Together, as one world, we will all witness the change that *must* happen if we are to have true peace."

After a quick nod from Arthur, the assistants set to work, and each Chief Overseer extends their right arm. Silence descends like a fog. The assistants wipe the flats of the Chief Overseers' arms, and with expert precision, they stick them, releasing the contents of the serum. Then, the ten assistants waste no time in retreating from the stage and backing away from the platform.

I watch the Chief Overseers, not daring to take my eyes away. For a long minute, nothing happens and no one speaks, but then Eden Nova doubles over, gasping and holding her stomach. The cameras zoom in to her. Panting, she looks up at the sky as if something were hovering right in front of her. A piercing cry splits the stage. Eden begins to claw at her blonde hair and yowl like a wild animal. Her already tall stature begins to grow, filling out with muscle, and her thin, sharp jawline stretches. The people behind the cameras gasp, the other Chief Overseers back away from her, and Arthur's expression turns to malicious delight.

After a few more seconds of the odd transformation, Eden stills, huffing madly. She's grown to a monstrous height—easily ten feet—and her arms and legs ripple with muscle. Her clothing has ripped, barely keeping itself in place against her massive frame, and her hair has darkened to ash gray. With untamed eyes and sharp, pointed teeth, she looks like a wolf-human hybrid, and it's terrifying.

Everyone watches Eden, fearful of what she might do. The woman takes in a few deep and intentional breaths, and after examining her palms, she shrinks down to her normal size, fitting back into the tatters of her outfit.

Abruptly, there's a crack to my right so loud that I scream, clapping my hands over my ears. Lightning explodes into the sky, shattering bolts in a forked pattern of devastating power. Ava Ply gapes at her hands, a curious smile crossing her lips. She steps forward to the bitter edge of the stage, and as the cameras hone in on her, she releases a second prong of lightning. It rockets into the heavens, flashing so bright it hurts.

Another scream. Another round of gasps from the camera crew. Victor Quill is on his hands and knees, coughing violently. His body seizes, his spine arches, and his eyes roll back in his skull. But the disconcerting movements are over in a flash, and as he stands to his feet, his arms and legs become like jelly, flexing and stretching *way* beyond what is humanly possible. He tips into a backbend, folding himself in half. Like some mutant rubber band, the man twists his limbs around and twirls his torso, seeming to tie himself into a knot before undoing the position and righting himself once more.

Clang.

The sound of metal hitting metal rings out. Silver Chessens, now true to his name, has bulging arms made entirely of shiny silver metal. His fists have grown too, and he hits them against each other, testing their strength.

Clang. Clang. Clang.

As he continues, more of his body turns to silver until he's covered in the substance; a complete metal man. With intention and a set of focused breaths, he holds his palms out, and the silvery metal starts to recede, seeming to leach back into his skin.

Suddenly, the floor of the stage begins to shine, as if the very molecules of the platform were producing light. It's dazzling. Like diamonds. And its source: Sylee Hasten. She's down on her knees with her palms to the stage, wide-eyed and mesmerized, gawking at the beauty of the sparkling light emanating from beneath her. She stands, and the moment her palms disconnect from the floor, it stops glowing. She turns and walks toward Arthur's podium, taking hold of it. The instant that her skin connects with the object, it shines like a brilliant star.

Arthur moves out of her way, collecting his briefcase and motioning me to back up with him. I obey, and we move away, giving Sylee space.

Once more, a shriek fills the air, raising the hairs on the back of my neck. I have to keep my own ability in check by digging my fingernails into my palms. Tess Bane is writhing on the stage, curled in a fetal position. She rolls over in her fit, coming dangerously close to the edge, and when she stops moving, I fear the worst has happened. But then she lifts her face up, and as she pushes herself up from the stage, her head splits into two . . . then her shoulders . . . then her torso . . . until a duplicate Tess climbs out of herself like a snake shedding its skin. The two of them face each other in shock, poking and prodding at each other like one might not be real.

A deep, rumbling roar bursts forth. From the end of the stage, a lion prowls forward, licking its chops and curling its lips to expose canines four inches long. It has a muscular body, talon-like claws, and a thick dark mane. The animal snarls and leans back on its hind legs, ready to pounce in my direction. My self-preservation kicks in, and I hold out my hand, on the edge of freezing it in place, but Arthur grabs my wrist.

"Don't," he says, right as the creature leaps.

The metamorphosis that happens next hurts my brain. In mid-air, the lion transforms back into a man, snout shrinking into a nose, mane reverting into hair, and paws changing into hands. Faruk Hadi stands before us, panting and clutching his chest, but wearing a giddy excitement on his face that was never there before.

Something cold tickles my face, and I swat at it, thinking a fly may have landed there, but when I look up, a shower of snowflakes dances through the air. In fact, the entire stage is now under a light snowfall. Flakes drift around like magic, controlled by the delicate fingertips of Mizzen Frank. The small man flutters his hands, sending tufts of white crystals from his palms to create a snow globe effect. It's enchanting. Spellbinding.

Pop.

Purple light flashes in my peripheral vision, and I turn

toward it. It's coming from Sebastian Windward. The old man has his hands cupped to his chest, an orb force field held within as if it were a small rodent he'd picked up from the floor. It expands slowly, enveloping his whole body. Then, with a second loud pop, the orb bursts and dissipates as if it had never been there.

Amidst all the chaos of the power display, the amazed looks of the camera crew, and the growing excitement of the Chief Overseers, Aleda Sagespark stands as still as a statue. A deeply devilish look overshadows her face, like she's working out something in her mind. She doesn't double over or cry out, she doesn't thrust her hands forward in a display of power, and she doesn't look sick to her stomach like some of the others. She simply watches the show.

Then, I see her close her eyes and hold her palms open in front of her stomach, inhaling deeply. Finally, the stance clicks in my brain. She's feeling the power underneath her skin. She's focusing on it, allowing herself to soak in the vibrations. The symbol of the New World Order—the golden woman—it's a natural pose one might take when experiencing the thrill of an ability for the first time. It's meant to represent the moment of taking the serum . . .

This horrifying realization along with Aleda's unnatural calmness makes me shrink back behind Arthur. It's the same kind of calmness she displayed as she was persuading me to give up my power—one that switched into savage, murderous triumph as she aimed the gun in my face with the intent to kill. What power did Arthur give her?

As if sensing my gaze, Aleda's attention snaps to me, and my blood turns to ice. She gives me a toothy leer and strides over to Arthur.

"How does the power feel?" he asks.

"Invigorating," she replies with a heaving chest. She pulls her shoulders back and gives Arthur an enchanted and sinister look. It's something I've never seen from her, as if whatever was in that concoction finally made her see the light. To my surprise, she holds out her hand. "You were right. I've never felt alive until this very moment."

Arthur's hungry grin of satisfaction makes my skin crawl. He grabs her hand and shakes it, keeping his eyes steady on her. Then, he slips an envelope into her hands. She opens it and takes a moment to read over the message within.

"You have a lot of work to do," Arthur says. "Are you ready to close out the show, my dear?"

She cracks a wolf-like smile and leans into him to whisper in his ear. "I've never been more ready for anything in my life."

Then, she pulls away from him and inhales deeply, closing her eyes and twitching her palms. It's a tactic I recognize and one I use myself to draw power from my chest into my hands.

"Then, by all means. The stage is yours." Arthur gives her a deep bow, gesturing her toward the podium.

When Aleda Sagespark steps up to it, a hush falls over everyone present. The other Chief Overseers stop what they're doing, the cameras pan to the center of the stage, and I hold my breath, ready to witness the closing of this serum ceremony.

Aleda's spindling hands grasp either side of the podium, and she stares the cameras down with a look that could kill. When she opens her mouth, magic-filled, fear-instilled words flow from her lips, and my knees almost give out.

"Citizens of the world," she calls out with conviction. "What you have just witnessed is the dawn of a new age. Arthur Evandrum and his associates have developed a serum that gives *power*, and I, along with my colleagues, have stepped into the decision to take this power with bravery and forward thinking. We all have the biomarker. We are now Pure Ones. And we invite each and every one of you to join us until the world stands as one, with power-filled blood, hand in hand with one another."

I gape at her, feeling the effects of the spell. Like a knife, Arthur's words to Aleda dig into my mind: "I want you to become a Pure One. I want you to take the serum live in front of the whole world. And I want you to convince the other Chief Overseers to take it too. Then I want you to convince everyone in Area 19 to take it ... and then I want you to convince *all* citizens to take it ... until every last person has a biomarker flowing through their veins."

My heartbeat thuds into my ears as the realization crashes over me. Arthur Evandrum gave Aleda Sagespark the power of his silver tongue ...

Aleda's voice continues, strong and undeterred. She clutches the envelope Arthur gave her in a vice-like grip.

"From this day forward, the Pure Ones will work to transition each Testing Center into a Power Distribution Center. There, you may take a dose of the serum for yourself. Now, I would like to speak to my fellow Chief Overseers. We are an elect group. A handful of grains among the sands of humanity. Though the ten of us here on this stage were the first to take the serum, I sincerely hope we are not the last. With your leadership, we can change the world."

Aleda bears down on the crew of people filming her, her presence seeming to reach through the lens of the camera.

"I promise you, though you may think I've lost my mind, you have not tasted how sweet this power truly is. I will admit . . . I was skeptical of Evandrum's offer at first, entrenched in my ways and filled with hate. But what I thought was a plague is actually a gift. I understand now. What runs in my veins is the very pinnacle of what humanity should be. We were wrong, my friends. The biomarker is not our destruction, it is our salvation. And I urge you to take it. You have seen an incredible display of power today, but that is only the beginning! We are the leaders, bravely stepping into this unknown with dignity so we can light the way for our fellow man. May you have the courage to do as we did, so that the citizens in your Areas may follow in your footsteps."

Aleda's voice rises, drawing in every ear. I can't help the way I hang on each word, yearning for more. It captivates me, and it's horrifying. It's like the times Arthur used his ability full force . . . there's no choice but to fall into the melody of the way she weaves her words together.

"Doses of the serum will be flown all across the globe so that every Power Distribution Center has a sufficient supply. In the coming months, all of you, great and small, will have this opportunity. Citizens, think about where your loyalties lie. The time of the Diseased Ones is over. Emerge with us into the brave new world of the Pure Ones or be lost to the darkness of the past. The choice is yours. No one will force you to take it, but you may soon find yourself to *be* as people with powers once *were*: utterly *alone.*"

With that, Aleda Sagespark steps away from the podium, and the cameras cut, ending the live feed. As soon as Aleda stops speaking, I'm able to come out of the enchanted stupor. I keep myself angled behind Arthur, using him as a shield to shift the attention off of me as, one by one, the Chief Overseers approach him to marvel over their new found power.

I watch the spectacle in silence. All of the emotionless and commanding men and women here have shifted. They are still terrifying, but now there's a new level of it laced behind their eyes. The same hunger I've seen in Arthur Evandrum is hidden in them as well. They've tasted power, and it has exhilarated them. If I'm being honest, it exhilarated me too. The display of abilities was incredible and awe-inspiring even to me—and I've been around people with powers for a while now. I can't imagine what the citizens of the world may think. Perhaps they are fearful—some likely are—but Aleda's silver-tongued speech was dangerously convincing. Her words probably ensnared those of weaker resolve.

What scares me most about all of this is not the blatant display of intimidating abilities given to some of the most dangerous society members, but Arthur's choice to make a dose of his own ability and give it to Aleda Sagespark. Of the ten Chief Overseers, she was the only one to get a type two ability—one that requires other people to work.

Type twos are more powerful than type ones. That's something Jonah taught me the first time he ever gave me a lesson. I can see the strategy behind this. The other nine were simply props for Arthur's show, but Aleda Sagespark, by the very nature of her blood, is now a part of Arthur's inner circle. He sees her as a major player, and now he has the Chief Overseer of the Capitol City's Power Distribution Center in his pocket.

Yet again, Arthur's proven he can play the field of people as pawns in his endgame of taking over the world, and I'm left feeling as powerless as ever.

30

THE REST OF THE DAY WRAPS UP IN A SERIES OF MEETINGS and instructions. Arthur gives the Chief Overseers an expected timeline of dose deliveries and tells them that their Power Distribution Centers will be the focus of the first wave of serum shipments. Then, he sends them back to their respective Areas, each with their own private jet and pilot. Thankfully, I'm able to take a short break from the chaos of "security duty" when they leave.

I collapse into a chair in the now-empty conference room B with a weary body and a grumbling stomach. All I want to do is get something to eat and pass out in the Beechcraft for a few short hours of respite before returning to the mountain.

With the sun well past the horizon and the night creeping into late, I wonder how much longer we'll be here. I wish Arthur would hurry up with whatever he's doing. He's disappeared into the Military Base with Wren, leaving me alone.

A half hour passes. Then an hour. I finally decide to get up and walk into the grand foyer to stretch my legs. As I do, Arthur and Wren emerge from a door at the far end of the room. Relieved, I stride over to them, and with as much respect as I can muster with my tired voice, I ask, "Are we going back to the mountain now?"

"Yes," Arthur says.

My heart leaps into my throat. The plan to get Maddy slams its way into my chest, and for a moment, I can't breathe. I'm hours away from gathering Jonah, Ashton, and Hazel, and forcing Wren to do my bidding under Arthur's nose. Sweat collects in my palms and buzzing enters my face, but more than anything else, wrath courses beneath my skin, waiting to be released.

As the three of us walk out onto the airstrip toward the Beechcraft, my mind is consumed with thoughts of what I'm going to do when I finally confront Arthur. With all my heart, I want to let the creature take over and do it for me. I could kill him in a blind rage, muted and distant from the experience, lost to the darkness of my own power. It would be so easy that way. She could shield me from the reality of actually taking a life . . .

But the other part of me wants to make the decision myself. To purposefully watch as my power destroys him. I'm caught in a war of raging anger and uncertainty. And then there's the smallest sliver in me that wonders if I have the strength to kill Arthur at all.

"Timewire!" Wren barks, jerking me out of my thoughts. "Get in."

"Sorry," I murmur.

I climb the stairs of the Beechcraft and settle into my spot in the back. Arthur wastes no time in gently tucking the white briefcase under his seat near the cockpit. To my dismay, he doesn't sit. Instead, he walks over, taking the seat opposite me.

His invasive stare leaches into me, and I shift uncomfortably, though I keep my face as impassive as ever. "Tell me, Hollis, what is your assessment of today?"

I press my lips together. As much as I hate to admit it, I don't have to think of my response, and I don't have to lie. "I think it was a success. The serum was incredible to witness, and Aleda . . . I think she convinced a lot of people."

Arthur can't hide his smug look. It saturates his face. He rests back in his seat, and his thumb traces the tip of his chin. "Do you know how long I've been working toward this moment?"

"A long time," I say, not daring to offer a number, though from Arthur's memories, I know he's been working to get people with powers back into society for at least a decade.

He nods slowly, studying me intently. "I'd say you were no older than five when I started this." A half-hearted chuckle that's more of a huff escapes his mouth, and he shakes his head. "To think our paths would cross in the way they have . . . that I would rely so heavily on a *society* girl to accomplish overturning the entire system. The irony doesn't escape me."

I have no idea where Arthur's going with this, so I don't respond.

"It's been an incredibly long road. And despite your brazen arrogance and naivety at the start of our partnership, you've been a real help to me. It seems that a firm hand was all you needed to get your priorities straight."

I flinch at the gravelly timbre of his tone.

"You've done well, puppet master."

I try to don a look of thankfulness, but the sour taste on my tongue makes it difficult. I don't like that he's praising me. Everything about it feels wrong. So once more, I choose to remain silent.

"I think it's time you take a break. You've done a lot, and you need to rest. Be with your friends. Enjoy the victory we've accomplished. For now, you've done all that I've required you to do."

My mouth parts in surprise. "Are you serious?"

The question escapes me before I can guise it in caution, and my longing peeks through.

"Yes," he replies. He dips his head ever so slightly. "There is more work to be done, of course, but not now. The world isn't going to change overnight. It will take time to fly doses of the serum to the first ten Power Distribution Centers, and there will be more broadcasts to come to convince those who are more reticent to comply with these changes. But for now, you've earned time to yourself."

My heart thuds in my chest. For a moment, I can't find my words, and I fumble with figuring out what to say. "I . . . um . . . thank you, Mr. Evandrum."

There's a long pause between us, and Arthur looks out the window of the Beechcraft into the pitch black of night. When he speaks again, it's hushed and pensive. "I've only dealt harshly with you to teach you, I hope you know that."

To teach me? I have to force the boiling rage in myself to stay under the surface. All he's ever wanted from me is my complete and unquestioning compliance. And he's killed, kidnapped, manipulated, and tortured to get it—even going as far as purposefully letting me walk into Camille's holo-tech trap and allowing "the cards to fall where they may." At no point was his intention to teach me. It was to control me. Plain and simple.

"I couldn't have done this as quickly without your help," he continues in a voice that's kind and soft. "You've been instrumental."

The way he's acting reminds me of the meeting where he told me that he took no pleasure in stealing Maddy away from me. In that same meeting he said that I had the potential to be one of the most influential leaders in history, and he also asked me if, given time, I'd be willing to do what he wants without coercion. He thinks he's tamed me, but he doesn't know what I'm about to do. I swore he would never break me, and I've kept that promise to myself. Through all of this, I've worked to free myself and Maddy. Arthur never truly forced me to be on his side, even though outwardly it appears that way. I've played my part well.

"You understand why I've put you through what I have, don't you?" he asks.

The only word I can force from my lips is "Yes." Anything more and I might slip.

"Good," he replies. "I'm hoping to put it in the past, as our continued partnership is what's best for all. Don't you agree?"

I let out a deliberate but silent breath, not taking my eyes off Arthur. "Of course. I would like that very much actually."

A small grin hides at the corner of his mouth. "I'm glad you see it that way. Before your father's execution, you offered me a handshake to new beginnings. I didn't believe you. But I think you finally understand things, don't you?" He presses his lips together, scrutinizing me, and then he says something that nearly breaks my stonewall façade. "I'm ready to offer you the same thing you offered me." He sticks his hand out, and my throat closes up. "To new beginnings?"

Though everything in me is screaming "no," I grab his hand and shake it, repeating the same thing Arthur said to Rosalie when she was disguised as me. "To new beginnings."

■   ■   ■

When the Beechcraft touches down at the mountain, a buzz enters my body. It's a heightened sense of anticipation that floods my veins and doesn't leave. I can't believe what I'm about to do. As we taxi to the hangar, I clutch my duffle bag, mostly to give my shaking hands something steady to hold on to.

Each minute feels like an eternity, but when the engines finally turn off and the door to the plane opens, I rise to my feet and walk down the steps, freeing myself from the interior. Arthur holds the white briefcase close and bids me goodnight, stalking off without another word. Right as I'm about to do the same, Wren's voice stops me.

"Timewire."

I close my eyes tightly and center myself a moment before opening them and turning back around.

"Yes?"

"You did a good job. It's not my place to say something like that in front of Evandrum, but I wanted you to know."

My heartbeat quickens, another dose of anxiety weaving its way through me. "Thank you, Wren. That means a lot."

For all the things this woman has done for me, I hate what I'm about to do to her, but it's the only way to get Maddy, and I'll do whatever it takes for him. Perhaps she will forgive me someday.

"Get some rest," Wren says. "You really have earned it."

"Yes ma'am," I say, taking her dismissal to stride over to the exit of the hangar that leads to the interior of the mountain fortress. I need to gather Jonah, Ashton, and Hazel before I take control of Wren.

It doesn't take me long. The first person I go to is Jonah, and I ask him to get the others and meet me in the training room. Twenty minutes later, the four of us are gathered on the training mat. We hash out the details of the plan one last time, and when there's nothing left to go over, I look each of them in the eye for a long moment.

"Are we ready to do this?" I ask.

Ashton nods, balling up his fists. "Let's go get Maddy."

I give a determined nod. Before I make a move toward the door, I walk up to Jonah and wrap my arms around him. He embraces me back. The encouragement he gave me at the start of this mess comes back to me like a wave of strength, and it fills me with purpose: "You are strong. Unbreakably so."

"I've got you," Jonah says. "Every step of the way, I'm here with you."

I blow out air between pursed lips, releasing the hug and

igniting my hands with tingling. To tell the truth, I'm so relieved Jonah is doing this with me. To know that his power and his guidance are there if I need them gives me the confidence that we're going to pull this off.

I stretch my hands out, allowing the tendrils of my power to sense Wren. "She's still in the aircraft hangar."

"Hazel, it's time," Jonah says.

She nods shakily, flowering her hands open to envelop herself, Jonah, and Ashton, leaving me as the only visible one in our party.

"Let's go. Follow me and keep quiet," I say.

The trudge through the mountain feels like a fever dream. Every step I take makes me feel like someone will whip around a corner and confront us. But no one stops me. I don't see a single person on my way back to the hangar. The late night is in our favor, as it seems the whole mountain is asleep.

When I reach the double doors, I pause, drawing in one last deep breath before taking the plunge into a decision I can't take back. I enter into the large concrete space, spotting Wren by the Beechcraft. With quick steps, I march forward, adrenaline and tingling mixing together in my limbs. She looks up at my approach, a curious expression shadowing her face.

"Timewire, what is it?" she asks.

My pulse slams through my chest. Five seconds of no response hangs between us, and then, with a slash of my palm, I grab Wren with the full force of my ability, and the creature closes her mouth. Her eyes light up in surprise, and then horror flickers across her face.

"Get on the Beechcraft!" I command, compelling her to action.

She springs into motion, forced to follow the order. The fold-out stairs open, and I direct her into the cabin of the plane. With everything she has, she fights my hold. I can feel the strain of it under my fingertips, but there's nothing she can do to refuse me. Her attempts are futile.

When the two of us are inside, I wait a moment, allowing time for Jonah, Ashton, and Hazel to board. Even though I can't see them, I can sense them, and when the three are safely on board, I shut the door to the Beechcraft. Hazel still keeps the group concealed.

I push tingling into Wren, and the creature materializes by my side, hovering in coils of ash black mist. She fuels my desire to get into the skies as quickly as possible. With intention, I channel my instructions into the woman bound under my control.

"You are going to take me to the Area 7 Testing Center," I snarl.

Wren's eyes widen, and more fighting ensues under my fingertips, but outwardly she doesn't move a muscle.

"You will not alert *anyone* to what's happening, especially Arthur. I'm getting Maddy back, and you're going to help me. If anyone comes on that radio when we taxi and take off, you will lie about what you're doing." I shove my hand forward, and more control washes over me. It's invigorating, like being able to breathe, and the wrath that's been stockpiling in my body comes out. I don't hurt Wren, but I pour everything I have into her. "And if there's any kind of help signal in this plane, you will not touch it. Get in the cockpit and get us off the ground!"

Wren jolts as though I've punched her and turns on her heels to enter the cockpit. With stiffened and strained movements, she sits and begins to tap on buttons. The sound of the engines whirring skyrockets my confidence. I've done it. I've taken control of Wren Zayla.

"I'm coming Maddy," I say under my breath.

I take the seat next to Wren, watching her movements like a hawk. There's so many buttons, levers, and lights that it's impossible for me to understand what she's doing, but I hold fast to my ability because she can't disobey the puppet master who commands her.

The Beechcraft begins to move, pulling out of its spot in the hangar. Wren is still viciously trying to break my control, but it feels like nothing more than a tickle under my fingertips, barely perceivable.

Over the next five minutes, every movement Wren makes against the control panel is intentional, led by the overbearing presence of my command. It's so freeing to finally unleash the beast. I am the puppet master, and she is my puppet.

Control. Pure and untainted control. *Finally.*

It's only when we've taken to the sky without incident and the mountain begins to shrink in the distance that the intense pulsing down my arms relaxes a bit. The creature hisses in my ear, relishing in the hold she has. I stand, walking back into the cabin.

"You can show yourselves now," I say to my companions.

With a rippling of the air around the seats in the back, Jonah, Ashton, and Hazel appear. Ashton jumps to his feet, swearing at the top of his lungs and brushing his hands through his dirty blond hair.

"We did it!" he exclaims.

"Let's not celebrate too early," Hazel says, a nervous sheen of sweat forming against her dark brown hairline.

"Hollis, how long are we expected to be in the air?" Jonah inquires.

"Let me ask," I say, turning back toward the cockpit. I shimmy into the seat next to Wren, a bold vengeance in my countenance. I give a twitch of my palm. "How long does it take to fly to the Area 7 Testing Center?"

A gritted, forced reply leaves her lips. "One hour and forty-seven minutes."

I stare at her for a long moment, and the smallest amount of guilt creeps in. I'm not sure what it will accomplish, but I want to have one last conversation with her before this is over. Against my better judgment, I say, "I'm going to open your mouth so you can talk."

I hold my hand up, flourishing my palm.

Wren gasps, taking a hard swallow. "Are you insane!? What are you doing? I promise you, you have *not* thought this through!" Her hands grip the yoke of the plane so hard it stretches the skin on her knuckles.

"I promise you, I *have*!" I counter. "I'm not doing Arthur's bidding anymore, Wren. I can't. I'm getting Maddy out of that lab. I'm going to end the serum production, and I'm going to put a stop to Arthur's twisted vision for the future. I don't care what Aleda said about the serum being a 'choice.' You and I both know

Arthur intends to force citizens to take it at the penalty of their own lives. That's not right, Wren. Arthur's plan leads to a massacre of people who don't have powers, plain and simple. And I refuse to stand by and watch as history repeats itself."

"Hollis!" she cries. "Don't do this!"

The severity of her tone makes me jump, but I compose myself quickly. "You can't stop me. This is happening! I've worked every moment since Maddy's kidnapping to find him, and I'm taking him back. Arthur's insurance against me has just run out. I'm no longer his pet puppet master."

"HOLLIS!" The way she barks my name stabs me with fear. "I'm begging you! We need to turn this plane around *right now*."

I shake my head fervently. "No!"

But something about her tone sets me on high alert. I cast my hand toward her, forcing more power through my fingertips. "Does Arthur know we've taken off? Does he know about this?"

"No," she growls.

"Does anyone know about this?"

"No."

"Is there something waiting for us at the Testing Center? Something Arthur's set up against me?"

"There's nothing waiting for you."

Relief floods me, though jitters have suddenly claimed my hands, betraying my nerves. As long as Arthur doesn't find out about this until after we extract Maddy, we'll be fine.

This conversation is over. I sweep my hand forward, closing her mouth once more. The look behind her eyes is one of absolute horror. Another round of silent fighting commences, but Wren can't break my hold. My control is absolute.

"I'm doing this, Wren. I'm sorry you had to get caught up in it," I say, gazing at her with compassion and regret. "You really have treated me with kindness, and for that, I thank you."

I get up from my seat in the cockpit, making my way back to the cabin where my three companions wait. Ashton is pacing up and down the aisle, Hazel is standing all the way in the back, nervously chewing on her thumb nail, and Jonah is sitting in one of the plush leather chairs.

"We'll be there in less than two hours," I say.

Ashton stops pacing. His normally bold swagger has evaporated. While he doesn't look scared, he doesn't appear confident either. "Can we talk it out one more time?" he asks, dropping into the seat across from Jonah.

"I'd like that too," Hazel says, joining them by sitting down as well.

"Sure," Jonah replies. "When we land, Hazel will make the four of us disappear. Hollis, you'll keep Wren bound under your power in the Beechcraft, waiting and ready to go. We'll walk into the Testing Center and go to the eighth floor. When we locate Maddy's room, we'll enter the code Hollis got from Maddy—"

"3-3-4-6-7," I cut in.

Jonah nods. "Then Hazel will conceal Maddy with her power as well. The five of us will walk out, board the Beechcraft, and get back in the air. If everything goes smoothly, no one will know what's happened until we're gone."

Ashton lets out the breath he was holding, looking at Hazel. "Let's hope the only person's power we need is yours. But remember, Hollis, Jonah, and I have your back if you need us."

"Yes," she affirms, shaking out her hands in an attempt to calm herself. She clutches her chest. "My heart is racing."

"Mine too," Ashton says.

I look between the two of them. "Remember, they don't know we're coming. We have surprise on our side, and that's all we need."

Jonah clears his throat. "Hollis, this man, Jenkins . . . the one that watches Maddy. Is there anything else you can remember about him? Anything at all?"

I shake my head. "I told you everything Maddy told me. I don't know what his power is, all I know is that we can't let him touch us. Maddy was adamant."

Jonah puts a hand to his chin. "Let's hope we don't run into him. I may be able to take on powers that are near me, but I don't know what a power is until I try it for myself."

Hazel points up to the cockpit. "Why not make Wren tell us? I'm sure she knows."

The simplicity of this nearly makes me smack my forehead, but when I walk to the cockpit and force my question over Wren, she tells me she doesn't know—a statement I find as odd as ever. How could Wren Zayla, one of Arthur's inner circle, *not* know?

"What do you mean you don't know?" My hand gives another flick, commanding her to answer.

Wren snarls out her reply. "It may surprise you to know that I'm not intimately familiar with the powers of every single Pure One, Timewire. I've been stationed in Area 19 for the past decade, not Area 7."

"But Maddy's keeper?" I reiterate. "The person responsible for the boy who's blood is running this whole operation?"

"I don't know."

I give a grunt of frustration, leaving her silent again as I trek back to the cabin. "She doesn't know."

Hazel and Ashton both look at each other.

"And you believe her?" Ashton asks, aghast. "She's obviously lying!"

"She can't lie to me." I wave my palm in the air. "My power compels the truth from people. She doesn't know."

"Look," Jonah says, pulling everyone's attention to himself. "Truthfully, it doesn't matter what power Jenkins has. We know what Maddy told us. Don't let him touch anyone. Maybe we won't run into him at all. But if we do, we have power enough to deal with it."

"I suppose so," I say.

I shake out my hands in the same manner Hazel did a minute ago. More than anything, a resolute desire to see Maddy safe is driving me. All tiredness is gone from my body, leaving only single-minded determination in its place. Wren is going to land this plane soon, and I'll have to live with what happens as a result of this choice. But I'm ready for it. I'm the puppet master. I'm the leader. And Maddy is *mine*.

31

Wren lands the plane outside the city to keep our arrival a secret. I leave her where she is, stiff and silent under the creature's hold, with instructions to do nothing until we return. Fortunately for us, the Area 7 Testing Center isn't far from the edge of the city's layout, so maintaining my hold over Wren from a distance is doable.

Under the cover of darkness and Hazel's invisibility, we slink down the streets unnoticed. The only sound is an occasional footfall that lands too hard, but there's no one out to hear us. It's strange, being under Hazel's power. It's like a cloak draped over the four of us. Inside her protective bubble of shifted air, we can see each other, but no one can see us.

We take a left at the street transit stop at the end of the block, and when we do, the Area 7 Testing Center looms into view. Even in the dark, it's daunting. Floodlights illuminate the marble steps and grand entrance, casting shadows up the high glass walls that reach into the night sky.

"Not a sound," I whisper.

We ascend the stairs slowly, and when we reach the top, I hold my hand up to stop everyone. The light coming from the large lobby makes it easy to peer through the glass. There's a security guard behind the welcome desk, and he looks like he's one nod away from falling asleep. If the doors were to open, it would most certainly jerk him out of his stupor. I'd rather avoid that sort of suspicion.

I look from Jonah to Ashton to Hazel. "Follow my lead. Stop when I stop. Go when I go."

They all nod in agreement. With a channeled burst of power, I call the creature out, and she emerges, wrapping herself like a shield around my chest. Her head hovers over my right shoulder as if poised to strike anyone who would dare come near me. Her hiss turns into words that fuel my strength.

I will protect you.

I raise my hand, focusing my ability into the security guard's arm. With a small flick, I give his wrist a tug, and it smashes into a stack of papers, which knocks into his cup of coffee. There's a violent crash, and the porcelain shatters against the tile flooring behind his desk. The man curses, stooping down to deal with the mess.

The second his head ducks under the rim of the desk, I pull open the Testing Center double doors, and the four of us slip in. The man is so preoccupied with his mishap that he doesn't notice a thing.

Without a sound, we make our way toward the leftmost side of the lobby, where the entrance to the stairwell starts. Thankfully, this Testing Center isn't any different from Area 19's floor plan. The cookie-cutter nature of society's most cherished institution means I know this place well, even though I've never stepped foot here.

The security guard is still on the floor gathering the shards of his broken cup, so I waste no time in grasping the handle of the door that leads into the stairwell and ushering my three companions through. The timing is perfect. The moment the door closes behind us, I sense the security guard's gaze as he rises up from his crouched position. There's no change in his heartbeat or breath. We got by him undetected.

The spiral steps in front of me seem to reach out and grab hold of my throat. They cast me back to the nightmare of when I was fleeing for my life from Camille. This place . . . This horrid place . . . I shake the thought from my head with force. Camille is dead. No one is chasing me.

Up and up we go, around the spiral until we reach level eight. Again, I let the invisible strands of my power do the work before I dare open the door. The creature prowls through the people present. Three souls . . . one that feels intimately familiar.

An overwhelming wave of emotion crashes into me, and my eyes well with happy tears. I press a hand to my mouth to stop myself from making a sound. Finally, after being separated for seven tortuous weeks, I can sense the small and delicate heartbeat of the boy with the golden light.

But I don't move. Not yet.

Jonah, Ashton, and Hazel all stand behind me, waiting patiently for my lead. There are two more people I have to take into account, and currently, one of them is far too close to the stairwell for us to make a move. If the door to the level opened seemingly on its own, that would definitely raise suspicion.

I stand there with a hammering heartbeat, unsure of how to proceed. So I hone in on the person closest to us, collecting more details. It's a woman. She's holding a glass beaker, pouring liquid out into a sink. My hearing turns sharp as the creature expands my senses.

Water rushes over the woman's hands as she rinses out the piece of glassware. She sets it upside down on a plastic drying rack, grabbing the next beaker from the workbench and swirling it under the gentle flow. It seems that she's not going anywhere any time soon.

Just as I'm about to hone in on the second person, I hear a man's voice as sharply as if he were standing next to me.

"Tawni, could you come here for a moment?" he calls. My power shifts to him to assess. He's standing at the other end of the level in an office.

The woman begrudgingly turns off the water. "What?"

"I said, could you come here?"

The woman tisks in annoyance. "Jenkins, if this is another one of your stupid puzzles, I'm reporting you. I don't give a damn about your word games. I have work to do."

When he doesn't reply, she abandons the dirty beakers and strides away from the stairwell, her heels clicking madly against the tile.

Now's our chance. I turn the handle, pulling the door in toward myself. My three companions get through first, and I follow. Recognition again throws me into a flurry of nightmarish memories. I know this layout. There are three see-through glass laboratories that span the length of the level, and it reminds me of the puppets under Camille's control clutching needles, knives, scissors, and scalpels, ready to tear me to pieces.

Sweat creeps down my back.

Focus, Hollis, my ability snarls.

My fingertips move deliberately through the air, and Maddy's presence comes into sharper focus. I can sense him at the end of a small hallway that's tucked past the three glass laboratories. Unfortunately, Jenkins and Tawni are in the office that's right next to Maddy's room.

The four of us sneak forward, keeping against the leftmost wall.

"We're behind schedule," Jenkins grumbles, his voice carrying clearly. "Look." I feel him point to something I can't see. "Here's the projected doses for the first ten Power Distribution Centers. Evandrum sent this a few hours ago."

There's a sharp intake of breath.

"We're ten thousand doses behind?" Tawni blurts. "The boy can't take that kind of stress. We're stretching him thin as it is."

"I know."

"Then tell Evandrum we can't complete the order by his deadline."

There's a beat of silence as the four of us creep all the way up to the office. I can see the keypad situated on the deadlock to Maddy's room. It's ten feet away, just past the door where Jenkins and Tawni stand. But I hold us steady because the voice growls at me.

Wait.

There's a sudden shuffling of footsteps, and Jenkins walks out of the office, coming so close to me that he misses me by a mere foot.

"I'm not telling Evandrum anything," he replies coldly.

Tawni clicks after him, her short stubby legs having a hard time keeping up with Jenkins' long ones. "*You're* in charge of the boy! We can't produce that many doses by the deadline. It's simply impossible!"

"Then you tell him."

The two of them head toward the glass laboratory that's closest to the stairwell.

"Do you want him to die?" Tawni asks, catching his arm. "Because that's what's going to happen. You realize that, right?"

Jenkins pulls out of her grip, entering the glass laboratory, and she follows him with a frustrated huff. I can still see them, but they're so engrossed in their argument that I know this is our moment. I leap into action, striding over to the keypad and tapping in the code Maddy gave me. The deadbolt lights up, and a soft click comes from the handle.

My heart leaps into my throat at the noise, but Jenkins and Tawni haven't noticed. They're still going at it, their voices getting louder and more heated.

I push the door in just wide enough for the four of us to get through, and then I leave it open, but only a sliver. I don't want to accidentally lock us in this room. When I turn around, I'm greeted by the same stark white room of Maddy's dreamspace, but this time it's a reality. There in the corner, half covered by a blanket on the small bed—which is the only piece of furniture in the room—is Maddy, and he's sound asleep, his blond curls plastered against his pallid forehead. He looks sickly and bony. Dark circles rim his eyes, a layer of grime resides under his fingernails, and bruises from the needle marks cover his arms.

Affection for him, stronger than I've ever felt before, takes hold of me, and the creature coils her misted body tighter. Still under the invisibility of Hazel's shield, I approach Maddy, gently touching his hand. He stirs almost instantly, his eyelids fluttering open. I don't want to scare him or have him call out, so with a soft push of my ability, I close his mouth and stiffen him under my command.

"Maddy, it's me, Hollis," I whisper. "I'm here to rescue you, but you have to be quiet. Okay?"

I can feel a quiver shoot through him, and his eyes go wide. Immediately, he begins to tear up, but I don't release him from my power yet.

"Hazel, shield him in with us," I say, keeping my voice as low as possible.

There's a shudder of air molecules around the small boy, and like a lost lamb finally coming home, he's invited into the fold, cloaked under the protection of Hazel's power. The moment he can see us, I hold my finger up to my lips, then I withdraw my power from his body. He sinks into me, and I wrap my arms around him, lifting him from the bed and holding him tight to my chest.

He clings to my neck, crying quietly. Little sobs wrack his body, though he stifles them well. I can tell he's trying his best to stop his tears, but the emotion of the moment is too much for him to handle. The poor baby is completely overwhelmed.

"I'm here," I whisper. "You're safe now. We're going to get you out."

I stand from the bed, clutching him securely against my hip, and he grabs onto me even tighter. Now all we have to do is get the hell out of here . . .

A pair of thick footfalls causes me to jump, and my heartbeat jackhammers violently. With the senses of my power, I can feel Jenkins approaching the office again, and Tawni isn't far behind. My eyes dart to the crack I left in the door.

"You're the team lead!" Jenkins says angrily, whipping into the office. "It's *your* responsibility, not mine. I may be in charge of the kid, but I'm not the leader. I'm done having this conversation."

"You're infuriating!" Tawni retorts, entering the office space close behind him.

Their backs are turned away from the opening. I can feel them. I almost take the opportunity to plunge back through the door and onto the level, but before I can make my move, Jenkins' annoyed voice suddenly turns deadly.

"Wait a minute . . . what the hell?"

"What?" Tawni snaps.

All I can feel with the strings of my power is Jenkins slowly lifting a forefinger to point at something directly in front of him. "Maddy . . ." he croons to himself, drawing out the ending syllable of his name for far too long. "How did you get that door open?"

Faster than humanly possible, he launches out of the office, pushing past Tawni to stand directly in front of the cracked sliver to Maddy's room. He shoves the door open and fills the entire entryway with his towering presence. When his dark eyes rove over the space, they pass directly through us, but his posture shifts in surprise when he doesn't see Maddy. All thoughts of doing this mission without anyone noticing vanish. Jenkins is involved now, and so is Tawni. I can't let them raise an alarm.

Just as I'm about to swipe my hand, the smallest whimper leaves Maddy's mouth, and several things happen at once. Jenkins lunges at the noise, swinging his hand through the air directly at *me*. The creature tugs me out of the way, and in the same instant, she seizes Jenkins, but not before his palm makes contact with Hazel's shoulder. The effect is instantaneous. Hazel collapses to the floor and the shield of invisibility around us bursts.

Jenkins' eyes bulge in realization as he sees the five of us materialize.

My ability bursts through his body. I channel it with so much force that I slam him into the wall with the strength of my control. I extend a hand to grab Tawni too, silencing her and forcing her into the small room. Control cements my hold over the two of them, and the creature rattles with pleasure over her new victims.

"Oh my God . . . Hazel!" Ashton cries.

When I turn to look, what I see sends fear all the way down to my bones. Hazel's skin has shrunken against her skull, her hair has turned brittle, and her muscles have atrophied. She's nothing but skin and bones, and her sunken eyes appear hollow. It looks like she's been starved to death.

Maddy screams, causing my ears to ring. He grabs me so tight I can barely breathe.

Jonah springs into action, stooping down to check Hazel's pulse. "She's alive. But barely." He looks up at me with urgency. "Hollis, we have to get out of here! And we have to take those two with us." He points to Jenkins and Tawni. "We can't leave them here now that they've seen us."

"Can you shield us if Hazel is like this?" I ask, taking in her skeletal state. Bile rises up my throat.

"Yes, but if she dies, so does our invisibility."

His statement jabs panic through my chest. If that happens while we're still in the Testing Center, then our cover is up. Even if we don't run into anyone, there are security cameras everywhere. I may be able to take two hostages with us, but I can't take on this whole Testing Center and get back to the mountain in secret.

"Ashton, help me!" Jonah urges.

Ashton gives Jonah a hand in hoisting Hazel from the floor, and the two of them support her tiny frame between themselves. With a rippling of the air, Jonah shrouds the seven of us in Hazel's power. It flickers for a moment, to my dismay, but holds strong.

I call the two puppets to my side, tucking them in with our group so that we're tight knit. I hug Maddy against my chest, whispering in his ear. "You have to stay quiet, okay? You can't make a sound. We're invisible to people right now, but they can still hear us." Then I lock eyes with Jonah and Ashton. "Let's go."

I lead the charge, exiting Maddy's room. Since there's no one else on level eight, I don't bother to hide the sound of my feet. It's only when we get to the stairwell that I step more lightly. By the time we make it down the spiral, Ashton and Jonah are breathing heavily with the strain of carrying Hazel. I stop our group in front of the door leading to the lobby—one, to give Jonah and Ashton a moment to stop panting, and two, to scope out the space. The same security guard is still there, but this time, he's wide awake. I can see him through the small window installed in the door.

My mind blanks out as I try to think of how we're going to get past him without him noticing . . .

Abruptly, the bubble of shifted air around us trembles, flickering like a broken wall screen. Jonah strains with the effort of keeping us concealed, and his frantic whisper sends frisson down my arms.

"Hollis, we have to move, or we're going to lose this shield."

Our invisibility fluctuates again, and this time, it's enough to catch the security guard's eye. Before I can even react, Ashton's hands have cut through the air to suppress the security guard's ability right as the man splays his palms in our direction. An alarmed look crosses the guard's face, and his brow furrows in confusion.

"What the—" he begins.

Without hesitation, I wrap the ropes of my power around the man's body, closing his mouth. I watch as he jerks behind his desk. Then, I open the door to the stairwell, and all of us spill into the lobby. With a flick, I force the man to his feet, compelling him to my side, and Jonah casts a wave of illusion over him. Silent and bound like the other two, the security guard falls into line, and our entourage leaves through the double doors of the Testing Center.

"Thanks for that," I say to Ashton.

It's not until we're three blocks down that the claws of panic release their hold over me. The pitch black of night helps us hide amidst the failing shield of Hazel's ability. More and more, it glitches, throwing us in and out of view. But no one is out on the streets.

"How's Hazel?" I ask, huffing madly from supporting Maddy's weight.

"Not good," Jonah replies. "I can feel the strength leaving her. She doesn't have much time."

"What the hell did that guy do to her?" Ashton asks, grunting.

Jonah shakes his head. "I don't know."

"We just have to get to the Beechcraft," I say.

With all my heart, I hold this thought close like a prayer, willing it to be so. Block after block, I repeat it in my head, until finally, the edge of the city comes into view, and with it, the plane that's flown me all across the world.

There's a distinct hum of bugs in the air, playing their medley in the cool breeze. Stars peek out behind swaths of gray clouds. And as our footsteps thud across the cracked dirt beyond the city limit, an owl hoots from somewhere in the distance.

I practically run the last stretch to the Beechcraft, even with Maddy slowing me down. I haul him up the fold-out steps, gulping the air as I do so. A stitch has entered my chest, stabbing me. I set Maddy down in the seat nearest the cockpit and turn toward my trio of puppets. Without restraint, I yank them roughly into the plane, forcing them all the way into the back and leaving them seated on the floor.

Jonah and Ashton climb in next, carrying Hazel up, and when they're in, I pull the door to the Beechcraft shut, sealing the airlock. As Jonah and Ashton carefully lay Hazel down in the aisle, I cast a hand toward the cockpit, and Wren jolts.

"Get us in the air!" I cry. "Now! And take us back to the mountain."

The engines start up, rumbling beneath us, and yet another string of tension vanishes. We did it. We got Maddy out of the Testing Center . . .

I spin around, immediately moving to tend to Maddy, but he's not seated anymore. He's standing and pointing toward the back of the plane. More specifically, he's pointing toward Jenkins. The small boy's ghost-like appearance sends razor blades of panic back through me.

I stoop down to his level. "Maddy, what is it?"

"He can fix her. He can undo it." Maddy's eyes land on Hazel, whose death-like state has only gotten worse. She looks like she's moments away from taking her last breath. Immediately, I step around Hazel and march to the back of the plane, puppeting Jenkins to his feet. I slice my hand over his heart.

"What did you do to her?" I demand.

He spits through clenched teeth, choking out his words because of the force I'm using. "I depleted—all of the—calories and energy reserves from—her body."

So that's what Jenkins was doing to Maddy. Every time they would take his blood, Jenkins would replenish Maddy's energy with his ability and strengthen his body so that they could take more and more. A near never-ending supply of healthy blood from an otherwise sickly and used-up little boy.

I practically lift Jenkins from his feet with the ferocity of my next command. "Undo it!" I throw him to his knees next to Hazel's shrunken form. "Jonah, Ashton, get away from her!"

They obey me, scrambling out of Jenkins' way. The man places his hand on Hazel's chest, and color comes back to her ashen cheeks. At the same time, her face and limbs begin to fill out, muscle being restored and atrophy disappearing. Within ten seconds, a spark of energy comes back to Hazel's eyes, and her chest expands with life.

"Hazel!" I exclaim.

I twitch my fingertips, ordering Jenkins away from her and back to his spot on the floor with the others.

Hazel clutches the collar of her shirt, gazing around at us. She turns over and coughs violently. "I thought I was dead."

"We thought you were too," Ashton admits.

"Beck is going to kill me when he finds out about this," she huffs.

"Maybe he doesn't need to know?" Ashton offers.

She gives a half-hearted laugh. "Maybe you're right. It would only worry him."

Now that Hazel is no longer dying, I walk over to Maddy and scoop him up in my arms, sitting down with him in the nearest leather chair. My heart is so happy, it could burst. I can't believe he's really in front of me. We hug for a full minute. Tears spill down both of our faces. The boy with the golden light is safe at last.

"I told you I would come for you," I murmur.

His little body shivers, and I hold him close, gently moving dirty curls from his face. Maddy looks absolutely spent.

"Here," I say, shifting his position on my lap. "Lean your head against my shoulder and sleep. You're safe now."

Maddy looks up at me, and his eyelids droop with exhaustion. "Do you promise?"

"I promise."

He doesn't need any more coaxing. He passes out in my lap in no time at all, and I cherish this moment of sweet rest.

I glance out of the window of the Beechcraft, a steady storm of wrath brewing up from the depths of my soul to collect in my fingertips. It's so tangible and so palpable that my vision begins to tunnel and my hands begin to burn.

The familiar hiss of the creature lingers in my ear. She says one word, and one word only: *Kill.*

"Arthur Evandrum," I growl. "Here comes the monster you made."

—

32

—

Maddy sleeps on my chest for the next hour, but with the mountain fast approaching, I gently wake him. We don't have long before we land, and I need to prepare myself.

"We're almost back home, Maddy," I say, feeling an odd twinge in my stomach at the concept. The mountain, as strange as it is to admit, has become my home. I wonder if I'll always consider it my home when this is over.

Maddy rubs his eyes and sniffles, giving a big stretch of his arms before sitting up on my lap. Though he still looks tired and sickly, an energetic happiness has entered his voice, and he gives me a big smile. "Is Vivi going to be there when we land?"

I smile back at him. "No, but you're going to see her later today. I have to take care of some things first. And you're going to stay with Jonah and Ash. But when I'm done, you can see her."

"Yay! Duck bill! Duck bill!" he chimes, lighting up.

This simple chant brings me so much warmth, and I squeeze him into another hug. I can't help it. Before Maddy's kidnapping, he spent a lot of time with Vianne, and her favorite trick to use with him was morphing her face into a duck bill and passing off a surprisingly good impression of a quack. She never ceased to elicit fits of laughter from him—and Maddy's laughter is a magic all on its own.

"Maddy."

He looks up at me with his bright blue eyes.

"I'm going to tell you something, and I want you to listen carefully. Okay?"

"Okay." His little hand reaches out and grabs mine, and his attention cleaves to me.

As I look into his frail face, so much anger for the people who hurt him thrashes inside me, but I keep it down. I want him to know that he's more than a prop, and I want him to know that he matters—not because of his power, but because of who he is.

"You're going to be okay now. No one is going to take your blood anymore or lock you up. And no one is going to use you for your power ever again." I squeeze his hand. "You are special and you matter, and it's not just because you have the golden light. You matter because you're the only person in the world like you. You matter because you have your own thoughts and your own voice. I want you to know that even though evil people have done evil things to you, you're not here on this earth for the purpose of being *used*. Your story is bigger than that. And I'm so sorry that you've been a part of something so dark. If I could take all the pain away, I would." I pause, collecting myself to fight through the growing lump in my throat. "I want you to know that you have a family and that you are *not* alone. I promise you as long as I have breath in my body, I will fight for you. Because you deserve the chance to be a person and not just a power."

I lean in and kiss the top of his head, clinging to his hand still. "I love you, little one."

Maddy nuzzles his head into me affectionately, wrapping his arms around my neck. "I love you, Hollis."

I soak in the embrace, tears collecting in my eyes. When he unhooks his arms, I gently nudge him to stand up. I rise from the chair, stretching my limbs from the stiffness of being in one position for so long. "I have to talk with Jonah and Ash. We'll be landing soon. You should try and get some more rest."

Maddy clambers back up into the seat I've vacated, leaning his head against the window, and I walk down the aisle to join Jonah, Ashton, and Hazel. Hazel is dozing in her chair, no doubt spent from her near-death experience, but Jonah and Ashton are wide awake. I walk up to the bolted-in table that's anchored between them.

"We're almost there," I say, graven.

"What's your plan?" Jonah asks.

"As we're landing, I'm going to take control of Arthur from the air. I'm going to take control of Terrace too and anyone else I need to so I can face him without interruption. I'd like you and Ashton to stay with Maddy. Keep him in the Beechcraft and out of sight until this is over."

Ashton fiddles with a hangnail on his thumb, looking up at me with a somber expression. "Have you decided what you're going to do to Arthur?"

A slow and purposeful breath escapes me, and my hands

charge with tingling. After wrestling with myself over the decision, getting Maddy back finally tipped the scales of my uncertainty. There's no way Maddy would ever be safe with Arthur alive. His desire to create this serum is too strong, and his true followers are too loyal to his vision for the future. I'm ending this today. Arthur Evandrum is going to pay for what he's done with his life. I'll deal with the fallout of this decision later.

"Yes," I breathe out, my voice sure and steady. "I'm going to kill him."

It's the first time I've said the words out loud in front of Jonah, but he doesn't look surprised. He simply stares at me, a deep soberness in his features.

"Ashton told me about your struggles with this decision," Jonah says.

My heartbeat increases with a spike of worry for what he might say next. Out of anyone's opinion, Jonah's matters the most to me. If he condemns the idea, it won't change my mind, but his support would give me peace.

He puts a hand to his chin, his brow creasing. "I never thought I would say something like this, but . . . I think your decision is the right choice. My only regret is that this decision had to fall on your shoulders, Hollis."

Relief sweeps through me at his response, and I grab his hand, giving it a firm squeeze. My mouth curves into a half-smile that's more lamentful than anything else. "You taught me well. You once said no one would expect anything from a sixteen-year-old girl, but it was my decision to prove them wrong. Well? This is it, isn't it? It all falls on me, the way it was always going to with a power as strong as mine."

There's a tightness in my chest that's maintaining its hold, but more than anything, strength and raw power overwhelm the nerves in me. I'm ready to face him, and I'm ready to end this.

"I'm going to get an ETA from Wren," I say, turning on my heels to walk down the aisle past Maddy.

As I scoot into the cramped cockpit, the early signs of dawn clothe the sky with a dim glow. The sun isn't above the horizon yet, but its rays work to lighten the sleeping earth below.

I flick my hand toward Wren. "How far are we?"

"Sixteen minutes."

I don't allow her to say anything more. I exit the cockpit, rolling my shoulders out and pacing the length of the aisle a few times to give my pent-up energy an outlet. Every minute that passes, the tingling in my hands builds until I'm sure I'm going to explode from the intensity of the sensation.

When the plane starts its descent, my stomach drops. We're mere minutes from touching down. Maddy moves from his seat to be with Ashton, Jonah, and Hazel, and I summon the creature out of me, willing her into existence. As she forms in mid-air, her coal-red eyes lock on to mine. All she does is bow low before coiling on my back.

I stand at the ready in front of the door to the Beechcraft and close my eyes tight, centering myself on the feel of the power beneath my skin. I extend a hand out in front of my chest. The tethers of the creature snake down to the ground with precision, and I begin to search the people present at the mountain. With lightning speed, my ability stalks through the souls.

The plane inches closer to the runway.

Thirty seconds out.

Twenty seconds out.

Ten seconds out . . .

My eyes fly open as my heart drops into my abdomen. I turn to Jonah, and all the blood leaves my cheeks. "I don't feel Arthur. He's not there."

The Beechcraft's wheels hit the pavement, and flaps along the wings open up, causing me to take a step to catch my balance.

"What do you mean, he's not there?" Ashton asks, ashen faced.

"I don't sense him. He's not physically there!" I say.

Hollis, pay attention! The voice rasps in a manner I've never heard before, turning my blood cold. My hands tingle, and my hearing heightens tenfold. Even though I can't see what's in front of us from my position in the cabin, I hear the rumbling of trucks across the airstrip, and they're headed straight for the Beechcraft, fanning out in a line to block the plane. They come so fast that I whip my hand toward Wren, forcing her to stop the progress of our taxi to avoid crashing into them.

There's a sudden jerk as the Beechcraft halts, and I stumble sideways, nearly falling over but managing to catch myself on the seat next to the door.

"Why have we stopped?" Hazel squeaks. "We're not back to the hangar yet."

Adrenaline spikes through me as I peer through the windows of the Beechcraft. Sure enough, I can make out the tail end of a fleet of trucks parked on the runway. Past that, I'm unable to see anything else. It's still too dim outside. Only the early pricks of dawn have peeked through.

"There are trucks blocking the plane," I say, doing my best to keep panic from my voice. For the smallest fraction of a second, I consider what I should do, but my hesitation to act immediately with Jenkins at the Testing Center almost got Hazel killed. I have no idea what's happening here, but I'm not taking any chances, so with a slice of my hands, I reach out to grasp control of every person on the airstrip. They freeze under my fingertips, trapped beneath the creature's grip.

Just as I'm about to charge into the cockpit to confront Wren, Maddy walks down the aisle toward me. He looks like he's trying not to cry. His mouth is puckered shut, his little arms shake with intensity, and he's ghostly white.

I stoop down to his level. "Maddy, what's wrong?"

A small pause hangs between us . . .

He reaches out, clamping both of his hands around my forearm with incredible force. The golden light bursts from his palms, arcing high with molten beauty, and I cry out in shock. Warmth leaves my fingertips and power vanishes from my chest. The underlying hum of tingling in my body, so present a moment ago, now snuffs itself out, and the coiled creature on my back shrieks as she disappears, sucked into the golden light that tucks itself back into Maddy's hands.

"Maddy! What—"

Abruptly, Jonah launches forward, but he doesn't grab Maddy. Instead, he walks straight past him, pulling down the lever to open the Beechcraft's door.

"Jonah, what are you doing!?" I demand, panicked.

The fold-out stairs extend automatically, and before I can

process what's just happened, the plane is swarmed with men. They push past Jonah and file into the cabin. Two of them grab me forcefully and pull me down the steps, out into the brisk early morning air. My arms are yanked behind my back, and cuffs click around my wrists. Then, a hand twists through my hair, pulling my head back so hard I scream.

Pinned between the two men, with my heart ramming itself mercilessly against my ribcage, I watch as Jonah, Ashton, Hazel, and Maddy walk unaccompanied down the Beechcraft's steps. It's only when I notice their stiffened movements and pressed-shut mouths that I realize . . .

All of them are being puppeted.

A horrified cry wrenches itself from my throat, and I flail against the guards. They nearly fall to their knees in an effort to keep me restrained, and when they pull me upright again, I'm face to face with Arthur Evandrum.

His hands move through the air rhythmically, controlling my companions and forcing them to kneel on the hard pavement. The rest of the men exit the Beechcraft, helping Wren, Jenkins, Tawni, and the security guard off of the plane with careful steps. I'm so shocked that I'm momentarily unable to compel words from my own lips.

Arthur leers, examining his hands in deep fascination. His fingers stroke the air in a trance of infatuation. "My, my, this power truly is incredible. Wouldn't you agree, Hollis?"

I strain against my captors. Even though I'm cuffed, I'm so forceful with them that I almost wrench myself from their grip. "Arthur! You—"

He flicks his hand, closing my mouth and stilling me under his command. "Oh, it's not time for you to talk quite yet, my dear."

The force of my own power is suffocating. It feels like a sock has been jammed into my mouth, and the coiling pressure of the stillness in my body is stifling. It's the worst sensation I've ever felt. Everything building in me wants to scream, but I can't. I'm bound to the power of the puppet master who controls me.

"Keep a hold of her," Arthur instructs.

The guards' nails dig into my flesh even though I can't move a muscle.

Arthur approaches me, an evil smirk on his face. "Hollis Timewire," he tuts, his voice dripping with triumph. "Successfully stealing *my* little Maddy. Bravo."

He slow-claps, and the sound of it echoes across the airstrip. When he stops, his expression darkens to something dangerous and feral, and his eyes crawl over every inch of me. Then he strikes me full across the face with a blow that makes my left ear ring. The sting from his hand turns my vision fuzzy, but still nothing in my body moves at all. I'm completely at his mercy.

"Did you really think you could take him from me!?" he bellows, his spit landing on my cheek. "Did you really think I wouldn't know the whereabouts of my most prized possession at all times!?" His chest heaves in his anger, but then he collects himself, smoothing out the front of his white suit jacket. "Let's see how many people you've enlisted for help." He turns, looking to someone beyond my field of vision. "Terrace, suck out every ounce of information she possesses."

Into my view, the rat-like man stalks forward, and though I fight with my entire self, nothing I do can break Arthur's hold. Terrace's amber eyes bore deep into my hazel ones, and like a never-ending flow, everything I've done to get Maddy back leaves my body: the identities of the people in the band of rebels, our holodeck meetings, the mission to steal Arthur's memories, the foreknowledge I had of the serum and its purpose, the plan to kill Arthur . . . all of it leaves me against my will. When Terrace finishes leaching every last piece, he turns toward Arthur with a shaky look on his face. What he just discovered has disturbed him deeply. His throat bobs, and he pulls at the collar of his shirt.

"There's a lot more people involved in this than we thought."

"How many?" Arthur asks.

"Let's just say I'd like to commission the entire guard to help us out on this one."

The snarl that leaves Arthur's throat injects fear down to the sinews of my flesh. "I want *every last one* of these traitors out on this runway. GO!" he spits. "Bring them to me!"

Terrace, Erwin, and five other guards carrying guns immediately make a beeline toward the mountain aircraft hangar, which is becoming more visible in the growing light of dawn.

My breath comes out more rapidly, but my chest isn't expanding or contracting. It's locked in place, and slowly, the panic attack taking over my body darkens the periphery of my vision. I feel like I'm going to pass out, trapped in this pit of suffocation that promises no end.

The sound of hacking and retching reaches my ears. Wren, Jenkins, Tawni, and the security guard are on their hands and knees, breathing in huge gulps of air. They all look sick—Wren in particular because she was trapped under my ability all night—and the remaining guards tend to them, checking to see if they're alright.

Arthur's stale breath in my face elicits a gag from me that's stifled under the power of his puppetry. "I truly thought you had changed, Hollis. It's such a shame. All this wasted potential." His fingers trace the side of my cheek slowly, stopping over the jagged knife wound Camille gave me. He tucks a strand of my hair behind my ear, and the sensation makes me want to vomit. "You were shaping up to be such a good little soldier."

With all that I am, I fight him, trying everything I can to break out of his control and call the creature to my fingertips. But my power is gone. Nothing is left in my body. Not even a shiver passes through me.

Arthur flexes his dominant hand, no doubt feeling my attempts to break his control. He leans in until his lips are against my ear. "How does it feel to be totally and completely powerless?" The vibrations of his voice make the hairs all across my neck stand on end. He maintains his offensively close stance. "I'm going to let you in on a little secret, Hollis. Until last week, I was planning to kill you once the first ten Power Distribution Centers were fully operational. Even with Maddy as leverage, you've been a thorn in my side. But when you started to show your support and Terrace kept coming up blank with no ulterior motives to report, I thought . . . maybe you'd truly joined the cause. Maybe I would let you live after all. But here you are, in all your shiny true-colored glory, standing at my doorstep with *my* Maddy in hand."

He leans away from my ear, grabbing hold of my lower jaw. His fingernails pierce my skin, and his voice rises in volume, transitioning from a snarl to a growl.

"I don't know how you managed to hide so much from me, but I can guarantee you this: I'm going to kill you today. But first, I'm going to make you watch as I dispose of every last person involved in this coup. I've worked for far too long and struggled through far too much to have a *filthy* society-loving *traitor* stop me from achieving the world I've been dreaming of! Your time is up, puppet master."

He releases my face, breathing in power with the crisp morning breeze, and I shudder under his puppetry, still completely trapped. A wicked grin lights his features as he relishes in the taste of his new ability.

Arthur flicks his fingertips, forcing Jonah, Ashton, and Hazel to get up and walk away from Maddy. They move to a new spot on the pavement, kneeling down again in a line. Maddy joins Arthur's side, and Arthur places a spindly hand on his little shoulder, angling him toward the opening of the aircraft hangar.

"Come, young Maddy. Let's wait together for the traitors to arrive."

The next few minutes feel like an eternity. The pressure squeezed across my entire body makes me feel like I'm being strangled to death. I can't scream, and I can't move. All I can do is blink and breathe, but even that is difficult because the smothering threads of Arthur's power have shoved their way down my throat.

In the distance, barely visible inside the mouth of the aircraft hangar, a blob of bodies emerges onto the airstrip, surrounded by guards who all have their guns pointed toward the group.

"Here they come," Arthur sing-songs, eyeing me. "More puppets for me to practice with."

As they move forward, crying reaches my ears. People are clinging to one another, and the guards are shouting at them to move, pushing and striking the slower people at the rear.

Arthur steps forward, tossing his head back and forth like an athlete before a marathon. He lifts his hands up, fingertips splayed. "Let's see what I can do with the *famed* Hollis Timewire's biomarker running through my veins!"

With a slash, he attempts to take the band of rebels under his command, though not every single person falls prey to the coils of his control. A number of stragglers cry out in alarm when the mechanical and stiffened movements overtake their captured companions.

With panting and maddened breaths, Arthur tries again, throwing his hands forward to bind the remaining victims to his will. The pure adrenaline of the moment elicits a dark cackle from his lips. He pulls his hands toward his chest, forcing the puppets forward until they reach the place where Jonah, Ashton, and Hazel kneel.

I nearly pass out when I spot my friends. Keith, Candice, Ben, Rosalie, Vianne, and Olivia are mixed in with a spattering of other familiar faces: Siena Rose, Yang, Delphi, Beck, Mr. Stuart, Libbie, Audrey . . .

Vianne's cheeks are smeared with tears, and so are Rosalie's and Candice's. But Keith, Ben, and Olivia look like they fought.

There's a budding bruise on Ben's cheekbone, Keith's lower lip has been split open and is bleeding profusely, and Olivia's chin sports a nasty gash.

Arthur's hands dance through the twilight, and every single person under his power kneels to the pavement, all huddled in a silent group. The guards form a semicircle behind them, guns trained inward. Wren, who is now up from her hands and knees, joins them, though she doesn't have a weapon in her hand. With a flick, Arthur leaves everyone bound in place and calls out instructions to his guards in a loud voice.

"If anyone escapes, shoot them!" He inhales deeply, clapping his hands together twice. "Well, well!" he shouts, huffing from the exertion he just used. "Let's see who we've got here." He saunters over to the very end of the first row of puppets and drops down to his knees in front of Olivia Turrick. Pure spite is written into her face. If she were free, I'd have no doubt that she would launch herself at him and sink her teeth into his neck. But she's as still as everyone else.

"Miss Olivia Turrick," Arthur says softly. "Once a society girl, always a society girl, huh? After everything I've done for you . . ." He gives the tiniest flick of his pointer finger, and the two of them rise to their feet together. "Didn't I already deal with you, my dear? I thought removing your power would be enough to keep you out of my way, but apparently not."

"She's the one who organized this," Terrace says. "All these people are here because of her."

Arthur's eyes dart between his nephew and Olivia, and his face fills with rage, but then it tempers, and his mouth splits into a cruel smile, an idea visibly lighting up his countenance. He cups Olivia's chin in his hand and says, "You're already powerless. I think it's time for your comrades to join you."

He jerks his hand, and she's forced to walk a few paces away from the group. Then, he pushes her down to her knees again, leaving her there.

"I'm not taking any more chances, Hollis," he snarls. "You and your friends are far too slippery, but this should take care of that!" With a snap of his fingers, Maddy walks over to Jonah.

My eyes widen in horror as Maddy's hand reaches out to touch Jonah's forehead. The golden light expands between them, bursting with vibrancy and sucking the power from his body. I writhe under the control wrapped around me, but to no avail. Next, Maddy's hand is on Ashton. More golden light showers around them, ripping the ability from Ashton's chest. And then Maddy moves to Keith.

I scream and scream, but nothing at all leaves my mouth. It's like my voice box has been torn from my throat, and all the while, my heart is on fire and my hands are burning, but not with power. All that's left in me is sheer petrifying panic.

Over and over again, Arthur's hands cut through the air as he puppets Maddy, forcing him to use the golden light. Power after power is stripped away, tucking itself under Maddy's skin, and everyone kneels there helpless, unable to do a thing but silently watch the show.

By the end of it, Arthur is panting and wild, gasping for air as though he'd run for miles on end. Sweat clings to his hairline and upper lip from the strain of using his power. He beckons

Maddy to his side, and when I catch sight of the little boy's face, it crushes my spirit. He's sobbing. With red eyes and a trembling pressed shut mouth, he looks like he would collapse if he was not held up by the strings of Arthur's command.

Arthur takes a moment to smooth himself out, sweeping his hair back and tugging on the folds of his jacket. Then he walks up and down the first row of prisoners with a manic vengeance in his eyes, visibly scouring over them.

He calls to the guards who are holding me. "Bring her over here." They drag my stiffened body closer to Arthur and then stop when he says, "That's far enough."

Arthur reaches over to the holster on the guard's hip, pulling out his handgun and cocking it back. Then he walks up to Keith, sticking the gun to his forehead. My heart rams itself so wildly against my ribcage that I swear I feel like I'm going to die.

Arthur casts a hand toward my body, and his power leaves me. Immediately, I begin to tremble and thrash violently against the hands securing me, and the cuffs bite into my wrists. Tears blur my vision. My lungs feel like they're going to shred from how rapidly I'm breathing. In my frenzied hysteria, my captors buckle in an effort to keep me restrained. Their grips clamp even tighter around my arms, and the hand that twisted through my hair earlier is back, anchoring my head in place. Pain jabs all the way through my skull.

Arthur watches this with a sick glee on his face, and when I've been thoroughly pinned, he says, "Beg me for mercy."

"Arthur, p-please!" I cry. "Forgive me! Don't kill h-him! Please! Please don't take him away f-from me!"

His mouth curls with pleasure, and he digs the barrel of the gun in deeper, pushing Keith's head back an inch.

Muted screams come from behind where Keith kneels. It's Candice, and she's physically quaking in an effort to stand to her feet. Surprised by her ability to move anything at all, Arthur's hand cuts through the air, silencing her once more. This sudden, small break in his absolute control seems to shake him, but he brushes it off, keeping the gun in place against Keith's head.

"Arthur, please!" I sob. "I'll do a-anything you want! I promise. P-please don't take him from me! Please!"

There's a long moment where Arthur's cruel eyes burrow into me. It's a look filled with so much hatred that it sucks the breath from my body. He speaks slowly and barely above a whisper. "You love him, don't you."

Keith and I hold each other's gaze. His eyes are glistening with tears. In all the time I've known him, he's never cried. He's always been so strong and steady, but now he's afraid. However, even through his fear, the look he gives me is one of strength and deep affection.

My chest spasms in an effort to get enough oxygen. "Yes, I love him. P-please don't do this! I'll give you anything!"

In the pause that spans the next few seconds, I can see the whole life I wanted to build with Keith slip away . . .

"You have nothing left to give me," Arthur snarls.

The gun fires, and I scream.

The sound shreds my throat like I've swallowed fragments of glass . . . but when I look at Keith, he's still kneeling on the pavement, exactly where he had been seconds ago—and he's completely untouched.

The gun in Arthur's hand is smoking, and it takes my brain a few moments to catch up with what I'm seeing. Wren is in front of Arthur, brute-like and panting, having just pushed the gun out of the way . . . and as I follow the trajectory of the barrel, my heart seizes and my mouth parts, though not a sound escapes me.

Maddy is standing curled forward with his little hands pressed against his stomach. A dark crimson stain spreads through his fingertips. Arthur's wild eyes widen in shock, and so do Wren's. A deathly silence falls across the airstrip as the little boy, now free of Arthur's power, takes a single step forward before collapsing to the ground.

There's a great shudder beneath our feet, and with a burst of concentrated light, a shining sphere of pure gold above Maddy's chest expands from a pinpoint to the breadth of twelve feet in the blink of an eye. Helixes of sparkling amber swirl in chaotic patterns at the orb's boundary as it pulses in even beats. Specks of gold skitter across the earth and through the air. It's like a fire made of the most pure form of flame.

A strand of gold reaches out from the top of the sphere and shoots toward me. When it reaches me, it splits into three tendrils. One wraps itself around my body, and the other two rip the guards away from me, hurtling them to the pavement. Then, the light lifts me into the air, pulling me inside the sphere toward Maddy and gently setting me down next to his crumpled form. The strand twists itself around my wrists, disintegrating the metal cuffs. Then, the gold retreats back into the boundary of the sphere, which still pulses alive with sparks of untamed power.

"Maddy!" I cry. "No, no, no!" My hands press to the bullet

wound, and his blood springs up over my fingertips. "Don't you die on me! Don't you dare die on me!"

Maddy's body gives a violent shudder. One of his little hands grabs onto mine, vice-like and purposeful, and with his other hand, he holds my wrist. "Don't be afraid."

Without warning, his eyes burn bright gold, fiercer than the sun. They're so blinding that I have to turn away from the force of the radiance. The light from all around the sphere matches the intensity, growing in an ever-building crescendo of illumination.

From the depths of Maddy's chest, a smaller orb emerges. It's like a sundrop, uncontaminated and brilliant beyond measure. The drop floats up from Maddy's chest and into mine, and when it makes contact with my skin, warmth showers over my entire body. I lift my face to the sky, and light explodes from it, beaming into the heavens in a column of magnificent glory. Tingling fills my limbs, power courses through my blood, and the creature bursts forth with a screech. But instead of a snake-like body made of misted black, she's transformed, stretching out wings made of shining gold. Her coal-red eyes have been replaced with ones that look like diamonds, and her thin form has now thickened out with limbs and claws.

She's turned from a serpent to a dragon. She dives, entering my body, and sparks fly from the sphere.

My hands are now shining as bright as Maddy's eyes. In the pulsing beats of the sphere, I feel the presence of so many abilities, all spiraling in the boundary of the orb. Their essence. Their uniqueness. Their form. All of it burns like an unquenchable flame, and a singular, powerful instinct takes over. My hands move in a rhythmic beauty, sweeping with the most delicate of movements, and the orb spurts out a thread of light. It corkscrews through the air until it finds its place in Jonah's chest. His face and hands shine gold. Then another corkscrew spirals forth, shooting into Keith's chest, and he radiates gold too. Over and over again, the sphere ejects the threads at the will of my fingertips until every last person on their knees is shining like the sun. The brilliance is so overpowering that the guards have now stepped back in sheer terror.

The power and lifeforce of the threads sear the ends of my fingertips. Then, they flash and dissipate, leaving behind shimmering specks that waft through the air like pieces of ash.

The sphere shrinks until it's the size of an apple, hovering right in front of me. Tears trace my face as I stare at it. There's so much warmth and light in this small piece of magic. It's devastatingly beautiful—an essence of pure innocence no one could look away from even if they tried. I reach out for the light, taking it into my hands, and when it makes contact with my skin, it melds into my palms, vanishing from sight.

Maddy curls his fist around two of my fingers, and a tear traces down his cheek, falling into his blond curls. He speaks in the smallest and softest whisper. "Don't be sad."

And then his tiny body turns deathly still . . .

33

The astonished looks from everyone on the airstrip, guard and rebel alike, suspend us all in a moment of quiet. It's like time has stopped. No one moves, and no one speaks. The first beams of sunlight crack across the sky, and like a spell, the sunrise breaks through the shock of the crowd.

There's a beastly yowl that comes from the pit of Arthur Evandrum's throat, and then several things happen at once: his deranged eyes land on me, he raises the gun toward my chest, and Olivia Turrick launches herself forward—but in the span of the time it takes Arthur's finger to pull the trigger, there's a violent flash of blue, and Olivia's orb of teleportation swallows every member in the band of rebels whole. Before I can even take a breath, I'm plunged into darkness, whisked away from the mountain.

The crushing, cold sensation of being teleported wracks my body, but it only lasts for a few seconds. With a forceful bang, my back slams into dirt as sky appears above me and pine trees materialize around me. My lungs lurch, momentarily unable to draw breath. I'm so disoriented that all I can do is lie there for several seconds, stunned.

As my senses return, a face peeks into my field of view. It's Olivia. She's panting, and tears trace her cheeks. She holds out a hand to me, and I take it. She helps me sit up. Nearly sixty people are here with us. Some are on their hands and knees, some are huddled together, and some are flat on their back. Every member of the band of rebels made it here.

Here . . .

My eyes rove my surroundings, and recognition for this place shatters my heart into a thousand pieces. We're on the bank of the river next to the clearing just outside the tree dome. This was the place my people called home less than five months ago, and this muddy bank was the place where I kneeled weeping for Jonah when the boy with the golden light gave me back my power.

"Maddy," I whisper.

Wordlessly, Olivia pulls me to my feet. My body feels sluggish—drained of all substance. She leads me forward to a patch on the upper bank that's covered in shoots of wild flowers. There, in the midst of the group, lying still with his eyes to the sky, is Maddy. When I reach his tiny frame, I sink to my knees.

The silence of death is so strong that even nature herself seems to quiet in respect. My eyes blur with grief. I can't take a breath. My lungs are stuck shut for a long time. Or maybe it's not long at all.

With gentle hands, I scoop Maddy's body up in my arms, cradling him. His eyes are blank. I stare at them like the golden light might spark up, but they're void and empty. Nothing at all remains. I bow my head over his, fingers tracing the stain on his shirt, and then I begin to sing, gently brushing his golden curls from his forehead. My voice comes out in a hushed lullaby, carrying the tune on the wind like magic. It wafts through the trees and floats along the river.

> Sleep, little one, safe in my arms
> Dream of a place where worries can't swarm
> In morning's light, you'll be strong as can be
> For healing and love surround you, you see

With all my strength, I keep my voice from breaking, weaving the notes with intention and care. Like he can hear me.

> Though you're weary tonight
> I promise tomorrow you'll be alright
> And with the sunrise, you'll fix your eye
> To gaze at an endless cerulean sky

The breeze and birds seem to join in, whistling and singing like they've lost him too. The words continue to flow from my trembling lips.

> Once night dances away on silver streams
> And flows under moonlight's sparkling beams

> You'll wake anew as light greets your face
>
> Chasing all aches far from this place

My voice grows stronger on the last verse as my tears land on Maddy's shirt, dripping from my nose and chin.

> Sleep, little one, safe in my arms
>
> Dream of a place where worries can't swarm
>
> In morning's light, you'll be strong as can be
>
> For healing and love surround you, you see

I hug him tight to my body and let out a quiet sob. It squeezes my chest and hurts so bad I wouldn't be surprised if my broken heart decided to give up and die right alongside him. I can't even begin to accept this. Maddy. Gone . . .

As tenderly as I can and with all the affection I own, I take my fingertips and close his eyes. Then I lean down and kiss the top of his head.

Soft crying reaches my ears. It comes from all around me, and the chorus of weeping only digs the knife of death in deeper, because there was nothing any of us could do to protect him . . .

Vianne is kneeling in front of me, her porcelain features flush with grief. She grabs Maddy's hand, holding it for a few moments, and then dips down to kiss his palm. Silently, her face transforms, growing a duck bill. She puts Maddy's hand to it, holding it there for a few seconds, and then the bill melds back into her face. When it slips away, she tucks his hand back onto his little chest.

Ashton is behind her, his arms holding her in comfort, and

Keith is kneeling behind me, arms around my own. We all say nothing. The only thing we have to offer each other is our tears.

More of my friends gather. Ben and Candice kneel by Maddy's head, Rosalie with them. Jonah is here too, and so is Olivia. They all extend a hand to gently lay on the boy whose golden light saved us all . . .

"Let me through!" a familiar voice insists.

There's a scuffle, and the sound of several heavy blows causes a spattering of grunts.

"You don't understand! We're not safe! You have to let me through!"

To my horror, I see Wren Zayla wrestling with three men. They gain the upper hand, arresting her arms, but her fingertips splay out with power, and the three of them double over in pain, relinquishing their hold. Yelling and cursing ensues as more people join in to try and subdue her.

Vianne quickly takes Maddy from my lap, and I rise to my feet, rage festering deep to my soul. My hands, fueled with the wrath of my newly returned ability, slash through the air, taking Wren under my command and silencing her. She stops struggling.

"Get away from her!" I shout.

The people who had joined the brawl move back.

My chest is heaving, and stars flicker at the periphery of my vision. I lock eyes with Olivia. "What is this?" I demand. "You brought her with us?"

Olivia quells under the intensity of my voice. "She saved Keith. She betrayed Arthur. Leaving her there would've been a death sentence."

I round on Wren. With a wild cut through the air, I force her to kneel. Everything inside of me wants to let the creature take over, save for one thing . . .

"What do you mean we're not safe?" I release her mouth, allowing her to talk freely. "You better speak quickly, Wren. My mercy is at its breaking point!"

Wren gasps, sucking in air, and her eyes move to the crumpled form of the boy in Vianne's arms. "There's a tracker in Maddy's left shoulder. That's how Arthur knew he had left the Testing Center. You have to let me remove it, or he'll find us. Please, Hollis! Let me help."

I stand over the woman, the power in me vibrant and alive. I raise my hand high into the air as if to strike her, but then it falls, and with it, I release her.

"Everyone, move out of the way!" I order.

Except for Vianne, the band of rebels retreats from Maddy, giving Wren space. I catch Wren's wrist, and she halts.

"If you do anything other than remove that tracker, I swear, it'll be the last thing you *ever* do."

Wren lifts her hands as a sign of surrender. Keeping her eyes on me, she withdraws a knife from her belt slowly. Several people cry out in protest, but I hold a hand up. Wren kneels next to Maddy and carefully turns him in Vianne's lap so that she can reach his shoulder. As much as I want to look away, I don't. I watch Wren like a hawk as she cuts a slit in Maddy's shirt and then makes a small incision in his left shoulder blade. Sure enough, a bead of silver lies underneath his skin. Wren pulls the tracker out and places it in the dirt, piercing it with the tip of the blade before tossing the knife to my feet. I kick it further away from her, and Jonah dips down to retrieve it.

"Get away from Maddy!" I snarl at her, and she listens, standing up and backing away from the boy. My eyes pool with tears, and anger curls in my belly. "You knew all along? You knew Arthur would be able to track us?"

Her brow turns upward as she nods in confirmation.

I place a hand to my forehead in regret, and I have to cover my mouth to stifle a sob. I questioned Wren on the plane, and when she was so insistent upon us turning back, it scared me. I didn't ask the right questions. I could've compelled more information from her, but I didn't. The reality of Maddy's death crashes over me again, and I clutch my chest, wanting to scream.

Olivia walks up to me. "Hollis, we can't stay here. I'm teleporting everyone to a new place. Now!" She calls out to the band of rebels in a loud voice. "We're leaving! It's not safe here! Grab someone's hand. It makes traveling easier."

Olivia's right. Given how long that tracker was active, Arthur could know where we are. I take one last look at the stream and then give her a firm nod.

"Get us out of here."

She grips my hand, and the blue orb expands around us, capturing everyone within its electric glow. Then, I'm crushed into darkness again. The journey is quick, but it leaves me with nausea. I'm sick with grief, but I'm also drained from the amount of adrenaline in my body and the near scrape with death.

The new setting is much more open than the forest. We're somewhere in a desert area with large boulders and tufts of dried-out shrubbery. It's not the best place to regroup or rest, but Olivia simply wanted to get us away from the stream where the smashed remains of the bug lay in the mud.

I take in the haggard people all around me, and then my eyes land on Wren. So many conflicting feelings surge through me, but I don't have the space in my brain to deal with her right now.

I walk up to the three men who had wrestled with her before she cut out the tracker and give them instructions. "Tie her up. I don't have the strength to keep her under my power."

They nod to one another and move to Wren. Two of them remove their belts. When they push her down to a sitting position by the nearest boulder, she doesn't fight them. All she does is stare at me, sorrow cast across her face. The men tie her hands behind her back. Then they tie her feet together by the ankles.

Just as I'm about to walk away, she calls my name . . .

"Hollis." Her voice is thick with feeling—something rare for her typical soldier-hardened tone. "I'm sorry about Maddy."

A sob lodges itself in my esophagus. I can't do this right now. I turn away from her as my eyes brim with sadness.

Keith is standing a few yards off, and I run to him. All over again, I fall into tears. I hug him, clinging to his chest, and he embraces me back, resting his chin on the top of my head. For a long time, we simply stand there in each other's arms, not saying a word.

Arthur was going to take him from me. The fact that he's alive right now is a miracle. The fact that *any* of us are alive right now is a miracle. My eyes travel across the dust, landing on Wren, one of Arthur's most trusted informants. What had changed in the span of the last seven weeks to make her betray him? What spark of sense had come over her? Or was it simply the fact that she finally saw Arthur for who he truly is? A cold-hearted, power-hungry monster. Whatever it was, there's no denying it: Wren Zayla's decision to push the gun out of the way saved us all.

Keith's still hugging me like he'll never let go, and I bury my head in his chest. We stand there together, both numb. I honestly don't know what to do with myself. Existing right now is nothing but pain that cuts deep to the bone.

Vianne is still cradling Maddy, with Ashton and Jonah by her side. Ben, Candice, and Rosalie are huddled with them too. The girls are weeping, and the boys are silent.

Olivia approaches me tentatively. "What do we do now?"

I bite my lower lip, holding back the cry of anguish that wants to rip itself from my throat. "I don't know. I . . . don't know."

My brain is a mesh of one agonized thought after another. I can't even begin to process what should happen next. It's too much. I gently push Keith away, backing up a few paces to get some air. I press my fingertips to my forehead, and my heart beats more rapidly, my pulse pounding up into my ears.

I back away even farther and then lean over to vomit onto the cracked ground. My stomach empties itself entirely. When I'm done, I wipe my mouth with the back of my hand, standing up again. My body feels like it has nothing left to give. All I want to do is collapse in the dirt and fall into oblivion.

Just as I'm about to walk away from the pile of sick, something catches my attention. A small speck of blue light appears right in front of me, and my brow furrows.

Flash.

In a brilliant display of blinding light, a blue orb materializes in the span of a microsecond, and a pair of strong arms grab me around the waist, lifting me from my feet. Arthur Evandrum's wild and demented face is right in front of my own. I don't even have time to scream before he pulls me into the black void, teleporting me away.

34

I SKID STOMACH-FIRST ACROSS A GRAVELLY SURFACE, AND granules of grit bite into my arms. Before I can even process where I am, hands grab hold of my ankles, dragging me several feet and flipping me onto my back.

Arthur stands over me with a crazed look, pointing the barrel of the gun that killed Maddy into my face. With a screech and a burst of golden light, the creature emerges from my chest to fling her wings around me, and I'm thrown sideways as the gun fires, missing me by mere inches.

My ears immediately begin ringing.

In a surge of movement, the creature hauls me to my feet, giving me the half-second I need to take in my surroundings. My heart plummets all the way to my toes. I'm standing on the rooftop of Area 19 Testing Center . . .

Arthur aims the gun again with a shriek of madness, but this time, I barrel straight into him, tackling him around the waist as the second shot fires. Even though I'm much smaller than he is, my momentum is enough to knock him off balance, and we crash against the roof, tumbling over each other and landing a few feet from the towering drop-off of the edge.

My hands cut through the air, but when nothing happens, horror rips through me. Just as with Camille, Arthur is now impervious to my power. My biomarker has made him immune to me. As the reality of this nightmare sinks in, a singular thought consumes me: get the gun.

With a cry, I claw over him, reaching for the weapon in his hand, but he overpowers me, rolling around until he's on top of me. For a third time, he points the gun in my face, but again, the creature yanks me away at the last second, causing Arthur to pitch forward on his hands and knees due to the force of me sliding out from underneath him.

Unsteadied from the sudden jerk of movement, he fumbles the gun, and it skids a few feet, dropping off the side of the Testing Center and into the abyss below.

"NO!" he roars.

Arthur turns to me with a murderous look, and my eyes widen in fear as he rises from the gravel. He tears off his white suit jacket, discarding it over the edge of the building and flexing his hands, as if feeling power.

I scramble up, backing away from him. My heart is pounding so hard that stars hang in my vision, and the ringing in my ears from the gunfire hasn't stopped. I look around, desperate for some kind of escape. The door to the roof of the Testing Center is a dozen feet away, so I sprint toward it, but when I reach the handle and pull, it doesn't budge.

"There's nowhere to run, Hollis, except for right off the edge like your mother!" he taunts, stalking after me.

I run, but he's too quick. He grabs a fistful of my hair, and with that leverage, he throws me down. Before I can move again, he casts a hand toward me. I half expect to freeze in place—even though that shouldn't be possible now that I have my ability back—but what happens instead is far worse.

Blinding pain rips through every ligament, bone, and muscle in my body. The agony is so great that it feels like I'm on fire, and the creature is sucked back into my chest. I scream and scream, writhing across the ground, twisting and clawing at myself until I'm sure I'm going die. Then Arthur pulls his hand back, and the pain ceases. Splotches of black and blue smear everywhere I look, and I'm left panting, flat on my back.

"Wren's power is a fascinating one, isn't it?" he leers, examining his hands. "To be able to cause any sensation I want in someone's body . . . the possibilities are endless!"

He shoves his hand forward again, and this time, my arms feel like every bone in them has been shattered. Just when it feels like I can't take a second more of the torture, the pain withdraws from my limbs. I curl onto my side, coughing and sputtering. My lungs spasm as I push myself to my hands and knees, taking huge inhales of cold air.

Arthurs claps in an eerie rhythm, his tone growing more maddened. "That a girl, Hollis! Big, deep breaths! Since I can't shoot you, we're just getting started!"

He stoops to grab my wrists, tugging me all the way up to my feet with a burst of brutish strength. I shriek, kicking out, but he pins me against his body, pressing a hand over my mouth and pushing me all the way to the bitter edge of the building. I cling to his arms, my feet slipping precariously.

"Or maybe I'll push you over the edge," he snarls into my ear. "You've ruined *everything*! I was about to change the world! And now my blood supply is gone!"

I scream against the hand smothering my face, straining my body to jam my elbow into his ribs, but this does nothing to shake him. His grip only cements further, and his nails dig into my cheek.

"What was your plan for killing me, Hollis?" he growls. "Were you going to shoot me? Or tear me apart with your power? I didn't think you had it in you!" He holds me there as my feet scrape to find purchase, and then his lips brush my ear. "What was it you said to Camille at the Testing Center? I believe it was . . . 'There can only be *one* puppet master.'"

I scream again, but it's barely audible over the suffocation of Arthur's hand. I'm scarcely able to get in a breath through my nose, and I'm beginning to feel faint. I twist and fight, slipping against the brim of the building, but every attempt I make to wriggle free is met with the ever-growing energetic fury of Arthur's madness as he keeps me pinned to himself.

"Haven't you learned yet? No matter the cost, I *always* win!"

Suddenly, there's a brilliant flash of blue and a mighty tug. Both of us jerk violently, but instead of me tumbling forward over the edge of the Testing Center, I'm pulled backward. Arthur's hands fall away from me, and when I turn around, my heart leaps in hope at what I see . . .

"Stay away from my girlfriend!"

With a powerful swing, Keith punches Arthur in the jaw, and he reels back, stunned by the force of the blow.

"Keith, NOW!" Olivia cries.

Keith dives toward me, his arms open wide, and in that moment, I know exactly what he's going to do. I hook my arms around his neck as he barrels forward, and in the span of a second, he launches us both over the side of the Testing Center. Wind whips my face, and I scream, but Keith's strong hands keep me close to his chest as he flies us down from the towering heights.

Moments later, our feet touch the pavement of the street, and we nearly collide with Jonah. My heart soars as I see him, and then my gaze lands on Ashton, Vianne, Candice, and Ben. My friends have come for me. Blue flashes violently to my right, and Olivia appears next to us, but before anyone can move, a second orb of blue materializes on the lower flight of steps that lead up to the glittering glass doors of the Testing Center.

Arthur Evandrum steps out of the bubble as it bursts. If he could breathe fire, I have no doubt it would be spewing from his mouth. His bloodshot eyes dart to the people at my back, and he flexes his hands, his chest rising and falling with ferocious rage.

"I may not be able to control you, Hollis, but I can still control *them*!"

Arthur's hands cut through the air, and with a cry, mine do too. The creature manifests from my chest, and her mighty wings of shimmering gold expand at my back. With a tug, Arthur and I fall into a deadlock, vying for control of the people behind me. But I'm more experienced than he is, and I steal them away with ease.

I bare my teeth, feeling strength in every cell of my body from the presence of the dragon. "You may have taken my blood, Arthur!" I snarl. "But you're no puppet master!" I swipe my hands, freeing my friends from the stillness of my ability. "They're *mine*!"

A wall of fire erupts from Candice's palms. It's so large and so hot that all of us have to leap back from the inferno. The flames crash against the steps of the Testing Center, cracking the marble, but Arthur is no longer standing there.

Flash.

Arms snatch me from behind.

"Hollis!" Jonah shouts, diving forward at the last second. He grabs my arm right as the electric blue of Arthur's power engulfs us. Crushing cold leads to blinding light, and Jonah and I are spit out of the orb. We tumble across black asphalt. All around us, tall glass buildings rise into the heavens, displaying a different part of the city.

Hands close around my throat as Arthur straddles me, and I nearly black out from the force being applied to my windpipe. My fingers scrape across Arthur's forearms, and my feet kick out.

Splotches of purple are everywhere.

My lungs cry for air.

Stars . . .

There's a grunt and a yell, and then oxygen rushes back into me, clearing the fog from my brain. Jonah has tackled Arthur, knocking him off of me, and the two of them roll across the ground. It takes my vision a moment to clear, but when it does, all I see is a fit of fists as the men grapple with each other.

I don't understand . . .

Why isn't Jonah using his power?

I know *I'm* unable to puppet Arthur because we now carry the same exact biomarker, but Jonah should be able to control him by taking on either of our powers. Dread slices into me like poison. Something isn't right.

The fistfight ends abruptly as Arthur gains the upper hand, casting his hand over Jonah's body. Jonah yells out in agony, writhing under the torture. His back arches, his teeth clench, and his hands claw across his chest. His cry is so loud that my heart feels like it's going to rip itself from my chest.

"NO!" I screech.

Though I'm still flat on the ground, I'm consumed with an overwhelming instinct to act on something I don't even know is possible. I throw my hands forward, and the golden creature flies through the air directly at Jonah, spreading her wings out and curling around Jonah's torso. She bares teeth made of pure, dazzling diamond and lets out a roar that only I can hear. Then Jonah stops thrashing.

He's able to push himself to his hands and knees. For a split second, both men look at me in bewilderment, confused by what's just happened because neither of them can see the beast protecting Jonah like a shield.

The small pause in the fight breaks as blue light shatters across the street.

It seems to flash from every reflective surface. The rest of my friends are here again, tumbling out of Olivia's orb. There's a whip of wind and blur of super speed as Ben clotheslines Arthur with his arm. This slams him into the pavement with such force that he gasps, momentarily dazed.

"Jonah!" I cry.

I run to him, closing the distance between us as another whip of wind is thrown across my face. Ben is running so fast he's creating a torrent of air that bears down on all of us, but the brunt of it is concentrated on Arthur.

Upon reaching Jonah, I call the creature back to me, and she uncurls from his chest, springing onto my arm and nestling on my back. I help him to his feet.

"What's wrong?" I shout to him over the wind. "Why can't you use your ability? Is it still gone?"

He shakes his head. "No, I have my power, but I can't take on Arthur's abilities. Or yours."

My heart rams itself into my chest in horror. "What? Why?"

"I don't know! Both of you feel different to me now. My power can't latch on! Every time I try, the buzzing dies in my fingerti—"

There's a war cry that shatters the torrent of air, and abruptly, all the wind stops. Arthur is now up, hands outstretched, and once again, all of my friends are under his command. They drop to their knees. Jonah's face flushes beet red in the span of two seconds. He can't breathe. None of them can. Arthur has puppeted their lungs, forcing suffocation over them.

Power shoots from my chest, down my arms, and into my hands. I crack through Arthur's control, taking them back and freeing them from the stillness.

Everyone's chests expand with breath. Olivia and Keith

double over with coughing, and Ben falls to his hands and knees, vomiting on the asphalt. The impact of being forced to stop running so suddenly has ripped his shirt clean off, and he looks like he's been walloped across the chest.

Jonah, Vianne, Ashton, and Candice, however, all launch into an attack.

Candice throws a barrage of fireballs in tandem with Jonah. Their combined heat is searing hot. At the same moment, Ashton and Vianne slash their palms through the air. Arthur dives out of the way, narrowly missing the bulk of the fire, but it still manages to singe his clothing. What he can't escape is the full brunt of Vianne's metamorph ability. Angry red boils erupt across his neck and arms, and he howls in pain.

Vianne's hands move again as she advances on him, and Arthur's face mutates. His lips grow fat, his hair sucks back into his skull, and his cheeks bulge as if the bones in his face have expanded. Wild shrieking splits the air.

"I can't hold him!" Ashton shouts, his arms trembling. He looks like he's throwing everything he has into his suppression, but then a blinding flash of blue light spews forth, and Arthur vanishes from the street.

"Damn!" Vianne cries. "I had him!"

"Where did he go?" Candice says, panting and gazing around at the tall buildings.

"Hollis, stay close to us!" Jonah shouts.

He and Keith both usher me into the middle of the group. They surround me, shielding me at the center. All of them are at the ready, scouring the city for any sign of Arthur, but the streets are empty. The golden creature snarls on my back, her wings tucked, and my hands ignite with tingling. If it were anyone else, I'd be able to find them with my heightened senses, but I can't sense Arthur even if I tried.

"Ashton, what happened?" I ask.

Sweat drips from his brow as he clutches his chest. He's still trying to breathe properly. "Arthur has too many abilities. I can't suppress all of them. Every time I try, they seem to slip out of my grasp."

"How many abilities?" I press him. "Can you sense them?"

"Five."

"Five?" Keith repeats.

Both Ben and Candice swear at the top of their lungs.

My mind immediately takes stock of what I've seen. He has his silver tongue, Olivia's blue orb, Wren's pain power, and my puppet master ability. My stomach ties itself in knots. What else did he take? But the more pressing question is . . . why hasn't he used his fifth ability yet? The only thing I can think of is Arthur's inexperience balancing so many powers in his body. Perhaps he's relying on the powers he's had more practice with. Even still, Ashton's statement is chilling. We're fighting him eight to one, but that has done nothing to deter him.

Vianne's hair changes from scarlet to purple to emerald. "What do we do now?"

"I could teleport us to him," Olivia suggests, but Jonah shakes his head.

"I don't think that's a good idea. He could be anywhere, and if we teleport to a place where there are more powers to deal with, that could be bad. He wants Hollis. He'll come back."

"So we just stand here like sitting ducks?" Ashton counters. "Shouldn't we at least teleport the hell away from here?"

Olivia throws up her hands. "Where would we go? Arthur can teleport to a person just by thinking of them—same way I can. He'll find us no matter where I take us."

I feel faint as my eyes bounce from building to building. Not a hint of blue light lingers anywhere. Even though I'm the most powerful person in this group, I can't help but feel powerless. I can't fight Arthur. The only thing I can do is shield my friends.

There's a hiss in my ear, and a forked tongue of gold flickers past my cheek. *You are not powerless.*

I stare into the dragon's diamond eyes, confused. The way she's looking at me takes hold of my heart. There's something in that stare. Something she wants to teach me. I can feel it deep in my spirit.

"What do you mean?" I ask her barely above a whisper.

She doesn't respond. Instead, her scales shine bright gold.

My friends keep around me, all of us on high alert. As the seconds turn into a minute, and the minute turns into two, my anxiety rises to new levels. Jonah's right. Arthur wants me. There's no doubt in my mind that he's coming back. But standing in this tight-knit circle feels helpless.

"There!" Vianne calls, pointing to the nearest street transit stop.

Fifty yards down the street, a spark of blue light forms. My friends form a wall in front of me, hands at the ready. The blue orb expands, growing larger and larger. It practically fills the whole street, and it shines so brightly I have to strain my eyes to keep them trained forward. The creature snarls, and I channel tingling into my hands.

But then, the orb implodes with a violent streak of light, vanishing from sight. Arthur hasn't appeared. In fact, there's nothing left behind by the orb at all . . .

Flash.

A new flare of blue expands directly next to Olivia, and Arthur snatches her around the waist, tugging her backward. All of us cry out in alarm, but no one is able to grab hold of her before she's teleported away.

In the retina-burning aftermath of the orb's illumination, we're all left standing in a heart-pounding silence. Arthur's just taken our only means of travel away from us.

35

"Find her!" I call to the creature. She leaps into the air, flying away through the city in a blur of gold, and the threads of my power snake out in tandem with the dragon, searching for any trace of Olivia's scent—any hint of her heartbeat. When I come up empty, my heart drops to the pit of my stomach. I turn to my friends as the dragon flashes back to my side. "She's not here. She's gone."

"Jonah, what do we do?" Vianne cries, spinning around. "He's going to kill her! We have to help her!"

I look to Jonah, hoping against hope that he will know our next move—that he will have some brilliant idea on how to find her—but the ashen look on his face tells me all I need to know. There's nothing we can do for her now. Arthur could have taken her anywhere. All I know is that she's somewhere beyond the scope of what my power can sense.

Candice's hands ignite with flame, and she screams, throwing a fireball into the nearest building. It crashes through the window, and an inferno starts within. She hurls two more fireballs, her chest heaving with anger.

"Candice, stop!" Ben says, running up to her. "Stop!"

He wrestles with her for a moment before she yields, falling into his arms with a sob. He holds her close. I can tell he's doing his best to keep it together, but his eyes are welling with tears.

Suddenly, I'm overwhelmed. No. Not Olivia too. I can't lose her too. But as my mind moves down every conceivable angle of how Olivia could escape him, they all come up with nothing, because if she hasn't teleported herself back by now, Arthur has gained control over her. All I can imagine is the horrible way in which she's dying right at this very moment.

My pulse spikes with panic, and I clutch my chest, backing away a few paces. My vision streaks and tunnels around the edges. "He's going to come back for me. He's going to grab me, and you won't be able to follow!"

Keith moves to me and grasps my hand. "We're not going to let that happen."

Ashton approaches me as well. "We'll keep you safe. I can focus on suppressing his teleportation. I may not be able to suppress his other powers, but I promise you: he's not taking you anywhere."

Jonah nods firmly. "I'll double on Ashton's suppression. We've got you."

I look at Ashton. "You can feel which one of his powers to suppress?"

He nods.

"Do you have any idea what his fifth power is?"

"I can't pin it down. The other four feel distinct to me, but the fifth doesn't."

My blood runs cold. A non-distinct power? What could Arthur have taken? But we don't get to continue our conversation. My gaze lands across the deserted street, and fear jumps down my throat. There, behind the nearest street transit stop, a blue speck appears. All of my friends surround me with their hands on guard, and Keith keeps a firm grip on my arm just above the elbow. He's not taking any chances with a surprise grab.

"What do we do?" Ben asks.

Vianne squares her shoulders, a dark look befalling her. "We kill him."

The orb grows steadily larger as thick electric lines of blue swirl at its boundary. I charge my hands with tingling, readying myself to protect who I need to.

"Keith! Ben! You stay with Hollis," Jonah says. He withdraws a knife from his belt, and I immediately recognize it as the one Wren used to cut out Maddy's tracker. The orb continues to grow to massive proportions, practically taking up the width of the entire street. "Don't hesitate! If any of you have the opportunity to take him out, do it."

The orb ruptures, and out steps Arthur with an animalistic energy. His sleeves are rolled up, and specks of blood pepper his front. My stomach churns at the sight. It has to be Olivia's . . . It's not enough blood for me to immediately assume her death, but I can't conceive of how she's still alive. I want to tear him limb from limb, but I don't move, keeping by Keith's side.

Arthur calls out to us in a loud voice. "Now that *that's* taken care of, I can finish what I started!" He licks his lips like a lion would before ripping into fresh meat. His arms bulge, and his hands flex. "Oh, Hollis! Why don't you come out from behind your friends and face me? If you do, I promise I'll make their deaths quick."

Vianne and Candice move together in a torrent of power. A flurry of fire flies through the air, but just as it's about to collide with Arthur, a second streak of fire towers up, shielding him from the attack. And when the flames die, Arthur appears untouched—even by Vianne's metamorph ability.

Vianne shrieks, backing away, her hands flying to her face. Her scars have erupted all across her cheeks and neck, but she's also covered in boils from head to toe, and Arthur leers with pleasure, breathing in a deep lungful of cold morning air.

My eyes widen in horror as the realization crashes over all of us. Arthur's fifth power is Jonah's . . .

Ashton and Jonah both launch into action, their hands cutting through the air to suppress Arthur's power. Immediately, the boils all over Vianne disappear. Arthur leaps, slashing his palms toward them, but nothing happens. Then there's a spark of blue, but that dissipates before the orb can even form. Arthur's feral eyes snap to Jonah and Ashton. Both of them are shaking with the tension of keeping Arthur's powers under check.

Crack.

A violent noise issues from the depths of the building Candice had lit on fire earlier, and glass shatters across the street, narrowly missing us . . . it's enough of a distraction for one of Arthur's powers to peek through.

He sends flames zipping down the middle of the street directly at me. The fire cracks the asphalt, tearing a scorched path across the ground. Ben grabs me around the waist and pulls me out of the way in a burst of super speed. In seconds, the two of us are easily a hundred feet away from the blaze, and Keith is no longer by my side.

There's a blast of wind, and Ben gives a shout of surprise. Arthur has crossed the expanse of pavement to get to us in under a second, and he wastes no time in striking Ben across the face. The blow lands hard, and Ben stumbles back, his nose immediately spurting blood.

I take off, running away from him, but he catches up to me with a whip of wind, grabbing me by the arm. With a cry, I swing my free fist toward his face, but he catches my wrist. A spark of blue starts up, but once again, it fails under the force of Ashton and Jonah's suppression.

Shouting echoes from down the street as all of my friends run toward me. Ben flashes to my side, jumping onto Arthur's back and hooking his arms around his neck—it's enough for me to wrench myself free—but with a shout of pain, Ben releases Arthur, falling to the asphalt and writhing under the torture ripping through his body.

The dragon roars, flinging herself from my back to curl around Ben at the direction of my fingertips. Ben gasps as if coming up from a swim, now shielded from the pain.

"NO!" Arthur yells, enraged.

But before Arthur can reach for me again, Keith flies directly overhead, his arms outstretched. I grab onto him as he makes a pass, and he lifts me from my feet to whisk me away. Ben sprints his escape as well. Arthur's eyes track Keith through the sky, and his hands raise to strike at him.

"Shield him!" I cry to the creature.

She latches onto Keith right as Arthur's fingertips twitch. When nothing happens, Arthur grinds his teeth, tearing at his hair and letting out a frustrated yell.

In seconds, Keith and I safely land back on the ground next to Jonah and the others.

"Jonah, you have to focus on suppressing Arthur's ability to copy powers," Keith says, wildly out of breath. "He's too strong otherwise. We're not going to be able to pin him down if he can run like Ben or shoot fire like Candice."

Jonah looks to Ashton, who's sweating profusely with the strain of keeping a lid on Arthur's teleportation. "Can you hold the blue orb at bay by yourself?"

Though he looks like he's about to pass out, he grits his teeth and nods. "I can hold him."

A scorching shriek splits the air, and fire billows down the street. It travels so fast toward us that I'm sure we're going to burn up, but Candice lifts her hands, throwing her own shield of fire back to protect us. The collision of the infernos looks like two massive waves crashing high into the heavens. It shatters more glass from the surrounding buildings, and all of us have to cover our heads as shards of debris fall to the pavement.

Jonah grips the knife in his right hand while flexing his left. "Vianne, Candice, Ben, with me! Ashton, Keith, you stay with Hollis."

In a blur of super speed, both Jonah and Ben cross the distance between themselves and Arthur, and then Jonah throws his hand out, switching powers to suppress Arthur's ability to copy. My hand flings forward as well, and the dragon detaches herself from Keith to charge after Jonah. A flash of gold is all I see before she wraps herself around him, wings spread wide with protection. Vianne and Candice take off after them too, sprinting down the burned and cracked city street.

There's a flash of silver as the weapon comes down directly at Arthur's chest, but Arthur is too quick. He grabs Jonah's wrist, and the two of them grapple with the blade. Ben joins in as well, doing his best to deter Arthur from gaining the upper hand. As the three of them wrestle, every attempt Arthur makes to control them or torture them fails, and though Jonah strains, he's able to stop Arthur from calling flames or running away.

Vianne reaches the tussle next, and she throws her hands forward. Arthur's face mutates, becoming disfigured and angry red. A howl of pain comes from his mouth, but it's not enough for him to relinquish his fight for the weapon. If anything, it makes him more aggressive. He lands a punch directly to Ben's nose, knocking him back, and then he kicks out at Jonah, landing a foot on Jonah's knee and twisting the knife from his grip. Jonah cries out and goes down—hard—landing flat on his back. There's a whizz as the weapon flies at Jonah's face, but Candice screams, sending a fireball directly into Arthur—and this time, it hits, sending him flying through the air.

Arthur rolls like a log several times over, and this snuffs out the flaming spots on his clothing, but the fire has done its damage. Patches of skin on his chest are now blistered and raw, and his shirt has fallen off of him in charred tatters.

The wild scream of rage that splits the air next causes the hairs all along my arms to stand on end. Arthur's hands shatter outward, and Vianne and Candice fall to the ground in agony, screaming as pain slices through their bodies. Ben, who's already on the asphalt, writhes with them too. The only person protected from the pain is Jonah because the dragon is still guarding him, but he's gritting his teeth, clutching his injured knee.

Another spark of blue appears, but Ashton extinguishes it, and this is when Arthur's attention hones in on him. There's a cold, calculated look that crosses Arthur's face, like a predator locking on to prey, and I can see it behind his eyes: he's going after Ashton next.

Before I can call the dragon back, Arthur's hands slash, and this time, all of us fall to the ground in pain. I scream, feeling the stab of a hundred knives throughout my body. In the distance, the creature shrieks, and I can feel her vanish from Jonah's chest as she's sucked back into mine. The boys twist and contort next to me, all of us caught in the torment of the power.

There's a streak of blue, and Arthur emerges from the orb to stand directly over me. I gasp as he grabs me by the wrists, yanking me up, and for that split second, the pain in my body ceases—and that's all I need to call the creature out again. She flings herself over Keith and Ashton just in time for them to grab onto one another, and as the blue orb expands to steal me away, Keith's hand reaches out to grasp Arthur's ankle.

Flash.

All four of us vanish from the street, sucked into the teleportation of the orb's clutches. The cold darkness coughs us out onto a gravelly surface, and Keith, Ashton, and I topple over one another. Wind whips across my face, and cold bites into my exposed skin. We're on the roof of another building, but it's not the Testing Center. I don't even know if we're in the same city . . .

"Ashton, watch out!" Keith cries.

Arthur leaps onto Ashton before he can get up, wrestling with his hands, but try as he might, he can't force the torture back over his body because Ashton is suppressing him with everything he's got. Keith jumps to his feet to charge across the five feet of space between himself and the fight.

With a mighty blow, Keith's fist makes contact with the side of Arthur's jaw, and it's enough to shake him off of Ashton. Keith grabs Ashton, hauling him to his feet, and the two of them back away, taking a defensive stance in front of me. My hands burn with tingling, and I direct the dragon to stand between them, its wings wide, casting a shimmer of golden light onto both of them.

Arthur spits blood into the gravel of the rooftop as he rises to his feet, panting wildly. The burns on his chest look severe, but they haven't slowed him down. His eyes bounce between the three of us. Ashton is shaking from head to toe in his efforts to keep Arthur's powers at bay. The only solace we have is that Arthur can't take on any of the abilities that are no longer with us, but I have no idea how we're going to beat him by physical strength alone.

Again, panic rips into me, weakening my resolve. The only reason I haven't collapsed is because of the copious amounts of adrenaline thundering through my veins and the vibrations of the creature in my limbs.

I feel powerless . . .

Once more, right as the thought crosses my mind, the creature snarls. *You are not powerless.* Her words sink into me—odd and enchanting, shrouded in a meaning I'm failing to grasp. Her diamond eyes flash as she bares her teeth, and she seems to shine even brighter, the gold of her power mesmerizing.

"You're quite a powerful young man," Arthur says, leering at Ashton through his labored breaths. He cocks his head to the side, scrutinizing him. "I must admit, I'm impressed. But I can feel you slipping. You don't have much left in you. Why don't you walk away? Let me have Hollis, and you can live. I'll give you a place of honor at my side."

Ashton raises his hands even higher, maintaining his defensive stance. He grits his teeth and digs his heels into the gravel of the roof. "Rot in hell, Arthur!" he spits. "Keith, take Hollis. Get out of here while I can still hold him."

Keith shakes his head. "We're not leaving you."

"We're not going anywhere," I affirm. A surge of golden light sparks from the creature, and power wells up through my chest and into my hands.

Arthur simpers in a mocking tone. "How touching. The two fools who chose to die by Hollis Timewire's side." He breathes in a deep chestful of air, seeming to center himself on the feel of the abilities beneath his skin. "Last chance for mercy, boys."

Ashton curls his hands into fists. "Fuck your mercy!"

An evil smile splits Arthur's lips, and it makes him look more beast-like than human. He squares his shoulders, tossing his head back and forth. Then his hands spread wide. "Have it your way then."

In a growl of madness, Arthur dives toward Keith, tackling him around the waist. The two of them fall to the roof, and Arthur ends up on top of him. He strikes Keith over and over again, and Ashton leaps in, grabbing Arthur's dominant fist to hold him at bay. But with a powerful uppercut, Arthur knocks Ashton back to continue his assault. I scream, jumping into the fray as well, but a punch to my jaw sends me reeling back, causing my upper lip to split open against my teeth. Blood drips into my mouth, and the metallic taste churns my stomach.

My vision swims, and I double over on my hands and knees, trying not to pass out. All I can hear is the sound of blow after blow landing.

There's shouting.

Cursing.

Stars flicker around my periphery.

The creature pulls me out of the fog, giving me an extra boost of clarity and dampening the sensation of pain that's riddled my face. What I see when I rise to my feet nearly makes my heart stop. Keith is lying motionless on the roof, bloodied and beaten, and Arthur is now on top of Ashton, strangling him.

"NO!" I cry, charging back in. I leap onto Arthur, doing my best to pry his hands away from Ashton, who's turning purple-faced with suffocation. But nothing I do tears Arthur away. Ashton falls limp under his hands, and when he does, his suppression extinguishes.

Arthur's chest heaves with victory, and then he turns his bestial energy toward me, his eyes alight with wicked pleasure. "It's time to end this, Hollis."

He snatches me by the wrists, his grip so strong that I feel like my bones are going to break. I shriek, fighting and kicking him. Throwing my head down, I sink my teeth into his right arm, and he yells, loosening his grasp, but before I'm able to wrench myself free, agony rips across my skin. The torture is back, consuming every part of me, and I drop to the gravel, screaming until my throat is raw. He lets it go on for far longer than before, relishing in my torment. Just as I'm about to black out, he pulls his hand back, calling the pain out of my body.

I lie on the roof, unable to move. My body is limp with shock. Though the ability is no longer ravishing my flesh, I can still feel the lingering aftereffects. I have nothing left in me to give. There's no more fight. No more chances. No more options of escape. I'm going to die now. I just hope I see Maddy and my mother and father on the other side. Although fear should be clawing its way through me, I feel a strange sort of peace. It covers me like a veil. Maybe dying isn't that scary after all. Maybe dying is simply the next adventure full of better things than what this short and painful life had to offer.

Arthur hauls me up by the back of my head, knotting his hand through my hair and securing me into a standing position. He pins me against himself—my back to his chest—and then he walks us all the way to the edge of the building, practically carrying me because of how numb my body has gone. He leans in, talking right against my ear.

"When this is over, I'm going to make sure everyone knows that *you* killed the boy with the golden light—that you snuck into the lab and kidnapped him, and that you took his life on *purpose* to ruin us all. You'll be remembered only as a terrorist. Everyone will loathe the very thought of you, and your legacy will go down as a dark stain against the progress of humanity. There won't be a child born in the new world that doesn't know your name from the pages of our history books. Both great and small, for generations to come, will know that there was no *light* in you at all. And I will be celebrated for finally ridding the world of the plague that is Hollis Timewire."

My hands move to cling onto his arms—one last burst of effort to avoid the towering depths of the cityscape below. Tingling showers through my limbs and face, and one last time, the creature emerges from my chest to hover right in front of me. She's dazzling gold with eyes brighter than the sun, and in her face, all I see is something beautiful and pure. The light from her body showers over me, casting me in wonderful warmth. The sensation spreads through me as her wings spread wide. Then, the tip of her tail moves to touch the center of my forehead, and the moment it does, a memory sparks in me as clearly as if I had been sucked back in time:

"Maddy, come here," I say softly. "It's okay to be sad sometimes."

"I don't like sadness," he sniffles. "It's cold. But the golden light makes me feel warm. Sissy made me feel warm."

"I know. Sadness is cold, and my power is warm. I've felt that too."

"How do you stop feeling sad?" he asks.

"I remember that I have people like you in my life. Then I don't feel so sad anymore . . . and new friends that come in unexpected ways . . ."

"New friends?"

"Yes. There are a lot of wonderful people here with special powers just like Sissy. We all have our own unique type of light. Many aren't gold like yours, Maddy, but the light is still there in all of us. Remember that."

"I'll remember."

My mind is pulled back to the present, and as I stare into the shimmering eyes of the creature, my own glisten with tears. Her body flashes bright gold, and my lips part as understanding crashes over me.

You are not powerless, she hisses.

"The golden light," I whisper.

The instant I utter the words, my hands shine gold like the sun, and Arthur gasps. Though he can't see the creature, he can see the light. Warmth flows through my entire body, and it gives me a boost of strength. Without hesitation, I clamp my hands around Arthur's arms. A flash of brilliance, luminescent like the stars, fires between us, lighting up the entire sky. In horror, Arthur tries to pull away from me, but I don't relinquish my grip. The golden light pours from my palms, latching itself onto Arthur's chest and face and entering into his mouth. As the golden light works its way through him, I feel a new sensation in my hands: a powerful tug. Energy is being sucked into my skin, and one by one, the abilities in Arthur's blood leach out of him, pooling beneath my palms and traveling into my chest.

The molten beauty gleams for a few more seconds before tucking itself back into my hands and vanishing from sight.

There's a full three seconds of utter silence . . .

Arthur shoves me, and the creature roars, wrapping herself around my torso to jerk me back from the edge as I fall to my hands and knees, narrowly avoiding the plunge. There's a moment of stunned quiet as he examines his hands. His face is pale, brow covered in sweat, and the burns across his skin catch the light of the growing morning.

A low rasp escapes his mouth. "What have you done?"

The dragon clings to my back. Golden wings unfurl behind me, and she flashes her diamond teeth as I rise to my feet, feeling the vibrations of my ability course through me. When Arthur turns, I slice my palms through the air, and he stiffens under the beast. Control fills me to the brim, building from my core to flood my fingertips with insatiable power. I move my hands in sync, forcing him to take a step back so that he's at the bitter edge. So much tingling washes over me that I can feel every cell in Arthur's body.

I walk up to him, getting within inches of his frozen frame. His mouth is pressed shut and his face is contorted. All the wrath I've been storing up inside of me spills forth, and I clamp my fists shut, forcing the air from his lungs and pressing the coils on my ability around his neck. His eyes turn bloodshot and his face grows steadily more purple. I can feel him suffocating under my fingertips. I can feel his brain beg for oxygen. I can sense his heartbeat race and his body writhe, though outwardly he can't move at all. A trail of blood starts from his nose, and beads of sweat lick his disheveled hairline. I look him directly in the eye, and all I see there is fear . . .

"This is for my mother, you son of a bitch."

I pull my hands apart like I'm drawing open a curtain, and Arthur jerks violently, falling backward off the towering heights of the building to land with a bone-shattering squelch on the asphalt below.

I stand at the brim of the sheer drop for only a second more before stepping back to clutch my chest. Tears have wetted my face, and I touch them, feeling them at the ends of my fingertips. The sensation sinks into me, and I breathe in through my nose.

I'm alive.

Alive . . .

"Keith," I murmur.

I turn on my heels to run to him. He's still lying unmoving on the rooftop, and when I reach him, I suck in a hasty breath, dropping down next to him. His nose looks broken, one of his eyes is purple, and his lips are a bloody mess. "Keith!" I cry out. My fingers immediately trace his neck. For a moment, I can't breathe, but when I sense a subtle heartbeat beneath his warm skin, I let out a sob of relief, bowing my head over his chest.

Tears fleck down my face, completely out of my control, and I scan the layout of the roof. There's a door, but even from here, I can see that it's chained shut. How am I going to get down? Keith and Ashton need help.

I sit back on the gravel, running my hands through my tangled hair to fight against the adrenaline-fraught attempts of my body to push me into hyperventilation.

Abruptly, there's a flash that comes from directly behind me. I spin around, jumping to my feet, my heart jolting on high alert again. I throw my hands up, ready for the fight to begin anew, but what I see causes me to cry out in disbelief.

"Olivia!"

I run to her, throwing my arms around her neck. She nearly buckles under the force of the hug, but she fights me off, her eyes darting madly around the rooftop. But when she doesn't see Arthur, she looks at me.

"He's dead," I say.

Her brow turns upward as if she was fighting off a sob, but then she lets one out anyway and returns the embrace with just as much ferocity, squeezing me around the ribs until it feels like she might crack one.

"You're alive!" she exclaims.

We stand there, clinging to each other out of sheer incredulity. When we break apart, I take in her appearance. Blood trails from her ears and nose, and the whites of her eyes are bloodshot. She looks like she's been strangled to death.

"What happened? How did you get away?"

"I didn't," she replies. "Arthur puppeted me. He forced all the air out of me and held me there until I passed out. I thought I was going to die—it certainly felt like I was dying—but he didn't hold me long enough. And when I woke up, I teleported straight to you."

I laugh out loud. It's a laugh of disbelief and happiness, filled with a dose of feeling completely overwhelmed. I place a hand to my forehead and the other to my busted lip. I spit blood onto the rooftop, feeling violently ill. Though the creature is still running energy through my body, I'm on the verge of collapsing. I can feel it.

"We have to get the boys help," I say, pointing to Keith and Ashton. "Jonah and the others too. They might be hurt. We have to get them to Beezee."

As far as my feelings for what side Beezee has chosen, I'll reserve judgment until after my friends are well. I need her power, and I'll force her to help if need be.

"Hollis," a faint voice calls.

"Keith!" I sprint to his side again, and when I get to him, I cradle his head in my lap, leaning down to kiss his bloodied lips. A sob gets stuck in my throat, but I choke through it. "It's going to be okay. You're okay. We're going to get you help. Olivia is here."

His eyes flutter, and he coughs, his breathing labored.

"Olivia, grab Ashton. Let's go," I press her.

She hurries over to Ashton, stooping down to take hold of his wrist. Olivia then gives me the most comforting look she can, and as I hold Keith in my arms, the creature shimmers by my side. Her golden light fills me with warmth. When the blue orb expands around us, she tells me wordlessly that everything will be alright.

___

36

___

I sit by the side of Keith's hospital bed in the medical ward in Sector 10, gently stroking his hair as he sleeps. Pumped full of pain killers and only partially healed, he's not been conscious for more than five minutes at a time for the past forty-eight hours.

In the two days since Arthur's death, so much has happened that it's a wonder I'm not unconscious in bed myself. However, since the only real injuries I sustained were scrapes along my knees and arms, a busted lip, and some mild bruising around my neck, I've been able to ignore Beezee's incessant urges to rest.

When Olivia teleported us back to the mountain, we came with the whole band of rebels in tow. Immediately, I used my power to take control of the entire guard—including Terrace, Hugo, Erwin, and anyone else I perceived to be a threat. Within the span of an hour, the band of rebels had disarmed and imprisoned Arthur's forces, stuffing Sector 2—the prison block of the mountain fortress—to its bursting point. Many of the cells, which were only intended for one occupant, were double and triple bunked. Eli Stone, the lead Council member, was freed from his incarceration. He was the only person on the Council who didn't pledge his allegiance to Arthur after Camille's death, and he paid dearly for it. Malnourished and hanging on by a thread, he was transferred to the medical ward to receive care. Darren Mitchell and Pierce Bodegard were also freed and granted forgiveness for their attempts on my life back in the forest.

During the hasty transition, Delphi had taken it upon herself to create a temporary new guard from the band of rebels and a handful of trusted volunteers. They armed themselves with the stolen weapons and created groups to patrol the Sectors and keep order. Sector 2 became the most heavily guarded part of the mountain, with the medical ward and the aircraft hangar as a close second and third. Beezee wasn't imprisoned, due to her ability, but she was confined to Sector 10, and a handful of her assistants were allowed to stay in the medical ward with her—all of them under constant supervision.

After much deliberation, Maddy's body was brought to the medical ward and carefully placed in the Sector's morgue until proper arrangements could be made.

The entire mountain went in lockdown and all communication with the outside world was promptly cut off. No one, including the people staffed at the Area 7 Testing Center and the ten Chief Overseers who had been given powers, knew of Arthur's death yet. Jonah, along with a few others, had decided that this piece of information needed to break at the correct time, or else more chaos could ensue. And that was why, after a hasty and heated discussion, Olivia was sent to collect Arthur's body from the street and bring it back to the mountain. He was then promptly and unceremoniously burned in one of the incinerators in the waste Sector . . .

I space in and out of focus as I continue to stroke Keith's hair.

Now that the mountain is under our control, it's time for me to make some difficult decisions. Once news of Arthur's death breaches these walls, there will be so much more to deal with than simply sifting through restructuring how the mountain should operate. There is so much to consider—questions that demand answers. What do we do with the Testing Centers and the rest of Arthur's loyal followers that reside out in society? What about the Military Bases? How do we deal with the prisoners locked up at PC-7A? What should happen to the ten Chief Overseers that took the serum, and what are we supposed to do with the doses of serum that already exist? Who should be in charge now? What about Arthur's guards, his inner circle, and the scientists at the lab in Area 7? The list of pressing questions is long and daunting, and unfortunately, a fair few of them require immediate attention.

I can't stop my mind from reeling. My eyes are irritated and red from how much I've wept. Every time I think of Maddy, the crushing loss takes hold of me, and I feel like I can't breathe. I've half convinced myself that this is one big nightmare—like if I slept for any amount of meaningful time, I might wake up to Maddy's smiling face and his little hand pulling me up from bed to go eat breakfast. But he's gone, and the hole in my heart is something I don't even know how to begin dealing with.

Keith's steady breathing pulls me out of the pit of my

spiraling thoughts. I'm so glad he's alive. He and Ashton were in critical condition upon their arrival to the mountain, but Beezee told me they are both doing much better than she initially expected them to. Vianne has been in and out of this room just as much as I have, taking whatever spare time she has to sit by Ashton's side. When she's not here, she's with Jonah, having taken an active role in the temporary leadership of this time of transition. Candice has been checking up on her brother relentlessly too. She's been so worried that Vianne has opted to drag her into meetings to give her something to do so she doesn't lose her mind.

I sigh when I see the clock hanging over the exit. It's time for me to talk to Wren before dragging myself into yet another meeting with Jonah and the band of rebels. Wren was imprisoned with the rest of Arthur's guards, but what she did for us won't leave me. It keeps nagging at my heart, and before I make any other society-altering decisions as the temporary leader of this place, I have to decide what to do with her. I don't want to leave Keith right now, but there's too much to do. Jonah has helped me with the aftermath of the takeover in more ways than I can count, but I'm still the one with the power to enact the type of change we need to keep the world from crumbling into chaos. Realistically, we can't keep Arthur's death a secret for long. I told myself I was prepared to deal with the fallout of my decision to confront Arthur, and here I am, more broken than ever before, having to keep the shards of myself together while simultaneously hoping the world doesn't shatter because of what I've done.

I lean in to Keith, kissing him tenderly on the forehead. "I'll be back soon," I whisper.

I get up and walk to the exit of the hospital wing, passing Ashton's bed on the way. He's heavily drugged and sleeping just like Keith. Deep bruising lines his neck, making him look like a corpse. It's so discolored it's gruesome. I'm truly astonished that both he and Keith made it out of the fight. Arthur beat Keith within an inch of his life and strangled Ashton to the point where he likely won't come out of this without some impairment—at least that was Beezee's initial assessment. After a healing session though, Beezee revised her statement, saying that she's hopeful Ashton will make a "mostly" full recovery— whatever that means.

The two guards manning the exit let me pass with nods of respect, and as I walk down the hall to leave Sector 10, I pass Beezee, who's being escorted by two more guards. Based on the large medical bag she's carrying, she's about to check up on the boys. I don't say a word to her, but our brief eye contact is enough for her to avert her gaze. That's another thing I'm going to have to decide. What happens to Beezee-Day Jones? What is she guilty of concerning Maddy? At the very least, she knew of Arthur's plan to take him and use him for his blood. And she was the one who suggested the ability census as a guise for procuring Maddy's blood. The ability census also resulted in Arthur being able to build up his power inventory for batch doses of the serum. Beezee is not blameless by any means.

I shake the thought from my head, opting to forgo thinking about her. For now, Beezee is the least of my concerns.

I weave my way through the mountain, heading toward Sector 2, where the holding cells are. The people I run into either stare at me like I'm a spectacle, shrink back in unease, or offer me encouraging looks. Not everyone in the mountain is on my side, but a surprising number have come forward in the past forty-eight hours to align themselves with us. It turns out there were a lot more people who didn't approve of the serum than we initially thought—and a fair amount who felt like they had no choice but to go along with Arthur's plans from the beginning. Delphi was right when she said that the band of rebels had a voice to speak up for the future of the mountain. Most of the friends and family of those involved in the coup against Arthur changed their loyalty upon discovering the truth behind the serum. All things considered, this quick shift gave everyone hope.

It's the people who were intimately involved in what was going on behind the scenes that I'm most worried about. Those are the people I have to make decisions regarding.

Sector 2's gloomy cave-like entrance gives way to bright fluorescent lighting past the door. Armed guards are stationed at every block, keeping a watchful eye over the prisoners. Most of them look over at me upon my arrival.

Siena Rose, who is deep in conversation with Yang, pauses their talk. "Yang, hold on a minute," she says. There's a quick pattering of footsteps as she approaches me. "Hollis, what do you need?"

"I need to talk to Wren. Who has the passcode to her cell?"

"I have all the passcodes." She gives me a quizzical look. "Why do you need the passcode to talk to her? She can hear you through the glass you know."

"I want to speak to her alone . . . about what she did."

Siena's hooded eyes flash, and she purses her lips. "I don't think that's a good idea."

"Please don't argue with me." I keep my tone firm but civil. "Let Wren out. And I don't need an armed guard escort either." I let my fingers flitter through the air. "I can take care of myself."

She bites her upper lip and crinkles her nose, twisting a piece of her thick raven hair between her fingertips. "Fine," she relents.

She treads past me to move deeper into the cell block, and I follow her. Faces peer out at me through thick panes of glass, but I don't look at any of them. I don't want to see their disdain for me or witness their anger and fear. I must guard what energy I have left and reserve it for the task at hand.

Siena stops at the cell labeled H-13. Wren is lying on the cot within, but the moment she sees me, she sits up.

"Are you sure about this?" Siena asks.

"Yes."

She sighs, typing in the code to the door's control panel. There's a hiss and a popping noise as the glass panel opens, sliding into the frame of the cell.

Wren looks from me to Siena and then back again, uncertainty written across her expression. I can see it in her face: she doesn't know whether seeing me is a good thing or a bad thing. I can also tell from the subtle proddings of my ability that she isn't going to fight whatever is about to happen.

"Walk with me," I say to Wren.

She promptly listens, exiting the cell. When she does, some of the guards who were present when Wren stopped Arthur from shooting Keith call out to her from inside their cells. Some yell "traitor," others taunt her, and some threaten to kill her. The aggression displayed toward Wren is sickening, and it rivals that of a starving pack of wolves. If it was not for Olivia's decision to teleport Wren alongside the band of rebels when we escaped Arthur, she most certainly would be dead.

Wren doesn't say a word to anyone as we leave the cell block. When some of the band of rebels protest my decision to take Wren out of Sector 2, I simply hold my hand up to dismiss their reservations. I'm not going to explain myself to anyone right now. As we exit, Wren stays by my side, waiting patiently for me to speak first. I can sense the slight increase in her heartbeat the longer I keep silent, and when we finally emerge from the gloom into the well-lit hallway beyond the exit, I decide to begin.

"What you say to me today is going to determine what I do with you, Wren."

The daunting nature of this statement sobers her even more. We continue our stroll down the concrete hallway as I gather my thoughts. They are raging in me like a wildfire. Grief for Maddy mixes with gratitude for what Wren did to save our lives. It's completely overwhelming.

I stop walking, and Wren stops too. My eyes burn with fresh tears, and I clamp my hands into fists, digging my fingernails into my palms. "Did you know about Arthur taking doses of the serum for himself?"

Her brow creases in response to the pained look on my face. "No."

I have to take several deep breaths to calm the storm of wanting to sob my eyes out again.

"Why did you push the gun out of the way?"

My voice grows thick with sadness despite my every effort to shove it down. I look her in the eye, and she swallows hard. There's several seconds of silence, and then Wren's lips part. "Because I finally realized I was on the wrong side."

Tears slip down my face. I wipe them away with my fingertips, but more come, and I bury my head in my hands, overcome. Maddy pervades my thoughts again, and I want to scream at the injustice of it all. He didn't deserve to die. I should hate Wren, but I don't. I should want to tear her to pieces for taking Maddy away from me, but I can't. Arthur was going to kill us all, and Wren is one of the reasons I'm still breathing.

"I remember what you said to me on our first mission together," Wren murmurs. "You told me that how we treat people matters . . . that how we do things matter. I thought you were foolish, but you weren't. You were right."

She pauses, seeming to collect herself. Her mouth thins out into a line. The hardened look I'm so used to is now nowhere on her face. The only thing I see in her is sorrow.

"I truly thought Evandrum was leading a revolution and not a massacre, but the closer we got to stepping back into society, the more I came to realize that the only thing Arthur wanted was control, and it didn't matter who he had to step over to get it. I didn't want to believe he had changed. When Arthur started this, he was so hopeful and filled with ambition. He was a *good* man at the beginning, and his motives were noble. No one believed him when he said we could rejoin society. It sounded crazy. But over time, he convinced us it was possible—that we could all change the world if we were only brave enough to stand with him. It was incredible how he rallied everyone to the cause, how he slipped us into society, and how he planted the foundations that allowed us to do what we've done. I grew to believe in him—all of us did—because no one had the vision he did, and no one had the strength and cunning to bring it to fruition. But somewhere along the way, he lost himself, and I . . . I told myself that he was still the same as he was before—that his intentions were good at heart. I was holding on to the man he used to be, and not seeing him for the man he had become."

Her breath comes out strained.

"It took me all the way up until he pointed that gun at Keith's head for me to finally see the darkness in him."

Her brow furrows in sadness, and her voice catches.

"I never meant for Maddy to . . . I'm so sorry, Hollis. What happened to him wasn't fair."

She lowers her gaze from my face. For such a powerful and strongly built woman, I've never seen her so meek.

"Wren, look at me," I say.

She fights with herself for a moment before meeting my eyes again.

It takes all of my willpower to speak, but I mean what I'm about to say, and Wren needs to hear it.

"Thank you for saving us. If you hadn't defied Arthur, we'd all be dead. And I know Maddy . . . that you didn't mean for him to . . . I know."

I suppress a sob, pinching the skin in between my eyebrows. Wren seems repentant, which truly makes my heart glad. If I'm being honest, having her by my side to help me wade through the mess of navigating the new world without Arthur makes me so much less anxiety-ridden. But there will be pushback if I allow Wren into the fold. I know it. With a single decision, Wren has made herself an outcast to Arthur's loyal followers, and at the same time, her track record is enough to give everyone in the band of rebels pause. But I don't think I can do this without her. She has more pull with the people out in society than I do. They know her, and many of them respect her. Only the guards present when Arthur was going to kill us know about her act of defiance. She could help me change things for the better. From our talks on the Beechcraft, we're not so different, she and I. We both want to see a world where people with powers can live freely. It was our underlying approaches that were different. But now that Wren has seen the light and made such a life-altering decision, I want her with us.

This is going to cause an uproar, but there's too much at stake for me to care what people think of this decision.

"Wren, I want your help," I say earnestly. "With Arthur dead, there's so much to navigate that I'm . . . it's overwhelming. I'm the one in charge of everything, but . . . this is beyond what I'm capable of. I need your expertise. Your experience. You're a good leader, Wren. Arthur wouldn't have placed you so high up in his ranks if he didn't see that in you. There's going to be a lot of angry people who won't like this, but I don't care. You have a place with us. I *want* you with us. I want you to help me undo what Arthur's done."

Her eyes widen, and her mouth parts in mild shock. From her face, it's clear she wasn't expecting me to say this. She was probably expecting me to tell her that she's set for execution for her crimes of association with Arthur and for the bullet that ended Maddy's life.

"I'm going to tell you something I haven't told anyone yet. When Maddy died . . ." My throat tightens again, and my eyes well over with fresh tears. I let air out from between my lips slowly and start again. "When Maddy died, he gave me the golden light. I don't understand it fully, but he meant for me to have it. And I know deep down that I'm supposed to use it to fix this." I pause, gearing up for my request and hoping against hope that Wren will agree. "I want you by my side. I'm going to have Olivia teleport me to the ten Chief Overseers, and I'm going to take their powers back. They were never meant to have abilities, and regardless of what the future holds, we can't step into it with this perverted idea that those with the biomarker are 'pure' and those without it are not. So . . . will you stand with me?"

Wren stares at me blankly. It's like she's struggling to process the grace I'm extending her. Still, written all over her expression is grief for what she's done—and it's a grief that goes deeper than Maddy. It's sorrow for the ways she helped Arthur hurt so many people in his pursuit for power. It's a look that says she knows she can't take any of it back. But I can also see in her a desire to right the wrongs, even though it won't erase the past.

"Of course I'll stand with you," she says soberly. "I don't . . ." Wren stifles the sadness in her tone, but it still seeps through. "I don't deserve your mercy."

My heart breaks at the pain in her face. I myself once carried those same feelings after my betrayal led to the bombing of the underground compound. I didn't deserve Jonah's mercy or the

Council's decision to allow me a probationary period of reform. It's only because of Jonah's grace and understanding that I got another chance to do better. To be better. He was the one person who still saw something good in me, and he extended the forgiveness I needed to change from the inside out. Now I have the chance to be that person for Wren.

I take in a deep breath, speaking with a gentle voice. "I think if we all got what we deserved, the world would be a very dark place."

A reserved smile forms on her face. "I suppose you're right."

"I have to take you back now," I say. "To your cell. I can't let you out without talking to the others."

"I understand."

There's a moment of silence, and she stares at the concrete floor, leaning up against the wall of the hallway.

"Things will get better," I encourage.

These words are more for me than her. With all my heart, I cling to them. Because things have to get better. Now that Arthur is dead, we stand on the unknown, but at least the future holds hope that people, regardless of their blood status, can live—that no one is less than simply because of the presence or absence of the biomarker. No Diseased Ones and no Pure Ones.

I gaze at her for a long moment. "Please don't tell anyone about the golden light. It's my secret to share, and I don't feel like sharing it right now."

Wren gives me a gentle nod. "I won't tell a soul. You have my word."

"Thank you." I sigh, placing a hand to my forehead and

rubbing circles there to help ease the tension of a budding headache. "Let's go."

Wren follows me back to Sector 2. Again, she endures the cursing and yelling of her prison mates, but she doesn't acknowledge them. She simply slips back into her cell and sits on her cot.

"I'll be back for Wren later," I tell Siena Rose and Yang.

They both nod, and then I leave the prison Sector behind, trailing my way through the mountain.

Suddenly, a small tug beneath my fingertips prods me forward.

"What?" I ask the creature.

The tug nudges me again, and her hiss sounds in my mind. *Sector 15.*

The only thing there is Arthur's office. My hands move in a gentle arc, and I call the dragon from my chest. She appears in front of me in all her golden glory, staring at me with those dazzling diamond eyes.

"I don't want to go to Sector 15," I say.

But she simply gazes at me with a look that I can't refuse. Something is pricking at me, compelling me to listen to her.

"Fine," I say begrudgingly. I flick my hand, and she disappears, melding back into me.

Ten minutes later, the panel in front of Arthur's office door blinks, ready to accept my palm print. After a moment's hesitation, I bring my hand up to it, and the door slides into the wall to admit me.

The wall screens at the far end of the room are off, and the atmosphere of the space is eerily silent. My eyes wander over the surface of the oval table to the chair that once belonged to the man who did so much evil in his climb to the top. A lot happened in this office . . . within these walls. This place is filled with darkness despite its shining white color.

I walk a few paces into the room, and memories of how trapped I felt under Arthur's coercion wash over me, slamming into my chest and squeezing my lungs.

"Why did you bring me here?" I ask the creature.

Another tug pulls on my fingertips.

It's only when I look at Arthur's leather chair again that I notice the smallest sliver of a handle poking up above the lip of the oval table.

I approach the chair with tentative steps, pulling it out from its tucked-in spot. When I do so, my heart plummets all the way to my feet.

The white briefcase . . .

With jittery fingers, I grasp the handle of the case, placing it on top of the oval table. Then I click open the clasp and lift the lid up.

There, sitting on a cushion of custom cut out foam, are five syringes of serum, all labeled:

Hollis Timewire—Puppet Master

Wren Zayla—Sensation Mimicry

Olivia Turrick—Teleportation

Jonah Luxent—Duplicate Powers

Ashton Teel—Suppression

The first four vials are empty, but the last—Ashton Teel's—is full. I stare at the case with my mouth ajar, feeling sick to my stomach. At what point had Arthur started to take doses of the serum for himself? At what point did he take *my* power?

Like an answer falling from the heavens, my mind goes back to the moment Arthur was late entering the Beechcraft. He looked haggard and violently ill. I had never seen him in such a state. He must have had a severe reaction to one of the doses in this case, and the one that caused it was probably mine. Besides, the timing of it would make the most sense. Arthur was about to give the Chief Overseers doses of the serum. Why would he do that unless he could guarantee that *he* was more powerful than *them*? Giving Aleda Sagespark his own power seemed like a bold and risky move to me, but he was one step ahead of her, like he always was—leaps and bounds in front of those he used.

I stare at the last dose, both saddened and angered. I lift the syringe from the case and place it on the floor. Then, with a hard stomp, I shatter it underneath the heel of my boot, and the dark liquid splatters out across the floor as the glass crunches.

I promised Maddy no one would ever use his blood again, and I'll be damned if I don't keep that promise.

—

37

—

True to my word, I speak with Jonah and the rest of the band of rebels about Wren. As I expected, I'm met with severe disapproval. Most of them don't trust her and urge me to keep her locked up, but I press the matter, bringing up what she did for us by defying Arthur. I also explain that Wren seems repentant and that we should be a people of grace and understanding—that we *have* to be in order to move forward.

"I can't do this without her," I insist when more objections are raised. This has become my mantra. "She has military *and* leadership experience. She's the only one who might be able to convince some of Arthur's people to join us instead of fight us. We can't lock up everyone who followed Arthur. We don't have the resources to do that. Besides, that's not who we are. We have to find another solution, and Wren can help. I want her to sit in on our meetings too. I need her input."

Thankfully, Jonah, Olivia, Vianne, and a few others take my

side by the end of the discussion. Ben, Candice, and Rosalie still seem on the fence, but their vehement protests have died down. I can tell that most of the band of rebels feels shaky about my decision. However, I assure everyone that Wren is *my* responsibility and I will keep her in check.

With a quick trip to Sector 2, I collect Wren and bring her back with me. The atmosphere among the band of rebels sobers with her entrance, but I ignore this.

During the next part of the meeting, we hash out who we should take into custody to avoid an insurrection when news of Arthur's death breaks. Right away, Wren proves her usefulness, extending our current list—which only consisted of George, Warden Kane, Jenkins, and Aleda Sagespark—to include the current leader of the Area 19 Military Base, General Myers, along with the other Generals presiding over the rest of the Military Bases. In addition, anyone Arthur personally appointed to a position of power is added to the list too—an insight we wouldn't have gotten had it not been for Wren.

When the meeting finishes, Olivia, Wren, and I get ready to teleport. After a brief shuffle of prisoners in Sector 2, empty cells await those who made it onto our list. Today's mission is about apprehending the prominent people in Arthur's regime.

It's a long and draining day. Olivia teleports me and Wren from Military Base to Military Base, and I use my ability to capture the Generals. We get in and out unnoticed—though it's only a matter of time before everyone knows. Next, Olivia takes us to PC-7A, and I capture Warden Kane. Then we go to the lab at Area 7 to collect George and the other scientists. One by one,

Wren breaks the news of Arthur's death to them and explains that they are now prisoners until fair trials can be set to determine the extent of their crimes.

When the only person left on the list is Aleda Sagespark, I tell Olivia about the golden light. The look of shock on her face quickly changes to overwhelming heartache for Maddy. As I explain my plan for the ten Chief Overseers, she doesn't prod me for more information, and she doesn't ask me anything about the golden light. All she does is grab my hand with a sad smile and say, "Let's go."

With all my heart, I'm grateful for her support. Only a true friend would know not to push me to talk about the golden light right now, and Olivia's as true of a friend as they come.

The trips are quick. I puppet the Chief Overseers to keep them from hurting us or calling out for help, and then with the guidance of the creature, I use the golden light to take away their powers. Each time, the light is incredible to behold, and it tugs at my heart, simultaneously filling me with wonder and deep anguish for the little boy we lost.

At long last, the day wraps up, and we return to the mountain with Aleda in hand. After confining her to her cell in Sector 2, I bid Wren and Olivia goodnight and collapse onto my bed in the training room to catch a few hours of sleep before the tasks of leadership demand my attention again.

■   ■   ■

"Hollis."

Gentle hands coax me awake, and my eyes blink open. A haze

of sleepy fog meshes across my vision, and it takes me a few seconds to see clearly. Jonah is sitting at the end of my bed, cane in hand. He wears a brace around his knee and looks just as tired as I feel.

"I'm so sorry to wake you up," he says. "But we need you again. We're going to discuss the broadcast."

The broadcast. My stomach twirls in discomfort. It's almost time to tell the world about Arthur, and when we do, we also need to lay out our plans for the future. We can't leave society unguided now that people with powers are out in the open. We must propose a path of reform—a way forward without the serum.

I groan, pulling the blanket up over my face, but I only leave it there for a moment before peeking my head out again and sitting up.

"At least I slept," I murmur half-heartedly. "I haven't been able to sleep much since Maddy."

Every time I say his name, it chokes me. My eyes fill with tears, and I have to grab Jonah's hand to anchor myself to something real.

"We're going to have his funeral tomorrow," Jonah says soberly.

This statement tugs a sob from me, and I lean against his arm, completely drained. I can't say goodbye. How am I supposed to accept this? How do I grieve and lead at the same time? I've mourned people before, but no amount of experience when it comes to loss prepares you for the next person who leaves.

"How am I supposed to do this?" I say through my tears. I look into Jonah's weary face. "How do I say goodbye to Maddy?"

His voice deepens with sorrow. "You don't. The people we love have a way of staying with us. Time will make it hurt less, but Maddy will always be with you, Hollis."

I sniffle, wiping my nose on the back of my hand. We sit there without speaking for nearly a minute, and I'm inundated with sadness. It physically hurts. It's like a knife digging itself deeper and deeper into my flesh.

Once more, I'm overwhelmed by what Maddy did for us in the moments of his death—what he did for *me*. Maddy saved me on the airstrip, but he also saved me in the end. The golden light is a part of me now, and that means that Maddy is too. Only *I* know what happened to Arthur on that rooftop. I'll never forget the golden light bursting from my palms to suck the powers from his body. Surprisingly, no one has pressed me for details about his death. Perhaps they've been too afraid to, or maybe they've been respectful of my space and decided not to pry.

In any case, I haven't talked about it with anyone. But sitting here now, with my teacher by my side, I feel the urge to share. Jonah is my family. He's the only father I have left, and the circumstances of Arthur's death is something I don't want to carry alone.

"I have to tell you something," I say.

I rise to my feet and move a few paces away from Jonah, holding my hands out in front of my stomach. Then my palms shine bright gold like the sun, and he shields his face from the light, squinting at the intensity. I let the gold linger there for a moment more before commanding it back into my skin.

Jonah's mouth parts in shock.

"As I was holding Maddy . . . when he was dying . . . I could feel all of your abilities in the sphere. They were so vibrant and alive. And somehow, I knew what to do. It was like Maddy was teaching me. I directed the abilities back into everyone with my hands. It was a connection point—something only our two powers could have done." Tears trace my face. "It was beautiful. The light was so pure and good. He gave me the golden light so I could save everyone. The creature . . . she's gold now. Every time I look at her, I feel like Maddy is with me. That's what happened to Arthur in the end. I took his powers away, and then I . . . I forced him to step off the edge of the roof."

For a long moment, all Jonah can do is stare at me. Compassion and grief come across his face; he wears them like a cloak. During the fight, he did his best to protect me, and when Arthur teleported me away, he must have felt helpless. In the end, I stood against Arthur without my friends, but I was never truly alone. I had the golden light.

"I'm sorry I wasn't able to . . ." he trails off, unable to finish his sentence.

I shake my head. "You protected me. You all did. Besides, it's done now. Arthur's dead. There's no use in thinking about what could have been."

His hands grip the end of his cane with vice-like intensity, and then a strange expression crosses his face, as if he were considering something for the first time.

"The golden light," he murmurs softly. "That's why I wasn't able to take on your power."

"What do you mean?" I ask.

"When we were fighting Arthur, I couldn't copy his powers. But I also couldn't copy yours. I didn't understand why, but . . . I think I do now." He shakes his head in disbelief. "My power, at its core, is meant to copy a single biomarker. But you and Arthur . . . you both had multiple abilities."

We both look at each other, astonished. Once again, Jonah's understanding of the nuances of an ability amazes me. He's taught me so much, and I've come to respect and deeply appreciate the study of abilities.

The broadcast comes to the forefront of my attention again, and the strength in my body dissipates. I sink to the floor, sitting down on the rug at Jonah's feet. I'm still so exhausted. That nap wasn't long enough, and I feel like I could spend another half hour crying my eyes out. But now is not the time for more tears. I have to be a leader again.

This moment feels unreal. Despite all odds, we did it. Arthur's regime is over. No one else will die because of their decision to refuse the serum. We can truly create a world where all people are treated equally—where your blood doesn't matter.

I twist a thread from the carpet around my finger, staring at it as it coils. "Jonah, I know there's a lot we have to cover in this broadcast, but I think we need to talk about what we call ourselves. We can't be the Pure Ones anymore. It's not right. We're not better than people who don't have powers. We can't be the Diseased Ones either. There's too much fear and hate in that term." Conviction rises in my chest, and I look up into his eyes. "I think we need to call ourselves something that reminds people that powers are important but still holds respect for those who don't have the biomarker. Something that says we're claiming our lives and our rights. That we have a place and a voice in this world." My brow furrows as I search for the right word. The smallest hint of a tug pulls at my heart, and I think again of the golden light and of Maddy. He gave me power when I needed it the most. He made me stronger despite everything that did its best to break me. My lips part as the word comes to me, and a sad smile forms on my face. "The Empowered Ones. That's what I think we should call ourselves."

Jonah's pensive look turns into a smile. "I think that's perfect, Hollis."

He stands and then holds his hand out to me. I take it, and he helps me to my feet.

"This is turning out to be the longest week of my life," I say with a sigh. "Let's get this over with so I can see Keith again."

"How is he doing?"

"He's been sleeping mostly, but that's good. His body needs the rest. His left cheekbone is broken, and so is his nose. Beezee's been able to mend some of the damage, but he's still . . ."

My throat closes around my next words. I have to force my brain to shut off its spiraling thoughts concerning Keith. He's alive. He's safe. He'll be okay. That's all I have space to tell myself.

Jonah leans on his cane heavily as we begin our trek through the mountain, and his footsteps echo off the concrete walls.

"Keith is in good hands," he says.

I nod, mostly to reassure myself, though I can't help the worry that creases my brow. I stifle a cry behind my hand, taking in uneven breaths. Jonah stops in his tracks and pulls gently on my shoulder. When I turn toward him, he holds his arms open wide, and I sink into the hug as he holds me firm in a comforting embrace.

"I know the path forward is going to be difficult," he says softly. "You have an impossible amount of tasks to face, and you're going to have to make more difficult decisions, but I want you to remember that you are *strong*, that you *deserve* to be here, and that you are *not* alone. *You* did this. You changed things for the better when the whole world was against you, and you never gave up your good heart along the way. You've grown into an incredible young woman, Hollis, and I am so proud of you."

He squeezes me tighter, and when the embrace ends, I look up at him with tears in my eyes. "Thank you, Jonah."

He gives me a weary smile. "I love you."

"I love you too."

He sighs. "Are you ready to go?"

Determination settles in me, and even though I'm riddled with exhaustion, a new spring forms in my step. "Yes. Let's go. I'm sure everyone is waiting for us by now."

■　　■　　■

The meeting lasts way longer than I want it to, but by the end, we have a solid outline for what we want to present to the world.

The agenda includes the following:

(1) Denounce Arthur and publicly condemn his plan for the serum

(2) Destroy all existing doses of the serum

(3) Free the military personnel imprisoned at PC-7A

(4) Hold fair and public trials for all of Arthur's inner circle

(5) Share our vision for a free and equal world

(6) Explain the plan to transition the Testing Centers into Education Centers

(7) Introduce ourselves as the Empowered Ones

The idea of calling ourselves the Empowered Ones is met with great enthusiasm, which makes my heart happy. With the meeting done and the day stretching into late afternoon, I excuse myself so I can go see Keith. My body is screaming at me to sleep, but I ignore it. I'd rather sit in the medical ward and let my thoughts wander. At least around Keith I don't feel like I'm losing my mind, and it puts me at ease to hear his breathing.

Just as I'm about to enter through the double doors of Sector 10, a familiar voice stops me.

"Oh Hollis, there you are!"

I turn to see a scarlet-cheeked Siena, huffing and completely out of breath. She presses two fingers into the stitch in her side.

"What's up?" I ask, concerned.

"Terrace wants to speak with you."

Unease clenches my stomach into a knot. "What about?"

"I don't know. He won't say. But I can't get him to shut up about it. So I told him I'd go find you."

I bite my lower lip as my hand hovers over the push bar leading to the medical ward. I'd rather go sit with Keith, but I know my curiosity would get the best of me. What could Terrace possibly want?

"You don't owe him anything," Siena says, swiping strands of hair from her face. "I told him as much. But he's been insisting for the past two days. I probably shouldn't have given in, but here I am."

I hesitate for only a second longer before begrudgingly withdrawing my hand from the door. "I'll talk to him."

The whole time we walk to Sector 2, I wrack my brain for what this could be about. Is Terrace going to ask me for a second chance? Would he so easily switch sides? Does he want to talk to me about Maddy? Or prod me about Arthur's death? Any avenue my mind moves down seems unlikely. Terrace is as much of a snake as Arthur was. He knew about Arthur's plan to kill my mother. He knew about Camille's trap for me too. He's ratted out and betrayed the secrets of so many people. I can't overlook that. He doesn't get the same mercy as Wren. His own actions have put him here, and I'm determined to make him live with it.

When we arrive at Sector 2, Siena leads me all the way to the last row of cells and then excuses herself. Terrace is lying in the cell labeled Z-40, and when I approach the glass, a smile curls his thin mouth. His amber eyes trace me from top to bottom, and my skin crawls. Though he doesn't look anything like his uncle, his mannerisms are eerily similar. He gets off his cot and stalks up to the glass, standing across from me.

"Hollis Timewire," he muses, his voice slippery. "Look at you . . . *alive* and well."

"What do you want, Terrace?" I ask coldly.

"Not even a hello?"

"Don't waste my time!" I snap.

"Wouldn't dream of it." He makes a fist and puts it up against the glass over his head, leaning forward to examine me. He sneers. "I've been following my uncle for as long as I can remember, and I've *never*, in all my years, seen someone stand up to him the way you did."

I stare at him with a hardened expression. I would think he's giving me a compliment if it wasn't for his aggressive stance and rugged tone.

"You . . ." His invasive gaze burrows into me, but I stare back at him without flinching, knowing beyond a shadow of a doubt that the creature is shielding me from his power. I can feel her beneath my skin, protecting me. "The *only* reason you're still breathing is because of sheer dumb *luck*. Not because of talent or vision. You're nothing but a society girl plucked by random chance from the masses. You were an accident bred from your mother's desperate desire to conceive."

"I don't have to listen to this. I didn't have to come here," I say, glaring at him. "Maybe I shouldn't have."

I start to back away, now realizing that this visit was probably a bad idea, but Terrace's next words stop me in my tracks.

"Oh, Hollis, I thought you were all about people speaking their minds. Or was that just talk? You can't handle a little honesty?"

He cocks his head, challenging me. When I don't respond, he continues, growing even more heated in his aggression.

"We could have made the world safe again! We had a real chance! But *you* . . . you had to ruin everything! You couldn't help it, could you? Everywhere you go, *everything* you touch, leads to destruction. The massacre of people with powers is going to happen again, Hollis! Just give it time. Humans are stupid. We forget and we repeat our same mistakes. At least Arthur saw that and tried to do something about it. Forcing everyone to take the biomarker was the *only* way to ensure our survival, but now that chance is gone. All that's left is your silly notion of coexistence." He simpers, pulling his pitch up to mock me. "'Oh, let's make a world where we can teach people that the Diseased Ones aren't bad!' Well, here we are, puppet master! Now we have to try to teach stupid people stupid things because that's the only option we have left."

Anger stirs in my belly, and I step closer to the glass. "I don't give a damn about what you think of me, Terrace. Your opinion is irrelevant. You don't get a say in what happens anymore. And it doesn't matter if I'm alive because of luck, does it? I'm here, and Arthur's not. You've lost."

Terrace chuckles. "I suppose I have, but so have you." His mocking smile deepens. "Maddy was a casualty you didn't anticipate. Poor helpless Maddy—caught up in the pit of your destruction along with the rest of us."

My hand moves faster than I have time to think, and I seize Terrace with the coils of my ability. He visibly stiffens, his eyes bulge, and his mouth clamps shut. I only hold him there for a second, but with all the aggression I can muster, I growl at him. "Don't you *dare* talk about Maddy! Keep his name out of your slimy mouth!"

I withdraw my power from his body, and he gulps, stepping back from the glass. He gives me a wary look but then shakes it off, tugging at the collar of his shirt. His voice slides back into a snake-like tone.

"There you go again, Hollis, always allowing your emotions to drive you. It's ironic, the way you feel things so deeply. Don't you think? Given your upbringing, I would've expected you to be more reserved, but you're not. You're still a child, throwing a fit with that big power of yours when things don't go your way."

I pull back on the tingling at the end of my fingertips, battling the urge to grab him again to shut him up. I can't let him get under my skin any more than he already has, so I bite my tongue.

He tilts his head and then his eyes narrow. "I have a question for you. If you would be so kind as to oblige poor-little-locked-up me."

"What question?" I ask in a more tempered tone.

"I've been mulling it over, all those meetings where I looked you in the eye and saw only complete and total compliance. I should have known something was wrong, but I convinced myself that you had finally fallen into line." His mouth puckers in disgust, and his nostrils flare. "How did you hide things from me? No one can hide things from me when I pull information through eye contact. How is it that *you*, despite every constraint Arthur put in place, managed to plot so much without my knowledge?"

I gaze at him with contempt in my heart, but I don't let it show on my face. I can tell that this question has been burning a hole right through his chest. He's questioning his ability, his *one* point of usefulness to his uncle's regime. His entire identity is wrapped up in his power—his pride of being a snitch and always having the inside scoop. But I'm not going to give him the satisfaction of an answer. He doesn't get to know this secret.

"That's a real puzzle, isn't it?" I say.

Terrace launches himself at the glass with lightning speed, slamming his fist against it, and I can't help but jump back.

"TELL ME!" he yells. "How did you hide things from me?"

Though my heart is pounding, I approach the glass again, getting within inches of his rat-like face. "I don't have to answer to you anymore, Terrace. I'm finally free."

The golden dragon materializes by my side, crouching low and baring her diamond teeth at Terrace with a snarl. I can feel the intensely protective nature of our bond. It's alive and present, and it showers me with warmth.

"I'll see you at your trial."

Abruptly, I turn away from him and begin to walk down the row of cells.

"COME BACK!" he bellows, pounding his fist on the glass. "You don't get to walk away from me! Answer the question!"

I ignore him, but his voice still follows me, growing even louder until all of the prisoners in block Z look up.

"Mark my words, Hollis Timewire! Somehow, someday, you'll meet the same sticky end as your parents! You can't escape your own reputation, puppet master. You'll always be the leader of the second Terror War!"

38

THE LIGHT OF DAWN PEEKS UP OVER THE HORIZON TO CAST
gold across the dirt-packed earth. A sizable group of us are huddled
together around a dug out grave. We're standing just past the
airstrip, with the mountain in the distance, and we're here to say
goodbye to Maddy.

Because the prison Sector and the medical ward couldn't
remain unsupervised, the temporary guard had to reorganize
itself to accommodate everyone who wanted to attend. The
grave had also been dug the night before in preparation.

Early this morning, Maddy's body was moved from the
morgue to a modest wooden coffin and walked in a silent
processional all the way out to the grave.

I stand between Jonah and Vianne, holding both of their
hands. Ben, Candice, Olivia, and Rosalie are on the other side of
the oval of people. Both Keith and Ashton are still too injured
to join us, and it breaks my heart. I know they would want to be
here for this.

I feel paralyzed. All I can do is stare down at the little box in the earth . . .

I haven't stopped crying since I woke up. The heaviness in my heart is crushing. Unbearable. I'm not sure how I'm going to survive it. I got to look at him before the coffin was closed. He was so small and peaceful . . . like he was sleeping.

I grip both Jonah and Vianne's hands even harder to keep myself steady. This war was never meant for someone so young, but just like me, Maddy was used for his ability with no regard for the person behind it. Maddy was here a hundred years ago when all this started, and he was so close to seeing it all end. The boy with the golden light . . . the last tragic casualty of a massacre that killed so many.

I close my eyes, feeling the morning breeze tickle my face. I breathe it in, feeling alive.

Alive . . .

Anguish rips into me, and I lean my head on Jonah's arm to sob.

The funeral proceeds in a simple manner. Jonah opens the time by asking everyone to think of something they can remember Maddy by. He then goes on to speak about how he was a boy filled with life and light, even through the darkest of times. Jonah's words flow with kindness and grace, and they paint a beautiful picture of the little boy. Then, the time opens up for anyone to speak.

A few of the band of rebels who didn't know Maddy as well thanked him for giving them back their powers. A few more wished him well in whatever the next life would hold. Then my friends speak up.

"He was a tough kid," Olivia says, her brow furrowed. "I think when things get bad, it's easy to see the negative in life, but Maddy never lost his happiness. And that's something rare. He brought a lot of people together too. He was really special. I'm proud that I got to fight for him. It's not fair that he had to leave us so soon, but I know his memory will keep us all strong."

Vianne's melodic voice joins in next. "He had the best laugh." Tears brim in her silver eyes. "I used to play this game with him where I would transform my face into a duck's bill. He thought it was the funniest thing. It would make him laugh. And his laugh was like magic. It was so wonderful you'd swear you'd never hear anything better. He was just . . . so full of joy. I didn't know him for long, but I'm better because of him." She looks down into the hole. "Thank you for teaching me to laugh more, little one. I'm so sorry you never got to grow up. I promise I'll keep you in my heart, always."

Candice sniffles, wiping her nose on the back of her hand. "Having Maddy around was like having a little brother. He just became part of the family so fast, like he'd always been with us. I know Keith felt that way too."

"If you were down," Ben adds, "he had a way of making you feel happy again. He was always smiling."

"At the Ability Festival," Rosalie murmurs. "I remember how he kept staring at all the lights. He always loved the lights. It captured his attention in a way nothing else could . . . I think that's what I've learned from him. To love the lights and to be a light for people when they're going through the dark. I won't forget you, Maddy."

When no one else speaks up, I take a step forward, letting go of Vianne's hand to wipe my eyes. It's my turn now. I don't know how to begin. I feel like anything I say isn't going to be enough. How could I get everyone to understand what he meant to me? What he did for me? I'm a different person because of Maddy. He changed my life in more ways than one, and knowing that I have to keep going without him makes me feel like my heart is going to stop.

I open my mouth to begin, but my voice feels like it's been stolen from me. Grief closes my throat. With a gentle nudge, my ability tingles beneath my palms, and then the golden dragon appears. She gazes at me, and calm descends, filling me with comfort. With her presence, I'm reminded once again that I'll never truly be alone. A little piece of Maddy lives on in me, and so, with shaking lips, I find my voice again, and the dragon fuels me with strength as I address the little wooden coffin.

"Maddy, when I met you, I was in a really dark place. I didn't want my power. I didn't know who I was, and I had a lot of growing up to do. When you took my power away all those months ago, I lost a piece of myself I never knew I needed. And when you gave me my ability back, it made me realize that being a puppet master isn't something to be afraid of. It's who I am. You made me whole again when I needed it the most. You helped save me, and you helped me save others too. You taught me so much when my heart was broken and my spirit was crushed. You taught me not to be sad . . ."

I swallow, and more tears slip down my face.

"The last thing you said to me was, 'Don't be sad.' And I'm

trying, little one. I am. Right now, it hurts a lot. I don't want to say goodbye to you. I miss you so much, and I'm so sorry I couldn't protect you. I tried, Maddy. I tried to save you like you saved me. I don't know how you did it, but I know what you gave me in your last moments . . . and what you gave me saved me again."

In my mind's eye, the golden light flashes all across the rooftop . . .

"It's like you were there, watching over me. I know it. I told you once that everyone has their own unique type of light. Before I met you, my light was dark, but now it's gold. It's gold, Maddy. And you did that. Every time I see the light, I'm going to remember you. I'm going to be a force for good in this world. I promise. I love you, Maddy. You will always be a part of me."

I release Jonah's hand and walk over to the pile of dirt off to the side of the grave. Stooping down, I grab a handful of earth and toss it on top of the coffin. The rest of the band of rebels follows suit, casting fistfuls of dirt onto the little box.

And then it's over.

The men who dug the grave grab their shovels and cover the coffin, packing Maddy into the earth. With each shovelful, I want to tell them to stop. I'm not ready. This can't be it. But my voice is gone. All I can do is stand there and watch.

Once the grave is thoroughly covered, groupings of people leave the gravesite in silence until only my friends and I are left. Vianne and Jonah are still by my side, and Olivia, Ben, Candice, and Rosalie all shuffle around the freshly packed earth to join me.

"I have to go back," Olivia says solemnly. She's looking at me like I might break. "Hollis, don't worry about doing anything today. Just . . . take your time with this. You don't have to be the leader right now. We can take care of things for a bit."

Candice comes up to me and gives me a hug that I only half-register. She whispers in my ear. "Maddy loved you a lot."

She moves out of the way so Rosalie can hug me too. "I'm so sorry, Hollis," she murmurs through her tears.

Ben gently touches my shoulder, giving me a silent look of compassion as Rosalie finishes her embrace. Then Ben, Candice, and Rosalie join Olivia's side to begin the trek across the airstrip back to the mountain.

Jonah moves in next, wrapping me up in his warm embrace. "We'll put up a grave marker tomorrow. Try to eat something today if you can. I'll see you inside when you're ready."

And just like that, he leaves me alone with Vianne. She doesn't move in for a hug. Instead, she stays by my side and knits her fingers together with mine. For a while, both of us stare at the spot where Maddy was buried, and my mind spirals into thoughts of grief that feel like knives stabbing me all over. More tears flow down my face, blurring my vision and plugging up my nose.

I wipe my cheeks with my free hand, doing my best to breathe properly.

"I don't know how to do this," I whisper. "I feel like if I walk away . . . if I leave him . . . then it will finally feel real."

Vianne squeezes my hand. "I know."

My fingers move up to my face to trace the scar there. Vicious thoughts swirl through my head, taking me back to the moment I left the mountain—the moment I decided to go to Camille. That's when Arthur took Maddy. If I had only stayed. If I had only agreed to the assassination. If I had only . . .

Stop, Hollis, the creature whispers. *You can't change this. It is a part of you now.*

Warmth centers at my core, and a calming sensation descends over me, but it does nothing to dampen the intensity of the heartbreak I'm feeling. I know I can't turn back time. Nothing can. Not even the golden light.

"This feels like another scar," I say. "It won't ever heal all the way. I just have to carry it with me."

Vianne looks at me with compassion. Her hair changes from ghostly white to shiny silver, and then, like a mirage melting away, her scars flower across her face and neck. "I've been thinking a lot about scars lately." Her brow furrows. "When we were living in the forest, I remember the day you ran after me when I lost control of my ability. I was embarrassed that my scars were visible. I wanted you to leave me alone, but you didn't."

She takes a steadied breath.

"It was something about you not walking away . . . it finally got me to open up about my scars. That was the first time I ever admitted out loud that I hide my scars because I'm ashamed I couldn't save my parents. I've always seen my scars as something that makes me a coward. But now . . . I think I finally see them the way I'm supposed to. They're proof that I made it out alive. They're proof that I'm strong. That I'm a fighter."

Tears form in her eyes, and one slides down her cheek, falling down into the divot of one the claw marks on her face.

"I don't know why I survived the dogs that night when my parents didn't, but now I think it was because I was meant to fight *with* you, Hollis . . . and I was meant to fight for a better world. I was supposed to meet Maddy. Everything that's happened . . . I was supposed to be a part of it. If my parents were able to see me today, I know they would be proud of me."

"They would be," I affirm.

Her voice catches, and sadness deepens her tone. "I'm going to miss him so much, Hollis."

"Me too."

She looks at me with glassy eyes. "We fought for him. Didn't we?" Her tone is unsure, and I can hear the strain of a sob she's fighting to keep down.

"We did," I say. "We all did. We gave Maddy a family. We gave him a home just like we said we'd do when we rescued him from the Area 19 Testing Center. It wasn't for long, but it mattered. He knew we loved him. He knew we cared. We made a difference."

She nods, and her lower lip trembles. More tears fall down, tracing paths through the deep scars that line her face and neck.

"I think I'm ready, Hollis."

"To go back?" I ask.

She shakes her head. "Not yet. I want to stay here a little longer." Her breathing turns shaky, and she purses her lips to blow out air. "I think I'm ready to stop hiding my scars."

My lips part, and I stare at her in surprise.

"That day by the river you told me that if I was ever ready to show them, you'd support me. You told me I was beautiful, scars and all. I never thought I'd want to, but . . ."—Her fingertips sweep down her neck gently.—"I want people to see them. I want to wear them. They're mine, and they matter. They're part of me and my story. Just like Maddy was. Just like you are."

My heart fills with a mix of respect and admiration for the girl standing by my side—for how she's changed and grown.

"I'm proud of you, friend," I say, gathering her into a hug.

She hugs me back, and as we stand there in each other's arms in the growing light of the morning, the gold of the sun casts itself onto Maddy's grave, lighting up the dirt. And for a moment, it feels like Maddy is here with us, joining in the hug to say: everything is going to be alright.

■　■　■

"Hollis, we're going to start in fifteen minutes. Are you ready?" Wren asks, peeking her head through the cracked doorway of Candice's bedroom. "Everyone's waiting in Sector 3."

"Almost," I say. "I'll be out in a minute."

She nods and then slips away, leaving me alone.

I stare into a mirror that's been propped up against the wall. It's on a desk pushed into the corner, and I sit in a chair facing my reflection. The makeshift vanity is strewn with various items: a brush, a tube of soft pink lipstick, hair pins and hair ties, compact powder, eyeliner, and blush. Candice offered to help me apply a thin layer of makeup, but I declined, opting to try it myself. The only thing I managed to do, however, is get a tint of color on my pale lips and hide the dark circles under my eyes with the powder.

My blonde hair is pulled back into a loose braid that cascades over my left shoulder, and as I take in my complexion, I decide I'm happy with it. At least I look like I've slept, even though I haven't. The scar on my left cheekbone is tempered as well, the powder paling the saturation of the jagged line but doing nothing to hide it.

I'm wearing a V-neck wine red blouse, navy blue slacks, and black flats. The outfit feels much fancier than what I'd normally wear, and it makes me look like I put time and effort into my appearance.

With a sigh, I rise from the vanity and make my way to the door. This is it. Today's the day we broadcast ourselves to the world. No more Arthur, no more serum, and no more Pure Ones. Nerves of anticipation flutter through me. We're on the verge of a new world—one that I helped create.

I'm only doing a part of the broadcast. Jonah and Wren are going to talk through the majority of the changes that will occur as a result of Arthur's death—with Wren taking the lead in condemning Arthur's actions. Olivia is going to talk about the Education Centers, and I'm going to announce us as the Empowered Ones.

As I walk through the empty concrete halls leading to Sector 3, a strange feeling comes over me. It's one of hope and strength. On the morning of my sixteenth birthday, I never would've imagined this path. I never would've conceived of all the things that would happen to me. I'll be seventeen in twenty-three days, and it will be the year 2648 in five days. So much has happened. So much has changed.

The girl I was in the white van on her way to take the blood Test doesn't exist anymore. I remember reciting the words of the pledge in a spiral of emotion-suppressed panic, hoping against hope that I wouldn't be the one in ten million. The pledge was my promise of allegiance to a government who did its best to wipe me from the face of the earth. It was full of empty words and meaningless declarations. But to this day, three phrases still stay with me. One: "Today, my life changes for the better." Two: "Today, I become accountable to the world." And three: "Today, I help change the world."

That was never true for me back then. Even though I believed in my government, I never mattered to them. I was a cog in the machine of an emotionless society built on obedience and conformity at all costs. I was nameless and faceless, just like I was supposed to be—and I was brainwashed into believing that my service to the world order would make a difference.

Funny how those three phrases turned out to be true in the end.

By some stroke of fate, my life *has* changed for the better. Today, I *am* going to become accountable to the world, and I *have* changed the world.

Looking back over everything that's brought me here, I'm overwhelmed by it all. I had to struggle and learn the meaning of loss. I had to discover how to feel and what it means to love. I had to fight through the carnage of my own decisions and wade through the consequences of having a devastating and sought-after power. But I came out stronger, I found my people, and I found my purpose.

As I make it to the double doors of Sector 3, the creature appears next to me, her golden glory basking me in light. I enter into the large concrete space. This was the hangar Olivia teleported me and my friends to all those months ago. It's barren, save for a raised platform at the far end that's been set up for the broadcast.

Chatter echoes around the room, off the walls, and up onto the stone balcony. My footsteps tap along, adding to the noise as I approach the small crowd. A group of cameramen are all busy setting up their equipment, and as I pass them by, my eyes search around until I find Jonah. He's wearing a gray suit with a white undershirt, and his dark brown hair is combed back. His beard is also trimmed. The clothes compliment him well, and I'm taken aback by how professional he looks.

I walk up to him and nudge his shoulder. "You clean up well," I tease.

He chuckles, taking in my appearance with a smile. "So do you."

"Are you ready?"

"As ready as I'll ever be. And you?"

The golden dragon pulses energy through my body, giving me a surge of confidence. "I am." I stare at Jonah for a long moment. "I can't believe this. A year ago, I didn't even know you, and I had so much fear and hate in my heart for the Diseased Ones . . . and now, you're my family, and I'm going to announce to the world that we're the Empowered Ones. It doesn't feel real."

Jonah beams at me. "A year ago, I never imagined that we'd be stepping back into society. I never thought I'd live to see a day like this, let alone be a part of it." He scratches his chin, a pensive look befalling him. "I remember the day Tiffany rescued you and brought you underground with us ... how you were so scared and alone. I knew you would have to learn to do life all over again, and I admitted to Tiffany soon after you arrived that I didn't think you'd change your mind about us." There's a beat of silence, and then he says, "Little did I know that I had just met the person who would change the world for us."

My eyes brim with happy tears, and I smile through them. "You never stopped believing in me even when everyone was against me. You're one of the reasons I'm here, Jonah. Don't ever forget that."

"You were worth believing in."

He pulls me into a hug, and I wrap my arms around him. My hearing fixates on the background chatter again as we end the embrace, and then Wren jumps up onto the platform.

"Alright people," she calls out, and a hush falls over the crowd gathered in the hangar. "Let's get this broadcast started."

I climb up to the platform with Olivia and Jonah, and all of us take our places behind the podiums. The cameras fix their lenses on Jonah and Wren, gearing up for the start of broadcast.

I look out at the faces gazing up at us, and hope fills my heart. My friends have come to watch, and just seeing them gives me courage. Later, I'm going to sit by Keith's bed and tell him all about this. Maybe we can eat a meal together, or maybe—if he feels well enough—I can walk him around in a wheelchair to get some fresh air. Whatever we do, I just want to be with him, and when I get the chance, I want to tell him about the golden light.

The dragon stands by my side, shining bright gold and bolstering me with a deep sense of belonging. My heart rate rises ever so slightly, and the hum of my ability tingles beneath my fingertips. I feel that incredible sense of control. Once more, the golden light surges from the creature, letting me know that Maddy is with me, and as the cameraman counts down to start the broadcast, my heart fills with purpose for the new world to come.

Epilogue

1 YEAR and 23 DAYS later

I'M SITTING AT THE OVAL TABLE ACROSS FROM WREN AND Jonah in the newly refurbished office of Sector 15. We're halfway through a long and arduous meeting. We're discussing what memories would be most important to preserve in our efforts to memorialize the true history of the Empowered Ones. It was Rosalie's idea—a brilliant one—and we've taken to the new project with enthusiasm. We're calling it The Memory Collective. The plan is to identify the people whose memories are vital to telling our story, catalog the memories into a digital format by recording the projections as Rosalie displays them, and then organize it all into a timeline. That way, Education Centers across the world will have access to them, and the memories will live on long past our time.

The fact that we're finally talking about instituting a tangible program for the Education Centers is an honest miracle.

The first nine months following Arthur's death were filled with more chaos than order. Challenges for how to restructure society arose at almost every turn. Citizens were still deeply fearful and prejudiced, and pockets of resistance cropped up in droves around the world, which took the form of protests, vandalism, and in some cases, riots. When the first set of Education Centers opened, it was nearly impossible to get anyone to step through the doors.

But we persevered, always with the message: we are one

society again. We also never let up on our dedication to the idea that education is the greatest weapon we could wield.

As the presence of the Empowered Ones became normalized—and no harm came to citizens from anyone with a power, despite the unrest—people grew curious. It started with the youth, then slowly, the curiosity trickled up to the older generations. It seemed that people were finally open to learning from us.

And so, the restructuring began.

Jonah spearheaded the education projects aimed at teaching citizens the true history of the last one hundred years, Wren took on the mighty task of overseeing all active Education Centers, and I filled whatever role circumstances demanded. Peacekeeper. Event coordinator. Broadcast spokesperson.

Progress has been slow—grueling even. But now, with The Memory Collective project underway, a new spark has formed in our determination to keep knitting together the fragments of the new world . . .

There's a sharp rap on the office door that stops our meeting mid-conversation. Both Wren and Jonah exchange amused glances from their seats as I swivel in my chair to face the noise. When the door slides into the wall, Keith's smiling face appears. He's dressed in a faded blue flannel and jeans, and his dark hair falls unkempt around his ears and across his forehead.

I'm unable to suppress the grin that tugs at my mouth.

"What are you doing here?" I ask, as if I don't already know. I shoot a playfully indignant look at both Wren and Jonah, and then I turn my attention back to Keith. "Does she really think it's still a secret?"

Keith laughs. "Can you at least pretend? For Candice's sake? She's worked so hard."

"Oh, I'll pretend," I say with spirited seriousness. "I promise. I'll be the most surprised person in the room."

Jonah grins and then nods his head in Keith's direction. "We can keep talking about the memories later. Go. We'll be there soon." He gives me a quick wink, and I shake my head in amusement.

I rise to my feet, tugging at the folds of my burgundy sweater and brushing a strand of hair from my face. I join Keith at the office door, and then we both slip out.

"Hi," I say.

"Hey."

I wrap my arms around his neck, giving him a deep kiss. He kisses me back. He tastes like mint and smells like fresh laundry. Twisty, wonderful feelings flutter down into my stomach, and when we break apart, Keith stares at me with a sweet smile. He's grown quite a lot taller in the past year. His hair is longer, and it has started to curl around the edges. His nose, which was badly broken, never healed correctly, and it's slightly crooked now, but to me, it only adds to his charm and gives him a rugged look he didn't have before.

"Happy birthday, Hollis," he says. "You look beautiful."

Heat creeps through my cheeks; I'm sure I'm blushing. I'm only dressed in a sweater and grungy jeans that I threw on after rolling out of bed to start a day full of meetings. I didn't even brush my hair. But I soak in the compliment anyway. "Thanks."

He cups my face in his hands and gives me another tender

kiss. With the subtle proddings of my ability, I can feel that he's suddenly nervous. There's the slightest bit of trembling beneath his fingertips, and I'm not sure why.

"Ready to be surprised?" he asks.

I giggle. "Oh, I've *been* ready."

He grabs my hand, and we skitter through the mountain halls, laughing at how cute it is that Candice thinks she's been able to pull this off without my knowledge. All through this past week, she's been increasingly jumpy and secretive. Two weeks ago, when Ben mentioned in an offhand slip-of-the-tongue comment that vanilla cake would be his go-to flavor, Candice nearly cracked one of his ribs with her elbow to shut him up. And there's been a surprising number of random people that have asked me what my favorite things are in every conceivable category. Never Candice though—of course.

"Where are we going?"

Keith shakes his head. "I'm not going to ruin the only part of this you don't know about."

"Fair enough."

He pulls me along, and a budding excitement grows in my stomach until it feels like I'm nervous. But it's not an anxious nervous. It's a good kind of nervous. I've never had a real party thrown for me before. My birthday was acknowledged back in society, but it was never made into a celebratory occasion. You just got older. But here, it seems that birthdays are a big deal—a reason to party and have fun. I honestly have no idea what to expect.

"We're almost there," Keith says, taking us down another set of halls.

At this point, I know where we're headed. We're in Sector 7, and my training room is just ahead. When we approach the metal door, Keith grabs the handle and slides the door into the wall. The only thing I see past him is darkness, and my eyes strain as we step into the room.

I put on my best confused voice. "Keith, why are all the lights off?"

Before he can reply, there's a burst of sound and a twinkle of soft lighting. A chorus of voices call out as the shifted air shield of Hazel's ability uncloaks the guests from their invisibility.

"SURPRISE!"

I gasp, and it's actually genuine. My training room is unrecognizable. Strings of lights hang across the ceiling like stars and drape down the walls like willow branches. It casts the room in a soft glow as if we were under the night sky. Standing round tables covered in silver fabric are spaced out to the left of the training platform, and a dozen couches sit end to end in a wide arc to the right. In front of the couches, there are platters of food and drinks on large glass coffee tables. In addition, dark fabric dividers have sectioned off my private living space so that it's out of sight. But it's more than just the elaborate set up that makes me gawk at the reveal. It seems that everyone from the former band of rebels is here.

"Oh my goodness!" I exclaim, pushing a bit more surprise into my tone. "What—what is this?"

Candice rushes forward to barrel me with a hug, and I brace myself for the impact. "It's your surprise party! Happy birthday, Hollis!"

She releases me and then wastes no time in pulling me further into the room. The next two people I see make me smile like an idiot.

"Olivia! Rosalie!" I beam at them as they both move in for a quick hug. "Aren't you two busy running Area 19's Education Center? I thought you told me you weren't visiting the mountain for another month!"

"We lied," Olivia chimes.

"We weren't going to miss your party, obviously," Rosalie says, giving Candice a sly glance. "Candice would have our heads. Besides, I'll be meeting with Jonah and Wren about The Memory Collective project anyway."

"Oh, so your visit *isn't* just for me?" I tease, giving her a fake stern look.

Just then, Ben bounds up to us in an energetic flurry of movement, nearly knocking over Candice in his excitement. He wears a mischievous grin, and then cascades a deck of cards nimbly through his long fingertips. "Let's get this party started!"

I eye the cards with playful skepticism. "A card trick? Really Ben?"

"Of course," Ben says matter-of-factly. He wears a smug look drenched in over-eagerness. "I fought for the Candice-approved honor of kicking off the party with some *magic*." His eyebrows jump up and down his forehead, and he lets his fingers flitter through the air as if scattering dust. He gives his girlfriend a quick wink and then calls out to the room. "Gather 'round everyone! We're going to start things off with a spectacular trick of mental proportions! And Hollis, the lovely birthday girl, is going to be my assistant!"

Keith laughs as Ben pulls me away from him and ushers me up to the training platform. I can already feel the color deepening in my face as everyone crowds closer to the staged area. As my eyes scour the guests, I spot a few more familiar faces: Yang, Siena Rose, Hazel, Beck, and Delphi. Then I spot Vianne and Ashton. Vianne gives me a small wave, her hair bursting through different shades of purple. Ashton waves as well, shifting his stance to lean on his cane.

Ben shuffles the deck of cards in several different flashy ways that seem to defy gravity, and then he stops, fanning the cards out to me. "Okay, Hollis. Go ahead and pick any card you want."

My hand hovers over the deck and moves to the far right. I pull a card out and look at it.

"It's blank." I clap a hand over my mouth, mortified that I just said that out loud without waiting for further instruction. "Oh no . . . did I just ruin the trick?"

Ben shakes his head with a chuckle. "They're all blank." With a showy wave of his hand, a pen appears in his palm as if plucked from thin air, which garners a few "ooh's" and "aah's" from the onlookers. "I'm going to try some magic with your thoughts, Hollis. A little mind reading! I want you to think of a word—any word—and I want you to write that word on your card. Don't let me see it, but you may show it to the audience."

Immediately, my mind hurls back to the first time I ever participated in a magic trick with Ben Bryson. He had me write my name on a card, and the trick ended with a shocking display of public affection.

"You're not going to try and kiss me again, are you?" I ask guardedly. I fold my arms across my chest.

"And have Candice light my pillow on fire?" he says in mock seriousness. He places a hand over his heart. "Nope. Wouldn't dream of it."

"You guys make me sound like a terrorist!" Candice huffs in irritation.

"Only joking," Ben says with a twinkle in his eye. "Love you, Candy Cane."

There's a sprinkle of laughter from the crowd, and Candice's stern look melts into a smile.

"Okay, Hollis, write your word on the card and show everyone."

Uncapping the pen, I scrawl across the card's surface, taking care to keep it shielded from Ben. Then I hold it up for the room to see.

Vanilla Cake

"Okay, the pen please." Ben holds his hand out while still looking away from me. I give the pen back, Ben caps it, and he shoves it into his pocket. He fans the deck out once more and says, "Place the card anywhere into the deck. Facedown."

I slide the card in. Then he gathers the deck together in his palm, but he keeps my card sticking out from the stack slightly.

"I'm not even going to touch your card with my hands," Ben says. He sweeps a small stack of cards from the bottom of the deck. "I'm going to tuck your card into the deck with other cards so there's no chance of me tampering with it. Is that fair?"

I nod, keeping an eagle eye out for the ruse.

Ben lightly taps my card into the deck with the cards in his hand and then places the excess cards on top of the stack when he's done.

"Hold out your hand," Ben instructs.

I open up my palm, and Ben places the entire deck onto it.

"Now, the magic!" he calls out in a spooky voice, waving his hand above the cards. "Hollis, I want you to think of what you wrote down in your mind, and I'm going to take a card from the top of the deck."

His fingers grasp the top card, and he shows it to the room. It's blank. He digs in his pocket for the pen while giving me a mysterious and scrutinizing look.

"Hmmm . . . I'm sensing you didn't only write down one word," he murmurs.

My stomach flips. What? How did he know that? He flicks the cap off the pen, eyeing me up and down.

"In fact, I think you're referencing my slip up the other week?"

I gape at him as he scribbles on his own card. His eyes light up with victory as he turns the card around, displaying his handwriting to the crowd.

Vanilla Cake

"Is that what you wrote on your card?" he asks with a grin.

"Yes!" I say shakily, my mouth open in a dumbfounded 'O.'

Everyone cheers at the completion of the trick, and Ben takes a grandiose bow. He then pats me on the back with a goofy grin. "Happy birthday, Hollis."

"How on earth did you do that? I was watching you the whole time! There's no way you could've seen my card."

Ben shrugs. "I can read minds. My power has evolved."

He jumps down from the platform, and I follow suit. "You're really not going to tell me?"

"Good luck with getting him to spill," Candice says. She joins his side and nudges him. "He won't tell me either, and I've pestered him to death."

Keith shuffles through the group, coming up behind me and hooking his arms around my waist. "You know, Hollis, you could just make Ben tell you with your power."

Ben blanches slightly. "Hey, that's not cool! A magician never reveals his secrets!"

I laugh. "Don't worry, Ben. I'm not going to force you to tell me. That was an amazing trick."

Just then, a burst of giggling comes from the couches. Yang, with a flute of pink liquid in hand, stumbles forward, nearly knocking Siena Rose over. Siena holds her own flute, a smirk curling her mouth. It's as if she can feel my eyes on her, because her attention snaps to me. She lifts a second glass from the tray of drinks on the coffee table and saunters over.

"Here, birthday girl," she says, thrusting the bubbly pink drink into my hand. "Drink up."

"Oh, I need to see this," Ashton says, shuffling over to us. He taps his cane against the concrete with a sly smile.

I look between Ashton and Siena. "What's in the drink?"

Ashton smirks. "Well, it's not alcohol, if that's what you're wondering."

"I'm eighteen. I can drink alcohol," I shoot back. "That's not what I'm asking." I scan Siena suspiciously. "Siena, what did you put into the drinks?"

Her hooded eyes flash with mischief, and she takes a lazy sip of her own drink. It doesn't appear to have any effect on her, but

I'm assuming that's because she can neutralize her own power.

"I call it a giggling gulp," she says. "It's just a little something to loosen people up. You know? Lower the inhibitions. Loosen the tongue." Her prankish look deepens. "It doesn't make your head feel fuzzy, I promise. It just makes you feel good."

I glance at the frothy liquid, watching the bubbles creep up the side of the glass.

"Come on, Hollis. It's your party. You should loosen up," Ashton teases.

My gaze bounces between Siena and Ashton as I consider it . . .

"How about this? I'll take a glass if you do, Ash." I smirk as Ashton's eager expression falters. "If anyone needs to loosen up, it's you. You're always brooding. It wouldn't kill you to enjoy yourself every once in a while, and maybe smile every now and then."

I say this in a tone that's half joking and half serious.

Ashton sours, his brow crunching together.

The statement is a little unfair, but it's not untrue. Though he tries to hide it, the impact of what happened a year ago is still affecting him. The lack of oxygen to his brain during the skirmish left him with low muscle strength in his left leg and a lingering tremor in his right hand. Initially, he wasn't even able to walk. To be fair, it's a miracle he survived at all with a nearly crushed windpipe. But he's improved by leaps and bounds with the help of physical therapy and Beezee's healing sessions. Even with all the progress, I can tell that he's still down on himself about having to rely on a cane to get around.

We've become close friends over the past year, and I've gotten to know him well. Ashton has surprised me in a lot of ways. He's taken an active role in the mountain's leadership from the moment his health permitted it. He's even expressed interest in working at PC-7A, which now holds all of the people found guilty during the trials we held in the months following Arthur's death.

Despite being crappy at hiding his feelings about his physical condition, Ashton has integrated himself into the cheerful atmosphere of our friend group quite seamlessly. And, as Maddy once informed me, he's funny. It's in a dark humor and well-timed sort of way, but I've grown fond of his gloomy and monotone deliveries of some spectacularly grim jokes.

I cock my head to the side, looking Ashton up and down. "Well? Are you going to drink one?"

His sour look tempers, and then he slides an eyebrow up as his mouth curls into a smile. "Alright, I'll take a glass," he says, putting a hand to his chin. "But I'll only drink if you help me convince Wren to drink too."

There's a moment of silence, and then all of us burst into laughter at the idea of breaking Wren out of her work-oriented and rigid shell.

"Now *that*, I would *love* to see!" I chortle. "Deal." I stick out my hand and Ashton shakes it. Siena wastes no time in ushering all of us over to the table filled with bubbly pink drinks.

Olivia and Rosalie are already there, laughing and talking with Yang, who's halfway through an impersonation of Wren giving instructions in a stern voice. All three of them have clearly imbibed, and the effect of the drink is obvious. Rosalie has gone bright pink in the face, Olivia is giggling in a manner I've never heard from her before, and Yang is more boisterous than usual.

I snatch up a glass, handing it to Ashton. "Bottoms up, Ash."

His glowering expression is back, but it's cloaked in a reserved smile. He lifts his glass up, and we clink. Then we swallow the few gulps of bubbly liquid together.

The sensation is immediate. A warm feeling slides down my esophagus and settles into my stomach, and everything in me relaxes. I didn't even know I was tensing my shoulders until the liquid hit me. On top of that, I'm all of a sudden giddy. It's like a well of energy at my core springing up to my lips. I let out a giggle.

Ashton looks like he's swallowed a sour candy. His mouth puckers as he fights a laugh, but he can't hold back. A mirthful noise escapes him, and it's so odd to hear that I cackle. Soon, everyone grabs a glass, and we move to the couches, dipping into the platters of meats, cheeses, and dried fruits.

Over the next hour, my friends and I lounge, eat, and talk while people come up to me in intervals to wish me happy birthday. The giggling gulps last in spurts of fifteen minutes, and I find myself reaching for more when the effects wear off.

We play a game called "Truth or Dare," which unlocks everyone's devilish side and really should just be called "Dare," because no one picks "Truth" the whole time. Candice dares Ben to lick the wall. Then Ben dares Candice to lick his shoe. Keith dares me to down two glasses of the bubbly pink drink at the same time—which makes me twice as silly—and then Olivia dares Rosalie to show everyone her most embarrassing moment using her ability. But what happens next makes the whole game. Ashton dares Vianne to eat raw garlic, which Olivia teleports away to grab. Then, Vianne dares Ashton to kiss her with tongue in front of everyone. The group howls with laughter, and Ashton looks like he wants to melt into the floor. When the intimate lip-locking finishes, Vianne pulls back from him, thrilled.

"Payback for the garlic," she says, her hair flickering through shades of bubblegum pink. "Thought you should get a taste of it too."

When Wren and Jonah arrive, all of us pounce on the opportunity to rope them into the fun. We shove glasses into their hands while we sip on our own, and when the bubbly liquid slides down Wren's throat, she becomes a completely different person. Her hardened military exterior melts away into that of a chortling schoolgirl who's experiencing her first taste of fun. It's hilarious, and I laugh so much my sides hurt.

As the party continues, Candice and Ben emerge with a huge rectangular cake with white frosting and golden sprinkles. On top of it, there's eighteen candles, and I stare at them as Candice lights the candles with her pointer finger. Ben hollers at everyone to gather around, and then a chorus of song bursts forth from the crowd to wish me a happy birthday. I've never heard the song before, and I'm momentarily caught off guard that everyone knows the words. They must have practiced it . . .

When the song ends, I'm left staring around at my friends with a dopey smile on my face. They're all gazing at me expectantly.

"What?" I say.

"Well, blow out the candles!" Candice says, gesticulating at me.

"Oh, um, right," I murmur, trying to pass off the blunder as if I knew what to do all along, but I can see in Keith's expression that look he gives me when I've done something adorably awkward.

I pucker and blow on the flames until they extinguish, and then everyone cheers.

Cake is served. The drinking continues. Keith smudges frosting on my nose, and I manage to get his cheek. Dancing breaks out on the training platform, and Siena and Yang lead the charge, pulling people up to join the chaos. Beck and Hazel steal the dance floor with their impressive moves. As the party carries on, bolstered by the music and conversation, I take it all in, and a deep sense of happiness settles into me. Finally, at long last, I feel like I'm allowed to be the kid I never got to be before.

"Hollis," Keith murmurs, gently tugging on the sleeve of my sweater. "I have a present for you. But I want to give it to you in private."

He stands from the couch, offering me his hand. I take it, and he pulls me up. I hiccup slightly, blushing in the semi-darkness of the training room at how giddy I feel from the endless pink drinks.

He ushers me along until we reach the door, and his hands fumble with the handle for a moment. His nervousness from before is back. His heartbeat has quickened, and perspiration has formed on his palms. He looks like he's had too much coffee.

When we're out of earshot of the party, back in the bright lighting of the hall, he grabs me gently by the back of the waist and pulls me in for a kiss. I reciprocate enthusiastically, and my lips crash into his. He tastes like the pink drink. The kiss lasts a delightfully long time, and I giggle when I feel his hands moving up through my hair. I pull away from him slightly. "Hmm, I like this present."

He chuckles. "I got you something besides a kiss."

He seems to take a moment to center himself. His breathing has turned shallow, and he throws his shoulders back, standing tall.

From the depths of his pants pocket, he pulls out a small black box and hands it to me. I stare at it for a second, and my heart jumps up into my throat. With delicate fingers, I open up the box, and inside is a simple silver band made of two twisted pieces of metal that weave together like two vines snaking around each other.

For a moment, I don't move. I simply gawk at the thing, unable to believe my eyes. "Is this . . . ? Are you . . . ?" I look up at Keith as the pounding of my heart travels up into my ears.

He hurriedly dives into speech, tripping over his words. "It's a ring. I know we're both still so young—I'm barely nineteen, you just turned eighteen—and we have so much time to figure things out. But, I just . . . every time I think about doing life without you, I don't want to. I love you, Hollis. I want to spend the rest of my life with you. And you don't have to say anything right now if you don't want to—or if you don't feel ready. We can wait. I can ask you again later, when we're older. If you want.

I—I just know I want to marry you someday. You're my person, and if you'll let me, I promise to be your person too. Every day. No matter what happens."

He smacks a hand to his forehead, mumbling something about forgetting to get down on one knee, which makes no sense to me.

I grab his hands, which are shaking slightly, and then I stare up into his brilliant blue eyes. My heart feels overwhelmed in the best possible way. With everything in me, I want this too. The biggest smile fills my face.

"Yes," I say simply.

"Y-yes?" he repeats. He looks completely taken aback. "As in, yes, you'll marry me?"

I nod, letting out a laugh of disbelief. "Yes, I'll marry you."

I pull the ring from its slot and slide it onto my left ring finger, admiring it in the light. A shower of happiness fills me to the brim, and a giddiness that has nothing to do with the pink drink bubbles up in me.

Keith's cheeks are flushed. He looks like he's been sucker-punched. "I . . . did we just get . . . are we engaged?"

I grin at him. "We are."

Keith runs a hand through his hair. "Holy crap," he breathes shakily, as if truly considering the magnitude of what he just asked me for the first time. "Oh man, Candice is going to absolutely lose her mind!"

I laugh. "She absolutely will."

I grab the front of his shirt and pull him into another kiss. It's tender at first, but then it grows in fervor until my desire for him drives me wild. I twist my hands through his hair, and he wraps his arms around me, lifting me off my feet for a moment.

When the kiss ends, I bite my lower lip and grin at him. Then I examine the silver twisted band on my finger. "This was a really good birthday present. I wonder if anyone will top it," I tease.

Keith laughs. "I certainly hope not!" His hand slips into mine and our fingers intertwine. "Shall we go back?"

"And show it off?" I ask, holding up my hand.

He flashes a handsome smile. "Of course."

With that, we walk down the hall toward the open door where the sounds of music and laughter float like a melody through the air, and as we enter back into the party, I finally know deep in my heart that happiness has found me at last.

ACKNOWLEDGEMENTS

I have a whole book series out! I can't believe I can actually say this now. WOW! This has been a long time coming. When I started this series back in 2017, I never imagined that it would launch my author career. And I also never imagined that I'd complete a project as huge as this. The Diseased Ones (Book 1) was initially going to be a standalone, but that changed real quick as I delved deeper into Hollis's world. As I crafted her story, the series expanded into a 3-book series, and then eventually a 4-book series. The things I have learned over the past seven years are wild. At twenty-eight years old, I'm a better writer, storyteller, and editor than I was at twenty-one. I've found a life-long passion to pursue, and I hope to have a long career of writing and publishing books.

This journey has been life changing. I've met so many wonderful people and made some amazing friends along the way.

Some HUGE thank you's are in order.

Thank you, God, for giving me the gift of storytelling and giving me the drive and passion to see something like this through. You've been faithful to me through the years, and I give all glory to you!

Steven, you've been such a wonderful and supportive husband through this whole process. All the way back with Book 1, you were there to help me brainstorm and edit and nerd out with me about Hollis's world. I truly could not have done this without you! Thank you for always pushing me to improve and thank you for being my number one fan.

To Acorn Publishing: Holly and Jessica, you ladies truly gave me the tools I needed to learn about independent publishing. Thank you for taking a chance on little-baby-writer me all those years ago. And thank you for walking alongside me through this whole process. What I've learned from you through our partnership has been so valuable, and I appreciate how you've cheered me on through the series.

Josh, your eye for storytelling is phenomenal! You're an amazing critique partner, and I appreciate how much time and care you spent on this book series. Thank you for all the DMs, video calls, and emails helping me hash out the details of how to make this story the best it could possibly be. Your notes gave me some ideas that wouldn't have made it into the series otherwise. You've become a dear friend to me. From the bottom of my storyteller heart, thank you for supporting me and my writing career!

Michelle and Gabby! I love you so much. You two are the best sisters a gal could ask for. Thank you for always being so excited to read my books in the early stages. It's been a blast talking about Hollis's story together through the years. So many different points of inspiration came from you ladies along the way.

Luke, thanks for brainstorming some of the biggest reveals in this book series with me. I will forever be in your debt! You're an incredibly kind and supportive brother. I love you and appreciate you so much.

Mom and Dad, thank you for encouraging me to pursue my passions. I love you! Thank you for helping me host book signing parties and coming to my B&N signings. It's been so much fun sharing my storytelling with you.

To Molly, Sky, and Danna: I appreciate your beta reader feedback and your attention to detail. Thank you so much for sticking with me through all four books! It's been an amazing journey with you ladies.

Tony, you always seem to catch the typos that slip through the cracks. Bravo! You're an amazing proofreader. Seriously, thank you for your critical eye and for being a fan of my series since Book 1.

Jillian, I'm still so grateful that you reached out to me all the way back in 2020 to ask about being the audiobook narrator for The Hollis Timewire Series. There's truly no one better I could have hired. I've loved working with you to bring the series to life in a new way. You've done phenomenal work, and your range of character voices is incredible. What a talent!

To my readers: with all my heart, thank you for trusting me as a storyteller and giving me a chance. You guys are the reason I write! I love writing high stakes, rip-your-heart-out, insanely plot-twisty stories. And you guys have given me a platform to do so. I hope you stick with me as I continue my author journey. I don't know what other stories are in store for me, but I promise you I will continue to write and release books. If you enjoyed "The Empowered Ones," consider leaving a review. Reviews help me reach more readers.

And with that, Hollis Timewire's story closes. It might seem strange for me to thank a character who I made up, but these characters have become my family, so here goes:

Hollis, thank you for what you gave me. Writing your story was always something I could fall back on when life got crazy or when I felt down. You were with me through my teaching career, through Covid, and through having a baby. I can't believe I have to say goodbye to you. Your story will always hold a special place in my heart, and through the years, as I grow older, I will definitely re-read these books. Only other storytellers will fully understand me when I say this but . . . you've become a dear friend, and I will cherish all that we went through together on the page. Goodbye, friend. I'm never going to forget you.